MYTH DIRECTIONS

HIT OR MYTH

ROBERT ASPRIN

ACE BOOKS, NEW YORK

MYTH DIRECTIONS/HIT OR MYTH

An Ace Book / published by arrangement with
Donning Company

PRINTING HISTORY
Ace mass-market edition / June 2002

Published by arrangement with Starblaze Editions of the
Donning Company/Publishers.
Myth Directions/Hit or Myth copyright © 2002 by Donning Company.
Myth Directions copyright © 1982 by Robert L. Asprin.
Hit or Myth copyright © 1983 by Robert L. Asprin.
Cover art by Walter Velez.
Cover design by Judith Murello.
Text design by Julie Rogers.

Visit our website at
www.penguinputnam.com
Check out the ACE Science Fiction & Fantasy newsletter!

ISBN: 0-441-00943-3

ACE®
Ace Books are published by The Berkley Publishing Group,
a division of Penguin Putnam Inc.,
375 Hudson Street, New York, New York 10014.
ACE and the "A" design
are trademarks belonging to Penguin Putnam Inc.

PRINTED IN THE UNITED STATES OF AMERICA

10 9 8 7 6 5 4 3 2 1

MYTH DIRECTIONS

I:

"Dragons and Demons and Kings, Oh my!"

—THE COWARDLY KLAHD

"This place stinks!" my scaly mentor snarled, glaring out the window at the rain.

"Yes, Aahz," I agreed meekly.

"What's that supposed to mean?" he snapped, turning his demon's speckled gold eyes on me.

"It means," I gulped, "that I agree with you. The King-dom of Possiltum, and the palace specifically, stink to high heaven—both figuratively and literally."

"Ingratitude!" Aahz made his appeal to the ceiling. "I lose my powers to a stupid practical joker, and instead of concentrating on getting them back, I take on some twit of an apprentice who doesn't have any aspirations higher than being a thief; train him, groom him, and get him a job paying more than he could spend in two lifetimes, and what happens? He complains! I suppose you think you could have done better on your own?"

It occurred to me that Aahz's guidance had also gotten me hung, embroiled in a magik duel with a master ma-gician, and recently, placed in the unenviable position of trying to stop the world's largest army with a handful of

down-at-the-heels demons. It also occurred to me that this
was not the most tactful time to point out these minor
nerve-jangling incidents.

"I'm sorry, Aahz," I grovelled. "Possiltum *is* a pretty
nice kingdom to work for."

"It stinks!" he declared, turning to the window again.

I stifled a sigh. A magician's lot is not a happy one. I
stole that saying from a tune Aahz sings off and on ...
key. More and more, I was realizing the truth of the jingle.
As the court magician to my king I had already endured
a great deal more than I had ever bargained for.

Actually the king of Possiltum isn't my king. I'm *his*
royal magician, an employee at best.

Aahz isn't *my* demon, either. I'm his apprentice, trying
desperately to learn enough magik to warrant my afore-
mentioned lofty title.

Gleep is definitely my dragon, though. Just ask Aahz.
Better still, ask anyone in the court of Possiltum. Anytime
my pet wreaks havoc with his playful romping, I get the
blame and J.R. Grimble, the king's chancellor, deducts
the damages from my wages.

Naturally, this gets Aahz upset. In addition to manag-
ing my magik career, Aahz also oversees our finances.
Well, that's something of an understatement. He shame-
lessly bleeds the kingdom for every monetary considera-
tion he can get for us (which is considerable) and watches
over our expenses. When it comes to spending our ill-
gotten wealth, Aahz would rather part with my blood. As
you might guess, we argue a lot over this.

Gleep is understanding though; which is part of the
reason I keep him around. He's quite intelligent and understanding for a baby dragon with a one word vocabulary. I spend a considerable amount of time telling him
my troubles, and he always listens attentively without interrupting or arguing or shouting about how stupid I am.
This makes him better company than Aahz.

It says something about one's lifestyle when the only
one you can get sympathy from is a dragon.

Unfortunately, on this particular day I was cut off from my pet's company. It was raining, and when it rains in Possiltum, it doesn't kid around. Gleep is too big to live indoors with us, and the rain made the courtyard impassable, so I couldn't reach the stables where he was quartered. What was more, I couldn't risk roaming the halls of the castle for fear of running into the king. If that happened, he would doubtless ask when I was going to do something about the miserable weather. Weather control was not one of my current skills, and I was under strict orders from Aahz to avoid the subject at all costs. As such, I was stuck waiting out the rain in my own quarters. That in itself wouldn't be so bad, if it wasn't for the fact that I shared those quarters with Aahz.

Rain made Aahz grouchy, or I should say grouchier than usual. I'd rather be locked in a small cage with an angry spider-bear than be alone in a room with Aahz when he's in a bad mood.

"There must be *something* to do," Aahz grumbled, begging to pace the floor. "I haven't been this bored since the Two Hundred Year Siege."

"You could teach me about dimension travel," I suggested hopefully.

This was one area of magik Aahz had steadfastly refused to teach me. As I mentioned earlier, Aahz is a demon, short for "dimension traveler." Most of my close friends these days were demons, and I was eager to add dimension traveling to my meager list of skills.

"Don't make me laugh, kid." Aahz laughed harshly. "At the rate you're learning, it would take more than two hundred years to teach it to you."

"Oh," I said, crestfallen. "Well—you could tell me about the Two Hundred Year Siege."

"The Two Hundred Year Siege," Aahz murmured dreamily, smiling slightly to himself. Large groups of armed men have been known to turn pale and tremble visibly before Aahz's smile.

"There isn't much to tell," he began, leaning against a table and hefting a large pitcher of wine. "It was me and another magician, Diz-Ne. He was a snotty little upstart . . . you remind me a bit of him."

"What happened?" I urged, anxious to get the conversation away from me.

"Well, once he figured out he couldn't beat me flat out, he went defensive," Aahz reminisced. "He was a real nothing magikally, but he knew his defense spells. Kept me off his back for a full two hundred years, even though we drained most of the magik energies of that dimension in the process."

"Who won?" I pressed eagerly.

Aahz cocked an eyebrow at me over the lip of the wine pitcher.

"I'm telling the story, kid," he pointed out. "You figure it out."

I did, and swallowed hard.

"Did you kill him?"

"Nothing that pleasant." Aahz smiled. "What I did to him once I got through his defenses will last a lot longer than two hundred years—but I guarantee you, he won't get bored."

"Why were you fighting?" I asked in a desperate effort to forestall the images my mind was manufacturing.

"He welshed on a bet." My mentor shrugged, hefting the wine again.

"That's all?"

"That's enough," Aahz insisted grimly. "Betting's a serious matter—in any dimension."

"Um—Aahz?" I frowned. "Weren't Big Julie and his men running from gambling debts when we met them?"

That's the army I mentioned earlier. Big Julie and his men were currently disguised as happy citizens of Possiltum.

"That's right, kid." Aahz nodded.

"Then that's why you said the loansharks would probably come looking for them," I declared triumphantly.

"Wrong," Aahz said firmly.

"Wrong?" I blinked.

"I didn't say they'd probably come looking," he corrected. "I said they *would* come looking. Bank on it. There are only two questions involved here: When are they coming, and what are you going to do about it?"

"I don't know about the 'when,'" I commented with careful deliberation, "but I've given some thought to what I'm going to do."

"And you've decided—" Aahz prompted.

"To grab our money and run!" I declared. "That's why I want to learn dimension travel. I figure there won't be anywhere in this dimension we could hide, and that means leaving Klah for greener, safer pastures."

Aahz was unmoved.

"If push comes to shove," he yawned, "we can use the D-Hopper. As long as we've got a mechanical means of traveling to other dimensions, there's no need for you to learn how to do it magikally."

"C'mon, Aahz!" I exploded. "Why won't you teach me? What makes dimension traveling so hard to learn?"

Aahz studied me for a long moment, then heaved a big sigh. "All right, Skeeve," he said. "If you listen up, I'll try to sketch it out for you."

I listened. With every pore, I listened. Aahz didn't call me by my given name often, and when he did, it was serious.

"The problem is that to travel the dimensions, even using pentacles for beacons—gateways—requires knowing your destination dimension . . . knowing it almost as well as your home dimension. If you don't, then you can get routed into a dimension you aren't even aware of, and be trapped there with no way out."

He paused to take another drink from the wine pitcher.

"Now, you've only been in one dimension besides Klah," he continued. "That was Deva, and you only saw the Bazaar. You know the Bazaar well enough to know it's constantly changing and rearranging. You *don't* know it well enough to have zeroed in on the few permanent fixtures you could use to home in on for a return trip, so effectively, you don't know any other dimensions well enough to be sure of your destination if you tried to jump magikally. That's why you can't travel the dimensions without using the D-Hopper! End of lecture."

I blinked.

"You mean the only reason I can't do it magikally is because I don't know the other dimensions?" I asked.

"That's the *main* reason," Aahz corrected.

"Then let's go!" I cried, leaping to my feet. "I'll get the D-Hopper and you can show me a couple new dimensions while we're waiting for the rain to stop."

"Not so fast, kid!" Aahz interrupted, holding up a restraining hand. "Sit down."

"What's wrong?" I challenged.

"Do you *really* think that possibility hadn't occurred to me?" he asked, an edge of irritation creeping into his voice.

I thought about it, and sat down again.

"Why don't you think it's a good idea?" I queried in a more humble tone.

"There are a few things you've overlooked in your enthusiasm," he intoned dryly. "First of all, remember that in another dimension, you'll be a demon. Now, except for Deva which makes its money on cross-dimension trade, most dimensions don't greet demons with flowers and red carpets. The fact is, a demon is likely to be attacked on sight by whoever's around with whatever's handy."

He leaned forward to emphasize his words. "What I'm trying to say is, it's dangerous! Now, if we went touring and ran into trouble, what do we have to defend ourselves? I've lost my powers and yours are still so undeveloped as to be practically non-existent. Who's going to handle the natives?"

"How dangerous is it?" I asked hesitantly.

"Let me put it to you this way, kid." Aahz sighed. "You spend a lot of time griping about how I keep putting your life in jeopardy with my blatant disregard for danger. Right?"

"Right." I nodded vigorously.

"Well, now I'm saying the trip you're proposing is dangerous. Does that give you a clue as to what you'll be up against?"

I leaned back in my chair and stretched, trying to make it look nonchalant.

"How about sharing some of that wine?" I suggested casually.

For a change, Aahz didn't ignore the request. He tossed the pitcher into the air as he rose and strode to the window again. Reaching out with my mind, I gently grabbed the pitcher and brought it floating to my outstretched hand without spilling a drop.

As I said, I *am* the court magician of Possiltum. I'm not without powers.

"Don't let it get you down, kid," Aahz called from the window. "If you keep practicing, someday we can take that tour under your protection. But until you reach that level, or until we find you a magikal bodyguard, it'll just have to wait."

"I suppose you're right, Aahz," I conceded. "It's just that sometimes . . ."

There was a soft BAMF! as the ether was rent asunder and a demon appeared in the room. Right there! In my private quarters in the Possiltum royal palace!

Before I could recover from my surprise or Aahz could move to intervene, the demon plopped itself onto my lap and planted a big, warm kiss full on my mouth.

"Hi, handsome!" it purred. "How's tricks?"

II:

"When old friends get together, everything else fades to insignificance."

—Wars, Famine, Pestilence, and
Death

"Tanda!" I exclaimed, recovering from shock sufficiently to fasten my arms around her waist in an energetic hug.

"In the flesh!" she winked, pressing hard against me.

My temperature went up several degrees, or maybe it was the room. Tananda has that effect on me—and rooms. Lusciously curvaceous, with a mane of light green hair accenting her lovely olive complexion and features, she could stop a twenty-man brawl with a smile and a deep sigh.

"He isn't the only one in the room, you know," Aahz commented dryly.

"Hi, Aahz!" my adorable companion cried, untangling herself from my lap and throwing herself into Aahz's arms.

The volume of Tananda's affections is exceeded only by her willingness to share them. I had a secret belief, though, that Tananda liked me better than she liked Aahz. This belief was tested for strength as their greeting grew longer and longer.

"Um . . . what brings you to these parts?" I interrupted at last.

That earned me a dark look from Aahz, but Tananda didn't bat an eye.

"Well," she dimpled, "I could say I was just in the neighborhood and felt like dropping by, but that wouldn't be true. The fact is, I need a little favor."

"Name it," Aahz and I declared simultaneously.

Aahz is tight-fisted and I'm chicken, but all bets are off when it comes to Tananda. She had helped us out of a couple of tight spots in the past, and we both figured we owed her. The fact she had helped us *into* as many tight spots as she had helped us out of never entered our minds. Besides—she was *awfully* nice to have around.

"It's nothing really," she sighed. "I have a little shopping to do and was hoping I could borrow one of you two to help me carry things."

"You mean today?" Aahz frowned.

"Actually, for the next couple days," Tananda informed him. "Maybe as long as a week."

"Can't do it." Aahz sighed. "I have to referee a meeting between Big Julie and General Badaxe tomorrow. Any chance you could postpone it until next week?"

"Ummm . . . you weren't the one I was thinking of, Aahz," Tananda said, giving the ceiling a casual survey. "I was thinking Skeeve and I could handle it."

"Me?" I blinked.

Aahz scowled.

"Not a chance," he declared. "The kid can't play step-and-fetch-it for you. It's beneath his dignity."

"No, it isn't!" I cried. "I mean, if it wouldn't be beneath *you*, Aahz, how could it be beneath me?"

"I'm not the court magician of Possiltum!" he argued.

"I can disguise myself!" I countered. "That's one of my best spells. You've said so yourself."

"I think your scaly green mentor is just a lee-tle bit jealous," Tananda observed, winking at me covertly.

"Jealous?" Aahz exploded. "Me? Jealous of a little . . ." He broke off and looked back and forth between Tananda and myself as he realized he was being baited.

"Oh—I suppose it would be okay," he grumbled at last. "Go ahead and take him—even though it's beyond me what you expect to find in this backwater dimension worth shopping for."

"Oh, Aahz!" Tananda laughed. "You're a card. Shopping in Klah? I may be a little flighty from time to time, but I'm not crazy."

"You mean we're headed for other dimensions?" I asked eagerly.

"Of course." She nodded. "We have quite an itinerary ahead of us. First, we'll hop over to—"

"What's an itinerary?" I asked.

"Stop!" Aahz shouted, holding up a hand for silence.

"But I was just—"

"Stop!"

"We were—"

"Stop!"

Our conversation effectively halted, we turned our attention to Aahz. With melodramatic slowness, he folded his arms across his chest.

"No," he said.

"No?" I shrieked. "But, Aahz . . ."

" 'But, Aahz' nothing," he barked back. "I said 'No' and I meant it."

"Wait a minute," Tananda interceded, stepping between us. "What's the problem, Aahz?"

"If you think I'm going to let my apprentice go traipsing around the dimensions alone and unprotected—"

"I won't be alone," I protested. "Tananda will be there."

"—a prime target for any idiot who wants to bag a demon," Aahz continued, ignoring my outburst, "just so you can have a beast of burden for your shopping jaunt, well, you'd better think again."

"Are you through?" Tananda asked testily.

"For the moment." Aahz nodded, matching her glare for glare.

"First of all," she began, "as Skeeve pointed out, if you'd bothered to listen, he won't be alone. I'll be with him. That means, second of all, he won't be unprotected.

Just because I let my membership with the Assassins Guild expire doesn't mean I've forgotten everything."

"Yeah, Aahz," I interjected.

"Shut up, kid," he snapped.

"Third of all," Tananda continued, "you've got to stop thinking of Skeeve here as a kid. He stopped Big Julie's army, didn't he? And besides, he *is* your apprentice. I assume you've taught him *something* over the last couple of years."

That hit Aahz in his second most sensitive spot. His vanity. His most sensitive spot is his money pouch.

"Well . . ." He wavered.

"C'mon, Aahz," I pleaded. "What could go wrong?"

"The mind boggles," he retorted grimly.

"Don't exaggerate, Aahz," Tananda reprimanded.

"Exaggerate!" my mentor exploded anew. "The first time I took Mr. Wonderful here off-dimension, he bought a dragon we neither need nor want and nearly got killed in a brawl with a pack of cut-throats."

"A fight which he won, as I recall," Tananda observed.

"The second time we went out," Aahz continued undaunted, "I left him at a fast-food joint where he promptly recruited half the deadbeats at the Bazaar for a fighting force."

"They won the war!" I argued.

"That's not the point," Aahz growled. "The point is, every time the kid here hits another dimension, he ends up in trouble. He draws it like a magnet."

"This time I'll be there to keep an eye on him," Tananda soothed.

"You were there the first two times," Aahz pointed out grimly.

"So were you!" she countered.

"That's right!" Aahz agreed. "And both of us together couldn't keep him out of trouble. Now do you see why I want to keep him right here in Klah?"

"Hmm," Tananda said thoughtfully. "I see your point, Aahz."

My heart sank.

"I just don't agree with it," she concluded.

"Damn it, Tananda . . ." Aahz began, but she waved him to silence.

"Let me tell you a story." She smiled. "There was this couple see, who had a kid they thought the world of. They thought so much of him, in fact, that when he was born they sealed him in a special room. Just to be sure nothing would happen to him, they screened everything that went into the room; furniture, books, food, toys, *everything*. They even filtered the air to be sure he didn't get any diseases."

"So?" Aahz asked suspiciously.

"So—on his eighteenth birthday, they opened the room and let him out," Tanda explained. "The kid took two steps and died of excitement."

"Really?" I asked, horrified.

"It's exaggerated a bit," she admitted, "but I think Aahz gets the point."

"I haven't been keeping him sealed in," Aahz mumbled. "There've been some real touch-and-go moments, you know. You've been there for some of them."

"But you *have* been a little overprotective, haven't you, Aahz?" Tananda urged gently.

Aahz was silent for several moments, avoiding our eyes. "All right," he sighed at last. "Go ahead, kid. Just don't come crying to me if you get yourself killed."

"How could I do that?" I frowned.

Tananda nudged me in the ribs and I took the hint.

"There are a few things I want settled before you go," Aahz declared brusquely, a bit of his normal spirit returning.

He began moving back and forth through the room, gathering items from our possessions.

"First," he announced, "here's some money of your own for the trip. You probably won't need it, but you always walk a little taller with money in your pouch."

So saying, he counted out twenty gold pieces into my hands. Realizing I had hired a team of demons to fight a war for five gold pieces, he was giving me a veritable fortune!

"Gee, Aahz . . ." I began, but he hurried on.

"Second, here's the D-Hopper." He tucked the small metal cylinder into my belt. "I've set it to bring you back here. If you get into trouble, if you *think* you're getting into trouble, hit the button and come home *right then*. No heroics, no jazzy speeches. Just hit and get. You understand me?"

"Yes, Aahz," I promised dutifully.

"And finally," he announced, drawing himself up to his full height, "the dragon stays here. You aren't going to drag your stupid pet along with you and that's final. I know you'd like to have him with you, but he'd only cause problems."

"Okay, Aahz." I shrugged.

Actually, I had figured on leaving Gleep behind, but it didn't seem tactful to point that out.

"Well," my mentor sighed, sweeping us both with a hard gaze, "I guess that's that. Sorry I can't hang around to see you off, but I've got more pressing things to do."

With that he turned on his heels and left, shutting the door behind him more forcefully than was necessary.

"That's funny," I said, staring after him. "I didn't think he had anything important to do. In fact, just before you showed up, he was complaining about being bored."

"You know, Skeeve," Tananda said softly, giving me a strange look, "Aahz is really quite attached to you."

"Really?" I frowned. "What makes you say that?"

"Nothing." She smiled. "It was just a thought. Well, are you ready to go?"

"As ready as I'll ever be," I declared confidently. "What's our first stop? The Bazaar at Deva?"

"Goodness, no!" she retorted, wrinkling her nose. "We're after something really unique, not the common stuff they have at the Bazaar. I figure we're going to have to hit some out-of-the-way dimensions, the more out-of-the-way the better."

Despite my confidence, an alarm gong went off in the back of my mind at this declaration.

"What are we looking for, anyway?" I asked casually.

Tananda shot a quick glance at the door, then leaned forward to whisper in my ear.

"I couldn't tell you before," she murmured conspiratorially, "but we're after a birthday present. A birthday present for Aahz!"

III:

*"That's funny, I never have any trouble
with service when I'm shopping."*

— K. KONG

Ever since he took me on as an apprentice, Aahz has
complained that I don't practice enough. He should
have seen me on the shopping trip! In the first three days
after our departure from Klah I spent more time practicing
magik than I had in the previous year.

Tananda had the foresight to bring along a couple of
translator pendants which enabled us to understand and
be understood by the natives in the dimensions we visited.
That was fine for communications, but there remained the
minor detail of our physical appearance. Disguises were
my job.

Besides flying, Aahz had taught me one other spell
which had greatly enhanced my ability to survive dubious
situations; that was the ability to change the outward appearance of my own, or anyone else's, physical features.
Tagging along with Tananda, this skill got a real workout.

The procedure was simple enough. We would arrive at
some secluded point, then creep to a spot where I would
observe a few members of the local population. Once I
had laid eyes on them I could duplicate their physical

form for our disguises and we could blend with the crowd. Of course, my nerves had to be calmed so I wouldn't jump out of my skin when catching a passing glance of the being standing next to me.

If from this you conclude that the dimensions we visited were inhabited by people who looked a little strange . . . you're wrong. The dimensions we visited were peopled by beings who looked *very* strange.

When Tananda decides to tour out-of-the-way dimensions, she doesn't kid around. None of the places we visited looked normal to my untraveled eyes but a few in particular stand out in my memory as being exceptionally weird.

Despite Tananda's jokes about rental agencies, Avis turned out to be populated with bird-like creatures with wings and feathers. In that dimension I not only had to maintain our disguises, I had to fly us from perch to perch as per the local method of transportation. Instead of traversing their market center as I had expected, we spent considerable time viewing their national treasures. These treasures turned out to be a collection of broken pieces of colored glass and bits of shiny metal which to my eye were worthless—but Tananda studied them with quiet intensity.

To maintain our disguises, we had to eat and drink without hands—which proved to be harder than it sounded. Since the food consisted of live grubs and worms, I passed on any opportunity to sample the local cuisine. Tananda, however, literally dove into (remember—no hands!) a bowlful. Whether she licked her lips because she found the fare exceptionally tasty or if she was attempting to catch a few of the wriggly morsels that were trying to escape their fate was not important; I found the sight utterly revolting. To avoid having to watch her, I tried the local wine.

The unusual drinking style meant that I ended up taking larger swallows than I normally would, but that was okay as the wine was light and flavorful. Unfortunately, it also proved to be much stronger than anything I had previously sampled. After I had nearly flown us into a rather large tree Tananda decided it was time for us to move to another dimension.

As a footnote to that particular adventure, the wine had two side effects: First, I developed a colossal headache, and, second, I became violently nauseous. The latter was because Tananda gleefully told me how they make wine on Avis. To this day I can't hear the name Avis without having visions of flying through the air and a vague tinge of air-sickness. As far as I'm concerned, when rating dimensions on a scale of ten, Avis will always be a number two.

Another rather dubious dimension we spent considerable time in was Gastropo. The length of our stay there had nothing to do with our quest. Tananda decided, after relatively few stops, that the dimension had nothing to offer of a quality suitable for Aahz's present. What delayed us was our disguises.

Let me clarify that before aspersions are cast on my admittedly limited abilities, the physical appearance part was easy. As I've said, I'm getting quite good at disguise spells. What hung us up was the manner of locomotion. After flying from tree to tree in Avis, I would have thought I was ready to get from point A to point B in any conceivable way. Well, as Aahz has warned me, the dimensions are an endless source of surprises.

The Gastropods were snails—large snails, but snails nonetheless. Spiral shells, eyes on stalks—the whole bit. I could handle that. What I couldn't get used to was inching my way along with the rest of the local pedestrians—excuse me, *pod*-estrians.

"Tanda," I growled under my breath. "How long are we going to stay in this god-awful dimension?"

"Relax, handsome," she chided, easing forward another inch. "Enjoy the scenery."

"I've been enjoying this particular hunk of scenery for half a day," I complained. "I'm enjoying it so much I've memorized it."

"Don't exaggerate," my guide scolded. "This morning we were on the other side of that tree."

I closed my eyes and bit back my first five or six responses to her correction. "How long?" I repeated.

"I figure we can split after we turn that corner."

"But that corner's a good twenty-five feet away!" I protested.

"That's right," she confirmed. "I figure we'll be there by sundown."

"Can't we just walk over there at normal speed?"

"Not a chance; we'd be noticed."

"By who?"

"Whom. Well, by your admirer, for one."

"My what?" I blinked.

Sure enough, there was a Gastropod chugging heroically along behind us. When it realized I was looking at it, it began to wave its eye-stalks in slow, but enthusiastic, motions.

"It's been after you for about an hour," Tananda confided. "That's why I've been hurrying."

"That does it!" I declared, starting off at a normal pace. "C'mon, Tanda, we're getting out of here."

Shrill cries of alarm were being sounded by the Gastropods as I rounded the corner, followed, shortly, by my guide.

"What's the matter with you?" she demanded. "We could—"

"Get us out—now!" I ordered.

"But—"

"Remember how I got my dragon?" I barked. "If I let an amorous snail follow me home, Aahz will disown me as his apprentice. Now, are you going to get us out of here, or do I use the D-Hopper and head for home?"

"Don't get your back up," she soothed, beginning her ritual to change dimensions. "You shouldn't have worried though, we're looking for cargo—not S-cargo."

We were in another dimension before I could ask her to explain why she was giggling. So it went, dimension after dimension until I gave up trying to predict the unpredictable and settled for coping with the constants. Even this turned out to be a chore. For one thing, I had some unexpected problems with Tananda. I had never noticed it before, but she's really quite vain. She didn't just want to look like a native—she wanted to look like an *attractive* native.

Anyone who thinks beauty is a universal concept should visit some of the places we did. Whatever grotesque form I was asked to duplicate Tananda always had a few polite requests for improving her appearance. After a few days of "the hair should be more matted," or "shouldn't my eye be a bit more bloodshot?" or "a little more slime under the armpits," I was ready to scream. It probably wouldn't have been so annoying if her attention to detail had extended just a little bit to my appearance. All I'd get was—"You? You look fine." That's how I know she's vain; she was more interested in her own appearance than mine.

That wasn't the only thing puzzling about Tananda's behavior. Despite her claim that we were on a shopping trip, she steadfastly avoided the retail sections of the dimensions we visited. Bazaars, farmers' markets, flea markets and all the rest were met with the same wrinkled nose (when there was a nose) and "we don't want to go *there*." Instead she seemed to be content as a tourist. Her inquiries would invariably lead us to national shrines or the public displays of royal treasures. After viewing several of these we would retire to a secluded spot and head off for the next dimension.

In a way this suited me fine. Not only was I getting a running, flying, and crawling tour of the dimensions, I was doing it with Tananda. Tananda is familiar with the social customs of over a hundred dimensions and in every dimension she was just that—familiar. I rapidly learned that in addition to beauty, morality varied from dimension to dimension. The methods of expressing affection in some of the dimensions we visited defy description but invariably make me blush at the memory. Needless to say, after three days of this I was seriously trying to progress beyond the casual friendship level with my shapely guide. I mean, Tananda's interpretation of casual friendship was already seriously threatening the continued smooth operation of my heart—not to mention other organs.

There was a more pressing problem on my mind, however. After three days of visiting strange worlds, I was hungry enough to bite my own arm for the blood. They say if you're hungry enough you'll eat anything. Don't you believe it. The things placed before me and called food were unstomachable despite starvation. I know; I tried occasionally, out of desperation, only to lose everything else in my stomach along with the latest offering. Having Tananda sitting across from me, joyfully chewing tentacled things that oozed out of her mouth and wriggled didn't help.

Finally I expressed my distress and needs to Tananda.

"I wondered why you hadn't been eating much," she frowned. "But I thought maybe you were on a diet, or something. I wish you'd spoken up sooner."

"I didn't want to be a bother," I explained lamely.

"It isn't that," she waved. "It's just that if I had known two dimensions ago, there were half a dozen humanoid dimensions nearby that we could have hopped over to. Right now, there's only one that would fit the bill without us having to go through a couple of extra dimensions along the way."

"Then let's head for that one," I urged. "The sooner I eat the better off we'll be." I wasn't exaggerating. My stomach was beginning to growl so loudly it was a serious threat to our disguises.

"Suit yourself," she shrugged, pulling me behind a row of hedges that tinkled musically in the breeze. "Personally, though, it's not a dimension I normally stop in."

Again the alarm sounded in the back of my head, despite my hunger. "Why not?" I asked suspiciously.

"Because they're weird there—I mean, *really* weird," she confided.

Images flashed across my mind of the beings we'd already encountered. "Weirder than the natives we've been imitating?" I gulped. "I thought you said they'd be humanoid?"

"Not weird physically," Tananda chided, taking my hand. "Weird mentally. You'll see."

"What's the name of the dimension?" I called desperately as she closed her eyes to begin our travels. The scenery around us faded, there was a rush of darkness, then a new scene burst brightly and noisily into view.

"Jahk," she answered, opening her eyes since we were there.

IV:

" 'Weird' is a relative, not an absolute term."

—Baron Frank N. Furter

You recall my account of our usual modus operandi on hitting a new dimension? How we would arrive inconspicuously and disguise ourselves before mingling with the natives? Well, however secluded Tananda's landing point in Jahk might be normally—it wasn't when we arrived.

As the dimension came into focus it was apparent that we were in a small park, heavily overgrown with trees and shrubs. It was not the flora of the place which caught and held my attention, however, it was the crowd. What crowd? you might ask. Why, the one carrying blazing torches and surrounding us, of course. Oh—that crowd!

Well, to be completely honest, they weren't actually surrounding us. They were surrounding the contraption we were standing on. I had never really known what a contraption was when Aahz had used the word in conversation, and being Aahz he wouldn't define the word when I asked him to. Now that I was here, however, I recognized one on sight. The thing we were standing on had to be a contraption.

It was some sort of wagon—in that it was large and had four wheels. Beyond that I couldn't tell much about it, because it was completely covered by tufts of colored paper. That's right, I said paper—light fluffy stuff that would be nice if you had a cold, runny nose. But this paper was mostly yellow and blue. Looming over us was some kind of monstrous, dummy warrior complete with helmet—also covered with tufts of blue and yellow paper.

Of all the things that had flashed across my mind when Tananda warned me that the Jahks were weird, the one thing that had not occurred to me was that they were blue-and-yellow-paper freaks.

"Get off the float!"

This last was shouted at us from someone in the crowd.

"I beg your pardon," I shouted back.

"The float! Get off of it!"

"C'mon, handsome," Tananda hissed, hooking my elbow in hers.

Together we leaped to the ground. As it turned out we were barely in time. With a bloodthirsty howl, the crowd surged forward and tossed their torches onto the contraption we had so recently abandoned. In moments it was a mass of flames the heat of which warmed the already overheated crowd. They danced and sang, joyfully oblivious to the destruction of the contraption.

Edging away from the scene, I realized with horror that it was being duplicated throughout the park. Wherever I looked there were bonfires set on contraptions, and jubilant crowds.

"I think we arrived at a bad time," I observed.

"What makes you say that?" Tananda asked.

"Little things," I explained, "like the fact they're in the middle of torching the town."

"I don't think so." My companion shrugged. "When you torch a town you don't usually start with the parks."

"Okay, then you tell me just what they're doing."

"As far as I can tell, they're celebrating."

"Celebrating what?"

"Some kind of victory. As near as I can tell, everyone's shouting—we won! We won!"

I surveyed the blazes again. "I wonder what they'd do if they lost?"

Just then a harried-looking individual strode up to us. His no-nonsense, business-like manner was an island of sanity in a sea of madness. I didn't like it. Not that I have anything against sanity, mind you. It's just that up 'til now we had been pretty much ignored. I feared that was about to change.

"Here's your pay," he said brusquely, handing us each a pouch. "Turn in your costume at the Trophy Building." With that he was gone, leaving us open-mouthed and holding the bags.

"What was that all about?" I managed to say.

"Beats me," Tananda admitted. "They lost me when they called that contraption a float."

"Then I'm right! It is a contraption," I exclaimed with delight. "I knew they had to be wrong; a float is airtight and won't sink in water."

"I thought it was made with ice cream and ginger ale?" Tananda frowned.

"With what and what?" I blinked.

"Great costumes—really great!" someone shouted to us as they staggered by.

"Time to do something about our disguises," Tananda murmured as she waved to the drunk.

"Right." I nodded, glad we could agree on something.

The disguises should have been easy after my recent experience in other dimensions. I mean the Jahks were humanoid and I had lots of ready models to work from. Unfortunately I encountered problems.

The first was pride. Despite the teeming masses around us, I couldn't settle on two individuals whose appearance I wanted to duplicate. I never considered myself particularly vain; I've never considered myself as being in top physical condition—of course, that was before I arrived in Jahk.

Every being I could see was extremely off-weight—either over or under. If a specific individual wasn't ribs-protruding thin to the point of looking brittle, he was laboring along under vast folds of fat which bunched and bulged at waist, chin and all four cheeks. Try as I might, I couldn't bring myself to alter Tananda or myself to look like these wretched specimens.

My second problem was that I couldn't concentrate, anyway. Disguise spells, like any other magik, require a certain amount of concentration. In the past I've been able to cast spells in the heat of battle or embarrassment. In our current situation I couldn't seem to get my mind focused.

You see there was this song—well, I think it was a song. Anyway the crowd acted like it was singing a rhythmic chant; the chant was incredibly catchy. Even in the short time we'd been there I'd almost mastered the lyrics—which is a tribute to the infectious nature of the song rather than any indication of my ability to learn lyrics. The point is that every time I tried concentrating on our disguises, I found myself singing along with the chant instead. Terrific!

"Any time you're ready, handsome."

"What's that, Tananda?"

"The disguises," she prompted, glancing about nervously. "The spell will work better when you aren't humming."

"I—er, um—I can't seem to find two good models," I alibi'd lamely.

"Are you having trouble counting up to two all of a sudden?" she scowled. "By my count you've got a whole parkful of models."

"But none I want to look like—want *us* to look like," I amended quickly.

"Check me on this," Tananda said, pursing her lips. "Two days ago you disguised us as a pair of slimy slugs, right?"

"Yes, but—"

"And before that as eight-legged dogs?"

"Well, yes, but—"

"And you never complained about how you looked in your disguise then, right?"

"That was different," I protested.

"How?" she challenged.

"Those were—well, things! These are humanoids and I know what humanoids should look like."

"What they *should* look like isn't important," my guide argued. "What matters is what they *do* look like. We've got to blend with the crowd—and the sooner the better."

"But—" I began.

"Because if we don't," she continued sternly, "we're going to run into someone who's both sober and unpreoccupied—which will give us the choice between being guest-of-honor at the next bonfire they light or skipping this dimension before you've had anything to eat."

"I'll try again," I sighed, scanning the crowd once more.

In a desperate effort to comply with Tananda's order, I studied the first two individuals my eyes fell on, then concentrated on duplicating their appearance without really considering how they looked.

"Not bad," Tananda commented dryly, surveying her new body. "Of course, I always thought I looked better as a woman."

"You want a disguise, you get a disguise," I grumbled.

"Hey, handsome," my once-curvaceous comrade breathed, laying a soft, but hairy, hand on my arm. "Relax, we're on the same side. Remember?"

My anger melted away at her touch—as always. Maybe someday I'll develop an immunity to Tananda's charms. Until then I'll just enjoy them. "Sorry, Tanda," I apologized. "Didn't mean to snap at you—log it off to hunger."

"That's right," she exclaimed, clicking her fingers, "we're supposed to be finding you some food. It completely slipped my mind again, what with this racket going on. C'mon, let's see what the blue-plate special is today."

Finding a place to eat turned out to be more of a task than either of us anticipated. Most of the restaurants we came across were either closed or only serving drinks. I half-expected Tananda to suggest that we drink our meal, but mercifully that possibility wasn't mentioned.

We finally located a little sidewalk cafe down a narrow street and elbowed our way to a small table, ignoring the glares of our fellow diners. Service was slow, but my companion sped things up a bit by emptying the contents of one of our pouches onto the tabletop thus attracting the waiter's attention. In short order we were presented with two bowls of steaming whatever. I didn't even try to identify the various lumps and crunchies. It smelled good and tasted better and after several days of enforced fasting, that was all that mattered to me. I glutted myself and was well into my second bowl by the time Tananda finished her first. Pushing the empty dish away she began to study the crowd on the street with growing interest.

"Have you figured out yet what's going on?" she asked.

"Murppg!" I replied through a mouthful of food.

"Hmmm?" She frowned.

"I can't tell for sure," I said, swallowing hard. "Everybody's happy because they won something, but darned if I can hear what they won."

"Well," Tananda shrugged. "I warned you they were weird."

Just then the clamor in the streets soared to new heights, drowning out any efforts at individual conversation. Craning our necks in an effort to locate the source of the disturbance, we beheld a strange phenomenon. A wall-to-wall mob of people was marching down the street, chanting in unison and sweeping along, or trampling, any smaller groups it encountered. Rather than expressing anger or resentment at this intrusion, the people around us were jumping up and down and cheering, hugging each other with tears of pure joy in their eyes. The focus of everyone's attention seemed to be sitting on a litter borne aloft by the stalwarts at the head of the crowd. I was fortunate enough to get a look at it as it passed by— fortunate in that I could see it without having to move. The crowds were such that I couldn't move if I'd wanted to, so it was just as well that it passed close by.

To say they carried a statue would be insufficient. It was the *ugliest* thing I had ever seen in my life and that included everything I'd just seen on this trip with Tananda. It was small, roughly twice the size of my head, and depicted a large, four-legged toad holding a huge eye-ball in its mouth. Along its back, instead of warts, were the torsos, heads and arms of tiny Jahks intertwined in truly grotesque eroticism. These figures were covered with the warty protrusions one would expect to have found on the toad itself. As a crowning touch, the entire thing had a mottled gold finish which gave the illusion of splotches crawling back and forth on the surface.

I was totally repulsed by the statue, but it was obvious the crowd around me did not share these feelings. They swept forward in a single wave, joining the mob and add-ing their voices to the chant which could still be heard long after the procession had vanished from sight. Finally we were left in relative quiet on a street deserted save for a few random bodies of those not swift enough to either join or evade the mob.

"Well," I said casually, clearing my throat. "I guess we know what they won, now. Right?"

There was no immediate response. I shot a sharp glance at my companion and found her staring down the street after the procession.

"Tanda," I repeated, slightly concerned.

"That's it," she said with sudden, impish glee.

"That's what?" I blinked.

"Aahz's birthday present," she proclaimed.

I peered down the street, wondering what she was looking at. "What is?" I asked.

"That statue," she said firmly.

"*That* statue?" I cried, unable to hide my horror.

"Of course," she nodded, "it's perfect. Aahz will have never seen one, much less owned one."

"How do you figure that?" I pressed.

"It's obviously one-of-a-kind," she explained. "I mean, who could make something like that twice?"

She had me there, but I wasn't about to give up the fight. "There's just one little problem. I'm no expert on psychology, but if that pack we just saw is any decent sample, I don't think the folks around here are going to be willing to sell us their pretty statue."

"Of course not, silly." She laughed, turning to her food

again. "That's what makes it priceless. I never planned to *buy* Aahz's present."

"But if it isn't for sale, how do we get it?" I frowned, fearing the answer.

Tananda choked suddenly on her food. It took me a moment to realize she was laughing. "Oh, Skeeve," she gasped at last, "you're such a kidder."

"I am?" I blinked.

"Sure," she insisted, looking deep into my eyes. "Why do you think it was so important for you to come along on this trip. I mean, you've always said you wanted to be a thief."

V:

"Nothing is impossible. Anything can be accomplished with proper preparation and planning."

—PONCE DE LEON

It was roughly twelve hours later, the start of a new day. We were still in Jahk. I was still protesting. At the very least, I was sure this latest madcap project was *not* in line with Aahz's instructions to stay out of trouble.

Tananda, on the other hand, insisted that it would not be any trouble—or it *might* not be any trouble. We wouldn't know for sure until we saw what kind of security the locals had on the statue. In the meantime, why assume the worst?

I took her advice. I assumed the best. I assumed the security would be impenetrable and that we'd give the whole idea up as a lost cause.

So it was, with different but equally high hopes, we set out in search of the statue.

The town was deathly still in the early morning light. Apparently everyone was sleeping off the prior night's festivities—which seemed a reasonable pastime, all things considered.

We did manage to find one open restaurant, however. The owner was wearily shoveling out the rubble left by the celebrating crowds, and grudgingly agreed to serve us breakfast.

I had insisted on this before setting out. I mean, worried or not, it takes more than one solid meal to counterbalance the effects of a three-day stretch without food.

"So," I declared once we were settled at the table. "How do we go about locating the statue?"

"Easy," Tananda winked. "I'll ask our host a few subtle questions when he serves our food."

As if summoned by her words, the owner appeared with two steaming plates of food, which he plopped on the table in front of us with an unceremonious *klunk*.

"Thanks," I nodded, and was answered with an unenthusiastic grunt.

"Say, could we ask you a couple questions?" Tananda purred.

"Such as?" the man responded listlessly.

"Such as where do they keep the statue?" she asked bluntly.

I choked on my food. Tananda's idea of interrogation is about as subtle as a flogging. I keep forgetting she's a long standing drinking partner of Aahz's.

"The statue?" Our host frowned.

"The one that was being carried up and down the streets yesterday," Tananda clarified easily.

"Oh! You mean the *Trophy*." The man laughed. "Statue. Hey, that's a good one. You two must be new in town."

"You might say that," I confirmed dryly. I had never been that fond of being laughed at—particularly early in the morning.

"Statue, trophy, what's the difference?" Tananda shrugged. "Where is it kept?"

"It's on public display in the Trophy Building, of course," the owner informed us. "If you want to see it, you'd best get started early. After five years, everyone in the city's going to be showing up for a look-see."

"How far is it to—" Tananda began, but I interrupted her.

"You have a whole building for trophies?" I asked with forced casualness. "How many trophies are there?"

"Just the one," our host announced. "We put up a building especially for it. You two must *really* be new not to know that."

"Just got in yesterday," I confirmed. "Just to show you how new we are, we don't even know what the trophy's for."

"For?" The man gaped. "Why, it's for winning the Big Game, of course."

"What big game?"

The question slipped out before I thought. It burst upon the conversation like a bombshell, and our host actually gave ground a step in astonishment. Tananda nudged my foot warningly under the table, but I had already realized I had made a major blunder.

"I can see we have a lot to learn about your city, friend," I acknowledged smoothly. "If you have the time, we'd appreciate your joining us in a glass of wine. I'd like to hear more about this Big Game."

"Say, that's nice of you," our host declared, brightening noticeably. "Wait right here. I'll fetch the wine."

"What was that all about?" Tananda hissed as soon as he had moved out of earshot.

"I'm after some information," I retorted. "Specifically, about the Trophy."

"I know that," she snapped. "The question is 'Why?' "

"As a thief," I explained loftily, "I feel I should know as much as possible about what I'm trying to steal."

"Who ever told you that?" Tananda frowned. "All you want to know about a target item is how big it is, how heavy it is, and what it will sell for. Then you study the security protecting it. Learning a lot about the item itself is a handicap, not an advantage."

"How do you figure that?" I asked, my curiosity aroused in spite of myself.

My companion rolled her eyes in exasperation.

"Because it'll make you feel guilty," she explained. "When you find out how emotionally attached the current owner is to the item, or that he'll be bankrupt without it, or that he'll be killed if it's stolen, then you'll be reluctant to take it. When you actually make your move, guilt can make you hesitate, and hesitant thieves either end up in jail or dead."

I was going to pursue the subject further, but our host chose that moment to rejoin us. Balancing a bottle and three glasses in his hands, he hooked an extra chair over to our table with his foot.

"Here we go," he announced, depositing his load in front of us. "The best in the house—or the best that's left after the celebrations. You know how that is. No matter how much you stock in advance, it's never enough."

"No, we don't know," I corrected. "I was hoping you could tell us."

"That's right." He nodded, filling the glasses. "You know I still can't believe how little you know about politics."

"Politics?" I blinked. "What does the Big Game have to do with politics?"

"It has everything to do with politics," our host proclaimed mightily. "That's the point. Don't you see?"

"No," I admitted bluntly.

The man sighed.

"Look," he said, "this land has two potential capitals. One is Veygus, and this one, as you know, is Ta-hoe."

I hadn't known it, but it seemed unwise to admit my ignorance. I'm slow, but not dumb.

"Since there can only be one capital at any given time," our host continued, "the two cities compete for the privilege each year. The winner is the capital and gets to be the center of government for the next year. The Trophy is the symbol of that power, and Veygus has had it for the last five years. Yesterday we finally won it back."

"You mean the Big Game decides who's going to run the land?" I exclaimed, realization dawning at last. "Excuse my asking, but isn't that a bit silly?"

"No sillier than any other means of selecting governmental leadership," the man countered, shrugging his bony shoulders. "It sure beats going to war. Do you think it's a coincidence that we've been playing the game for five hundred years and there hasn't been a civil war in that entire time?"

"But if the Big Game has replaced civil war, then what—" I began, but Tananda interrupted.

"I hate to interrupt," she interrupted, "but if we're going to beat the crowds, we'd better get going. Where did you say the Trophy Building was, again?"

"One block up and six blocks to the left," our host supplied. "You'll know it by the crowds. I'll set the rest of the bottle aside and we can finish it after you've seen the Trophy."

"We'd appreciate that." Tananda smiled, paying him for our meal.

Apparently she had succeeded in using the right currency, for the owner accepted it without batting an eye and waved a fond farewell as we started off.

"I was hoping to find out more about this Big Game," I grumbled as we passed out of earshot.

"No, you weren't," my guide corrected.

"I wasn't?" I frowned.

"No. You were getting involved," she pointed out. "We're here to get a birthday present, not to get embroiled in local politics."

"I wasn't getting involved," I protested. "I was just trying to get a little information."

Tananda sighed heavily.

"Look, Skeeve," she said, "take some advice from an old dimension traveler. Too much information is poison. Every dimension has its problems, and if you start learning the gruesome details, it occurs to you how simple it would be to help out. Once you see a problem *and* a solution, you feel almost obligated to meddle. That always leads to trouble, and we're supposed to be avoiding trouble this trip, remember?"

I almost pointed out the irony of her advising me to avoid trouble while en route to engineer a theft. Then it occurred to me that if the theft didn't bother her, but local politics did, I might be wise to heed her advice. As I've said, I'm slow, but not dumb.

As predicted, the Trophy Building was crowded despite the early hour. As we approached, I marveled anew at the physique of the natives—or specifically, the lack thereof.

Tananda did not seem to share my fascination with the natives, and threaded her way nimbly through the throng, leaving me to follow behind. There was no organized line, and by the time we got through one of the numerous doors, the throng was thick enough to impede our progress. Tananda continued making her way closer to the Trophy, but I stopped just inside the door. My advantage of height gave me a clear view of the Trophy from where I was.

If anything, it was uglier seen plainly than it had been viewed from a distance.

"Isn't it magnificent?" the woman standing next to me sighed.

It took me a moment to realize she was speaking to me. My disguise made me look shorter, and she was talking to my chest.

"I've never seen anything like it," I agreed lamely.

"Of course not." She frowned. "It's the last work done by the great sculptor Watgit before he went mad."

It occurred to me that the statue might have been done *after* he went mad. Then it occurred to me that it might have driven him mad—especially if he had been working from a live model. I became so lost in the horrible thought that I started nervously when Tananda reappeared at my side and touched my arm.

"Let's go, handsome," she murmured. "I've seen enough."

The brevity of her inspection gave me hope.

"There's no hope, eh?" I sighed dramatically. "Gee, that's tough. I had really been looking forward to testing my skills."

"That's good," she purred, taking my arm. "Because I think I see a way we can pull this caper off."

I wasn't sure what a caper was, but I was certain that once I found out I wouldn't like it. I was right.

VI:

"Now you see it, now you don't."

—H. SHADOWSPAWN

"**A**re you positive there was no lock on the door?" I asked for the twenty-third time.

"Keep it down," Tananda hissed, laying a soft hand on my lips, though none too gently. "Do you want to wake everybody?"

She had a point. We were crouched in an alley across from the Trophy Building, and as the whole idea of our waiting was to be sure everyone was asleep, it was counterproductive to make so much noise we kept them awake. Still, I had questions I wanted answered.

"You're sure?" I asked again in a whisper.

"Yes, I'm sure," Tananda sighed. "You could have seen for yourself if you had looked."

"I was busy looking at the statue," I admitted.

"Uh-huh," my partner snorted. "Remember what I said about getting over-involved with the target? You were supposed to be checking security, not playing art connoisseur."

"Well, I don't like it," I declared suspiciously, eager to get the conversation off my shortcomings. "It's too easy. I can't believe they'd leave something they prize as highly as that Trophy in an unlocked, unguarded building."

"There are a couple things you've overlooked," Tanda chided. "First of all, that statue's one of a kind. That means any thief who stole it would have some real problems trying to sell it again. If he even showed it to anyone here in Ta-hoe, they'd probably rip his arms off."

"He could hold it for ransom," I pointed out.

"Hey, that's pretty good," my guide exclaimed softly, nudging me in the ribs. "We'll make a thief of you yet! However, that brings us to the second thing you overlooked."

"Which is?"

"It's not unguarded," she smiled.

"But you said—" I began.

"Sshh!" she cautioned. "I said there would be no guards in the building with the Trophy."

I closed my eyes and regained control of my nerves, particularly those influenced by blind panic.

"Tanda," I said gently. "Don't you think it's about time you shared some of the details of your master plan with me?"

"Sure, handsome," she responded, slipping an arm around my waist. "I didn't think you were interested."

I resisted an impulse to throttle her.

"Just tell me," I urged. "First off, what *is* the security on the Trophy."

"Well," she said, tapping her chin with one finger, "as I said, there are no guards in the building. There is, however, a silent alarm that will summon guards. It's triggered by the nightingale floor."

"The what?" I interrupted.

"The nightingale floor," she repeated. "It's a fairly common trick throughout the dimensions. The wooden floor around the Trophy is riddled with deliberately loosened boards that creak when you step on them. In this case, they not only creak, they trip an alarm."

"Wonderful!" I grimaced. "So we can't set foot in the

room we're supposed to steal something out of. Anything else?"

I was speaking sarcastically, but Tananda took me seriously.

"Just the magikal wards around the statue itself," she shrugged.

"Magikal wards?" I gulped. "You mean there's magik in this dimension?"

"Of course there is," Tananda smiled. "You're here."

"I didn't set any wards," I exclaimed.

"That wasn't what I meant," Tanda chided. "Look, you tapped into the magikal force lines to disguise us. That means there's magik here for anyone trained to use it—not just us, anyone. Even if none of the locals are adept, there's nothing stopping someone from another dimension from dropping in and using what's here."

"Okay, okay," I sighed. "I guess I wasn't thinking. I guess the next question is, how are we supposed to beat the funny floor and the wards?"

"Easy," she grinned. "The wards are sloppy. Someone set up a fence instead of a dome when they cast the wards. All you have to do is levitate the Trophy over the wards and float it across the floor into our waiting arms. We never even have to set foot in the room."

"Whoa!" I cautioned, holding up a hand. "There's one problem with that. I can't do it."

"You can't?" She blinked. "I thought levitation was one of your strongest spells."

"It is," I conceded. "But that statue's heavy. I couldn't levitate it from a distance. It has something to do with what Aahz calls leverage. I'd have to be close, practically standing on top of it."

"Okay," she said at last. "We'll just have to switch to Plan B."

"You have a Plan B?" I asked, genuinely impressed.

"Sure," she grinned. "I just made it up. You can fly us both across the floor and over the wards. Then we latch onto the Trophy and fly back to Klah from inside the wards."

"I don't know." I frowned.

"Now what's wrong?" My guide scowled.

"Well, flying's a form of levitation," I explained. "I've never tried flying myself and someone else, and even if I can do it, we'll be pushing down on the floor as hard as if we were walking on it. It might set the alarm off."

"If I understand flying," Tanda pondered, "our weight would be more dispersed than if we were walking, but you're right. There's no point in taking the extra risk of flying us both across the floor."

She snapped her fingers suddenly.

"Okay. Here's what we'll do," she exclaimed, leaning forward. "You fly across to the Trophy alone while I wait by the door. Then, when you're in place, you can use the D-Hopper to bring yourself and the Trophy back to Klah, while I blip back magically."

For some reason, the thought of dividing our forces in the middle of a theft bothered me.

"Say . . . um, Tanda," I said, "it occurs to me that even if we set off the alarm, we would be long gone by the time the guards arrived. I mean, if they haven't had war for over five hundred years, they're bound to be a little sloppy turning out."

"No," Tananda countered firmly. "If we've got a way to completely avoid alerting the guards, we'll take it. I promised Aahz to keep you out of trouble, and that means—"

She broke off suddenly, staring across the street.

"What is it?" I hissed, craning my neck for a better look.

In response, she pointed silently at the darkened Trophy Building.

A group of a dozen cloaked figures had appeared from the shadows beside the building. They looked briefly up and down the street, then turned and disappeared into the building.

"I thought you said there wouldn't be any guards in the building!" I whispered frantically.

"I don't understand it," Tananda murmured, more to herself than to me. "It's not laid out for a guard force."

"But if there are guards, we can't—" I began, but Tananda silenced me with a hand on my arm.

The group had reemerged from the building. Moving more slowly than when we had first seen them, they edged their way back into the shadows and vanished from sight.

"That's a relief," Tananda declared, letting out a pent-up breath. "It's just a pack of drunks sneaking an after-hours look at the Trophy."

"They didn't act like drunks," I commented doubtfully.

"C'mon, handsome," my guide declared, clapping a hand on my shoulder. "It's time we got this show on the road. Follow me."

Needless to say, I didn't want to go, but I was even more reluctant to be left behind. This left me no choice but to follow as she headed across the street. As I went, though, I took the precaution of fumbling out my D-Hopper. I didn't like the feel of this, and wanted to be sure my exit route was at hand in case of trouble.

"In you go!" Tananda ordered, holding the door open. "Be sure to sing out when you're in position. I want to be there to see Aahz's face when you give him the Trophy."

"I can't see anything," I protested, peering into the dark building.

"Of course not!" Tananda snapped. "It's dark. You know where the Trophy is, though, so get going."

At her insistence, I reached out with my mind and pushed gently against the floor. As had happened a hundred times in practice, I lifted free and began to float toward the estimated position of the statue.

As I went, it occurred to me I had neglected to ask Tananda how high the wards extended. I considered going back or calling to her, but decided against it. Noise would be dangerous, and time was precious. I wanted to get this over with as soon as possible. Instead, I freed part of my mind from the task of flying and cast about in front of me, seeking the tell-tale aura of the magikal wards. There were none.

"Tanda!" I hissed, speaking before I thought. "The wards are down!"

"Impossible," came her response from the door. "You must be in the wrong spot. Check again."

I tried again, casting about the full extent of the room. Nothing. As I peered about, I realized my eyes were acclimating to the darkness.

"There are no wards," I called softly. "I'm right over the pedestal and there are no wards."

Something was tugging at my consciousness. Something I had seen was terribly wrong, but my attention was occupied scanning for the wards.

"If you're over the pedestal," Tananda called, "then drop down and get the Trophy. And hurry! I think I hear someone coming."

I lowered myself to the floor, gently as I remembered the creaky boards, and turned to the pedestal. Then it burst upon me what was wrong.

"It's gone!" I cried.

"What?" Tananda gasped, her silhouette appearing in the doorway.

"The Trophy! It's gone!" I exclaimed, running my hands over the vacant pedestal.

"Get out, Skeeve," Tananda called, suddenly full volume.

I started for the door, but her voice stopped me.

"No! Use the D-Hopper. Now!"

My thumb went to the activator button on the device I had been clutching, but I hesitated.

"What about you?" I called. "Aren't you coming?"

"After you're gone," she insisted. "Now get go—"

Something came flying out of the dark and struck her silhouette. She went down in a boneless heap.

"Tanda!" I shouted, starting forward.

Suddenly the doorway was filled with short silhouettes swarming all over Tananda's prone form.

I wavered for a moment in indecision.

"There's another one inside!" someone called.

So much for indecision. I hit the button.

There was the now familiar rush of darkness . . . and I was back in my quarters on Klah.

Aahz was seated at a table with his back to me, but he must have heard the *BAMF* of my arrival.

"It's about time!" he growled. "Did you enjoy your little—"

He broke off as he turned and his eyes took in the expression on my face.

"Aahz," I cried, stumbling forward. "We're in trouble."

His fist came down in a crash which splintered the table.

"I knew it!" he snarled.

VII:

"A friend in need is a pest."

—FAFHRD

"Now let's see if I've got this straight," Aahz grumbled, pacing the length of the room. "You got away without a scratch, but Tanda got caught. Right?"

"I couldn't help it!" I moaned, shaking my head. "They were all over her and you said—"

"I know, I know." My mentor waved. "You did the right thing. I'm just trying to get a clear picture of the situation. You're sure this was in Jahk? The weird dimension with the short, pale guys? Skinny or overweight?"

"That's right," I confirmed. "Do you know it?"

"I've heard of it," Aahz shrugged, "but I've never gotten around to visiting. It's talked around a bit on the gambling circuit."

"Must be because of the Big Game," I suggested brightly.

"What I can't figure," Aahz mused, ignoring my comments, "is what you two were doing there."

"Um . . . it was sort of because of me," I admitted in a small voice.

"You?" Aahz blinked, halting his pacing to stare at me. "Who told you about Jahk?"

"No one," I clarified hastily. "It wasn't that I asked to go to Jahk specifically. I was hungry, and Tanda said Jahk was the closest dimension where I could find something to eat."

"I know how that is," my mentor grimaced. "Eating is always a problem when you're traveling the dimensions— even the humanoid ones."

"It's even rougher when you aren't even visiting humanoid dimensions," I agreed.

"Is that a fact?" Aahz murmured, eyeing me suspiciously. "Which dimensions did you visit, anyway?"

"Um . . . I can't remember all the names," I evaded. "Tanda—um—felt there would be less chance of trouble in some of the out of the way dimensions."

"What did the natives look like?" Aahz pressed.

"Aren't we getting off the subject?" I asked desperately. "The real issue is Tanda."

Surprisingly, the ploy worked.

"You're right, kid." Aahz sighed. "Okay. I want you to think hard. You're sure you don't know who jumped her or why?"

My conversational gambit had backfired. The question placed me in a real dilemma. On the one hand, I couldn't expect Aahz to come up with a rescue plan unless he knew the full situation. On the other, I wasn't particularly eager to admit what we were doing when Tananda was captured.

"Um . . ." I said, avoiding his eyes. "I think I can remember a few things about those other dimensions after all. There was one where . . ."

"Wait a minute," Aahz interrupted. "You were the one who said we should focus on Tanda's problem. Now don't go straying off . . ."

He stopped in mid-sentence to examine me closely. "You're holding out on me, kid," he announced in a cold voice that allowed no room for argument. "Now give! What haven't you told me about this disaster?"

His words hung expectantly in the air, and it occurred to me I couldn't stall any longer.

"Well . . ." I began, clearing my throat. "I'm not sure, but I think the ones who grabbed Tanda were the city guardsmen."

"Guardsmen?" Aahz frowned. "Why would they want to put the grab on Tanda? All you were doing was getting a bite to eat and maybe a little shopping."

I didn't answer, taking a sudden interest in studying my feet in close detail.

"That *is* all you were doing, wasn't it?"

I tried to speak, but the words wouldn't come.

"What *were* you doing?" Aahz growled. "Come on. Out with it. I should have known it wasn't just . . . Hey! You didn't kill anyone, did you?"

Strong hands closed on my shoulders and my head was tossed about by a none too gentle shaking.

"We didn't kill anyone!" I shouted, the process difficult because my jaw was moving in a different direction than my tongue. "We were just stealing . . ."

"Stealing!?!"

The hands on my shoulders released their grip so fast I fell to the floor. Fortunately, I had the presence of mind to break my fall with my rump.

"I don't believe it! Stealing!" Aahz made his appeal to the ceiling. "All this because you tried to steal something."

My rump hurt, but I had other more pressing matters to deal with. I was desperately trying to phrase my explanation when I realized with some astonishment that Aahz was laughing.

"Stealing!" he repeated. "You know, you really had me going for a minute there, kid. Stealing! And I thought it was something important."

"You mean, you aren't mad?" I asked incredulously.

"Mad? Naw!" he proclaimed. "Like the old saying goes, 'you can take the boy out of thieving' . . . Heck! Most demons are thieves. It's the only way to get something if you don't have any native coinage."

"I thought you'd really be upset," I stammered, still unwilling to believe my good fortune.

"Now, don't get me wrong, kid," my mentor amended sternly, "I'm not overjoyed with your venture into thievery. You're supposed to be studying magik . . . the kind that will get you a raise as a court magician, not the kind that ends up with you running down a dark alley. Still, all things considered, you could have done a lot worse on your first solo trip through the dimension."

"Gee, thanks, Aahz." I beamed.

"So, let's see it." He smiled, extending a palm.

"See what?" I blinked.

"What you stole," he insisted. "If you came here direct from the scene of the crime, I assume you still have it with you."

"Umm . . . actually." I gulped, avoiding his eyes again. "I—that is, we didn't get it. It's still back in Jahk somewhere."

"You mean to say you went through all this hassle, got Tanda captured, and came running back here with your tail between your legs, and you didn't even bother to pick up what you were trying to steal?"

The storm clouds were back in Aahz's face. I realized I was on the brink of being in trouble again.

"But you said . . ." I protested.

"I know you aren't supposed to be a thief!" my mentor roared. "But once you set your hand to it, I expect you to at least be a successful thief! To think an apprentice of mine can't even put together a workable plan . . ."

"It was Tanda's plan," I offered weakly.

"It was?" Aahz seemed slightly mollified. "Well, you should have checked it over yourself before you joined in."

"I did," I protested. "As far as I can tell it should have worked."

"Oh, really?" came the sarcastic reply. "All right. Why don't you tell me all about this plan that didn't work after you okayed it."

He dragged up a chair and sat in front of me, leaving me little option but to narrate the whole story. I went over the whole thing for him; the plan, the nightingale floor, the magik wards, everything—except what we were trying to steal, and why. By the time I had finished, his jeering smile had faded to a thoughtful frown.

"You're right, kid," he admitted at last. "It should have worked. The only thing I can figure is that they moved your target somewhere else for safekeeping—but that doesn't make sense. I mean, why would they set up all the security arrangements if the target was going to be kept somewhere else? And that group hanging around the building before you went in sounds a bit suspicious."

He thought for a few more minutes, then sighed and shrugged his shoulders. "Oh, well," he proclaimed. "Nobody wins *all* the time. It didn't work and that's that. C'mon, kid. Let's get some sleep."

"Sleep?" I gasped. "What about Tanda?"

"What about her?" Aahz frowned.

"They're holding her prisoner in Jahk!" I exclaimed. "Aren't we going to try to rescue her?"

"Oh, that!" My mentor laughed. "Don't worry about her. She'll be along on her own in a little while."

"But they're holding her prisoner!" I insisted.

"You think so?" Aahz grinned. "Stop and think a minute, kid. How are they going to hold her? Remember, she can hop dimensions any time she wants. The only reason she didn't come back at the same time you did is that she got knocked cold. As soon as she wakes up, she'll be back. Mark my words."

Something about his logic didn't ring true, but I couldn't put my finger on it.

"What if they execute her before she wakes up?" I asked.

"Execute her?" Aahz frowned. "For what? The heist didn't work, so they've still got their whatever. I can't see anyone getting upset enough to have her executed."

"I dunno, Aahz," I said. "The whole city seemed pretty worked up over the Trophy, and . . ."

"Trophy?" Aahz interrupted. "You mean the Trophy from the Big Game? What does that have to do with anything?"

"That's . . . um, that's what we were trying to steal," I explained.

"The Trophy?" Aahz exclaimed. "You two didn't aim small, did you? What did you want with—no, on second thought don't tell me. That woman's logic always makes my head hurt."

"But now you see why I'm afraid they might execute her," I pressed, secretly relieved at not having to disclose the motive for our theft.

"It's a possibility," Aahz admitted, "but I still think they'd let her wake up first. Public trials are dramatic, especially for something as big as trying to steal the Big Game Trophy. Heck, Tanda's enough of a sport that she might even stick around for the trial before popping back here."

"You really think so?" I pressed.

"I'm sure of it," Aahz declared confidently. "Now let's get some sleep. It sounds like it's been a long day for you."

I grudgingly retired to my bed, but I didn't go to sleep immediately. There was still something eluding my mental grasp—something important. As I lay there, my mind began wandering back over my trip—the sights, the smells, the strange beings . . .

"Aahz!" I shouted, bolting upright. "Aahz! Wake up!"

"What is it?" my mentor growled sleepily, struggling to rise.

"I just remembered! I was handling our disguises for the whole trip."

"So what?" Aahz growled. "It's good practice for you, but . . ."

"Don't you see?" I insisted. "If I'm here and Tanda's unconscious in Jahk, then she hasn't got a disguise! They'll be able to see she isn't one of them—that she's a demon!"

There was a frozen moment of silence, then Aahz was on his feet, looming over me.

"Don't just sit there, kid," he growled. "Get the D-Hopper. We're going to Jahk!"

VIII:

"Once more into the breach..."

—ZARNA, THE HUMAN CANNONBALL

Fortunately, there *was* a setting for Jahk on our D-Hopper though Aahz had to search a bit to find it.

I wanted to go armed to the teeth, but my mentor vetoed the plan. Under cross-examination I had had to admit that I hadn't seen anyone in that dimension wearing arms openly except the city guards, and that was that. My ability to disguise things was weak when it came to metal objects, and swords and knives would have made us awfully conspicuous walking down the street. As Aahz pointed out, the one time you don't want to wear weapons is when they're more likely to get you into trouble than out of it.

I hate it when Aahz makes sense.

Anyway, aside from a few such minor squabbles and disputes, our departure from Klah and our subsequent arrival at Jahk was smooth and uneventful. In hindsight, I realize that was the last thing to go right for some time.

"Well, kid," Aahz exclaimed, looking about him eagerly, "where do we go?"

"I don't know," I admitted, scanning the horizon.

Aahz frowned. "Let me run this by you slowly," he sighed. "You've been here before, and I haven't. Now, even your limited brain should realize that that makes you the logical guide. Got it?"

"But I *haven't* been here before," I protested. "Not *here!* When Tanda and I arrived, we were in a park in Ta-hoe!"

At the moment, Aahz and I were standing beside a dirt road, surrounded by gently rolling meadows and a scattering of very strange trees. There wasn't even an outhouse in sight, much less the booming metropolis I had visited.

"Don't tell me, let me guess," Aahz whispered, shutting his eyes as if in pain. "Tanda handled your transport on the way in the first time. Right?"

"That's right," I nodded. "You made me promise to keep the D-Hopper set for Klah, and . . ."

"I know, I know," my mentor waved impatiently. "I must say, though, you pick the damnedest times to be obedient. Okay! So the D-Hopper's set for a different drop zone than the one Tanda uses. We'll just have to dig up a native guide to get us oriented."

"Terrific!" I grimaced. "And where are we supposed to find a native guide?"

"How about right over there?" Aahz smirked, pointing.

I followed the line of his extended talon. Sure enough, not a stone's throw away was a small pond huddled in the shade of a medium-sized tree. Seated, leaning against the tree, was a young native. The only thing that puzzled me was that he was holding one end of a short stick, and there was a string which ran from the stick's other end to the pond.

"What's he doing?" I asked suspiciously.

"From here, I'd say he's fishing," Aahz proclaimed.

"Fishing? Like that?" I frowned. "Why doesn't he just . . ."

"I'll explain later," my mentor interrupted. "Right now we're trying to get directions to Ta-hoe. Remember?"

"That's right!" I nodded. "Let's go."

I started forward, only to be stopped short by Aahz's heavy hand on my shoulder.

"Kid," he sighed, "aren't you forgetting something?"

"What?" I blinked.

"Our disguises, dummy," he snarled. "Your lazy old teacher would like to be able to ask our questions without chasing him all around the landscape for the answers."

"Oh! Right, Aahz."

Embarrassed by the oversight, I hastily did my disguise bit, and together we approached the dozing native.

"Excuse me, sir," I began, clearing my throat, "can you tell us the way to Ta-hoe?"

"What are you doing out here?" the youth demanded, without opening his eyes. "Don't you know the land between Veygus and Ta-hoe is a no-man's-land until the war's over?"

"What did he say?" Aahz scowled.

"What was that?" the youth asked, his eyes snapping open.

For a change, my mind grasped the situation instantly. I was still wearing my translator pendant from my travels with Tananda, but Aahz didn't have one. That meant that while I could understand and be understood by both Aahz and the native, neither of them could decipher what the other was saying. Our disguise was in danger of being discovered by the first native we'd met on our rescue mission. Terrific.

"Umm. Excuse me a moment, sir," I stammered at the youth.

Thinking fast, I removed the pendant from around my neck and looped it over my arm. Aahz understood at once, and thrust his hand through the pendant, grasping my forearm with an iron grip. Thus, we were both able to utilize the power of the pendant.

Unfortunately, the native noticed this by-play. His eyes, which had opened at the sound of Aahz's voice, now widened to the point of popping out as he looked from one of us to the other.

"Fraternity initiation," Aahz explained conspiratorially, winking at him.

"A what?" I blinked.

"Later, kid," my mentor mumbled tensely. "Get the conversation going again."

"Right. Ummm . . . what was that you were saying about a war?"

"I was saying you shouldn't be here," the youth replied, regaining some of his bluster, but still eyeing the pendant suspiciously. "Both sides have declared this area off-limits to civilians until after the war's over."

"When did this war start?" I asked.

"Oh, it won't actually start for a week or so," the native shrugged. "We haven't had a war for over five hundred years and everyone's out of practice. It'll take them a while to get ready—but you still shouldn't be here."

"Well, what are *you* doing here?" Aahz challenged. "You don't look like a soldier to me."

"My dad's an officer," the youth yawned. "If a Ta-hoer patrol finds me out here, I'll just tell 'em who my father is and they'll keep their mouths shut."

"What if a patrol from Veygus finds you?" I asked curiously.

"The Veygans?" He laughed incredulously. "They're even more unprepared than Ta-hoe is. They haven't even got their uniforms designed yet, much less organized enough to send out patrols."

"Well, we appreciate the information," Aahz announced. "Now if you'll just point out the way to Ta-hoe, we'll get ourselves off your battlefield."

"The way to Ta-hoe?" the youth frowned. "You don't know the way to Ta-hoe? That's strange."

"What's strange?" my mentor challenged. "So we're new around here. So what?"

The youth eyed him passively.

"It's strange," he observed calmly, "because that road only runs between Veygus and Ta-hoe. Perhaps you can explain how it is that you're traveling a road without knowing either where you're going or where you're coming from?"

There was a moment of awkward silence, then I withdrew my arm from the translator pendant.

"Well, Aahz," I sighed, "how do we talk our way out of this one?"

"Put your arm back in the pendant," Aahz hissed. "He's getting suspicious."

"He's *already* suspicious," I pointed out. "The question is what do we do now?"

"Nothing to it." My mentor winked. "Just watch how I handle this."

In spite of my worries, I found myself smiling in eager anticipation. Nobody can spin a lie like Aahz once he gets rolling.

"The explanation is really quite simple," Aahz smiled, turning to the youth. "You see, we're magicians who just dropped in from another world. Having just arrived here, we are naturally disoriented."

"My, what a clever alibi," I commented dryly.

Aahz favored me with a dirty look.

"As I was saying," he continued, "we have come to offer our services to the glorious city of Ta-hoe for the upcoming war."

It occurred to me that that last statement was a little suspicious. I mean, we had clearly not known about the war at the beginning of this conversation. Fortunately, the youth overlooked this minor detail.

"Magicians?" He smiled skeptically. "You don't look like magicians to me."

"Show him, kid," Aahz instructed.

"Show him?" I blinked.

"That's right," my mentor nodded. "Drop the disguises, one at a time."

With a shrug, I slipped my arm back into the translator pendant and let my disguise fall away.

"I am Skeeve," I announced, "and this"—I dropped Aahz's disguise—"is my friend and fellow magician, Aahz."

The effect on the youth couldn't have been greater if we had lit a fire under him. Dropping his pole, he sprang to his feet and began backing away until I was afraid he'd topple into the pond. His eyes were wide with fright, and his mouth kept opening and shutting, though no sounds came forth.

"That's enough, kid," Aahz winked. "He's convinced."

I hastily reassembled the disguises, but it did little to calm the youth.

"Not a bad illusion, eh, sport?" My mentor leered at him.

"I . . . I . . ." the youth stammered. Then he paused and set his lips. "Ta-hoe's that way."

"Thanks," I smiled. "We'll be on our way now."

"Not so fast, kid," Aahz waved. "What's your name, son?"

"Griffin . . . sir," the youth replied uneasily.

"Well, Griffin," Aahz smiled, "how would you like to show us the way?"

"Why?" I asked bluntly.

"Wake up, kid," my mentor scowled. "We can't just leave him here. He knows who and what we are."

"I know," I commented archly. "You told him."

". . . and besides," he continued as if I hadn't spoken, "he's our passport if we meet any Army patrols."

"I'd rather not . . ." Griffin began.

"Of course," Aahz interrupted. "There is another possibility. We could kill him here and now."

"I *insist* you let me escort you!" the youth proclaimed.

"Welcome, comrade!" I beamed.

"See, kid?" My mentor smiled, clapping me on the shoulder. "I told you you could settle things without my help."

"Ummm . . . there is one thing, though," Griffin commented hesitantly.

"And that is . . ." Aahz prompted.

"I hope you won't hold it against me if your services aren't accepted," the youth frowned.

"You doubt our powers?" My mentor scowled in his most menacing manner.

"Oh, it's not that," Griffin explained quickly. "It's just that . . . you see . . . well, we already have a magician."

"Is that all?" Aahz laughed. "Just leave him to us."

When Aahz says "us" in regard to magik, he means me. However bad things had gone so far, I had an uncomfortable foreboding they were going to get worse.

IX:

"War may be Hell . . . but it's good for business!"

—THE ASSOCIATION FOR MERCHANTS, MANUFACTURERS, AND MORTICIANS

Ta-hoe was a beehive of activity when we arrived. Preparations for the upcoming war were in full swing, and everybody was doing something. Surprisingly enough, most of the preparations were of a non-military nature.

"What *is* all this?" I asked our native guide.

"I told you," he explained. "We're getting ready for a war with Veygus."

"*This* is getting ready for a war?" I said, gazing incredulously about.

"Sure," Griffin nodded. "Souvenirs don't make themselves, you know."

There wasn't a spear or uniform in sight. Instead, the citizens were busily producing pennants, posters, and lightweight shirts with "Win the War" emblazoned across them.

"It's the biggest thing to hit Ta-hoe in my lifetime," our guide confided. "I mean, Big Game souvenirs are a stock item. If you design it right, you can even hang on to any overstock and sell it the following year. This war thing caught everybody flat-footed. A lot of people are complaining that they weren't given sufficient warning to cash in on it. There's a resolution before the council right now to postpone hostilities for another month. The folks who deal in knitted hats and stadium blankets are behind it. They claim that declaring war on such short notice will hurt their businesses by giving unfair advantage to the merchants who handle stuff like bumper stickers and posters that can be cranked out in a hurry."

I couldn't understand most of what he was talking about, but Aahz was enthralled.

"These folks really know how to run a war!" he declared with undisguised enthusiasm. "Most dimensions make their war profits off munitions and weapons contracts. I'll tell you, kid, if we weren't in such a hurry, I'd take notes."

It's a rare thing for Aahz to show admiration for anyone, much less a whole dimension, and I'd never before heard him admit there was anything he could learn about making money. I found the phenomenon unnerving.

"Speaking of being in a hurry," I interjected, "would you mind telling me *why* we're on our way to talk to Tahoe's magician?"

"That's easy," my mentor smiled. "For the most part, magicians stick together. There's a loyalty to others in the same line of work that transcends any national or dimensional ties. With any luck, we can enlist his aid in springing Tanda loose."

"That's funny," I observed dryly. "The magicians I've seen so far were usually at each other's throats. I got the definite impression they'd like nothing better than to see competing magicians, and us specifically, expire on the spot."

"There is that possibility," Aahz admitted, "but look at it this way. If he won't help us, then he'll probably be our major opponent and we'll want to get a fix on what he can and can't do before we make our plans. Either way, we want to see him as soon as possible."

You may have noticed Aahz's appraisals of a situation are usually far from reassuring. Some day I might get used

to that, but in the meantime I'm learning to operate in a
constant state of blind panic.

For a moment, our path was blocked by a crowd listening to a young rabble-rouser who spoke to them from
atop a jury-rigged platform. As near as I could make out,
they were protesting the war.

"I tell you, the council is withholding information from
us!"

A growl arose from the assemblage.

"As citizens of Ta-hoe, we have the right to know the
facts about this war!"

The response was louder and more fevered.

"How are we supposed to set the odds for this war,
much less bet intelligently, if we don't know the facts?"

The crowd was nearing frenzied hysterics as we finally
edged past.

"Who are these people?" I asked.

"Bookies." Griffin shrugged. "The council'd better
watch its step. They're one of the strongest lobbies in Ta-
hoe."

"I tell you, it's awe-inspiring," Aahz murmured dreamily.

"We've got to stand up for our rights! Demand the
facts!" the rabble-rouser was screaming. "We've got to
know the lineups, the battle plans, the . . ."

"They're barking up the wrong tree," Griffin commented. "They haven't gotten the information because the
military hasn't devised a plan yet."

"Why don't you tell them?" I suggested.

Our guide cocked an eyebrow at me. "I thought you
were in a hurry to see the magician," he countered.

"Oh, that's right," I returned, a little embarrassed by
the oversight.

"Say, Griffin," Aahz called. "I've been meaning to ask.
What started the war, anyway?"

For the first time since we'd met him, our youthful
guide showed an emotion other than boredom or fear.

"Those bastards from Veygus stole our Trophy," he
snarled angrily. "Now we're going to get it back or know
the reason why."

For a change, I didn't need an elbow in the ribs from Aahz to remember to keep quiet. I got one anyway.

"Stole your Trophy, eh?" my mentor commented innocently. "Know how they did it?"

"A pack of 'em pulled a hit-and-run raid the day after the Big Game," Griffin proclaimed bitterly. "They struck just after sundown and got away before the guardsmen could respond to the alarm."

The memory of the group entering and leaving the Trophy Building while Tananda and I waited flashed across my mind. That explained a couple questions that had been bothering me, like "where did the statue go?" and "how did the guards arrive so fast?" We hadn't triggered any alarms! The group from Veygus had—inadvertently setting us up for the guards!

"I'd think you'd take better care of the Trophy, if it means so much to you," Aahz suggested.

Griffin spun on him, and I thought for a minute he was actually going to throw a punch. Then, at the last moment, he remembered that Aahz was a magician and dropped his arms to his side. I heaved a quiet sigh of relief. I mean, Aahz is strong! I was impressed with his strength in my own dimension of Klah, and here on Jahk, *I* looked strong compared to the natives. If Griffin had thrown a punch, Aahz would have ripped him apart . . . literally!

"Our security precautions on the Trophy were more than adequate," our guide announced levelly, "under normal circumstances. The thieves had magikal assistance."

"Magikal assistance?" I said, finally drawn from my silence.

"That's right." Griffin nodded vigorously. "How else could they have moved such a heavy statue before the guards arrived?"

"They could have done it without magik," Aahz offered. "Say, if they had a lot of strong men on the job."

"Normally, I'd agree with you," our guide admitted, "but in this case, we actually captured the demon that helped them."

For a long moment there was silence. Neither Aahz nor I wanted to ask the next question. We were afraid of what the answer might be. Finally, Aahz spoke. "A demon, you say?" he asked, smiling his broadest. "What happened to it?"

His tone was light and casual, but there was a glint in his eye I didn't like. I found myself in the unique position of worrying about the fate of an entire dimension.

"The demon?" Griffin frowned. "Oh, the magician's holding it captive. Maybe he'll let you see it when you meet him."

"The magician? The one we're going to see?" Aahz pressed. "He's got the demon?"

"That's right," our guide answered. "Why do you ask?"

"Is she still unconscious?" I blurted.

The elbow from Aahz almost doubled me over this time, but it was too late. Griffin had stopped in his tracks and was studying me with a new intensity.

"How did you know it was unconscious?" he asked suspiciously. "And why do you refer to it as 'she'?"

"I don't know," I covered smoothly. "Must have been something you said."

"I said we'd captured a demon," he argued, "not how, and as far as its sex goes . . ."

"Look," Aahz interrupted harshly, "are we going to stand around arguing all day, or are you going to take us to the magician?"

Griffin stared at us hard for a moment, then shrugged his shoulders.

"We're here," he announced, pointing at a door in the wall. "The magician lives there."

"Well, don't just stand there, son," Aahz barked. "Knock on the door and announce us."

Our guide heaved a sigh of disgust, but obediently walked over and hammered on the indicated door.

"Aahz!" I hissed. "What are we going to say?"

"Leave it to me, kid," he murmured back. "I'll try to feel him out a little, then we'll play it by ear from there."

"What are we supposed to do with our ears?" I frowned.

Aahz rolled his eyes. "Kid . . ." he began.

Just then, the door opened, exposing a wizened old man who blinked at the sunlight.

"Griffin!" he exclaimed. "What brings you here?"

"Well, sir," our guide stammered, "I—that is, there are two gentlemen who want to speak with you. They say . . . Well, they're magicians."

The old man started at this and shot a sharp glance in our direction before he covered his reaction with a friendly smile.

"Magicians, you say! Well, come right in, gentlemen. Lad, I think you'd better wait outside here. Professional secrets and all that, you know."

"Um . . . actually, I thought I'd be on my way now," Griffin murmured uneasily.

"Wait here." There was steel in the old man's voice now.

"Yes, sir," our guide gulped, licking his lips.

I tried to hide my nervousness as we followed the magician into his abode. I mean, aside from the fact that we didn't have the vaguest idea of this man's power, and that we had no guarantee we'd ever get out of this place alive, I had nothing to worry about. Right?

"Aahz," I whispered. "Have you got a fix on this guy yet?"

"It's a little early to say," my mentor replied sarcastically. "In the meantime, I've got a little assignment for you."

"Like what?" I asked.

"Like, check his aura. Now."

One of the first things I had learned from Aahz was how to check auras, the field of magik around people or things. It seemed a strange thing to do just now, but I complied, viewing our host with unfocused eyes.

"Aahz," I gasped. "He's got an aura! The man's actually radiating magik. I can't do anything against someone that powerful."

"It's possible there is another explanation, kid," Aahz murmured. "He could be wearing a disguise spell like we are."

"Do you think so?" I asked hopefully.

"Well," my mentor drawled, "he's wearing a translator pendant, the same as we are. That makes it a good bet that he's not from this dimension. Besides, there's something familiar about his voice."

Our conversation ground to a halt as we reached our destination, a small room sparsely furnished with a large table surrounded by several chairs.

"If you'll be seated, gentlemen," our host said, gesturing to the chairs, "perhaps you'll be good enough to tell me what it is you wish to speak to me about."

"Not so fast," Aahz challenged, holding up a hand. "We're used to knowing who we're dealing with. Could you do us the courtesy of removing your disguise before we start?"

The magician averted his eyes and began to fidget nervously. "You spotted it, eh?" he grumbled. "It figures. As you've probably guessed already, I'm relatively new to this profession. Not in your class at all, if you know what I mean."

An immense wave of relief washed over me, but Aahz remained skeptical.

"Just take off the disguise, huh?" he insisted.

"Oh, very well." Our host sighed and began fumbling in his pocket.

We waited patiently until he found what he was looking for. Then the lines of his features began to waver . . . his body grew taller and fuller . . . until at last we saw . . .

"I thought so!" Aahz crowed triumphantly.

"Quigley!" I gasped.

"This *is* embarrassing," the ex-demon hunter grumbled, slouching down into his chair.

X:

"Old heroes never die; they reappear in sequels."

— M. MOORCOCK

Physically, Quigley was unchanged from when we first met him. Tall, long-boned and muscular, he still looked as if he'd be more at home in armor swinging a sword than sitting around in magician robes sipping wine with us. However, here we were, gathered in a conference which bore little resemblance to the formal interview I had originally anticipated.

"I was afraid you two would be along when I realized it was Tanda the guards captured," the ex-demon hunter grumbled.

"Afraid?" I frowned, genuinely puzzled. "Why should you be afraid of us?"

"Oh, come now, lad," Quigley smiled bitterly. "I appreciate your efforts to spare my feelings, but the truth of the matter is plain. My magikal powers don't hold a candle next to yours. I know full well that now that you're here you'll be able to take my job away from me without much difficulty. Either that, or make me look silly in front of my employers so that they'll fire me outright."

"That's ridiculous," I cried, more than slightly offended. "Look Quigley, I promise you we'll neither steal your job nor make you look silly while we're here."

"Really?" Quigley asked, brightening noticeably.

"You're being a little hasty with your promises, aren't you, kid?" Aahz interrupted in a warning tone.

"C'mon, Aahz," I grimaced. "You know that isn't why we're here."

"But, kid . . ."

I ignored him, turning back to Quigley.

"I promise you, Quigley. No job stealing, and nothing that will endanger your position. The truth is, I've already got a magician's job of my own. I'm surprised Tanda hasn't told you."

Strangely enough, instead of relaxing, Quigley seemed even more ill at ease and avoided my gaze.

"Well, actually, lad," he murmured uncomfortably, "Tanda hasn't said anything since she was turned over to my custody."

"She hasn't?" I asked, surprised. "That's funny. Usually the trouble is getting her to stop talking."

"Quite right." Quigley laughed uneasily. "Except this time—well—she hasn't regained consciousness yet."

"You mean she's still out cold?" Aahz exclaimed, surging to his feet. "Why didn't you say so? Come on, Quigley, wheel her out here. This might be serious."

"No, no. You misunderstand," Quigley waved. "She hasn't regained consciousness because I've kept a sleep spell on her."

"A sleep spell?" I frowned.

"That's right," Quigley nodded. "Tanda taught it to me herself. It's the first spell I learned, actually. Really very simple. As I understand it, all members of the Assassins Guild are required to learn it."

"Why?" Aahz interrupted.

"I never really gave it much thought." Quigley blinked. "I suppose it would help them in their work. You know, if you came on a sleeping victim, the spell would keep him from waking up until after you'd finished the job. Something like that."

"Not that!" Aahz moaned. "I know how assassins operate better than you do. I meant, why are you using a sleep spell on Tanda?"

"Why, to keep her from waking up, of course." Quigley shrugged.

"Brilliant," I muttered. "Why didn't we think of that?"

"Shut up, kid," my mentor snarled. "Okay, Quigley, let's try this one more time. Why don't you want to wake her up? I thought you two got along pretty well last time I saw you."

"We did," Quigley admitted, blushing. "But I'm a working magician now. If I let her wake up . . . well, I don't flatter myself about my powers. There would be nothing I could do to keep her from escaping."

"You don't want her to escape?" I blinked.

"Of course not. It would mean my job." Quigley smiled. "That's why I'm so glad you promised not to do anything that would jeopardize my position."

My stomach sank.

"Smooth move, kid," Aahz commented dryly. "Maybe next time you'll listen when I try to advise you."

I tried to say something in my own defense, but nothing came to mind, so I shut my mouth and used the time to feel miserable.

"Well, gentlemen," Quigley beamed, rubbing his hands together. "Now that that's settled, I suppose you'll be wanting to get on your way to wherever you're going."

"Not so fast, Quigley," Aahz declared, sinking back into his chair and propping his feet up on the table. "If nothing else, I think you owe us an explanation. The last time we saw you, you were a demon hunter, heading off through the dimensions with Tanda to learn more about magik. Now, I was under the distinct impression you intended to use that knowledge to further your old career. What brought you over to our side of the fence?"

Quigley thought for a moment, then shrugged and settled back in his own chair.

"Very well," he said. "I suppose I can do that, seeing as how we were comrades-in-arms at one point."

He paused to take a sip of wine before continuing.

"Tanda and I parted company with the others shortly

after we discovered your little joke. We thought it was quite amusing, particularly Tanda, but the others seemed quite upset, especially Isstvan, so we left them and headed off on our own."

The ex-demon hunter's eyes went slightly out of focus as he sank back into his memories. "We traveled the dimensions for some time. Quite a pleasant time, I might add. I learned a lot about demons and a little about magik, and it set me to thinking about my chosen line of work as a demon hunter. I mean, demons aren't such a bad lot once you get to know them, and magik pays considerably better than swinging a sword."

"I hope you're paying attention, kid," Aahz grinned, prodding my shoulder.

I nodded, but kept my attention on Quigley.

"Then," the ex-demon hunter continued, "circumstances arose that prompted Tanda to abandon me without money or a way back to my own dimension."

"Wait a minute," Aahz interrupted. "That doesn't sound like Tanda. What were these 'circumstances' you're referring to?"

"It was a misunderstanding, really," Quigley explained, flushing slightly. "Without going into lurid details, the end result involved my spending a night with a female other than Tanda."

"I can see why she'd move on without you," Aahz frowned, "but not why she'd take your money."

"Well, actually, it was the young lady I was with at the time who relieved me of my coinage," the ex-demon hunter admitted, blushing a deeper shade of red.

"Got it," Aahz nodded. "Sounds like along with magik and demons, there are a few things you have to learn about women."

I wouldn't have minded a few lessons in that department myself, but I didn't think this was the time to bring it up.

"Anyway," Quigley continued hastily, "there I was, stranded and penniless. It seemed the only thing for me to do was to go to a placement service."

"A placement service?" Aahz blinked. "Just where was this that you were stranded?"

"Why, the Bazaar at Deva, of course," the ex-demon hunter replied. "Didn't I mention that?"

"The Bazaar at Deva." My mentor sighed. "I should have known. Oh, well, keep going."

"There's really not that much more to tell." Quigley shrugged. "There were no openings for a demon hunter, but they managed to find me this position here in Jahk by lying about how much magik I knew. Since then, things have been pretty quiet—or they were before the guards appeared at my door carrying Tanda."

I was starting to wonder if *any* court magician was really qualified for his position.

"And you aren't about to let Tanda go. Right?" Aahz finished.

"Don't misunderstand," Quigley insisted, gnawing his lip. "I'd *like* to let her go. If nothing else it would do a lot for patching up the misunderstanding between Tanda and myself. Unfortunately, I just don't see any way I could let her escape without losing my job on grounds of incompetence."

"Say, maybe we could get you a job in Possiltum!" I suggested brightly.

"Kid," Aahz smiled, "are you going to stop that tongue of yours all by yourself, or do I have to tear it out by the roots?"

I took the hint and shut up.

"Thank you, lad," Quigley said, "but I couldn't do that. Unlike yourself, I'm still trying to build a reputation as a magician. How would it look if I left my first job in defeat with my tail between my legs?"

"You haven't got a tail," Aahz pointed out.

"Figure of speech." Quigley shrugged.

"Oh." My mentor nodded. "Well, if you think a hasty retreat from one's first job is unusual, my friend, you still have a lot to learn about the magik profession."

"Haven't I been saying that?" Quigley frowned.

I listened to their banter with only half an ear. The rest of me was floating on Quigley's implied compliment. I'm·

getting quite good at hearing indirect compliments. The direct ones are few and far between.

Come to think of it, I *was* getting a reputation as a magician. No one could deny we beat Isstvan at his own game—and I had actually recruited and commanded the team that stopped Big Julie's army. Why, in certain circles, my name must be . . .

"Bullshit!" Aahz roared, slapping his hand down on the table hard enough to make the chairs jump. "I tell you she didn't steal the damn Trophy!"

I collected my shattered nerves and turned my attention to the conversation once more.

"Oh, come now, Aahz," Quigley grimaced. "I traveled with Tanda long enough to know she's not above stealing something that caught her eye—nor are you two, I'd imagine."

"True enough," Aahz admitted easily, "but you can bet your last baseball card that if any of us went after your Trophy, we wouldn't be caught afterward."

"My last what?" Quigley frowned. "Oh, no matter. Look, even if I believed you I couldn't do anything. What's important is the *council* believes Tanda was involved, and they wouldn't even consider releasing her unless they got the Trophy back first."

"Oh, yeah?" Aahz smiled, showing all his teeth. "How many council members are there and how are they guarded?"

"Aahz!" Quigley said sternly. "If anything happened to the council, I'm afraid I'd see it as a threat to my job and therefore a direct violation of Master Skeeve's promise."

My mentor leaned back in his chair and stared at the ceiling. The heavy metal wine goblet in his hand crumpled suddenly, but aside from that there was no outward display of his feelings.

"Um . . . Quigley?" I ventured cautiously. I still had a vivid image in my mind of my tongue in Aahz's grasp instead of the wine goblet.

"Yes, lad?" Quigley asked, cocking an eyebrow at me.

"What did you say would happen if the Trophy were returned?"

Aahz's head swiveled around slowly until our gazes met, but his gold speckled eyes were thoughtful now.

"Well, I didn't say, actually," Quigley grumphed, "but that would change everything. With the Trophy back, the council would be ecstatic and definitely better disposed toward Tanda. . . . Yes, if the Trophy were returned, I think I could find an excuse to release her."

"Is that a promise?"

I may be ignorant, but I'm a fast learner.

Quigley studied me for a moment before answering. "Very well," he said at last. "Why do you ask?"

I shot a glance at Aahz. One eyelid slowly closed in a wink, then he went back to studying the ceiling.

"Because," I announced, relief flooding over me, "I think I've come up with a way we can free Tanda, protect your job, and stop the war in one fell swoop."

XI:

"What do you mean, 'You've got a little job for me'?"

— HERCULES

"**S**teal the Trophy back from Veygus. Just like that," Aahz grumbled for the hundredth time.

"We're doomed," Griffin prophesied grimly.

"Shut up, Griffin," I snarled.

It occurred to me I was picking up a lot of Aahz's bad habits lately.

"But I keep telling you, I don't know Veygus," the youth protested. "I won't be any help at all. Please, can't I go back to Ta-hoe?"

"Just keep walking," I sighed.

"Face it, son," Aahz smiled, draping a casual arm over our guide's shoulder. "We aren't going to let you out of our sight until this job's over. The sooner we get to Veygus, the sooner you'll be rid of us."

"But why?" Griffin whined.

"We've gone over this before," my mentor sighed. "This heist is going to be rough enough without Veygus hearing about it in advance. Now the only way we can be sure you don't tell anyone is to keep you with us.

Besides, you're our passport through the Ta-hoe patrols if we meet any."

"The patrols are easy to avoid," the youth insisted. "And I won't tell anyone about your mission, honest. Isn't there any way I can get you to trust me?"

"Well," Aahz drawled judiciously, "I guess there is one thing that might do the trick."

"Really?" our guide asked hopefully.

"What da ya think, Skeeve?" my mentor called. "Do you feel up to turning our friend here into a rock or a tree or something until the job's over?"

"A rock or a tree?" The youth gulped, wide-eyed.

"Sure." Aahz shrugged. "I wouldn't have suggested it myself. There's always a problem finding the *right* rock or tree to change back. Sometimes it takes years of searching. Sometimes the magician just gives up."

"Can't you guys walk any faster?" Griffin challenged, quickening his pace. "We'll never get to Veygus at this rate."

"I guess that settles that." I smiled, winking at Aahz to show I appreciated his bluff.

"Steal the Trophy from Veygus," my mentor replied, picking up his witty repartee where he had left it. "Just like that."

So much for changing the subject.

"C'mon, Aahz, give me a break," I defended glibly. "You agreed to this before I proposed it."

"I didn't say anything," he argued.

"You winked," I insisted.

"How do you know I didn't just get something in my eye?" he countered.

"I don't," I admitted. "Did you?"

"No." He sighed. "I winked. But only because it looked like the only way out of the situation *you* got us into."

He had me there.

"How we got into this spot is beside the point," I decided. "The real question is how are we going to steal the Trophy?"

"I see," Aahz grunted. "When you get us into trouble, it's beside the point."

"The Trophy," I prompted.

"Well . . ." my mentor began slowly, rising to the bait. "We won't be able to make any firm plans until we see the layout and size up the guards. How 'bout it, Griffin? What are we liable to be up against? How good are these Veygans?"

"The Veygans?" Our guide grimaced. "I wouldn't worry about them if I were you. They couldn't guard a pea if they swallowed it."

"Really inept, uh?" Aahz murmured, cocking an eyebrow.

"Inept? They're a joke." Griffin laughed. "There isn't a Veygan alive who knows how to spell strategy, much less use it."

"I thought you said you didn't know anything about Veygus," I commented suspiciously.

"Well . . . I don't actually," the youth admitted, "but I've seen their team play in the Big Game, and if that's the best they can muster . . ."

"You mean everything you've been saying was speculation based on the way their team plays?" Aahz interrupted.

"That's right." Griffin nodded.

"The same team that's been beating the pants off Tahoe for the last five years?"

Our guide's head came up as if he had just been slapped. "We won this year!" he declared fiercely.

"Whereupon they turned around and stole the Trophy right out from under your noses," my mentor pointed out. "It sounds to me like they may not be as inept as you'd like to think they are."

"They get lucky once in a while," Griffin muttered darkly.

"You might want to think it through a bit," I advised. "I mean, do you really want to go around claiming your team was beaten by a weak opponent? If Ta-hoe is so good and Veygus is so feeble, how do you explain five losses in a row? Luck isn't enough to swing the Game *that* much."

"We got overconfident," our guide confided. "It's a

constant danger you have to guard against when you're as good as we are."

"I know what you mean." Aahz nodded. "My partner and I have the same problem."

Well, modesty has never been Aahz's strong suit. Still it was nice to hear him include me in his brash statements. It made me feel like my studies were finally bearing fruit, like I was making progress.

"Aside from the military, what are we up against?" my mentor asked. "How about the magik you keep mentioning? Do they have a magician?"

"They sure do." Griffin nodded vigorously. "Her name's Massha. If you have any troubles at all, it will be with her. She's mean."

"Is that 'mean' in abilities, or in temperament?" Aahz cross-examined.

"Both," our guide asserted firmly. "You know, I've never been totally convinced our magician is as good as he claims to be, but Massha's a real whiz. I couldn't even start to count the fantastic things I've seen her do."

"Um . . . what makes you think her temperament is mean?" I asked casually, trying to hide my sagging confidence.

"Well, let me put it this way," Griffin explained. "If there was a messy job to be done, and you could think of three ways to do it, she'd find a fourth way that was nastier than the other three ways combined. She has a real genius for unpleasantness."

"Terrific," I grimaced.

"How's that again?" Our guide frowned.

"Skeeve here always likes a challenge," Aahz explained hastily, draping a friendly arm around my shoulders.

I caught the warning, even without him digging his talons in until they nearly drew blood. He did it anyway, making it a real effort to smile.

"That's right." I laughed to hide my gasp. "We've handled heavyweights before."

Which was true. What I neglected to mention and tried hard not to think about was that we survived the encounters by a blend of blind luck and bald-faced deceit.

"Good," Griffin beamed. "Even if you don't manage to steal the Trophy, if you can take Massha out of action, Ta-hoe can win the war easily."

"You know, Griffin," Aahz commented, cocking an eyebrow, "for someone who doesn't know Veygus, you seem to know an awful lot about their magician."

"I sure do," our guide laughed bitterly. "She used to be Ta-hoe's magician until Veygus hired her away. I used to run errands for her and . . ." He suddenly stopped in mid-stride and mid-sentence simultaneously. "Hey! That's right," he exclaimed. "I can't go along with you if you're going to see Massha. She knows me! If the Veygans find out I'm from Ta-hoe, they'll think I'm a scout. I'd get torn apart."

"Don't worry," I soothed, "we aren't going anywhere near Massha."

"Yes, we are," Aahz corrected.

"We are?" I blinked.

"Kid, do I have to explain it to you all over again? We've got to check out the local magikal talent, the same as we did when we hit Ta-hoe."

"And look where that got us?" I muttered darkly.

"Look where *who* got us?" Aahz asked innocently. "I didn't quite hear that."

"All right! All right!" I surrendered. "We'll go see Massha. I guess I'll just have to whip up a disguise for Griffin so he won't be spotted."

"She'll recognize my voice," our guide protested.

"Don't talk!" I ordered, without clarifying if it was an immediate or future instruction.

"This time, I think he's right," Aahz interrupted thoughtfully. "It would probably be wisest to leave Griffin behind for this venture."

"It would?" I blinked.

"Hey! Wait a minute," Griffin interjected nervously. "I don't *want* to be a rock or a stone."

"Oh, I'm sure we can work out something a bit less drastic." My mentor smiled reassuringly. "Excuse us for a moment while we confer."

I thought Aahz was going to pull me aside for a private conversation, but instead he simply slipped off his translator pendant. After a bit of browbeating, Quigley had supplied us with an extra, so now we each had one. Removing them allowed us to converse without fear of being overheard, while at the same time keeping Griffin within arm's length. I followed suit and removed mine.

"What gives, Aahz?" I asked as soon as I was free of the pendant. "Why the change in plans?"

"The job's getting a little too complex," he explained. "It's time we started reducing our variables."

"Our what?" I puzzled.

"Look!" Aahz gritted. "We're going to have our hands full trying to elude the military and this Massha gal without trying to keep an eye on Griffin, too. He can't be any great help to us, and if he isn't a help, he's a hindrance."

"He shouldn't be too much trouble," I protested.

"Any trouble will be too much trouble," my mentor corrected firmly. "So far, he's an innocent bystander we've dragged into this. That means if we take him into Veygus, we should be confident we can bring him out again. Now, are you that confident? Or don't you mind the thought of leaving him stranded in a hostile town?"

Aahz doesn't give humanitarian arguments often, but when he does, they always make sense.

"Okay," I sighed. "But what do we do with him? You know I can't turn him into a rock or a tree. Not that I would if I could."

"That's easy," Aahz shrugged. "You put a sleep spell on him. That should keep him out of mischief until we get back here."

"Aahz," I said gently, closing my eyes. "I don't know how to cast a sleep spell. Remember?"

"That's no problem," my mentor winked. "I'll teach you."

"Right now?" I questioned incredulously.

"Sure. Didn't you hear Quigley? It's easy," Aahz declared confidently. "Of course, you realize it isn't really a 'sleep' spell. It's more like suspended animation."

"Like what?" I blinked.

"It's a magikal slowing of the body's metabolism," he clarified helpfully. "If it were sleep as you perceive it, then you'd run into problems of dehydration and . . ."

"Aahz!" I interrupted, holding up a hand. "Is the spell easier than the explanation?"

"Well, yes," he admitted. "But I thought you'd like to know."

"Then just teach me the spell. Okay?"

XII:

"Out of the frying pan, into der fire."

—THE SWEDISH CHEF

Fortunately, the sleep spell was as easy to learn as Aahz had promised, and we left Griffin snoozing peacefully in a patch of weeds along the road.

We took the precaution of circling Veygus to enter the city from a direction other than Ta-hoe. As it turned out it was a pointless exercise. Everyone in Veygus was too busy with their own business to even notice us, much less which direction we were coming from.

"This is really great!" Aahz chortled, looking about the streets as we walked. "I could develop a real fondness for this dimension."

The war activities in Veygus were the same as we had witnessed in Ta-hoe, except the souvenirs were being made in red and white instead of blue and gold. I was starting to wonder if anyone was ever going to get around to actually fighting the war, or if they were all too busy making money.

"Look at that, Aahz!" I exclaimed, pointing.

There was a small crowd gathered, listening to a noisy orator. From what I could hear, their complaint was the same one we heard back in Ta-hoe: that the government's withholding information about the war was hampering the odds-makers.

"Yeah. So?" My mentor shrugged.

"I wonder if they're bookies, too," I speculated.

"There's one way to find out," Aahz offered.

Before I could reply, he had sauntered over to someone at the back of the crowd and engaged him in an animated conversation. There was nothing for me to do but wait . . . and worry.

"Good news, kid," he beamed, rejoining me at last.

"Tell me," I pressed. "I could use some good news right about now."

"They're giving three-to-one odds against Ta-hoe in the upcoming war."

It took me a moment to realize that was the extent of his information. "That's it?" I frowned. "That's your good news? It sounds to me like we've badly underestimated Veygus's military strength."

"Relax, kid," Aahz soothed. "Those are the same odds they're offering in Ta-hoe against Veygus. Local bookies always have to weight the odds in favor of the home team. Otherwise no one will bet against them."

Puzzled, I shook my head. "Okay, so they're actually evenly matched." I shrugged. "I still don't see how that's good news for us."

"Don't you see?" my mentor urged. "That means the bookies are operating independently instead of as a combine. If we play our cards right, we could show a hefty profit from this mess."

Even though annoyed that Aahz could be thinking of money at a time like this, I was nonetheless intrigued with his logic. I mean, after all, he *did* train me.

"By betting?" I asked. "How would we know which side to bet for?"

"Not 'bet for,' bet against," Aahz explained. "And we'd bet equal amounts against both sides."

I thought about this a few moments, nodding knowingly all the while, then gave up. "I don't get it," I admitted. "Betting the same amount for—excuse me, against—both sides, all we do is break even."

Aahz rolled his eyes in exasperation. "Think it through, kid," he insisted. "At three-to-one odds we can't do anything but win. Say we bet a thousand against each team. If Ta-hoe wins, then we pay a thousand in Ta-hoe and collect three thousand in Veygus, for a net profit of two thousand. If Veygus wins, we reverse the process and still come out two thousand ahead."

"That's not a bad plan," I said judiciously, "but I can see three things wrong with it. First, we don't have a thousand with us to bet . . ."

"We could hop back to Klah and get it," Aahz countered.

"Second, we don't have the time . . ."

"It wouldn't take that long," my mentor protested.

"Third, if our mission's successful, there won't be a war."

Aahz's mouth was open for a response, and that's where it stayed—open, and blissfully noiseless as he thought about my argument.

"Got you there, didn't I, Aahz?" I grinned.

"I wonder what the odds are that there won't be a war," he mused, casting a wistful eye at the crowd of bookies.

"C'mon, Aahz," I sighed, tugging bravely at his arm, "we've got a heist to scout."

"First," he corrected firmly, "we have to check out this Massha character."

I had hoped he had forgotten, but then, this adventure was not being typified by its phenomenally good luck.

We picked our way across Veygus, occasionally stopping people to ask directions, and arrived at last outside the dwelling of the town magician. It was an unimposing structure, barely inside the eastern limits of the city, and exuded an intriguing array of aromas.

"Not much of a hangout for a powerful magician, eh, Aahz?" I commented, trying to bolster my sagging courage.

"Remember where you were living when we first met?" my mentor retorted, never taking his eyes from the building.

I did. The one-room clapboard shack where I had first studied magik with Garkin made this place look like a veritable palace.

"What I can't figure out is why Massha settled for this place," Aahz continued, talking as much to himself as to me. "If what Griffin said is true, she could have had any place in town to work from. Tell you what, kid. Check for force lines, will you?"

I obediently closed my eyes and stretched out my mind, searching for those invisible currents of magikal power which those in the profession tap for their own use. I didn't have to look hard.

"Aahz!" I gasped. "There are four . . . no, five . . . force lines intersecting here. Three in the air and two in the ground."

"I thought so," my mentor nodded grimly. "This location wasn't chosen by accident. She's got power to spare, if she knows how to use it."

"But what can we do if she's that powerful?" I moaned.

"Relax, kid." Aahz smiled. "Remember, the power's there for anyone to use. You can tap into it as easily as she can."

"That's right," I said, relaxing slightly, but not much. "Okay, what's our plan?"

"I don't really know," he admitted, heading for the door. "We'll just have to play this by ear."

Somehow that phrase rang a bell in my memory. "Say—um—Aahz," I stammered. "Remembering how things went back in Ta-hoe, this time let's play it by *your* ear. Okay?"

"You took the words right out of my mouth." Aahz grinned. "Just remember to check her aura as soon as we get inside. It'll help to know if she's local or if we're dealing with imported help."

So saying, he raised his hand and began rapping on the door. I say "began" because between the second and third rap, the door flew open with alarming speed.

"What do you . . . well, hel-lo there, boys."

"Are . . . um . . . are you Massha, the magician?" Aahz stammered, both taken aback and stepping back.

"Can you imagine anyone else fitting the description?" came the throaty chuckle in response.

She was right. I had not seen anyone in Jahk—heck, in several dimensions—who looked anything like the figure framed in the open door. Massha was immense, in girth if not in height. She filled the doorway to overflowing—and it wasn't that narrow a door. Still, size alone doth not a pageant make. Massha might have been overlooked as just another large woman were it not for her garments.

Purple and green warred with each other across her tent-like dress, and her bright orange hair draped across one shoulder in dirty strings did nothing toward encouraging an early settlement. And jewelry! Massha was wearing enough in the way of earrings, rings and necklaces to open her own store. She wasn't a sample case, she was the entire inventory!

Her face was nothing to write home about—unless you're really into depressing letters. Bad teeth were framed by fleshy chapped lips, and her pig-like eyes peering from the depths of her numerous smile wrinkles were difficult to distinguish from her other skin blemishes.

I've seen some distinctive looking women in my travels, but Massha took the cake, platter, and tablecloth.

"Did you boys just come to stare?" the apparition asked, "or can I do something for you?"

"We . . . um . . . we need help," Aahz managed.

I wasn't sure if he was talking about our mission or our immediate situation, but either way I agreed with him wholeheartedly.

"Well, you came to the right place," Massha leered. "Step into my parlor and we'll discuss what I've got that you want—and vice-versa."

Aahz followed her into the building, leaving me no choice but to trail along. He surprised me, though, by dropping back slightly to seek my advice.

"What's the word, kid?" he hissed.

"How about 'repulsive'?" I suggested.

That earned me another dig in the ribs.

"I meant about her aura. What's the matter, did you forget?"

As a matter of fact, I had. Now that I had been so forcefully reminded, though, I hurriedly checked for magikal emanations.

"She's got—no, wait a minute," I corrected. "It isn't her, it's her jewelry. It's magikal, but she isn't."

"I thought so," Aahz nodded. "Okay. Now we know what we're dealing with."

"We do?" I asked.

"She's a mechanic," my mentor explained hurriedly. "Gimmick magik with her jewelry. Totally different than the stuff I've been teaching you."

"You mean you think I could beat her in a fair fight?"

"I didn't say that," he corrected. "It all depends on what kind of jewelry she's got—and from what we've seen so far, she's got a lot."

"Oh." I sagged. "What are we going to do?"

"Don't worry, kid." Aahz winked. "Fair fights have never been my specialty. As long as she doesn't know you're a magician, we've got a big advantage."

Any further questions I might have had were forgotten as we arrived at our destination. Having just left Quigley's dwelling, I was unprepared for what Massha used for an office.

To say it was a bedroom would be an understatement. It was the gaudiest collection of tassels, pillows, and erotic statues I had seen this side of the Bazaar at Deva. Colors screamed and clawed at each other, making me wonder if Massha were actually colorblind. As fast as the thought occurred to me, I discarded it. No one could select so many clashing colors by sheer chance.

"Sit down, boys." Massha smiled, sinking onto the parade-ground-sized bed. "Take off your things and we'll get started."

My life flashed before my eyes. While I had secretly dreamed of a career as a ladies' man, I had never envisioned it starting like this! If I had, I might have become a monk.

Even Aahz, with his vast experience, seemed at a loss.

"Well, actually," he protested. "We don't have much time . . ."

"You misunderstand me." Massha waved, fanning the air with a massive hand. "What I meant was, take off your disguises."

"Our disguises?" I blurted, swallowing hard.

In reply, she held aloft her left hand, the index finger extended for us to see. The third—no, it was the fourth—ring was blinking a brilliant purple.

"This little toy says you're not only magicians, you're disguised," she grinned. "Now, I'm as sociable as the next person but I like to see who I'm doing business with. In fact, I insist!"

As she spoke, the door behind us slammed shut and locked with an audible click.

So much for our big advantage.

XIII:

"If you can't dazzle them with dexterity,
baffle them with bullshit!"

—PROF. H. HILL

There was a long silent moment of frozen immobility.
Then Aahz turned to me with an exaggerated shrug.

"Well," he sighed, "I guess she's got us dead to rights.
There's no arguing with technology, you know. It never
makes mistakes."

I almost missed his wink, and even then I was slow to
realize what he was up to.

"With your permission, dear lady . . ." Making a half
bow at Massha, he began making a series of graceful
passes with his hand in the air in front of him.

It was all very puzzling. Aahz had lost all his magikal
powers back when . . . Then it hit me. Massha thought we
were *both* magicians! Aahz was trying to maintain the
illusion and could very well pull it off—if I got busy and
backed his move.

As inconspicuously as possible, I closed my eyes and
got to work stripping away his disguise.

"A Pervert!" Massha crowed in tribute to my efforts.
"Well, whatdaya know. Thought you walked funny for a
Jahk."

"Actually," Aahz corrected smoothly, "as a native of Perv I prefer to be called a 'Pervect.'"

"I don't care what ya *call* yourself," she winked lewdly, "I'm more interested in how ya act."

I was just beginning to enjoy my mentor's discomfort when Massha turned her attentions on me.

"How 'bout you, sport?" she pressed. "You don't say much, let's see what yer hiding."

I resisted an impulse to clutch wildly at my clothes, and instead set about restoring my normal appearance.

"A Klahd—and a young one at that," Massha proclaimed, cocking her head as she examined me. "Well, no matter, by the time old Massha's through with you . . . say!"

Her eyes suddenly opened wide and her gaze darted to Aahz, then back to me.

"A Klahd traveling with a Pervert . . . your name wouldn't be Skeeve, would it?"

"You've heard of me?" I blinked, both startled and flattered.

"Heard of you?" she laughed. "The last time I dropped into the Bazaar, that's all anyone was talking about."

"Really? What were they saying?" I urged.

"Well, the word is that you put together a team of six and used 'em to stop a whole army. It's the most effective use of manpower anyone's pulled off in centuries."

"It was actually eight, if you include Gleep and Berfert," I admitted modestly.

"Who?" She frowned.

"A dragon and a salamander," I explained. "It was such a successful venture I'd like to be sure everyone involved gets some credit."

"That's decent of you." Massha nodded approvingly. "Most folks I know in the trade try to hog all the glory when their plans work and only mention the help if they need someone to blame for failure."

"If you know Skeeve, here," Aahz smiled, elbowing his way into the conversation, "then surely you know who I am."

"As a matter of fact, I don't," Massha shrugged. "I

heard there was a loudmouthed Pervert along, but no one
mentioned his name."

"Oh, really?" Aahz asked, showing a suspicious number of teeth. "A loudmouthed Pervert, eh? And just who
did you hear that from?"

"Um . . . in that case," I interrupted hastily, "allow me
to introduce my friend and colleague, Aahz."

"Aahz?" Massha repeated, raising an eyebrow. "As
in . . ."

"No relation," Aahz assured her.

"Oh," she nodded.

"Mind if I have some wine?" my mentor asked, gesturing grandly at the wine pitcher on a nearby table. "It's
been a long dry trip."

This time I was ready, and covertly levitated the
pitcher into his waiting hand. The thought of embarrassing
him by leaving the wine where it was never entered my
mind. We were still in a tight spot, and anything we could
do to keep Massha off balance was a good gambit.

"So, what are a pair of big leaguers like you doing in
Jahk?" Massha asked, leaning back into her silken pillows. "You boys wouldn't be after my job, would you?"

It occurred to me that all the employed magicians I
was meeting shared a common paranoia about losing their
jobs.

"I assure you," Aahz interjected quickly, "taking your
job away from you is the furthest thing from our minds.
If nothing else, we couldn't pass the physical."

I almost asked "The physical what?" but restrained myself. Verbal banter was Aahz's forte, and for the time
being my job was to give him room to operate.

"Flattery will get you everywhere," Massha chuckled
appreciatively, "except around a direct question—and you
haven't answered mine. If you aren't looking for work,
what are you doing here?"

That was a good question, and thankfully Aahz had an
answer ready.

"We're just on a little vacation," he lied, "and dropped
by Jahk to try to make some of our money back in the
gambling set."

"Gambling?" Massha frowned. "But the Big Game is over."

"The Big Game," Aahz snorted. "I'll level with you. We don't know enough about spectator sports to bet on 'em, but we do know wars—and we hear there's one brewing. I figure if we can't bet more intelligently than a bunch of yokels who haven't seen a war in five hundred years, we deserve to lose our money."

"That explains what you're doing in Jahk." Massha nodded thoughtfully, "but it doesn't say what you're doing here—'in my office' here. What can I do for you you can't do for yourselves?"

"I could give you a really suggestive answer," Aahz smirked, "but the truth is, we're looking for information. From where we sit, magik could swing the balance one way or the other in this war. What we'd like is a little inside information as to how much of a hand you expect to have in the proceedings, and if you expect any trouble with the opposition."

"The opposition? You mean Ta-hoe's magician?"

She threw back her head and laughed. "I guarantee you, boys, I can handle . . . what's his name . . . Quigley . . . with one hand. That is, of course, providing that one hand is armed with a few of my toys."

She wiggled her fingers to illustrate her point and the ring colors glittered and danced like a malevolent rainbow."

"That's fine for the war," Aahz nodded. "But how about here in town? What's to keep Ta-hoe from stealing the Trophy back before the war?"

"Oh, I've got a few gizmos over at the Trophy Building that'll fry anyone who tries to heist it—especially if they try to use magik. Any one of 'em alone is fallible, but the way I've got 'em set, disarming one means setting off another. Nobody's taking that Trophy anywhere without my clearing it."

"Sounds good," my mentor smiled, though I noticed it was a little forced. "As long as you have total control on the Trophy's security, it isn't likely anything will go wrong."

"Not total control," Massha corrected. "The army's responsible for it when it's on parade."

"Parade?" I blurted. "What parade?"

"I know it's dumb," she grimaced. "That's why I refuse any responsibility for it. In fact, I had it written into my contract. I don't give demonstrations and I don't do parades."

"What parade?" Aahz repeated.

"Oh, once a day they carry the Trophy through the streets to keep the citizens fired up. You'd think they'd get tired of it, but so far everyone goes screaming bonkers every time it comes in view."

"I assume it has a military escort," Aahz commented.

"Are you kidding? Half the army tags along when it does the rounds. They spend more time escorting that Trophy around than they do drilling for the war."

"I see," my mentor murmured. "Well, I guess that tells us what we need to know. We should be on our way."

Before he could move, Massha was at the end of the bed, clasping his leg. "What's the hurry?" she purred. "Doesn't Massha get a little something in return for her information?"

"As a matter of fact," Aahz said, struggling to extract his leg, "there is something that might be valuable to you."

"I know there is," Massha smiled, pulling herself closer to him.

"Did you know that Quigley has summoned up a demon to help him?"

"He what?"

Massha released her hold on Aahz's leg to sit bolt upright.

"That's right," Aahz nodded, moving smoothly out of reach. "From what we hear, he's holding it captive in his workshop. I can't imagine any reason for his doing that unless he plans to use it in the war."

"A demon, eh?" Massha muttered softly, staring absently at the far wall. "Well, well, whatdaya know. I didn't think Quigley had it in him. I don't suppose you've heard anything about its powers?"

"Nothing specific," Aahz admitted, "but I don't think he'd summon anything weaker than he is."

"That's true." Massha nodded. "Well, I should be able to handle them both."

I recognized her tone of voice. It was the way I sound when I'm trying to convince myself I'm up to handling one of Aahz's plans.

"Say, Massha," my mentor explained, as if a thought had just struck him. "I know we're supposed to be on vacation, but maybe we can give you a hand here."

"Would you?" she asked eagerly.

"Well, it's really in our own best interest if we're betting money on the war," he smiled. "Otherwise we wouldn't get involved. As it is, though, I think we can get the demon away from Quigley, or at least neutralize it so it won't help him at all."

"You'd do that for me? As a favor?" Massha blinked.

"Sure," Aahz waved. "Just don't be surprised at anything we do and whatever you do, don't try to counter any of our moves. I won't make any guarantees, but I think we can pull it off. If we do, just remember you owe us a favor someday."

Anyone who knew Aahz would have been immediately suspicious if he offered to do anything as a favor. Fortunately, Massha didn't know Aahz, and she seemed both solicitous and grateful as she waved goodbye to us at the door.

"Well, kid," Aahz grinned, slapping me on the back. "Not bad for an afternoon's work, if I do say so myself. Not only did we scout the opposition, we neutralized it. Big bad Massha won't move against us no matter what we do, for fear of disrupting our plans against Quigley."

As I had restored our disguises before we emerged onto the street, Aahz's back slap didn't arrive on my back— and it hit me with more force than I'm sure he intended. All in all, it did nothing to improve my already black mood.

"Sure, Aahz," I growled. "Except for one little detail."

"What's that?"

"We can't steal Tanda away from Quigley because

he'd lose his job and we promised we wouldn't do anything to jeopardize his position. Remember?"

"Skeeve, Skeeve." My mentor chuckled, shaking his head. "I haven't overlooked anything. *You're* the one who hasn't thought things through."

"Okay," I snapped. "So I'm slow! Explain it to me."

"Well, first of all, as I just mentioned, we don't have to worry about Massha for a while."

"But—" I began, but he cut me off.

"Second of all," he continued, "I said 'free or neutralize.' Now, we already know Quigley isn't about to use Tanda in the war, so Massha's going to owe us a favor whether we do anything or not."

"But we're supposed to be rescuing Tanda," I protested, "and that means stealing the Trophy."

"Right!" Aahz beamed. "I'm glad you finally caught on."

"Huh?" I said intelligently.

"You *haven't* caught on." My mentor sighed. "Look, kid. The mission's still on. We're going to steal the Trophy."

"But I can't bypass Massha's traps at the Trophy Building."

"Of course not." Aahz agreed. "That's why we're going to steal it from the parade."

"The parade?" I blinked. "In broad daylight with half the army and the whole town watching?"

"Of course." Aahz shrugged. "It's the perfect situation."

It occurred to me that either my concept of a perfect situation was way out of line, or my mentor had finally lost his mind!

XIV:

"As any magician will tell you—Myth Directions is the secret of a successful steal."

—D. HENNING

"**D**on't you see, kid? The reason it's a perfect situation is that everyone's sure it can't be stolen!"

It was the same answer Aahz had given the last ten times I asked, so I gave him my usual rebuttal.

"The reason they're sure is because it *can't* be stolen. At least half the population of Veygus will be looking, Aahz, and they'll be looking right at the Trophy we're trying to steal! Someone's bound to notice."

"Not if you follow your instructions, they won't." My mentor winked. "Trust me."

I wasn't reassured. Not that I didn't trust Aahz, mind you. His ability to get me into trouble is surpassed only by his ability to bail me out again. I just had a hunch his bailing abilities were going to be tested to their limits this time.

I was about to express this to Aahz when a roar went up from the crowd around us, ending any hope for conversation. The Trophy was just coming into view.

We had chosen our post carefully. This point was the closest the procession came to the North wall of Veygus . . . and hence it was the closest the Trophy came to the gate opening onto the road to Ta-hoe.

In line with Aahz's plan, we waved our fists in the air and jumped up and down as the Trophy passed by with its military escort. It was pointless to shout, however. The crowd was making so much noise that two voices more or less went unnoticed, and we needed to save our lung power for the heist itself. Working our way to the back of the mob also proved to be no problem. By simply not fighting back when everyone else elbowed in front of us soon moved us to our desired position.

"So far, so good," Aahz murmured, scanning the backs in front of us to be sure we were unobserved.

"Maybe we should quit while we're ahead," I suggested hopefully.

"Shut up and start working," he snapped back in a tone that left no room for argument.

With an inward sigh, I closed my eyes and began making subtle changes in our disguises.

When I first learned the disguise spell, it was specifically to alter the facial features and body configurations of a being to resemble another. Later, after considerable practice, I learned to change the outward appearance of inanimate objects, providing they had once been alive. Aahz had seized this modification for a new application . . . specifically to change the configuration of our clothes. By the time I was done, we not only looked like Jahks, we were dressed in the uniforms of Veygan soldiers.

"Good enough, kid," Aahz growled, clapping me on the shoulder. "Let's go!"

With that, he plunged headlong into the crowd, clearing a path for me to emerge on the street behind the Trophy procession. Clearing paths through moveable objects, like people, is one of the things Aahz does best.

"Make way!" he bawled. "One side! Make way!"

Close behind him, I added my bellow to the din.

"Ta-hoers!" I called. "At the South wall! Ta-hoers!"

That's one of the things I do best—scream in panic.

For a moment, no one seemed to hear us. Then a few heads turned. A couple voices took up my call.

"Ta-hoers!" they cried. "We're being attacked."

The word spread through the crowd ahead of us like wildfire, such that when we reached the rearguard of the procession, it had ground to a halt. The soldiers milled about, tangling weapons with bodies around them as they tried simultaneously to scan the crowd, rooftops, and sky.

"Ta-hoers!" I shouted, pushing in among them.

"Where?"

"The South wall."

"Where?"

"The South wall."

"Who?"

"Ta-hoers!"

"Where?"

This nonsense might have continued endlessly, except for the appearance of an officer on the scene. He was noticeably more intelligent than the soldiers around him . . . which was to say he might have won a debate with a turnip.

"What's going on here?" he demanded, his authoritative voice silencing the clamor in the ranks.

"Ta-hoers, sir!" I gasped, still a bit out of breath from my performance. "They're attacking in force at the South wall!"

"The South wall?" The officer frowned. "But Tahoe is north of here."

"They must have circled around the city," I suggested hastily. "They're attacking the South wall."

"But Ta-hoe is north of here," the man insisted. "Why would they attack the South wall?"

His slow-wittedness was exasperating. It was also threatening to totally disrupt our plan, which hinged on momentum.

"Are you going to stand here arguing while those yellow and blue idiots take the city?" Aahz demanded, shouldering his way past me. "If everybody gets killed because of your indecision, the council will bust you back to the ranks."

That possibility wasn't very logical, so, of course, the

fool took it to heart. Drawing his sword, he turned to the men around him.

"To the South wall," he ordered. "Follow me!"

"To the South wall!"

The cry went up as the soldiers wheeled and dashed back down the street.

"To the South wall!" I echoed, moving with them.

Suddenly, a powerful hand seized my shoulder and slammed me against a wall hard enough to knock the air out of my lungs.

"To the South wall!"

It was Aahz, leaning back to keep me pinned between him and the wall as he waved the soldiers past.

At last, he turned his head slightly to address me directly.

"Where ya going?" he asked curiously.

"To the South wall?" I suggested in a small voice.

"Why?"

"Because the Ta-hoers . . . oh!"

I felt exceptionally stupid. I also felt more than slightly squashed. Aahz is no featherweight.

"I think better when I can breathe," I pointed out meekly.

The ground slipped up and crashed into me as Aahz shifted his weight forward.

"Quit clowning around, kid," he snarled, hauling me to my feet. "We've still got work to do."

As I've said before, Aahz has an enviable grasp of the obvious. A dozen soldiers were still clustered around the Trophy, its litter now resting on the ground. There was also the minor detail of the crowd of onlookers still milling about arguing over this latest change in events.

"What are we going to do, Aahz?" I hissed.

"Just leave everything to me," he retorted confidently.

"Okay." I nodded.

"Now here's what I want you to do . . ."

"What happened to 'leave everything to you'?" I grumbled.

"Shut up and listen," he ordered. "I want you to change my face and uniform to match that officer we talked to."

"But . . ."

"Just do it!"

In a moment the necessary adjustments were made and my mentor was on his way, striding angrily toward the remaining soldiers.

"What are you doing there?" he bawled. "Get to the South wall with the others!"

"But . . . we were . . . our orders are to guard the Trophy," the nearest soldier stammered in confusion.

"Defend it by keeping the Ta-hoers out of the city," Aahz roared. "Now get to the South wall! Anyone who tries to stay behind I'll personally charge with cowardice in the face of the enemy. Do you know what the punishment for that is?"

Apparently they did, even if I didn't. Aahz's question went unanswered as the soldiers sprinted off down the street toward the South wall.

So much for the Trophy's military escort. I did wonder, though, what my mentor planned to do about the milling crowd.

"Citizens of Veygus," Aahz boomed, as if in answer to my silent question. "Our fair city is under attack. Now, I know all of you will want to volunteer to help the Army in this battle, but to be effective you must be disciplined and orderly. To that end, I want all volunteers to line up here in front of me for instructions. Any who are unable to serve should return to their homes at this time, so the militia will have room to maneuver. All right, volunteers assemble!"

Within seconds, Aahz and I were left alone in the street. The crowd of potential volunteers had evaporated like water spilled on a hot griddle.

"So much for the witnesses." My mentor grinned, winking at me.

"Where'd they all go?" I asked, craning my neck to look around.

"Home, of course." Aahz smirked. "No one likes the draft—particularly when it affects them personally."

I wet my finger and tested the breeze. "There's not that much wind today," I announced suspiciously.

For some reason, this statement seemed to annoy my mentor. He rolled his eyes and started to say something, then changed his mind.

"Look, let's just grab the Trophy, okay?" he snarled. "That 'South wall' bit won't fool the Army forever, and I for one don't want to be here when they get back."

For once, we were in total agreement.

"Okay, Aahz." I nodded. "How do we get it out of the city?"

"That's easy." He waved. "Remember, I'm not exactly a weakling."

With that, he strode over to the Trophy and simply picked it up and tucked it under his arm, balancing it casually on his hip.

"But, Aahz . . ." I began.

"I know what you're going to say," he admonished, holding up a hand, "and you're right. It would be easier to steal a cart. What you're overlooking is that a cart is personal property, while the Trophy belongs to the whole city."

"But, Aahz . . ."

"That means," he continued hastily, "that everyone assumes someone else is watching the Trophy, so we can walk away with it. If we stole a cart, the owner would spot it in a minute and raise the alarm. Now, having successfully liberated the Trophy, it would be really dumb to get arrested for stealing a cart, wouldn't it?"

"I didn't mean how are we going to move it!" I blurted. "I meant how are we going to get it past the guards at the North gate?"

"What's that?" Aahz frowned.

"They aren't going to let us just walk past them carrying that Trophy, and I can't disguise it. It's a metal!"

"Hmmm . . . you're right, kid." My mentor nodded thoughtfully. "Well, maybe we can . . . oh, swell!"

"What is it?" I asked fearfully.

"The soldiers are coming back," he announced, cocking his head to listen. Aahz has exceptionally sharp hearing. "Oh, well, we're just going to have to do this the fast way. Break out the D-Hopper."

"The what?" I blinked.

"The D-Hopper!" he insisted. "We'll just take this back to Klah with us."

I hurriedly fumbled the D-Hopper out of my pouch and passed it to Aahz for setting.

"What about Tanda?"

"We'll use this gizmo to bring the Trophy back later and spring her," Aahz mumbled. "I hadn't figured on using this just now. There's always a possibility that . . . oh, well. Hang on, kid. Here we go."

I crowded close to him and waited as he hit the button to activate the Hopper.

Nothing happened.

XV:

*"—Or was it unlock the safe then swim
to the surface?"*

—H. HOUDINI

"**N**othing happened."

"I know it," Aahz groaned, glaring at the D-Hopper. "That's the trouble with relying on mechanical gadgets. The minute you rely on them, they let you down."

"What's wrong?" I pressed.

"The damn thing needs recharging," Aahz spat. "And there's no way we can do it before the Army gets here."

"Then let's hide until . . ."

"Hide where?" my mentor snapped. "Do you want to ask one of the citizens to hide us? They might have a few questions about the Trophy we're lugging along."

"Okay, you suggest something!" I snarled.

"I'm working on it," Aahz growled, looking around. "What we need is . . . there!"

Before I could ask what he was doing, he strode into a nearby shop, tugged an animal skin off the wall, and began wrapping it around the Trophy.

"Terrific," I observed dryly. "Now we have a furry Trophy. I don't think it will fool the guards."

"It will, once you disguise it." Aahz grinned.

"I told you, I can't," I insisted. "It's a metal!"

"Not the Trophy, dummy!" he snapped. "The skin. Get to work! Change it to anything. No . . . make it a wounded soldier!"

I wasn't sure it would work, but I closed my eyes and gave it a try. One wounded soldier—complete with a torn, bloodstained uniform and trailing feet.

"Not bad, kid." Aahz nodded, sticking the bundle under his arm.

As usual, I couldn't see the effects of my work. When I looked, I didn't see an officer of the guard with a wounded comrade under his arm. I saw Aahz holding a suspiciously lumpy package.

"Are you sure it's okay?" I asked doubtfully.

"Sure." Aahz nodded. "Just . . . oops! Here they come. Leave everything to me."

That had a suspiciously familiar ring to it, but I didn't have many other options at the moment. The soldiers were in sight now, thundering down on us with grim scowls set fiercely on their faces.

"That way! Quick! They're getting away."

Aahz's bellow nearly startled me out of my skin, but I held my ground. I'm almost used to his unexpected gambits—almost.

"After them!" Aahz repeated. "Charlie's hit!"

"Who's Charlie?" I frowned.

"Shut up, kid," my mentor hissed, favoring me with a glare before returning his attention to the soldiers.

They had slowed their headlong dash and were looking down the sidestreets as they came, but they hadn't changed course. The only fortunate thing was that the officer Aahz was impersonating was nowhere in sight.

"Don't you understand?" Aahz shouted. "They've got the Trophy! That way!"

That did it. With a roar of animal rage, the soldiers wheeled and started off in the direction Aahz had indicated.

"Boy," I murmured in genuine admiration. "I wouldn't

want to be holding that Trophy when they caught up with me."

"It could be decidedly unpleasant," Aahz agreed. "So if you don't mind, could we be on our way? Hmmm?"

"Oh! Right, Aahz."

He was already on his way, eating up great hunks of distance with his strong, hurried stride. As I hastened to keep up with him, I resolved not to ask about his plans for getting past the guards at the North gate. I was only annoying him with my constant questions, and besides, the answers only unsettled me.

As we drew nearer to the gate, however, my nervousness grew stronger and my resolve weaker.

"Ummm . . . do you want me to change the disguise on the Trophy?" I asked tentatively.

"No," came the brusque reply. "But you could mess us up a little."

"Mess us up?" I blinked.

"A little dirt and blood on the uniforms," Aahz clarified. "Enough to make it look like we've been in a fight."

I wasn't sure what he had up his sleeve, but I hastened to adjust our disguises. That isn't as easy as it sounds, incidentally. Try closing your eyes and imagining dirty uniforms in detail while walking down a strange street at a near-trot. Fortunately, my life with Aahz had trained me to work under desperate conditions, so I completed my task just as we were coming up on the gate.

As a tribute to my handiwork, the guard didn't even bother to address us directly. He simply gaped at us for a moment, then started hollering for the Officer of the Guard. By the time that member appeared, we were close enough to count his teeth as his jaw dropped.

"What's going on here?" he demanded finally, recovering his composure.

"Fighting in the streets," Aahz gasped in a realistic imitation of a weary warrior. "They need your help. We're your relief."

"Our relief!" The officer frowned. "But that man's unconscious and you look like . . . fighting, did you say?"

"We're fit enough for gate duty," Aahz insisted,

weakly pulling himself erect. "Anything to free a few more able-bodied men for the fighting."

"What fighting?" the officer screamed, barely suppressing an impulse to shake Aahz back to his senses.

"Riots." My mentor blinked. "The bookies have changed the odds on the war and won't honor earlier bets. It's awful."

The officer blanched and recoiled as if he had been struck. "But that means . . . my life savings are bet on the war. They can't do that."

"You'd better hurry," Aahz insisted. "If the mobs tear the bookies apart, no one will get their money back."

"Follow me! All of you!" the officer bellowed, though it wasn't necessary. The guards were already on their way. Apparently the officer wasn't the only one with money in the bookies' care.

The officer started after them, then paused to sweep us with an approving stare.

"I don't know if you'll get a medal for this," he announced grimly, "but I won't forget it. You have my personal thanks."

"Don't mention it, turkey," Aahz murmured as the man sprinted off.

"You know, I bet he *won't* forget this . . . ever." I smiled.

"Feeling pretty smug, aren't you, kid?" Aahz commented, cocking a critical eyebrow at me.

"Yes," I confirmed modestly.

"Well, you should." He laughed, clapping me on the back. "I think, however, we'd best celebrate at a distance."

"Quite right," I agreed, gesturing grandly to the open gate. "After you."

"No, after you!" he countered, imitating my gesture.

Not wanting to waste additional time arguing, we walked side by side through the now unguarded North gate of Veygus, bearing our prize triumphantly with us.

That should have been it. Having successfully recaptured the Trophy, it should have been an easy matter to return to Ta-hoe, exchange the Trophy for Tananda, and

relax in a celebration party back at Klah. I should have
known better.

Any time things seem calm and tranquil, something
happens to disrupt matters. If unforeseen outside complications don't arise, then either Aahz's temper flares or I
open my big mouth. In this case, there were no outside
complications, but there our luck ran out. Neither one of
us was to blame—we both were. Aahz for his temper, me
for my big mouth.

We were nearly back to the place where he had hidden
Griffin, when Aahz made an unexpected request.

"Say, kid," he said, "how about dropping the disguises
for a while?"

"Why?" I asked, logically.

"No special reason," he shrugged. "I just want to look
at this Trophy that's caused everyone so much trouble."

"Didn't you see it back at Veygus?" I frowned.

"Not really," my mentor admitted. "At first I was busy
chasing away the soldiers and the civilians, and after that
it was something big and heavy to carry. I never really
stopped to study it."

It took mere seconds to remove the disguises. They're
easier to break down than to build, since I can see what
the end result is supposed to look like.

"Help yourself," I announced.

"Thanks, kid." Aahz grinned, setting the Trophy down
and hastily unwrapping it.

The Trophy was as ugly as ever; not that I had expected it to change. If anything, it looked worse up close,
as Aahz was looking at it. Then he backed up and looked
again. Finally he walked around it, studying the monstros-
ity from all angles.

For some reason, his silent scrutiny was making me
uneasy.

"Well, what do you think?" I asked, in an effort to get
the conversation going again.

He turned slowly to face me, and I noticed his scales
were noticeably darker than normal.

"That's it?" he demanded, jerking a thumb over his
shoulder at the statue. "That's the Trophy? You got Tanda

captured and put us through all this for a dismal hunk of sculpture like that?"

Something clicked softly in my mind, igniting a small ember of anger. I mean, I've never pretended to admire the Trophy, but it *had* been Tananda's choice.

"Yes, Aahz," I said carefully. "That's it."

"Of all the dumb stunts you've pulled, this takes the cake!" my mentor raged. "You neglect your studies, cost us a fortune, not to mention putting everybody's neck on the chopping block, and for what?"

"Yes, Aahz," I managed.

"And Tanda! I knew she was a bit dippy, but this! I've got a good mind to leave her right where she is."

I tried to say something, but nothing came out.

"All I want to hear from you, apprentice, is why!"

He was looming over me now.

"Even feeble minds need a motive. What did you two figure to do with this pile of junk once you stole it? Tell me that!"

"It was going to be your birthday present!" I shouted, the dam bursting at last.

Aahz froze stock-still, an expression of astonishment spreading slowly over his face.

"My . . . my birthday present?" he asked in a small voice.

"That's right, Aahz," I growled. "Surprise. We wanted to get you something special. Something no one else had, no matter how much trouble it was. Sure was stupid of us, wasn't it?"

"My birthday present," Aahz murmured, turning to stare at the Trophy again.

"Well, it's all over now," I snarled savagely. "Us feeble-minded dolts bit off more than we could chew and you had to bail us out. Let's spring Tanda and go home. Maybe then we can forget the whole thing—if you'll let us."

Aahz was standing motionless with his back to me. Now that I had vented my anger, I found myself suddenly regretful for having ground it in so mercilessly.

"Aahz?" I asked, stepping in behind him. "Hey!

C'mon, we've got to give it back and get Tanda."

Slowly he turned his head until our gazes met. There was a faraway light in his eyes I had never seen before.

"Give it back?" he said softly. "Whatdaya mean, 'Give it back'? That's my birthday present!"

XVI:

". . . and then the fun began."

— N. Bonaparte

I had attended war councils before. I hadn't been wild about it as a pastime even then, but I had done it. On those occasions, however, our side was the only one with the vaguest skills in magik. This time, all three sides would have magicians in attendance. My joy knew definite bounds; in fact, I didn't want to be there at all.

"Maybe they won't come," I suggested hopefully.

"With their precious Trophy on the line?" Aahz grinned. "Not a chance. They'll be here."

"If they got the messages," I corrected. "Griffin may have just headed for the horizon."

My mentor cocked an eyebrow at me. "Think back to the days before you were an apprentice, kid," he suggested. "If a magician gave you a message to deliver, would you try to get away?"

"Well . . ." I conceded.

"They'll be here," he concluded firmly. "I just hope Quigley gets here first."

My last hope gone, I resigned myself to the meeting and turned my attention to our immediate surroundings.

"Can you at least tell me why we're meeting here?" I asked. "Why not in the forest where we'd have some trees to duck behind if things get ugly? What's so special about this statatorium?"

"That's stadium, kid," my mentor corrected, rolling his eyes. "And there're three good reasons to set up the meeting here. First of all, both the Veygans and the Ta-hoers know where it is. Second, they both acknowledge it as neutral ground."

"And third?" I prompted.

"You said it yourself." Aahz shrugged. "There's no cover. Nothing at all to hide behind."

"That's good?"

"Think it through, kid." My mentor sighed. "If we can hide behind a tree, so could someone else. The difference is, they have more people to hide."

"You mean they might try to ambush us?" I blinked.

"It's a possibility. I only hope that having the meeting in the open like this will lower the probability."

One thing I have to admit about Aahz. Any time I'm nervous, I can count on him to say just the right thing to convert my nervousness to near-hysteric panic.

"Um . . . Aahz," I began carefully. "Isn't it about time you let me in on this master plan of yours?"

"Sure." My mentor grinned. "We're going to have a meeting with representatives from both Veygus and Ta-hoe."

"But what are you going to say to them?" I pressed.

"You're missing the point, kid. The reason I'm meeting with both of them at once is because I don't want to have to repeat myself. Now, if I explain everything to you now, I'll only have to repeat myself at the meeting. Understand?"

"No," I announced bluntly. "I don't. I'm supposed to be your apprentice, aren't I? Well, how am I going to help out if I don't know what's going on?"

"That's a good point," Aahz conceded. "I wish you had raised it earlier. Because now it's too late. Our guests are arriving."

I turned to look in the direction he was pointing and

discovered he was right. A small group had emerged from one of the entrances halfway up the side of the stadium and was filing down the stairs toward the field where we were waiting. Watching them descend, I was struck again by the enormity of the stadium. I had realized it was large when we first arrived and I saw the rows and rows of seats circling the field. Now, however, seeing how tiny the group looked in this setting made me all the more aware of exactly how large the stadium really was. As we waited, I tried to imagine the seats filled with thousands upon thousands of people all staring down at the field and the very thought of it made me uneasy. Fortunately, the odds of my ever actually seeing it were very, *very* low.

The group was close enough now for us to distinguish between individuals. This didn't do us much good, though, as we didn't *know* any of the individuals involved. I finally recognized Griffin in their ranks, and from that figured out it was the Ta-hoe delegation approaching. Once I realized that, I managed to spot Quigley bringing up the rear. I would have recognized him sooner, but he was disguised as a Jahk, which threw me for a moment. Actually, it made sense. I mean, Aahz and I were currently disguised as Jahks, so it was only logical that Quigley would also be hiding his extra-dimensional origins as well. Sometimes it bothers me that I seem to habitually overlook the obvious.

"That's far enough!" Aahz boomed.

The group halted obediently a stone's throw away. It occurred to me it might be better if they were a little *more* than a stone's throw away, but I kept quiet.

"We're ready to discuss the return of the Trophy," one of the delegates called, stepping forward.

"We're not," my mentor retorted.

This caused a minor stir in the group and they began to mumble darkly among themselves.

"Aahz!" I urged.

"What I mean to say," Aahz added hastily, "is that what we have to say will wait until the other delegation arrives. In the meantime, I wish a word with your master magician."

There was a brief huddle, then Quigley came forward to join us. Even at a distance I could see he was upset.

"Hi, Quigley." Aahz grinned. "How's tricks?"

"I certainly hope you have an explanation for this," the ex-demon hunter snapped, ignoring the cordial greeting.

"Explanation for what?" my mentor countered innocently.

"You promised . . . or rather, Master Skeeve did . . . that you two wouldn't do anything to endanger my job."

"And we haven't," Aahz finished.

"Yes, you have!" Quigley insisted. "The council expects me to use my magik to get the Trophy away from you at this meeting. If I don't, I can kiss my job goodbye."

"Don't worry," my mentor soothed. "We've taken that into account."

"We have?" I murmured in wonder.

Aahz shot me a black look and continued.

"I guarantee that by the end of the meeting the council won't expect you to perform any magik against us."

"You mean you'll give the Trophy back voluntarily?" Quigley asked, brightening noticeably. "I must say that's decent of you."

"No, it isn't," Aahz corrected, "and we're not going to give it back. All I said was they wouldn't expect you to get it for them with magik."

"But—"

"The reason I wanted to talk with you," Aahz interrupted, "was to clarify a little something from our previous conversation."

"What's that?" Quigley frowned.

"Well, you promised to release Tanda if the Trophy was returned. Now, if Ta-hoe has a chance to take the Trophy back, and then doesn't do it, is the deal still on? Will you let her go?"

"I . . . I suppose so," the ex-demon hunter acquiesced, gnawing his lip. "But I can't imagine them not wanting it."

"Wanting something and being able to take it are two different things." Aahz grinned.

"But I'm supposed to be helping them with my magik!"

"Not this time, you aren't," my mentor corrected. "I've already told you that—"

"Is this a private chat, boys? Or can anybody join in?"

We all turned to find Massha lumbering towards us. The rest of the Veygus delegation waited behind her, having apparently arrived while we were talking to Quigley.

"Good God! What's that?" Quigley gasped, gaping at Massha's approaching bulk.

"That's Massha," I volunteered casually. "You know, the Veygans' magician!"

"That's Massha?" he echoed, swallowing hard.

"If you'll excuse us for a moment," Aahz suggested, "there are a few things we have to discuss with her before the meeting."

"Of course, certainly."

The ex-demon hunter beat a hasty retreat, apparently relieved at being able to avoid a face-to-face meeting with his rival.

"The council there tells me that was Quigley you were just talking to," Massha announced, tracking his flight with her eyes. "Is that true?"

"Umm . . . yes," I admitted.

"You boys wouldn't be trying to double-cross old Massha, would you?" Her tone was jovial, but her eyes narrowed suspiciously.

"My dear lady!" Aahz gasped. "You wound me! Didn't we promise to neutralize Quigley's demon for you?"

"You sure did."

"And it would be extremely difficult to engineer that without at least being on speaking terms with Quigley. Wouldn't it?"

"Well . . . yes."

"So no sooner do we start working on the project than you accuse us of double-crossing you! We should leave right now and let you solve your own problems."

I had to suppress a smile. Aahz looking indignant is a

comical sight at best. Massha, however, swallowed it hook, line and sinker.

"Now, don't be that way," she pleaded. "I didn't mean to get ya all out of joint. Besides, do you blame me for being a little suspicious after you up and made off with the Trophy?"

Aahz sighed dramatically. "Didn't we say not to be surprised at anything we did? Geez! I guess it's what we should expect, trying to deal with someone who can't comprehend the subtlety of our plans."

"You mean stealing the Trophy is part of your plan to neutralize the demon?" Massha asked, wide-eyed with awe.

"Of course!" Aahz waved. "Or it was. You see, Quigley got the demon to help get the Trophy away from Veygus. Now, if Veygus doesn't have the Trophy, he doesn't need the demon, right?"

"Sounds a little shaky to me." The sorceress frowned.

"You're right," Aahz acknowledged. "That's why I was so glad when the k . . . I mean, when Master Skeeve here came up with this new plan."

"I did?"

Aahz's arm closed around my shoulders in an iron grip which eliminated any thoughts of protest from my mind.

"He's so modest," my mentor explained. "You've heard what a genius tactician he is? Well, he's come up with a way to neutralize the demon . . . *and* give Veygus a good chance at retrieving the Trophy."

"I'm dying to hear it," Massha proclaimed eagerly.

"Me, too," I mumbled. Aahz's grip tightened threateningly.

"Then I guess we're ready to get started," he declared. "You'd better rejoin your delegation. Wouldn't want it to look like we're playing favorites. And remember . . . agree with us no matter what we say. We're on your side."

"Right!" she winked, and headed off.

"Say, um, Aahz," I managed at last.

"Yeah, kid?"

"If you're on Quigley's side *and* on Massha's side, who's on my side?"

"I am, of course."

I had been afraid he was going to say something like that. It was becoming increasingly clear that Aahz was going to come out of this in pretty good shape no matter how it ran. I didn't have much time to ponder the point, though.

Aahz was beckoning the groups forward to start the meeting.

XVII:

"I'm sure we can talk things out like civilized people."

—J. WAYNE

"I suppose you're all wondering why I called you here," my mentor began with a grin.

I think he intended it as a joke. I've gotten so I recognize his "waiting for a laugh" grin. Unfortunately, he was trying it on the wrong crowd. Jahks aren't generally noted for their sense of humor.

"I assume it's to talk about the Trophy," a distinguished individual from the Ta-hoe group observed dryly. "Otherwise we're wasting our time."

"Oh, it's about the Trophy," Aahz assured him hastily.

"Which you stole from us!" a Veygan contributed venomously.

"After you stole it from us!" the Ta-hoer speaker shot back.

"Only after you cheated us out of it at the Big Game."

"That call was totally legal! The rules clearly state . . ."

"*That* rule hasn't been enforced for three hundred years. There are four rulings on record which have since contradicted . . ."

"Gentlemen, please!" Aahz called, holding up his hands for order. "All that is water under the drawbridge, as well as being totally beside the point. Remember, neither of you currently have the Trophy. *We* do."

There was a moment of tense silence as both sides absorbed this observation. Finally, the Ta-hoer speaker stepped forward.

"Very well," he said firmly. "Name your price for its return. The Ta-hoe Council is prepared to offer . . ."

"Veygus will top any offer Ta-hoe makes."

"And Ta-hoe will double any offer that Veygus makes," the speaker shot back.

This was starting to sound pretty good to me. Maybe I've been hanging around with Aahz too long, but the potential financial benefits of our situation impressed me as being exceptionally good. The only foreseeable difficulty was Aahz's insistence that he was going to keep his birthday present.

"If you try anything, our magician will . . ."

"Your magician! We fired her. If she tries anything, *our* magician will . . ."

The raging debate forced its way into my consciousness again. That last bit sounded like it could get very ugly very quickly. I snuck a nervous glance at Aahz, but as usual he was way ahead of me.

"Gentlemen, gentlemen!" he admonished, raising his hands once more.

"Who are you calling a gentleman?"

"And ladies," my mentor amended, squinting at the source of the voice. "What-da-ya know. ERA strikes again."

"What's an eerah?" The Ta-hoe spokesman frowned, echoing my thoughts exactly.

"It seems," Aahz continued, ignoring the question entirely, "that our motives have been misconstrued. We didn't appropriate the Trophy to ransom it. Quite the contrary. It has been our intention all along to see that it goes to its rightful owners."

An ugly growl arose from the Veygans.

"Excellent!" beamed the Ta-hoe spokesman. "If you

won't accept a reward, will you at least accompany us
back to town as our guests. There's sure to be celebrating
and . . ."

"I said 'the rightful owner.' " Aahz smiled, cutting him
off.

The spokesman paused, his smile melting to a dangerous scowl. "Are you saying we aren't the rightful owners?" he snarled. "If you thought Veygus had a better
claim, why did you steal it in the first place?"

"Let me run it past you one more time," my mentor
sighed. "The Trophy's going to its *rightful* owner. That
lets Veygus out, too."

That took the spokesman aback. I didn't blame him.
Aahz's logic had me a bit confused, too . . . and I was on
his side!

"If I understand it correctly," Aahz continued grandly,
"the Trophy goes to the winning team—that wins the Big
Game—as their award for being the year's best team. Is
that right?"

"Of course." The spokesman nodded.

"Why do you assume the team that wins the Big Game
is the best team?" Aahz asked innocently.

"Because there *are* only two teams. So it follows logically that . . ."

"That's where you're wrong," my mentor interrupted.
"There *is* another team."

"Another team?" The spokesman blinked.

"That's right. A team that neither of your teams has
faced, much less beaten. Now, we maintain that until that
team is defeated, neither Ta-hoe nor Veygus has the right
to declare their team the year's best!"

My stomach did a flip-flop. I was getting a bad feeling
about this.

"That's ridiculous!" called the Veygus spokesman.
"We've never *heard* of another team. Whose team is this,
anyway?"

"Ours." Aahz smiled. "And we're challenging both
your teams to a game, a three-way match, right here in
thirty days . . . Winner takes all."

Bad feeling confirmed. For a moment, I considered altering my disguise and sneaking out with one of the delegations. Then I realized that option was closed. Both groups had stepped back well out of ear-shot to discuss Aahz's proposal. That put them far away, so that I couldn't join them without being noticed. With nothing else to do, I turned on Aahz.

"*This* is your plan?" I demanded. "Setting us up to play a game we know absolutely nothing about against not one but two teams who've been playing it for five hundred years? That's not a plan, that's a disaster!"

"I figure it's our best chance to spring Tanda *and* keep the Trophy." My mentor shrugged.

"It's a chance to get our heads beaten in," I corrected. "There's got to be an easier way."

"There was," Aahz agreed. "Unfortunately, you eliminated it when you promised we wouldn't do anything to endanger Quigley's job."

I hate it when Aahz is right. I hate it almost as much as getting caught in my own stupid blunders. More often than not, those two phenomena occur simultaneously in my life.

"Why didn't you tell me about this plan before?" I asked to hide my discomfort.

"Would you have gone along with it if I had?"

"No."

"That's why."

"What happens if we refuse your challenge?" the Ta-hoe spokesman called.

"Then we consider ourselves the winners by default," Aahz replied.

"Well, Veygus will be there," came the decision from the other group.

"And so will Ta-hoe," was the spontaneous response.

"If I might ask," the Ta-hoe spokesman queried, "why did you pick a date thirty days from now?"

"It'll take time for you to lay out a triangular field." My mentor shrugged. "And besides, I thought your merchants would require more than a week to prepare their souvenirs."

There were nods in both groups for that reasoning.

"Then it's agreed?" Aahz prompted.

"Agreed!" roared Veygus.

"Agreed!" echoed Ta-hoe.

"Speaking of merchandizing," the Ta-hoe spokesman commented, "what is the name of your team? We'll need it before we can go into production of the souvenirs."

"We're called 'The Demons,' " Aahz said, winking at me. In a flash I saw what his plan really was. "Would you like to know why?"

"Well . . . I would assume it's because you play like demons," the Ta-hoe spokesman stammered.

"Not 'like' demons!" My mentor grinned. "Shall we show them, partner?"

"Why not?" I smiled, closing my eyes.

In a moment, our disguises were gone, and for the first time the delegates had a look at what was opposing them.

"As I was saying," Aahz announced, showing all his teeth, "not 'like' demons."

It was a good gambit, and it should have worked. Any sane person would quake at the thought of taking on a team of demons. No sacrifice would be too great to avoid the confrontation. We had overlooked one minor detail, however. Jahks are not sane people.

"Excellent," the Ta-hoe spokesman exclaimed.

"What?" Aahz blinked, his smile fading.

"This should keep the odds even," the spokesman continued. "That's what we were discussing . . . whether you could field a good enough team to make a fight of it. But now . . . well, everyone will want to see *this* matchup."

"You . . . aren't afraid of playing against demons?" my mentor asked slowly.

Now it was the spokesman's turn to smile.

"My dear fellow," he chortled, "if you had ever seen *our* teams play, you wouldn't have to ask that question."

With that, he turned and rejoined his delegation as the two groups prepared to withdraw from the meeting.

"Didn't you listen in on their conversations?" I hissed.

"If you'll recall," Aahz growled back, "I was busy talking with you at the time."

"Then we're stuck," I moaned.

"Maybe not," he corrected. "Quigley! Could we have a word with you?"

The ex-demon hunter lost no time in joining us.

"I must say," he chortled. "You boys *did* an excellent job of getting me out of a tight spot there. Now it's a matter of pride for them to win the Trophy back on the playing field."

"Swell," Aahz growled. "Now how about your part of the deal? Ta-hoe has its chance, so there's no reason for you to keep Tanda."

"Mmm . . . yes and no," Quigley corrected. "It occurs to me that if I release her now, then you'll have the Trophy *and* Tanda, and would therefore have no motive to return for the game. To fulfill your promise, to give Ta-hoe a chance for the Trophy, the game will have to take place. *Then* I'll release Tanda."

"Thanks a lot," my mentor spat.

"Don't mention it." The ex-demon hunter waved as he went to rejoin his group.

"Now what do we do?" I asked.

"We form a team," Aahz shrugged. "Hey, Griffin!"

"What is it now?" the youth growled.

"We have one more job for you." My mentor smiled. "All you have to do is help us train our team. There are . . . a few points of the game that aren't very clear to us."

"No," said Griffin firmly.

"Now look, short stuff . . ."

"Wait a minute, Aahz," I interrupted. "Griffin, this time we aren't threatening you. I'm offering you a job at good wages to help us."

"What!?" Aahz shrieked.

"Shut up, Aahz."

"You don't understand," Griffin interrupted in turn. "Neither threats nor money will change my mind. I helped you steal the Trophy from Veygus, but I won't help you against my own team. I'd die before I'd do that."

"There are worse things than dying," Aahz suggested ominously.

"Let it drop, Aahz," I said firmly. "Thanks anyway, Griffin. You've been a big help when we needed you, so

I won't fault you for holding back now. Hurry up. The others are waiting."

We watched as he trotted off to join his delegation.

"You know, kid," Aahz sighed at last, "sometime we're going to have to have a long talk about these lofty ideals of yours."

"Sure, Aahz," I nodded. "In the meantime, what are we going to do about this game?"

"What else can we do?" My mentor shrugged. "We put together a team."

"Just like that." I winced. "And where are we going to find the players, much less someone who can tell us how the game is played?"

"Where else?" Aahz grinned, setting the D-Hopper. "The Bazaar at Deva!"

XVIII:

"What's the point-spread on World War III?"

—R. REAGAN

At several other points in this tale, I've referred to the Bazaar at Deva. You may be wondering about it. So do I . . . and I've been there!

Deva is the home dimension of the Deveels, acknowledged to be the best traders anywhere. You may find references to them in your folklore. Deals with Deveels are usually incredible and frequently disastrous. I've dealt with only two Deveels personally. One got me hung (not hung-over from drink—but hung up by the neck!) and the other sold me my dragon, Gleep. I like to think that makes me even, but Aahz insists I'm batting zero—whatever that means.

Anyway, there is a year-round, rock-the-clock Bazaar in that dimension where the Deveels meet to trade with each other. Everything imaginable and most things that aren't are available there. All you have to do is bargain with the Deveels. Fortunately, the Bazaar is large enough that there is much duplication, and sometimes you can play the dealers off against each other.

I had been here twice before, both times with Aahz.

This was, however, the first time I had been here when it was raining.

"It's raining," I pointed out, scowling at the over-hanging clouds. They were a dark orange, which was quite picturesque, but did nothing toward making getting wet more pleasant.

"I know it's raining," Aahz retorted tersely. "C'mon. Let's step in here while I get my bearings."

"Here," in this case, was some sort of invisible bubble enveloping one stall which seemed to be doing an admirable job of keeping the rain out. I've used magik wards before to keep out unwelcome intruders, but it had never occurred to me to use it against the elements.

"Buying or looking, gentlemen?" the proprietor asked, sidling up to us.

I glanced at Aahz, but he was up on his tiptoes surveying the surroundings.

"Um . . . looking, I guess."

"Then stand in the rain!" came the snarling reply. "Force fields cost money, you know. This is a display, not a public service."

"What's a force field?" I stalled.

"Out!"

"C'mon, kid," Aahz said. "I know where we are now."

"Where?" I asked suspiciously.

"In the stall of the Bazaar's rudest dealer," my mentor explained, raising his voice. "I wouldn't have believed it if I hadn't heard him with my own ears."

"What's that?" the proprietor scowled.

"Are you Garbelton?" Aahz asked, turning his attention on the proprietor.

"Well . . . yes."

"Your reputation precedes you, sir," my mentor intoned loftily, "and is devastatingly accurate. Come, Master Skeeve, we'll take our business elsewhere."

"But, gentlemen!" Garbelton called desperately, "if you'll only reconsider . . ."

The rest was lost as Aahz gathered me up and strode off into the rain.

"What was that all about?" I demanded, breaking stride

to jump a puddle. Aahz stepped squarely on it, splashing maroon mud all over my legs. Terrific.

"That? Oh, just a little smokescreen to save face. It isn't good for your reputation to get thrown out of places . . . particularly for not buying."

"You mean you hadn't heard of him before? Then how did you know his name?"

"It was right there on the stall's placard." Aahz grinned. "Sure gave him a turn, though, didn't I? There's nothing a Deveel hates as much as losing a potential customer . . . except for giving a refund."

As much as I care for Aahz and appreciate the guidance he's given me, he can be a bit stomach-turning when he starts gloating.

"We're still out in the rain," I pointed out.

"Ah, but now we know where we're going."

"We do?"

Aahz groaned, swerving to avoid a little old lady who was squatting in the middle of the thoroughfare chortling over a cauldron. As we passed, a large hairy paw emerged from the cauldron's depth, but the lady whacked it with her wooden spoon and it retreated out of sight. Aahz ignored the entire proceedings.

"Look, kid," he explained, "we're looking for two things here. First, we need to recruit some players for our team."

"How can we recruit for the team when we don't know the first thing about the game?" I interrupted.

"Second," my mentor continued tersely, "we have to find someone who can fill us in on the details of the game."

"Oh."

Properly mollified, I plodded along beside him in silence for several moments, sneaking covert glances at the displays we were passing. Then something occurred to me.

"Say . . . ummmm, Aahz?"

"Yeah, kid?"

"You never answered my question. Where are we going?"

"To the Yellow Crescent Inn."

"The Yellow Crescent Inn?" I echoed, brightening slightly. "Are we going to see Gus?"

"That's right." Aahz grinned. "Gus is a heavy bettor. He should be able to put us in touch with a reliable bookie. Besides, he owes us a favor. Maybe we can get him for the team."

"Good," I said, and meant it.

Gus is a gargoyle. He was part of the crew we used to stop Big Julie's army and I trust him as much as I do Aahz . . . maybe a little more. Anyone who's used the expression "heart of stone" to mean insensitive has never met Gus. I assume his heart is stone, the rest of him is, but he's one of the warmest, most sympathetic beings I've ever met. He's also without a doubt the stablest being that I've met through Aahz. If Gus joined our team, I'd worry a lot less . . . well, a little less. Then again, he might be too sensible to get involved in this madcap scheme. And as for the bookies . . .

"Hey, Aahz." I blinked. "What do we need a bookie for?"

"To brief us on the game, of course."

"A bookie from Deva is going to tell us how to play the game in Jahk?"

"It's the best we can do." Aahz shrugged. "You heard Griffin. Nobody in Jahk will give us the time of day, much less help us put a team together. Cheer up, though. Bookies are very knowledgeable in spectator sports, and the ones here in Deva are the best."

I pondered this for several moments, then decided to ask the question that had been bothering me since the meeting.

"Aahz? When you issued the challenge, did you really expect to play the game?"

My mentor stopped dead in his tracks and whirled to face me.

"Do you think I'd issue a challenge without intending to fight?" he demanded. "Do you think I'm a big-mouthed bluffer who'd rather talk his way out of trouble than fight?"

"It had crossed my mind," I admitted.

"Well, you're right." He grinned, resuming his stride. "You're learning pretty fast—for a Klahd. No, I really thought they'd back down when we dropped our disguises. That and I didn't think Quigley would see through the ploy and call our hand."

"He's learning fast, too," I commented. "I'm afraid he could become a real problem."

"Not a chance." My mentor snorted. "You've got him beat cold in the magik department."

"Except I've promised not to move against him," I observed glumly.

"Don't let it get you down," Aahz insisted, draping an arm around my shoulders. "We've both made some stupid calls on this one. All we can do is play the cards we're dealt."

"Bite the bullet, eh?" I grimaced.

"That's right. Say, you really are learning quick."

I still didn't know what a bullet was, but I was picking up some of Aahz's pet phrases. At least now I could give the illusion of intelligence.

The Yellow Crescent Inn was in sight now. I expected Aahz to quicken his pace . . . I mean, it *was* raining. Instead, however, my mentor slowed slightly, peering at a mixed group of beings huddled under a tent-flap.

"Hel-lo!" he exclaimed. "What have we here?"

"It looks like a mixed group of beings huddled under a tent-flap," I observed dryly, or as dryly as I could manage while dripping wet.

"It's a crap game," Aahz declared. "I can hear the dice."

Trust a Pervect to hear the sound of dice on mud at a hundred paces.

"So?" I urged.

"So I think we've found our bookie. The tall fellow, there—at the back of the crowd. I've dealt with him before."

"Are we going to talk to him now?" I asked eagerly.

"Not 'we,' " Aahz corrected me. "Me. You get in enough trouble in cleancut crowds without my taking you

into a crap game. You're going to wait for me in the Inn.
Gus should be able to keep an eye on you."

"Oh, all right."

I was disappointed, but willing to get out of the rain.

"And don't stop to talk to anyone between here and
there. Do you hear me?"

"Yes, Aahz." I nodded, starting off at a trot.

"And whatever you do, don't eat the food!"

"Are you kidding?" I laughed. "I've been here before."

The food at the Yellow Crescent Inn is dubious at best.
Even after dimension hopping with Tananda and seeing
what was accepted as food elsewhere, I wouldn't put anything from that place in my mouth voluntarily.

As I approached, I could see through the door that the
place was empty. This surprised me. I mean, from my
prior experience, there was usually a good-sized crowd in
there, and I would have expected the rain to increase the
number of loiterers.

Gus wasn't in sight, either; but the door was open, so
I pushed my way in, relieved to be somewhere dry again.
I shouldn't have been.

No sooner had I gained entry when something like a
large hand closed over the top of my head and I was
hoisted bodily from my feet.

"Little person!" a booming voice declared. "Crunch
likes little persons. Crunch likes little persons better than
Big Macs. How do you taste, little person?"

With this last, I was rotated until I was hanging face
to face with my assailant. In this case, I use the term
"face" loosely. It had felt like I was being picked up by
a big hand because I *was* being picked up by a big hand.
At the other end of the big hand was the first and only
troll it had been my misfortune to meet . . . and he looked
hungry.

XIX:

"Why should I have to pay a troll just to cross a bridge?"

—B. G. GRUFF

While I had never seen a troll before, I knew that this was one. I mean, he fit the description: tall, scraggly hair in patches, long rubbery limbs, misshapen face with runny eyes of unequal size. If it wasn't a troll, it would do until something better—or worse—came along.

I should have been scared, but strangely I wasn't. For some time now I had been ducking and weaving through some tight situations trying to avoid trouble. Now, Big Ugly here wanted to hassle me. This time, I wasn't buying.

"Why little person not answer Crunch?" the troll demanded, shaking me slightly.

"You want an answer?" I snarled. "Try this!"

Levitation is one of my oldest spells, and I used it now. Reaching out with my mind, I picked up a chair and slammed it into his face.

He didn't even blink.

Then I got scared.

"What's going on out here?!" Gus bellowed, charging out of the kitchen. "Any fights, and I'll . . . Skeeve!!"

"Tell your customer here to put me down before I tear off his arm and feed it to him!" I called, my confidence returning with the arrival of reinforcements.

I needn't have said anything. The effect of Gus's words on the troll was nothing short of miraculous.

"Skeeve?" My assailant gaped, setting me gently on my feet. "I say. Bloody good to make your acquaintance. I've heard so much about you, you know. Chumly here."

The hand which had so recently fastened on my head now seized my hand and began pumping it gently with each adjective.

"Ummm . . . a pleasure, I'm sure," I stammered, trying vainly to retrieve my hand. "Say, weren't you talking differently before?"

"Oh, you mean Crunch?" Chumly laughed. "Beastly fellow. Still, he serves his purpose. Keeps the riffraff at a distance, you know."

"What he's trying to say," Gus supplied, "is that it's an act he puts on to scare people. It's lousy for business when he drops in for a visit, but it does mean we can talk uninterrupted. That's about the only way you can talk to Chumly. He's terribly shy."

"Oh, tosh," the troll proclaimed, digging at the floor with his toe. "I'm only giving the public what it wants. Not much work for a vegetarian troll, you know."

"A vegetarian troll?" I asked incredulously. "Weren't you about to eat me a minute ago?"

"Perish the thought." Chumly shuddered. "Presently I would have allowed you to squirm free and run . . . except, of course, you wouldn't. Quite a spirited lad, isn't he?"

"You don't know the half of it," the gargoyle answered through his perma-grin. "Why, when we took on Big Julie's army . . ."

"Chumly!" Aahz exclaimed, bursting through the door.

"Aahz," the troll answered. "I say, this is a spot of all right. What brings you . . ."

He broke off suddenly, eyeing the Deveel who had followed Aahz into the inn.

"Oh, don't mind the Geek here." My mentor waved.

"He's helping us with some trouble we're having."

"The Geek?" I frowned.

"It's a nickname." The Deveel shrugged.

"I knew it," Gus proclaimed, sinking into a chair. "Or I should have known it when I saw Skeeve. The only time you come to visit is when there's trouble."

"If you blokes are going to have a war council, perhaps I'd better amble along," Chumly suggested.

"Stick around," Aahz instructed. "It involves Tanda."

"Tanda?" The troll frowned. "What has that bit of fluff gone and gotten herself into now?"

"You know Tanda?" I asked.

"Oh, quite," Chumly smiled. "She's my little sister."

"Your sister?" I gaped.

"Rather. Didn't you notice the family resemblance?"

"Well . . . I, ah . . ." I fumbled.

"Don't let him kid you," my mentor grinned. "Tanda and Chumly are from Trollia, where the men are Trolls and the women are Trollops. With men like this back home, you can understand why Tanda spends as much time as she does dimension hopping."

"That's quite enough of that," Chumly instructed firmly. "I want to hear what's happened to little sister."

"In a bit." Aahz waved. "First let's see what information the Geek here has for us."

"I can't believe I let you pull me out of a hot crap game to meet with this zoo," the Deveel grumbled.

"Zoo?" echoed Gus. He was still smiling, but then, he always smiled. Personally, I didn't like the tone of his voice.

Apparently Aahz didn't either, as he hastened to move the conversation along.

"You should thank me for getting you out," he observed, "before the rest of them figured out that you'd switched the dice."

"You spotted that?" the Geek asked, visibly impressed. "Then maybe it's just as well I bailed out. When a Pervert can spot me . . ."

"That's a Pervect!" Aahz corrected, showing all his teeth.

"Oh! Yes . . . of course," the Deveel amended, pinking visibly.

For his sake, I hoped he had some good information for us. In an amazingly short time he had managed to rub everyone wrong. Then again, Deveels have never been noted for their personable ways.

"So what can you tell us about the game on Jahk?" I prompted.

"How much are you paying me?" The Geek yawned.

"As much as the information's worth," Aahz supplied grimly. "Probably more."

The Deveel studied him for a moment, then shrugged.

"Fair enough," he declared. "You've always made good on your debts, Aahz. I suppose I can trust you on this one."

"So what can you tell us?" I insisted.

Now it was my turn to undergo close scrutiny, but the gaze turned on me was noticeably colder than the one Aahz had suffered. With a lazy motion, the Geek reached down and pulled a dagger from his boot and tossed it aloft with a twirl. Catching it with his other hand, he sent it up again, forming a glittering arch from hand to hand, never taking his eyes from mine.

"You're pretty mouthy for a punk Klahd," he observed. "Are you this mouthy when you don't have a pack of goons around to back your move?"

"Usually," I admitted. "And they aren't goons, they're my friends."

As I spoke, I reached out once more with my mind, caught the knife, gave it an extra twirl, then stopped it dead in the air, its point hovering bare inches from the Deveel's throat. Like I said, I was getting a little tired of people throwing their weight around.

The Geek didn't move a muscle, but now he was watching the knife instead of me.

"In case you missed it the first time around," Gus supplied, still smiling, "this 'punk Klahd's' name is Skeeve. The Skeeve."

The Deveel pinked again. I was starting to enjoy having a reputation.

"Why don't you sit down, Geek," Aahz suggested, "and tell the k . . . Skeeve . . . what he wants to know?"

The Deveel obeyed, apparently eager to move away from the knife. That being the case, I naturally let it follow him.

Once he was seated, I gave it one last twirl and set it lightly on the table in front of him. That reassured him somewhat, but he still kept glancing at it nervously as he spoke.

"I . . . um . . . I really don't have that much information," he began uncomfortably. "They only play one game a year, and the odds are usually even."

"How is the game played?" Aahz urged.

"Never seen it, myself," The Geek shrugged. "It's one of those get-the-ball-in-the-net games. I'm more familiar with the positions than the actual play."

"Then what are the positions?" I asked.

"It's a five-man team," the Deveel explained. "Two forwards, or Fangs, chosen for their speed and agility; one guard or Interceptor, for power; a goal-tender or Castle, who is usually the strongest man on the team; and a Rider, a mounted player who is used both for attack and defense."

"Sounds straightforward enough," my mentor commented.

"Can't you tell us anything at all about the play?" I pressed.

"Well, I'm not up on the strategies." The Geek frowned. "But I have a general idea of the action. The team in possession of the ball has four tries to score a goal. They can move the ball by running, kicking, or throwing. Once the ball is immobilized, the try is over and they line up for their next try. Of course, the defense tries to stop them."

"Run, kick, or throw," Aahz murmured. "Hmmm . . . sounds like defense could be a problem. What are the rules regarding conduct on the field?"

"Players can't use edged weapons on each other," the Deveel recited. "Any offenders will be shot down on the spot."

"Sensible rule," I said, swallowing hard. "What else?"

"That's it," the Geek shrugged.

"That's it?" Aahz exclaimed. "No edged weapons? That's it?"

"Both for the rules and my knowledge of the game," the Deveel confirmed. "Now, if we can settle accounts, I'll be on my way."

I wanted to cross-examine him, but Aahz caught my eye and shook his head.

"Would you settle for a good tip?" he asked.

"Only if it was a *really* good tip," the Geek responded dourly.

"Have you heard about the new game on Jahk? The three-way brawl that's coming up?"

"Of course." The Deveel shrugged.

"You have?" I blinked. I mean we had only just set it up!

"I have a professional stake in keeping up on these things."

"Uh-huh!" my mentor commented judiciously. "How are the odds running?"

"Even up for Ta-hoe and Veygus. This new team is throwing everyone for a loop, though. Since no one can get a line on them, they're heavy underdogs."

"If we could give you an inside track on this dark-horse team," Aahz said, looking at the ceiling, "would that square our account?"

"You know about the Demons?" the Geek asked eagerly. "If you do, it's a deal. With inside info, I could be the only one at the Bazaar with the data to fix the real odds."

"Done!" my mentor declared. "We're the Demons."

That got him. The Geek sagged back in his chair for a moment, open mouthed. Then he cocked his head at us.

"You mean, you're financing the team?"

"We *are* the team . . . or part of it. We're still putting it together."

The Deveel started to say something, then changed his mind. Rising silently, he headed for the door, hesitated with one hand on the knob, then left without saying a word.

Somehow, I found his reaction ominous.

"How 'bout that, kid," Aahz chortled. "I got the information without paying a cent!"

"I don't like the way he looked," I announced, still staring at the door.

"C'mon. Admit it! I just got us a pretty good deal."

"Aahz?" I said slowly. "What is it you always told me about dealing with Deveels?"

"Hmmm? Oh, you mean, 'If you think you've made a good deal with a Deveel . . . !' "

He broke off, his jubilance fading.

" 'First count your fingers, then your limbs, then your relatives!' " I finished for him. "Are you *sure* you got a good deal?"

Our eyes met, and neither of us were smiling.

XX:

"What are friends for?"

—R. M. NIXON

We were still pondering our predicament, when Chumly interrupted our thoughts.

"You blokes *do* seem to be having a bit of difficulty," he said, draping an arm around both of our shoulders. "But if it wouldn't be too much trouble, could you enlighten me as to what all this has to do with Tanda?"

Normally, this would sound like a casual request. When one pauses to consider, however, that the casual request was coming from a troll half again as tall as we were, and capable of mashing our heads like normal folks squash grapes, the request takes on a high priority no matter how politely it's phrased.

"Well, you know this game we're talking about?" Aahz began uneasily.

"Tanda's the prize," I finished lamely.

Chumly was silent. Then his grip on my shoulder tightened slightly.

"Forgive me." He smiled. "For a moment there I thought you said my little sister is the prize in some primitive, spectator brawl."

"Actually," Aahz explained hastily, trying to edge away, "the kid, here, was there when she was captured."

"But it was Aahz that got her involved in the game," I countered, edging in the other direction.

"You chaps got her into this?" the troll asked softly, his grip holding us firmly in place. "I thought you were trying to rescue her."

"Whoa! Everybody calm down!" Gus ordered, stepping into the impending brawl. "Nobody wrecks this place but me. Chumly, let's all sit down and hear this from the top."

I was pretty calm myself . . . at least, I wasn't about to start a fight. Still, Gus's suggestion was a welcome change in direction from the one the conversation was headed in.

This time, I needed no prompting to let Aahz do the talking. While he gets trapped in oversights from time to time, if given free rein, he can and has talked us out of some seemingly impossible situations. This was no exception. Though he surprised me by sticking to the truth, by the time he was done, Chumly's frozen features had softened to a thoughtful stare.

"I must say," the troll commented finally, "it seems little sister has done it to herself this time. You seem to have tried everything you could to effect her release."

"We could give the Trophy back," I suggested.

Aahz kicked me under the table.

"Out of the question," Chumly snorted. "It's Aahz's gift fair and square. If Tanda got herself in trouble acquiring it, that's bloody well her problem. You can't expect Aahz to feel responsible."

"Yes, I can," I corrected.

"No," the troll declared. "The only acceptable solution is to trounce these blighters soundly at their own game. I trust you'll allow me to fill a position on your team?"

"I'd had my hopes." My mentor grinned.

"Count me in, too," Gus announced, flexing his stone wings. "Can't let you all go into a brawl like this without my steadying influence."

"See, kid?" Aahz grinned. "Things are looking up already."

"Say, Aahz," I said carefully. "It occurs to me . . . you know that Rider position? Well, it seems to me we'd have a big psychological advantage if our Rider was sitting on top of a dragon."

"You're right."

"Aw, c'mon, Aahz! Just because Gleep's a bit . . . Did you say 'you're right'?"

"Right. Affirmative. Correct." My mentor nodded. "Sometimes you come up with some pretty good ideas."

"Gee, Aahz . . ."

"But not that stupid little dragon of yours," he insisted. "We're going to use that monster we got with Big Julie's army."

"But, Aahz . . ."

"But, Aahz nothing! C'mon, Gus! Close up shop here. We're heading for Klah to pick up a dragon!"

Now, Klah is my home dimension, and no matter what my fellow dimension travelers say, I think it's a pretty nice one to live in. Still, after spending extensive time in some other dimensions, however pleasantly familiar the sights of Klah seem, they do look a little drab.

Aahz had surprised me by bringing us well north of Possiltum, instead of at our own quarters in the royal palace. I inquired about this, and for a change my mentor gave me a straight answer.

"It's all in how you set the D-Hopper," he explained. "You've got eight dials to play with, and they let you control both which dimension you're going to as well as where you are when you arrive."

"Does that mean we could use it to go from one place to another in the same dimension?" I asked.

"Hmmm." Aahz frowned. "I really don't know. It never occurred to me to try. We'll have to check into it sometime."

"Well then, why did you pick this arrival point?"

"That's easy." My mentor grinned, gesturing at our colleagues. "I wasn't sure what our reception at the palace would be like if we arrived with a troll and a gargoyle."

He had me there. At the Bazaar disguises had been unnecessary, and I had gotten so used to seeing strange beings around me it had completely slipped my mind that our group would be a strange sight to the average Klahd.

"Sorry, Aahz." I flushed. "I forgot."

"Don't worry about it," my mentor waved. "If it had been important I would have said something to you before we left the Bazaar. I just wanted to shake you up a little to remind you to pay attention to details. The real reason we're here instead of at the palace is, we want to see Big Julie, and I'm too lazy to walk the distance if we could cover it with the D-Hopper."

Despite his reassurances, I got to work correcting my oversight. To redeem myself, I decided to show Aahz I had been practicing during my tour with Tananda. Closing my eyes, I concentrated on disguising Gus and Chumly at the same time.

"Not bad, kid," Aahz commented. "They're a little villainous looking, but acceptable."

"I thought it would help us avoid trouble if they looked a little mean," I explained modestly.

"Not bad?" Chumly snarled. "I look like a Klahd!"

"I think you look cute as a Klahd," Gus quipped.

"Cute? CUTE?" Chumly bristled. "Who ever heard of a cute troll? I say, Aahz, is this really necessary?"

"Unfortunately, yes," my mentor replied, his grin belying his expression of sympathy. "Remember, you aren't supposed to be a troll just now. Just a humble citizen of this lower than humble dimension."

"Why aren't you disguised?" the troll asked suspiciously, obviously unconvinced.

"I'm already known around here as the apprentice of the court magician," Aahz countered innocently. "Folks are used to seeing me like this."

"Well," Chumly grumbled, "there'll be bloody Hell to pay if anyone I know sees me looking like this."

"If anyone you know sees you like this, they won't recognize you," I pointed out cautiously.

The troll thought about that for a moment, then slowly nodded his head.

"I suppose you're right," he conceded at last. "Let's off to find this Big Julie, hmmm? The less time I spend looking like this, the better."

"Don't get your hopes too high," Aahz cautioned. "We're going to do our training in this dimension, so you might as well get used to being a Klahd for a while."

"Bloody Hell," was the only reply.

True to his plans for retirement, Big Julie was relaxing on the lawn of his cottage, drinking wine when we arrived. To the casual observer, he might seem nothing more than a spindly old man basking in the sun. Then again, the casual observer wouldn't have known him when he was commanding the mightiest army ever to grace our dimension. This was probably just as well. Julie was still hiding from a particularly nasty batch of loan sharks who were very curious as to why he and his men gave up soldiering . . . and hence their ability to pay back certain old gambling debts.

"Aye! Hello, boys!" he boomed, waving enthusiastically. "Long time no see, ya know? Pull up a chair and have some wine. What brings you out this way, eh?"

"A little bit of pleasure and a lot of business," Aahz explained, casually gathering to his bosom the only pitcher of wine in sight. "We've got a little favor to ask."

"If it's mine, it's yours," Julie announced. "Whatdaya need?"

"Is there any more wine?" I asked hastily.

Long years of experience had taught me not to expect Aahz to share a pitcher of wine. One was barely enough for him.

"Sure. I got lots. Badaxe is inside now getting some."

"Badaxe?" Aahz frowned. "What's he doing here?"

"At the moment, wondering what *you're* doing here," came a booming voice.

We all turned to find the shaggy-mountain form of Possiltum's general framed in the doorway of the cottage, a pitcher of wine balanced in each hand. Hugh Badaxe always seemed to me to be more beast than man, though

I'll admit his curly dark hair and beard when viewed in conjunction with his favorite animal skin cloak contributed greatly to the image. Of course, beasts didn't use tools, while Badaxe definitely did. A massive double-edged axe dangled constantly from his belt, at once his namesake and his favorite tool of diplomacy.

"We just dropped in to have a few words with Big Julie here," my mentor replied innocently.

"What about?" the general demanded. "I thought we agreed that all military matters would be brought to me before seeking Big Julie's advice. I *am* the Commander of Possiltum's army, you know."

"Now, Hugh," Julie soothed, "the boys just wanted to ask me for a little favor, that's all. If it involved the army, they would've come to you. Right, boys?"

Aahz and I nodded vigorously. Gus and Chumly looked blank. We had overlooked briefing them on General Badaxe and his jealousies regarding power.

"You see?" Julie continued. "Now, then, Aahz, what sort of favor can I do for you?"

"Nothing much." My mentor shrugged. "We were wondering if we could borrow your dragon for a little while."

"My dragon? What do you need my dragon for? You've already got a dragon."

"We need a *big* dragon," Aahz evaded.

"A big dragon?" Julie echoed, frowning. "It sounds like you boys are into something dangerous."

"Don't worry," I interjected confidently, "I'll be riding the dragon in the Game, so nothing . . ."

"Game?" Badaxe roared. "I knew it. You're going into a war game without even consulting me."

"It's not a war game," I insisted.

"Yes, it is," Aahz corrected.

"It is?" I blinked.

"Think about it, kid," my mentor urged. "Any spectator sport with teams is a form of wargaming."

"Then why wasn't I informed?" Badaxe blustered. "As commander of Possiltum's armed forces, any war games to be held fall under my jurisdiction."

"General," Aahz sighed, "the game isn't going to be played in this kingdom."

"Any military . . . oh!" Badaxe paused, confused by this turn of events. "Well, if it involves any members of my army . . ."

"It doesn't," my mentor interrupted. "This exercise only involves a five-man team, and we've filled it without drawing on the army's resources."

A bell went off in my mind. I ran a quick check, which only confirmed my fears.

"Um . . . Aahz . . ." I began.

"Not now, kid," he growled. "You see, general, all your paranoid fears were . . ."

"Aahz!" I insisted.

"What is it?" my mentor snarled, turning on me.

"We haven't got five players, only four."

XXI:

"We've got an unbeatable team!"

—SAURON

"Four?" Aahz echoed blankly.

"I count real good up to five," I informed him loftily, "and you, me, Gus and Chumly only make four. See? One, two, three . . ."

"All right! I get the message," my mentor interrupted, scowling at our two comrades. "Say, Gus! I don't suppose Berfert's along, is he?"

"C'mon, Aahz," I chided, "we can't claim a salamander as a team member."

"Shut up, kid. How 'bout it, Gus?"

"Not this time." The gargoyle shrugged. "He ran into a ladyfriend of his, and they decided to take a vacation together."

"A lady friend?" Aahz asked, arching an eyebrow.

"That's right." Gus nodded. "You might say she's an old flame."

"An old flame." The troll grinned. "I say, that's rather good."

For a change, *I* got the joke, and joined Gus and

Chumly in a hearty round of laughter, while Badaxe and
Julie looked puzzled.

Aahz rolled his eyes in exasperation.

"That's all I need," he groaned. "One member short,
and the ones I've got are half-wits. When you're all quite
through, I'm open to suggestions as to where we're going
to find a fifth team member."

"I'll fill the position," Badaxe said calmly.

"You?" I gulped, my laughter forgotten.

"Of course." The general nodded. "It's my duty."

"Maybe I didn't make myself clear," Aahz interjected.
"Possiltum isn't involved in this at all."

"But its magician and his apprentice are," Badaxe
added pointedly. "You're both citizens of Possiltum, and
rather prominent citizens at that. Like it or not, my duty
is to protect you with any means at my disposal—and in
this case, that means me."

I hadn't thought of that. In a way, it was kind of nice.
Still, I wasn't wild about the general putting himself in
danger on our account.

"Ummm . . . I appreciate your offer, general," I began
carefully, "but the game's going to be played a long way
from here."

"If you can survive the journey, so can I," Badaxe
countered firmly.

"But you don't understand!"

"Kid," Aahz interrupted in a thoughtful tone, "why
don't you introduce him to his potential teammates?"

"What? Oh, I'm sorry. General Badaxe, this is Gus,
and that's Chumly."

"No." My mentor smiled. "I mean *introduce* him."

"Oh!" I said. "General, meet the rest of our team."

As I spoke, I dropped the disguise spell, revealing both
gargoyle and troll in their true forms.

"Gus!" Big Julie roared. "I thought I recognized your
voice."

"Hi, Julie!" The gargoyle waved. "How's retirement?"

"Pretty dull. Hey, help yourself to some wine!"

"Thanks."

Gus stepped forward and took the two pitchers of wine

from the general's nerveless grip, passing one to Chumly. It occurred to me that I was the only one of the crew who wasn't getting a drink out of this.

The general was transfixed, his eyes darting from gargoyle to troll and back again. He had paled slightly, but to his credit he hadn't given ground an inch.

"Well, Badaxe," Aahz grinned, "still want to join the team?"

The general licked his lips nervously, then tore his eyes away from Gus and Chumly.

"Certainly," he announced. "I'd be proud to fight alongside such . . . worthy allies. That is, if they'll have me."

That dropped it in our laps.

"What do you think, Skeeve?" Aahz asked. "You're the boss."

Correction. That dropped it in my lap. Aahz had an annoying habit of yielding leadership just when things got sticky. I was beginning to suspect it wasn't always coincidence.

"Well, Lord Magician?" Badaxe rumbled. "Will you accept my services for this expedition?"

I was stuck. No one could deny Badaxe's value in a fight, but I had never warmed to him as a person. As a teammate . . .

"Gleep!"

The warning wasn't soon enough! Before I could brace myself, I was hit from behind by a massive force and sent sprawling on my face. The slimy tongue worrying the back of my head and the accompanying blast of incredibly bad breath could only have one source.

"Gleep!" my pet announced proudly, pausing briefly in his efforts to reach my face.

"What's that stupid dragon doing here?" Aahz bellowed, unmoved by our emotional reunion.

"Ask Badaxe," Julie grinned. "He brought him."

"He did?" My mentor blinked, momentarily stunned out of his anger.

I was a bit surprised myself. Pushing Gleep away momentarily I scrambled to my feet and shot a questioning glance at the general.

For the first time since and including our original confrontation, Hugh Badaxe looked uncomfortable. The fierce warrior who wouldn't flinch before army, magician, or demon couldn't meet our eyes.

"He was ... well, with you two gone he was just moping around," the general mumbled. "No one else would go near him and I thought ... well, that is ... it seemed logical that ..."

"He brought him out to play with my dragon," Julie explained gleefully. "It seems the fierce general here has a weak spot for animals."

Badaxe's head came up with a snap. "The dragon served the Kingdom well in the last campaign," he announced hotly. "It's only fair that *someone* sees to his needs—as a veteran."

His bluster didn't fool anyone. There was no reason why he should feel responsible for my dragon. Even if he did, it would have been easy for him to order some of his soldiers to see to my pet rather than attending to it personally as he had done. The truth of the matter was that he liked Gleep.

As if to confirm our suspicions, my pet began to frolic around him, waggling head and tail in movements I knew were reserved for playmates. The general stoically ignored him ... which is not that easy to do.

"Um ... general?" I said carefully.

"Yes?"

I was fixed by a frosty gaze, daring me to comment on the dragon's behavior.

"About our earlier conversation," I clarified hastily. "I'm sure I speak for the rest of the team when I say we're both pleased and honored to have you on our side for the upcoming war game."

"Thank you, Lord Magician." He bowed stiffly. "I trust you will find your confidence in me is not misplaced."

"Now that that's settled," Aahz chortled, rubbing his hands together. "Where's the big dragon? We've got some practicing to do."

Julie shrugged. "He's asleep."

"Asleep?" Aahz echoed.

"That's right. He got into the barn, ate up over half the livestock in the place. Now he's sleepin' like a rock, you know? Probably won't wake up for a couple of months at best."

"A couple of months!" my mentor groaned. "Now what are we going to do? The kid's got to have something to ride in the game!"

"Gleep!" my pet said, rolling on the ground at my feet. Aahz glared at me.

"He said it, I didn't," I declared innocently.

"Don't think we've got much choice, Aahz," Gus pointed out.

"If you aren't used to them, *any* dragon would seem rather frightening," Chumly supplied.

"All right! All right!" Aahz grimaced, throwing up his hands in surrender. "If you're all willing to risk it, I'll go along. As long as he doesn't drive me nuts by always saying . . ."

"Gleep?" my pet asked, swiveling his head around to see what Aahz was shouting about.

"Then we're ready to start practicing?" I asked hastily.

"As ready as we'll ever be, I guess," Aahz grumbled, glaring at the dragon.

"I know this isn't my fight," Big Julie put in, "but what kinda strategies have you boys worked up?"

"Haven't yet," my mentor admitted. "But we'll think of something."

"Maybe I can give you a hand. I used to be pretty good with small unit tactics. You know what I mean?"

The next few weeks were interesting. You notice I didn't say "instructive," just interesting. Aside from learning to work together as a team, there was little development among the individuals of our crew.

You could argue that with the beings we had on the team, there was little development to be done. That was their opinion. Nor was it easy to argue with them. With the exception of myself, their physical condition ranged from excellent to unbelievable. What was more, they were all seasoned veterans of countless battles and campaigns. From what we had seen of the Jahks, any one of our team was more than a match for five of our opponents—and together . . .

Maybe that's what bothered me: the easy assurance on everyone's part that we could win in a walk. I know it bothered Big Julie.

"You boys are over-confident," he'd scold, shaking his head in exasperation. "There's more to fighting than strength. Know what I mean?"

"We've *got* more than strength." Aahz yawned. "There's speed, agility, stamina, and with Gus along, we've got air cover. Then again, Skeeve there has a few tricks up his sleeve as a magician."

"You forgot 'experience,'" Julie countered. "These other guys, they've been playing this game for what? Five hundred years now? They might have a trick or two of their own."

With that stubborn argument, Julie would threaten, wheedle, and cajole us into practicing. Unfortunately, most of the practice centered around me.

Staying on Gleep's back was rough enough. Trying to keep my seat while throwing or catching a ball proved to be nearly impossible. Gleep was no help. He preferred chasing the ball himself or standing stock still while scratching himself with a hind leg to following orders from me. I finally had to cheat a little, resorting to magik to keep me upright on my mount's back. A little levitation, a little flying, and suddenly my riding skills improved a hundred fold. If Aahz suspected I was using something other than my sense of balance, he didn't say anything.

The problem of catching and throwing the ball was solved by the addition of a staff to my argument. Chumly uprooted a hefty sized sapling, and the general used his ever-present belt axe to trim away branches and roots. The result was an eleven foot club with which I could either knock the ball along the ground or swat it out of the air if someone had thrown or kicked it aloft. The staff was a bit heavier than I would have liked, but the extra weight moved the ball farther each time I hit it. Of course, I used a little magik to steer the ball, too, so I didn't miss often and it usually went where I wanted it to go.

Gleep, on the other hand, went where he wanted to go. While my club occasionally helped both to set him in motion and to institute minor changes in his direction once he was moving, total control had still eluded me when the day finally arrived for our departure.

The five of us (six including Gleep) gathered in the center of our practice meadow and said our goodbyes to Julie.

"I'm sorry I can't come with you, boys," he declared mournfully, "but I'm not as young as I used to be, you know?"

"Don't worry," Aahz waved, "we'll be back soon. You can come to our victory celebration."

"There you go again." Julie scowled. "I'm warning you, don't celebrate until after the battle. After five hundred years . . ."

"Right, Julie," Aahz interrupted hastily. "You've told us before. We'd better get going now or we'll miss the game. Wouldn't want to lose by default."

With that, he checked to see we were all in position and triggered the D-Hopper.

A moment later, we were back in Jahk.

XXII:

"No matter what the game, no matter what the rules, the same rules apply to both sides!"

—HOYLE'S LAW

The stadium had undergone two major changes since the last time Aahz and I were here.

First, the configuration of the field had been changed. Instead of a rectangle, the chalk lines now outlined a triangle with netted goals at each corner. I assumed that was to accommodate a three-way instead of a two-way match.

The second change was people. Remember how I said I didn't even want to imagine what the stadium would be like full of people? Well, the reality dwarfed anything my imagination could have conjured up. Where I had envisioned neat rows of people to match the military precision of the seats, the stands were currently a chaotic mass of color and motion. I don't know why they bothered providing seats. As far as I could tell, nobody was sitting down.

A stunned hush had fallen over the crowd when we appeared. This was understandable. Beings don't appear out of thin air very often, as we had assembled.

At Aahz's instruction, I had withheld any disguises from our team in order to get maximum psychological impact from our normal appearance. We got it.

The crowd gaped at us, while we gaped at the crowd. Then they recovered their composure and a roar trumpeted forth from a thousand throats simultaneously. The bedlam was deafening.

"They don't seem very intimidated," I observed dryly.

I didn't expect to be heard over the din, but I had forgotten Aahz's sharp ears.

"*Ave Caesar. Salutes e moratorium.* Eh, kid?" He grinned.

I didn't have the foggiest what he was talking about, but I grinned back at him. I was tired of staring blankly every time he made a joke.

"Hey, boss. We've got company," Gus called, jerking his head toward one side of the stadium.

"Two companies, actually," Chumly supplied, staring in the opposite direction.

Swiveling my head around, I discovered they were both right. Massha was bearing down on us from one side, while old Greybeard was waddling forward from the other. It seemed both Veygus and Ta-hoe wanted words with us.

"Hell-o boys," Massha drawled, arriving first. "Just wanted to wish you luck with your . . . venture."

This might have sounded strange coming from a supporter of the opposition. It did to me. Then I remembered that Massha thought we were out to neutralize Quigley's "demon." Well, in a way we were.

Aahz, as usual, was way ahead of me.

"Don't worry, Massha." He grinned. "We've got everything well in hand."

It never ceases to amaze me the ease with which my mentor can lie.

"Just be sure you stay out of it," he continued smoothly. "It's a rather delicate plan, and any miscellaneous moving parts could foul things up."

"Don't worry your green little head about that." She winked. "I know when I'm outclassed. I was just kinda hoping you'd introduce me to the rest of your team."

I suddenly realized that throughout our conversation,

she hadn't taken her eyes off our teammates. Specifically, she was staring sideways at Hugh Badaxe. This didn't change as Aahz made the proper introductions.

"Massha, this is Gus."

"Charmed, madam," the gargoyle responded.

"And Chum—er—Crunch."

"When fight? Crunch likes fighting," Chumly declared, dropping into his troll act.

Massha didn't bat an eye. She was busy running both of them up and down the general's frame.

"And this is Hugh Badaxe."

With a serpentine glide, Massha was standing close to the general.

"So pleased to meet cha, Hugh . . . you don't mind if I call you Hugh, do you?" she purred.

"Harmmph . . . I . . . that is," Badaxe stammered, visibly uncomfortable.

I could sympathize with him. Having Massha focus her attention on one was disquieting to say the least. Fortunately, help arrived just then in the form of the Ta-hoe delegate.

"Good afternoon, gentlemen," he chortled, rubbing his hands together gleefully. "Hello, Massha."

"Actually," she returned icily, "I was just leaving."

She leaned forward and murmured something in the general's ear before departing for her seat in the stands. Whatever it was, Badaxe flushed bright red and avoided our eyes.

"We were afraid you wouldn't arrive in time," Greybeard continued, ignoring Massha's exit. "Wouldn't want to disappoint the fans with a default, would we? When are you expecting the rest of your team?"

"The rest of our team?" I frowned. "I thought the rules only called for five players plus a riding mount."

"That's right," Greybeard replied, "but . . . oh, well, I admire your confidence. So there're only the five of you, eh? Well, well. That will change the odds a bit."

"Why?" I demanded suspiciously.

"Are the edges on that thing sharp?" the spokesman asked, spying the general's axe.

"Razor," Badaxe replied haughtily.

"But he won't use it on anyone," I added hastily, suddenly remembering the "no edged weapons" rule. I wasn't sure what the general's reaction would be if anyone tried to take his beloved axe away from him.

"Oh, I have no worries on that score," Greybeard responded easily. "As with all games, the crossbowmen will be quick to eliminate any player who chooses to ignore the rules."

He waved absently at the sidelines. We looked in the indicated direction, and saw for the first time that the field was surrounded by crossbowmen, alternately dressed in the blue and yellow of Ta-hoe and the red and white of Veygus. This was a little wrinkle the Geek had neglected to mention. He had told us about the rules, but not how they were enforced.

At the same time, I noticed two things which I had previously missed while scanning the stands.

The first was Quigley, sitting front and center on the Ta-hoe side. What was more important was that he had Tananda with him. She was still asleep, floating horizontally in the air in front of him. Apparently he didn't want to miss the game, and didn't trust us enough to leave her unguarded back at his workshop.

He saw me staring and waved. I didn't wave back. Instead, I was about to call Aahz's attention to my find when I noticed the second thing.

Griffin was at the edge of the field, jumping up and down and frantically waving his arms to get my attention. As soon as he saw I was watching him, he began vigorously beckoning to me.

Aahz was engrossed in conversation with the Tahoe spokesman, so I ambled off to see what Griffin wanted.

"Hello, Griffin." I smiled. "How've you been?"

"I just wanted to tell you," he gasped, breathless from his exertions, "I've changed sides. If there's anything I can do to help you, just sing out."

"Really?" I drawled, raising an eyebrow. "And why the sudden change of heart, not to mention allegiances?"

"Call it my innate sense of fair play." He grimaced. "I

don't like what they're planning to do to you. Even if my old team is involved, I don't like it."

"What are they planning to do to us?" I demanded, suddenly attentive.

"That's what I wanted to warn you about," he explained. "The two teams had a meeting about this game. They decided that however much they hated each other, neither side wanted to see the Trophy go to a bunch of outsiders."

"That's only natural," I nodded, "but what . . ."

"You don't understand!" the youth interrupted hastily. "They're going to double-team you! They've declared a truce with each other until they've knocked you off the field. When the game starts you'll be up against two teams working together against your one!"

"Kid! Get back here!"

Aahz's bellow reminded me there was another conference going on.

"I've got to go, Griffin," I declared. "Thanks for the warning."

"Good luck!" he called. "You're going to need it."

I trotted back onto the field, to find the assemblage waiting for me with expectant expressions.

"They want to see the Trophy," Aahz informed me with a wink.

"As per our original agreement," the Ta-hoe spokesman added stiffly. "It should be here to be awarded to the victorious team."

"It *is* here," I announced firmly.

"I beg your pardon?" Greybeard blinked, looking around.

"Show him, kid." My mentor grinned.

"All right," I nodded, "everybody stand back."

In many ways it was harder to produce the statue using magik than it would have been to do it with physical labor. I had to agree with Aahz, though, that this way was far more dramatic.

Stretching my levitation capacities to their utmost, I went to work. A large hunk of turf was lifted from the center of the field and set aside. Then the exposed dirt was shoved aside, and finally the Trophy rose into view. I let it hover in midair while I rearranged the dirt and replaced the turf, then let it settle majestically to rest in all its magnificent, ugly splendor.

The crowd roared its approval, though whether for my magik or the Trophy itself I wasn't sure.

"Pretty good," Aahz exclaimed, slapping me gently on the back.

"Gleep," my pet exclaimed, adding his slimy tongue to the offered congratulations.

"Very clever," Greybeard admitted. "We never thought to look there. A little rough on the field, though, isn't it?"

"It'll get torn up this afternoon anyway." My mentor shrugged. "Incidentally, when's game time?"

As if in answer to his question, the stands exploded in bedlam. I hadn't thought the stadium could get any noisier, but this was like a solid wall of sound pressing in on us from all sides.

The reason for the jubilation was immediately obvious. Two columns of figures had emerged from a tunnel at the far end of the stadium and were jogging onto the field.

The blue and yellow tunics of one column contrasted with the scarlet and white tunics of the other, but served nicely to identify them as our opponents. This, however, was not their most noteworthy feature.

The Ta-hoe team was wearing helmets with long, sharp spikes on the top, while their counterparts from Veygus had long, curved horns emerging from either side of their helmets giving them an animalistic appearance. Even more noticeable, all the players were big. Bigger than any Jahk I had encountered to date. Easily as big as Chumly, but brawnier with necks so short their heads seemed to emerge directly from their shoulders.

As I said earlier, I count real good up to five, and there were considerably more than five players on each team.

XXIII:

"Life is full of little surprises."

—PANDORA

As I was prone to do in times of crises, I turned to my mentor for guidance. Aahz, in turn, reacted with the calm levelheadedness I've grown to expect.

Seizing the Ta-hoe spokesman by the front of his tunic, Aahz hoisted him up until his feet were dangling free from the ground.

"What is this!!" he demanded.

Glaah . . . sakle . . ." the fellow responded.

"Um . . . Aahz?" I intervened. "He might be a little more coherent if he could breathe."

"Oh! Right," my mentor acknowledged, lowering the spokesman until he was standing once more. "All right. Explain!"

"Ex . . . explain what?" Greybeard stammered, genuinely puzzled. "Those are the teams from our respective cities. You can tell them apart by their helmets and . . ."

"Don't give me that!" Aahz thundered. "Those aren't Jahks. Jahks are skinny or overweight!"

"Oh! I see," the spokesman said with dawning realization. "I'm afraid you've been misled. Not all Jahks are alike. Some are fans, and some are players—athletes. The fans are . . . a little out of shape, but that's to be expected. They're the workers who keep the cities and farms running. The players are a different story. All they do is train and so on. Over the generations, they've gotten noticeably larger than the general population of fans."

"Noticeably larger?" Aahz scowled, glaring down the field. "It's like they're another species!"

"I've seen it happen in other dimensions," Gus observed, "but never to this extent."

"Well, Big Julie warned us about over-confidence." Chumly sighed.

"What was that?" Greybeard blinked.

"Want fight," Chumly declared, dropping back into character. "Crunch likes fight."

"Oh." The spokesman frowned. "Very well. If there's nothing else, I'll just . . ."

"Not so fast," I interrupted. "I want to know why there are so many players. The game is played by five-man teams, isn't it?"

"That's right," Greybeard nodded. "The extra players are replacements . . . you know, for the ones who are injured or killed during the game."

"Killed?" I swallowed.

"As I said," the spokesman called, starting off, "I admire your confidence in only bringing five players."

"Killed?" I repeated, turning desperately to Aahz.

"Don't panic, kid," my mentor growled, scanning the opposition. "It's a minor setback, but we can adapt our strategies."

"How about the old 'divide and conquer' gambit?" Badaxe suggested, joining Aahz.

"That's right." Gus nodded. "They're not used to playing a three-way game. Maybe we can play them off against each other."

"It won't work," I declared flatly.

"Don't be so negative, kid," Aahz snapped. "Sometimes old tricks are the best."

"It won't work because they won't be playing against each other . . . just us."

I quickly filled them in on what Griffin had told me earlier. When I finished, the team was uncomfortably silent.

"Well," Aahz said at last, "things could be worse."

"How?" I asked bluntly.

"Gleep?"

My dragon had just spotted something the rest of us had missed. The other teams were bringing their riding beasts onto the field. Unlike the players, the beasts weren't marked with the team colors . . . but then, it wasn't necessary. There was no way they could be confused with each other.

The Veygus beast was a cat-like creature with an evilly flattened head—nearly as long as Gleep, it slunk along the ground with a fluid grace which was ruined only by the uneven gait of its oversized hindlegs. Though its movements were currently slow and lazy, it had the look of something that could move with blinding speed when it wanted to. It also looked very, very agile. I was sure the thing could corner like . . . well, like a cat.

The Ta-hoe mount was equally distinctive, but much more difficult to describe. It looked like a small, armored mound with its crest about eight feet off the ground. I would have thought it was an oversized insect, but it had more than six legs. As a matter of fact, it had hundreds of legs which we could see when it moved, which it seemed to do with equal ease in any direction. When it stopped, its armor settled to the ground, both hiding and guarding its tiny legs. I couldn't figure out where its eyes were, but I noticed it never ran into anything . . . at least accidentally.

"Gleep?"

My pet had pivoted his head around to peer at me. If he was hoping for an explanation or instructions, he was out of luck. I didn't have the vaguest idea of how to deal with the weird creatures. Instead, I stroked his mustache in what I hoped was a reassuring fashion. Though I didn't want to admit it to my teammates, I was becoming less and less confident about this game . . . and I hadn't been all that confident to begin with.

"Don't look now," Gus murmured, "but I've spotted Tanda."

"Where?" Chumly demanded, craning his neck to see where the gargoyle was pointing.

Of course, I had seen Tananda earlier and had forgotten to point her out to the others. I felt a little foolish, but then, that was nothing new. To cover my embarrassment, I joined the others in staring towards Tananda's floating form.

Quigley noticed us looking his way and began to fidget nervously. Apparently he was not confident enough in his newfound powers to feel truly comfortable under our mass scrutiny. His discomfort affected his magik . . . at least his levitation. Tananda's body dipped and swayed until I was afraid he was going to drop her on her head.

"If that magician's all that's in our way," Gus observed, "it occurs to me we would just sashay over there and take her back."

"Can't," Aahz snapped, shaking his head. "The kid here promised we wouldn't do anything to make that magician look bad."

"That's fine for you two," the gargoyle countered, "but Chumly and I didn't promise a thing."

"I say, Gus," Chumly interrupted, "we can't go against Skeeve's promise. It wouldn't be cricket."

"I suppose you're right," Gus grumbled. "I just thought it would be easier than getting our brains beaten out playing this silly game."

I agreed with him there. In fact, I was glad to find something I could agree with. Chumly's argument about crickets didn't make any sense at all.

"It occurs to me, Lord Magician," Badaxe rumbled, "that the promise you made wasn't the wisest of pledges."

"Izzat so?" Aahz snarled, turning on him. "Of course, general, you speak from long experience in dealing with demons."

"Well . . . actually . . ."

"Then I'd suggest you keep your lip buttoned about Lord Skeeve's wisdom *and* abilities. Remember, he's your ticket back out of here. Without him, it's a long walk home."

Chastised, the general retreated, physically and verbally.

"Gee, thanks, Aahz."

"Shut up, kid," my mentor snarled. "He's right. It was a dumb move."

"But you said . . ."

"Call it reflex." Aahz waved. "A body's got to earn the right to criticize my apprentice . . . and that specimen of Klahdish military expertise doesn't qualify."

"Well . . . thanks, anyway," I finished lamely.

"Don't mention it."

"Hey, Aahz," Chumly called. "Let's get this . . . Trophy out of the center of the field and put it somewhere safe."

"Like where?" my mentor retorted. "We're the only ones in the stadium I trust."

"How about in our goal?" Gus suggested, pointing to the wide net at our corner of the triangle.

"Sounds good," Aahz agreed. "I'll be back in a second, kid."

I had gotten so used to the bedlam in the stadium that I barely noticed it. As my teammates started to move the Trophy, however, the chorus of boos and catcalls that erupted threatened to deafen me. My colleagues responded with proper aplomb, shaking fists and making faces at their decriers. The crowd loved it. If they loved it any more, they'd charge down onto the field and lynch the lot of us.

I was about to suggest to my comrades that they quit baiting the crowd, when General Badaxe beckoned me over for a conference.

"Lord Magician," he began carefully, "I hope you realize I meant no offense with my earlier comments. I find that I'm a trifle on edge. I've never fought a war in front of an audience before."

"Forget it, Hugh." I waved. "You were right. In hindsight it *was* a bad promise. Incidentally . . . it's Skeeve. If we're in this mess together, it's a little silly to stand on formality."

"Thank you . . . Skeeve." The general nodded. "Actually I was hoping I could speak with you privately on a personal matter."

"Sure." I shrugged. "What is it?"

"Could you tell me a little more about that *marvelous* creature I was just introduced to earlier?"

"Marvelous creature?" I blinked. "What marvelous creature?"

"You know . . . Massha."

"Massha?" I laughed. Then I noticed the general's features were hardening. "I mean, oh, *that* marvelous creature. What do you want to know?"

"Is she married?"

"Massha? I mean . . . no, I don't think so."

The general heaved a sigh of relief. "Is there a chance she'll ever visit us in Possiltum?"

"I doubt it," I replied. "But if you'd like I could ask her."

"Fine." The general beamed, bringing a hand down on my shoulder in a bone-jarring display of friendship. "I'll consider that a promise."

"A what?" I blinked. Somehow the words had a familiar ring to them.

"I know how you honor your promises," Badaxe continued. "Fulfill this pledge, and you'll find I can be a friend to prize . . . just as I can be an enemy to be feared if crossed. Do we understand each other?"

"But I . . ."

"Hey, kid," Aahz shouted. "Hurry up and get on that stupid dragon! The game's about to start!"

I had been so engrossed in my conversation with Badaxe I had completely lost track of the other activities on the field.

The teams from Ta-hoe and Veygus had retired to the sidelines, leaving five players apiece on the field. The cat and the bug each had riders now, and were pacing and scuttling back and forth in nervous anticipation.

At midfield, where the Trophy had been, a Jahk stood

wearing a black and white striped tunic and holding a ball. I use the word *ball* rather loosely here. The object he was holding was a cube of what appeared to be a black, spongy substance. A square ball! One more little detail the Geek had neglected to mention.

Without bothering to take my leave from the general, I turned and sprinted for Gleep. Whatever was about to happen, I sure didn't want to face it afoot.

XXIV:

"This contest has to be the dumbest thing I've ever seen."

— H. COSELL

I was barely astride Gleep when the Jahk at midfield set the ball down and started backing toward the sidelines.

"Hey, Aahz!" I called. "What's with the guy in the striped tunic?"

"Leave him alone," my mentor shouted back. "He's a neutral."

Actually, I hadn't planned on attacking him, but it was nice to know he wasn't part of the opposition.

I was the last of the team to get into place. Aahz and Chumly were bracketing me as the Fangs, Gus was behind me, waiting to take advantage of his extra mobility as Guard; and Badaxe was braced in the mouth of the goal as Castle. We seemed about as ready as we would ever be.

"Hey, kid!" Aahz called. "Where's your club?"

I was so engrossed in my own thoughts it took a minute for his words to sink in. Then I panicked. For a flash moment I thought I had left my staff back in Klah. Then I spotted it lying in the grass at our entry point. A flick of my mind brought it winging to hand.

"Got it, Aahz!" I waved.

"Well, hang onto it, and remember . . ."

A shrill whistle blast interrupted our not-so-private conference and pulled our attention down-field. The cat and the bug were heading for the ball at their respective top speeds, with the rest of their teammates charging along in their wakes.

The game was on, and all we were doing was standing around with our mouths open.

As usual, Aahz was the first to recover.

"Don't just stand there with your mouth open!" he shouted. "Go get the ball."

"But I . . ."

"GLEEP!"

What I had intended to point out to Aahz was that the cat was almost at the ball already. Realizing there was no way I could get there first, I felt we should drop back and tighten our defense. My pet, however, had other ideas.

Whether he was responding to Aahz's command to "get the ball" (which was unlikely), or simply eager to meet some new playmates (which was highly probable), the result was the same. He bounded forward, cutting me off in mid-sentence and setting us on a collision course with the cat.

The crowd loved it.

Me, I was far less enthusiastic. The cat's rider had the ball now, but he and his mount were holding position at midfield instead of immediately advancing on our goal. Presumably this was to allow his teammates to catch up, so he could have some cover. This meant he wouldn't have to venture among us alone.

That struck me as being a very intelligent strategy. I only wished I could follow it myself. Gleep's enthusiasm was placing me in the position I had hoped to avoid at all costs—facing the united strength of both of the opposing teams without a single teammate to support me. For the first time since our opponents had taken the field, I stopped worrying about surviving until the end of the game. Now I was worried about surviving until the end of the first play!

My hopes improved for a moment when I realized we would reach the cat and its rider well ahead of their teammates. The feeling of hope faded rapidly, however, as my rival uncoiled his weapon.

Where I was carrying a staff, he had a whip . . . a long whip. The thing was twenty feet long if it was an inch. No, I'm not exaggerating. I could see its length quite clearly as the rider let it snake out toward my head.

The lash fell short by a good foot, though it seemed much closer at the time. Its sharp crack did produce one result, however. Gleep stopped in his tracks, throwing me forward on his neck as I fought to keep my balance. An instant behind the whip attack, the cat bounded forward, its teeth bared and ears flat against its skull, and one of its forepaws darted out to swat my dragon on the nose.

Though never noted for his agility, Gleep responded by trying to jump backwards and swap ends at the same time. I'm not sure how successful he was, because somewhere in the middle of the maneuver, he and I parted company.

Normally such a move would not have unsettled me. When Gleep had thrown me in practice, I had simply flown clear, delicately settled to the ground at a distance. This time, however, I was already off balance and the throw disoriented me completely. Realizing I was airborne, I attempted to fly . . . and succeeded in slamming into the turf with the grace of a bag of garbage. This did nothing toward improving my orientation.

Lying there, I wondered calmly which parts of me would fall off if I moved. There was a distant roaring in my ears, and the ground seemed to be trembling beneath me. From far away, I could hear Aahz shouting something. Yes, just lying here seemed like an excellent idea.

"Up, kid!" came my mentor's voice. "Run!"

Run? He had to be kidding. My head was clearing slowly, but the ground was still shaking. Rolling over, I propped one eye open to get my bearings, and immediately wished I hadn't.

It wasn't in my head! The ground really was shaking! The bug was bearing down on me full tilt, displaying every intention of trampling me beneath its multiple tiny feet. It didn't even occur to me that this would be a ridiculous way to go. All that registered was that it was a way to go, and somehow that thought didn't appeal to me.

I sprang to my feet and promptly fell down again. Apparently I hadn't recovered from my fall as much as I thought I had. I tried again and got as far as my hands and knees. From there I had a terrific view of my doom thundering down on me, and there was nothing I could do about it!

Then Aahz was there. He must have jumped over me in mid-stride to get into position, but he was there, halfway between the charging bug and me. Feet spread and braced, knees bent to a crouch, he faced the charge unflinching. Unflinching? He threw his arms wide and bared his teeth in challenge.

"You want to fight?" he roared. "Try *me*."

The bug may not have understood his words, but it knew enough about body language to realize it was in trouble. Few beasts or beings in any dimension have the courage or stupidity to try to face down a Pervect when it has a full mad on, and Aahz was mad. His scales were puffed out until he appeared twice his normal breadth, and they rippled dangerously from the tensed muscles underneath. Even his color was a darker shade of green than normal, pulsing angrily as my mentor vented his emotions.

Whatever intelligence level the bug might possess, it was no fool. It somehow managed to slow from a full charge to a dead stop before coming within Aahz's reach. Even the frantic goadings from its rider's hooked prod couldn't get it to resume its charge. Instead, it began to cautiously edge sideways, trying to bypass Aahz completely.

"You want to fight?" my mentor bellowed, advancing toward the beast. "C'mon! I'm ready."

That did it! The bug put it into reverse, scuttling desperately backward despite the frantic urgings of its rider and the hoots from the crowd.

"I say, you lads seem to have things in hand here."

A powerful hand fastened on my shoulder and lifted. In fact, it lifted me until my feet were dangling free from the ground.

"Um . . . I can walk now, Chumly," I suggested.

"Oh, terribly sorry," the troll apologized, setting me gently on the ground. "Just a wee bit distracted is all."

"Gleep!"

A familiar head snaked into view from around Chumly's hip to peer at me quizzically.

"You were a big help!" I snarled, glad for the chance to vent my pent-up nervous energy.

"Gleep," my pet responded, hanging his head.

"Here, now," the troll chided. "Don't take it out on your mate, here. He got surprised, that's all. Can't blame him for getting a little spooked under fire. What?"

"But if he hadn't . . ." I began.

"Now are you ready to get rid of that stupid dragon?" Aahz demanded, joining our group.

"Don't take it out on Gleep," I flared back. "He just got a little spooked under fire is all."

"How's that again?" My mentor blinked.

"Gleep!" proclaimed my pet, unleashing his tongue in one of his aromatic, slimy licks. This time, to my relief Aahz was the recipient.

"Glaah!" my mentor exclaimed, scrubbing at his face with the back of his hand. "I may be violently sick!"

"The beast's just showing his appreciation for your saving his master." Chumly laughed.

"That's right," I agreed. "If you hadn't . . ."

"Forget it." Aahz waved. "No refugee from a wine-making festival's going to do his dance on my apprentice while I'm around."

For once, I knew what he was talking about. " 'Refugee from a wine-making festival'—that's pretty good, Aahz." I grinned.

"No, it wasn't," my mentor snarled. "In fact, so far this afternoon, *nothing's* been good. Why are we standing around talking?"

"Because the first play's over," Chumly supplied. "Also, I might add, the first score."

We all looked down field toward our goal. The field was littered with bodies, fortunately theirs, not ours. Whatever had happened, we had given a good accounting of ourselves. Stretcher bearers and trainers were tending to the fallen and wounded with well-practiced efficiency. The players still on their feet, both on the field and on the sidelines, were dancing around hugging each other and holding their index fingers aloft in what I supposed was some sort of religious gesture to the gods. Badaxe was sagging weakly against one of our four goalposts while Gus fanned him with his wings.

"The score," the troll continued casually, "is nothing to nothing to one . . . against us. Not the best of starts, what?"

For one instant I thought we had scored. Then I remembered that in this game, points are scored *against* a team. Therefore "nothing to nothing to one" meant we were behind by a point.

"Don't worry," Aahz snarled. "We'll get the point back, with interest! If they want to play rough, so can we. Right?"

"Quite right." Chumly grinned.

"Ummm . . ." I supplied hesitantly.

"So let's fire up!" my mentor continued. "Chumly, get Gus and Badaxe up here for a strategy session. Kid, get back on that dragon—and this time try to stay up there, huh?"

I started to obey, then turned back to him. "Ummm . . . Aahz?"

"Yeah, kid?"

"I didn't say it too well a minute ago, but thanks for saving me."

"I said forget it."

"No, I won't," I insisted defiantly. "You could have been killed bailing me out, and I just wanted you to know that I'll pay you back someday. I may not be very brave where I'm concerned, but I owe you my life on top of everything else and it's yours anytime you need it."

"Wait a minute, kid," my mentor corrected. "Any risks I take are mine, understand? That includes the ones I take pulling your tail out of the fire once in a while. Don't mess up my style by making me responsible for two lives."

"But, Aahz . . ."

"If I'm in trouble and you're clear, you skedaddle. Got it? Especially in this game. In fact, here . . ."

He fumbled in his belt pouch and produced a familiar object.

"Here's the D-Hopper. It's set to get you home. You keep it and use it if you have to. If you see a chance to grab Tanda and get out of here, take it! Don't worry about me."

"But . . ."

"That's an order, apprentice. If you want to argue it, wait until we're back in Klah. In the meantime, just do it! Either you agree or I'll send you home right now."

Our eyes locked for long moments, but I gave ground first.

"All right, Aahz." I sighed. "But we're going to have this out once we get home."

"Fine." He grinned, clapping me on the shoulder. "For now though, get on that stupid dragon of yours and try to keep him pointed in the right direction. We've got some points to score!"

XXV:

"If you can't win fair, just win!"

—U. S. GRANT

We needed to score some points, and to do that, we needed the ball.

That thought was foremost in my mind as we lined up again. One way or another, we were going to get that ball.

When the whistle sounded, I was ready for it. Reaching out with my mind, I brought the ball winging to my grasp. Before our team could form up around me, however, the whistle sounded again and the Jahk in the striped tunic came trotting toward us waving his arms.

"Now what?" Aahz growled. Then aloud, he called, "What's wrong, Ref?"

"There's been a protest," the referee informed him. "Your opponents say you're using magik."

"So what?" my mentor countered. "There's no rule against it."

"Well, not officially," the ref admitted, "but it's been a gentleman's agreement for some time."

"We're not gentlemen." Aahz grinned. "So get out of our way and let us play."

"But if you can use magik, so can your opponents," the striped tunic insisted.

"Let 'em," Aahz snarled. "Start the game."

A flash of inspiration came to me. "Wait a minute, Aahz," I called. "Sir, we're willing to allow the use of magik against us *if*, and only if, the magicians do it from the field."

"What?" The ref blinked.

"You heard him," Aahz crowed. "If your magicians join the team and take their lumps like our magician does, then they're free to use whatever skills and abilities they bring onto the field with them. Otherwise they can sit in the bleachers with the spectators and keep their magik out of it."

"That seems fair." The Jahk nodded thoughtfully. "I'll so inform the other teams."

"I say," Chumly commented as the referee trotted off. "That was a spot of clear thinking."

"Tactically superb," Badaxe nodded.

"That's the kind of generalship that beat Big Julie's army," Gus supplied proudly.

I waved modestly, but inside I was heady from the praise.

"Let's save the congratulations until after the game, shall we?" Aahz suggested icily.

It was an annoyingly accurate observation. There was still a long battle between us and the end of the game, and the other teams were already lining up to pit their best against our clumsy efforts. In grim silence, we settled down to go to work.

I won't attempt to chronicle the afternoon play by play. Much of it I'm trying to forget, though sometimes I still bolt upright out of a sound sleep sweating at the memory. The Jahks were tough and they knew their business. The only thing holding them at bay was the sheer strength and ferocity of my teammates and some inspired magik by yours truly.

However, a few incidents occurred prior to the game's climax which would be criminal neglect to omit from my account.

Gleep came of age that afternoon. I don't know what normally matures dragons, but for my pet adulthood arrived with the first play of the afternoon. Gone was the playfulness which led to my early unseating. Somewhere in that puzzling brain of his, Gleep thought things over and arrived at the conclusion that we had some serious business on our hands.

I, of course, didn't know this. When the ball ended up in my hands, I was counting on my other teammates for protection. Unfortunately, our opponents had anticipated this and planned accordingly. Three players each swarmed over Aahz and Chumly, soaking up incredible punishment to keep them from coming to my support. The two Riders converged on me.

I saw them coming and panicked. I mean, the cat was faster than us and the bug seemed invulnerable. Frantically, I looked around for some avenue of escape. I needn't have worried.

Instead of bolting, Gleep stood his ground, his head lowered menacingly. As the cat readied itself for a pounce, my pet loosed a jet of fire full in its face, singeing its whiskers and setting it back on its haunches.

I was so astonished I forgot to watch the bug moving up on our flank. Gleep didn't. His tail lashed out to intercept the armored menace. There was a sound like a great church bell gonging, and the bug halted its forward progress and began wandering aimlessly in circles.

"Atta boy, Gleep!" I cheered, balancing the ball on his back for a moment so I could thump his side.

That was a mistake. No sooner had I released the hold on the ball when one of the Jahks leaped high to pluck it from its resting spot. I took a wipe at him with my staff but he dodged to one side and I missed. Unfortunately for him, the dodge brought him within Chumly's reach.

The troll snaked out one of his long arms over the shoulder of a blocker, picked up the ball carrier by his head, and slammed him violently to the ground.

"Big Crunch catch," he called, winking at me.

The ball carrier lay still, and the stretcher team trotted onto the field again. The lineup of players on the sideline had decreased noticeably since the game started. In case you haven't noticed, things were pretty rough on the field.

"Tell me I didn't see that," Aahz demanded, staggering to my side.

"Um . . . Chumly's tackle or Gleep stopping the two Riders?" I asked innocently.

"I'm talking about your giving the ball away," my mentor corrected harshly. "Now that the dragon's coming through for us, you start . . ."

"Do you really think he's doing a good job?" I interrupted eagerly. "I always said Gleep had a lot of potential."

"Don't change the subject," Aahz growled. "You . . ."

"C'mon, you two," Gus called. "There's a game on."

"Got to go." I waved, guiding my pet away from my sputtering mentor. "We'll talk after the game."

Our defense finally solidified, and we meted out terrible punishment to any Jahk foolish enough to head for our goal with the ball in his arms. We even managed to score some points, though it took a little help from my magik to do it.

The first point we scored was against the Veygans. It was a variation of Aahz's original "divide and conquer" plan. The Veygans had the ball and were bringing it down-field when we plowed into them at midfield. As per my instructions, I waited until the brawl was getting heated, then used a disguise spell on Gus, altering his appearance so he looked like one of the Ta-hoe players, complete with a spiked helmet. Having been forewarned, the change didn't startle him at all. Instead, he started dancing around, waving his arms wildly.

"Here!" he shouted. "I'm open! Over here!"

The ball carrier was zig-zagging desperately with Aahz in hot pursuit. He saw an ally in a position to score and lobbed the ball to him without breaking stride. Gus gathered the ball in and started for the Veygus goal.

"Double-cross!"

The first shout was from Chumly, but the Veygus players quickly picked it up. Spurred by indignation, they turned on the Ta-hoe players who a moment ago had been their allies. The Ta-hoers were understandably surprised, but reacted quickly, defending themselves while at the same time laying down a blocking pattern for Gus.

The Veygan Castle had been up-field when the play broke, but the goal-tender braced himself as Gus swept down on him. The only pursuit close enough to count was Chumly, who appeared intent on hauling down the ball carrier from behind. At the crucial moment, however, he charged past the gargoyle and piled into the goal-tender. Gus scored untouched.

"That's zero to one to one now!" I crowed.

"Before you get too caught up in celebrating," Aahz advised, "you'd better do something about *that*!"

I followed his finger and realized that fights were breaking out throughout the stands. It seemed the fans didn't like the double-cross any more than the players had.

To avert major bloodshed, I removed Gus's disguise as he came back up the field. Within seconds, the fans and the opposing teams realized they had been had. Hostilities between the rival factions ceased immediately. Instead, they focused their emotions on us. Terrific.

The uniform change bit had been effective, but with the new attentiveness in the opposition, I was pretty sure it wouldn't work twice.

I'm particularly proud of our second goal, in that it was my idea from start to finish. I thought it up and executed it without the help or consultation of my teammates. Of course, that in itself caused some problems . . . but I'm getting ahead of myself.

The idea occurred to me shortly after my staff broke. I was swinging at the ball when one of the Ta-hoe players somehow got his head in the way. He was sidelined, but I was left with two pieces of what used to be a pretty good club. As we waited for play to resume, I found myself marveling anew at the sheer size of our opponents and wishing we had bigger players on our side. It occurred to me, too late of course, that I could have used disguise spells to make our team seem bigger when we first appeared. Now our rivals already knew how big, or to be specific, how small we were, so that trick wouldn't work.

I was starting to berate myself for this oversight, when the idea struck. If a disguise spell could make us look bigger, it could also make us look smaller. It was almost a good idea, but not quite. If one or all of us "disappeared" our opponents would notice immediately. What we needed was a decoy.

I found myself considering the two pieces of broken staff I was holding. There was a stunt I pulled once when we were fighting Big Julie. Then it had been a desperation gambit. Of course, we weren't exactly cruising along now.

"Get the ball to me!" I called to my teammates. "I've got an idea."

"What kind of an idea?" Aahz asked.

"Just get me the ball," I snapped back.

I didn't mean to be short with him, but if this plan was going to work, I needed all my concentration, and Aahz's banter wasn't helping.

Closing my eyes, I began to draw and focus power. At the same time, I began forming the required images in my mind.

"Head's up, kid!" Aahz shouted with sudden urgency.

My eyes popped open . . . and the ball was there. I wasn't quite as ready as I would have liked to have been but the time was now and I had to go for it.

I'll detail what happened next so you can appreciate the enormity of my accomplishment. In live time, it took no longer than an eyeblink to perform.

Dropping the two halves of the staff, I caught the ball with my hands. Then, I cast two spells simultaneously. (Four, actually, but I don't like to brag.)

For the first, I shrank the images of Gleep and myself until we were scant inches high. Second, I changed the appearance of the two staff halves until what was seen was full-sized reproductions of me astride my pet.

Once that was accomplished, I used my remaining energy to fly us toward the Ta-hoe goal. That's right, I said "fly." Even in our diminutive form, I wanted us well above the eye-level of our opponents.

Flying both Gleep and myself took a lot of effort. So much, in fact, that I was unable to animate the images we left behind. I had realized this before I started, but figured that suddenly stationary targets would only serve as a diversion for our real attack.

It seemed to work. We were unopposed until we reached the Ta-hoe goal. Then my mischievous sense of humor got the better of me. Landing a scant arm's length from the goalie, I let our disguises drop.

"Boo!" I shouted.

To the startled player, it appeared that we suddenly popped out of thin air. A lifetime of training fell away from him in a second, and he fainted dead away.

With a properly dramatic flourish, I tossed the ball into the goal.

One to one to one! A tie game!

The team was strangely quiet when Gleep and I triumphantly returned to our end of the field.

"Why the long faces?" I laughed. "We've got 'em on the run now!"

"You should have told us you had a gambit going," Gus said carefully.

"There wasn't time," I explained. "Besides, there's no harm done."

"That's not entirely accurate," Chumly corrected, pointing up field.

There was a pile of Jahks where I had left the staff pieces. The stretcher teams were busy untangling the bodies and carting them away.

"He was trying to protect you . . . or what he thought was you," Badaxe observed acidly.

"What . . ."

Then I saw what they were talking about. At the bottom of the pile was Aahz. He wasn't moving.

XXVI:

"Winning isn't the most important thing; it's the only thing!"

—J. Caesar

"**H**e'll be all right," Gus declared, looking up from examining our fallen teammate. "He's just out cold."

We were gathered around Aahz's still form, anxiously awaiting the gargoyle's diagnosis. Needless to say, I was relieved my mentor was not seriously injured. General Badaxe, however, was not so easily satisfied.

"Well, wake him up!" he demanded. "And be quick about it."

"Back off, general," I snarled, irritated by his insensitivity. "Can't you see he's hurt?"

"You don't understand," Badaxe countered, shaking his head. "We need five players to continue the game. If Aahz doesn't snap out of it . . ."

"Wake up, Aahz!" I shouted, reaching out a hand to shake his arm.

It was bad enough that my independent scoring drive had resulted in Aahz getting roughed up. If it cost us the game . . .

"Save it, Skeeve." Gus sighed. "Even if he woke up,

he wouldn't be able to play. That was a pretty nasty pounding he took. I mean, I don't *think* there's anything seriously wrong with him, but if he tried to mix it up with anyone in his current condition . . ."

"I get the picture," I interrupted. "And if we wake him up, Aahz is just stubborn enough to want to play."

"Right," the gargoyle nodded. "You'll just have to think of something else."

I tried, I really did. The team kept fussing over Aahz to stall for time, but nothing came to me in the way of a plan. Finally the referee trotted over to our huddle.

"How's your player?" he asked.

"Ah . . . just catching his breath." Badaxe smiled, trying to keep his body between the official and Aahz.

"Don't give me that," the stripe-tunicked Jahk scowled. "I can see. He's out cold, isn't he?"

"Well, sort of," Gus admitted.

" 'Sort of' nothing," the ref scowled. "If he can't play and you don't have a replacement, you'll have to forfeit the game."

"We're willing to play with a partial team," the gargoyle suggested hastily.

"The rules state you must have five players on the field. No more, no less," the official declared, shaking his head.

"All right," Badaxe nodded. "Then we'll keep him on the field with us. We'll put him off to one side where he won't get hurt and then we'll play with a four-man team."

"Sorry," the ref apologized, "but I can't let him stay on the field in that condition. It's a rough game, but we do have some ethics when it comes to the safety of the players."

"Especially when you can use the rules to force us out of the game," Gus spat.

I thought the slur would draw an angry response from the official, but instead the ref only shook his head sadly.

"You don't understand," he insisted. "I don't *want* to disqualify your team. You've been playing a hard game and you deserve a chance to finish it. I hate to see the game stopped with a forfeit . . . especially when the score's tied. Still, the rules are the rules, and if you can't field a full team, that's that. I only wished you had brought some replacements."

"We've got a replacement!" I exploded suddenly.

"We do?" Gus blinked.

"Where?" frowned the ref.

"Right there!" I announced, pointing to the stands.

Tananda was still floating in plain sight in front of Quigley.

"The captive demon?" the official gasped.

"What do you think we are? Muppets?" Gus snarled, recovering smoothly.

"Muppets? What . . . I don't think . . ." the ref stammered.

"You don't have to." I smiled. "Just summon the Tahoe magician and I'm sure we can work something out."

"But . . . Oh, very well."

The official trotted off toward the stands while the rest of the team crowded around me.

"You're going to have a woman on the team?" Badaxe demanded.

"Let me explain." I waved. "First of all, Tanda isn't . . ."

"She's not actually a woman," Chumly supplied. "She's my sister. And when it comes to the old rough and tumble, she can beat me four out of five times."

"She isn't? I mean, she is?" Badaxe struggled. "I mean, she can?"

"You bet your sweet axe she can." Gus grinned.

"Gleep," said the dragon, determined to get his two cents worth in.

"If you're all quite through," I said testily, "I'd like to finish. What I was about to say was that Tanda isn't going to play."

There was a moment of stunned silence as the team absorbed this.

"I don't get it," Gus said at last. "If she isn't going to play, then what . . ."

"Once she's here and revived, we're going to grab her and the Trophy and head back for Klah," I announced.

"The ref's about to hand us the grand prize on a silver platter."

"But what about the game?" Badaxe scowled.

I closed my eyes, realizing for a moment how Aahz must feel when he has to deal with me.

"Let me explain this slowly," I said carefully. "The reason we're *in* this game is to rescue Tanda and grab the Trophy. In a few minutes we're going to have them both, so there'll be no reason for us to keep getting our heads beaten in. Understand?"

"I still don't like quitting the field before the end of a battle," the general grumbled.

"For crying out loud!" I exploded. "This is a game, not a war!"

"Are we talking about the same field?" Chumly asked innocently.

Fortunately, I was spared having to formulate an answer to that one as Quigley chose that moment to arrive, Tananda floating in his wake.

"What's this the ref says about using Tanda in the game?" he demanded.

"That's right," I lied. "We need her to finish the game. Now if you'll be so good as to wake her up, we'll just . . ."

"But she's my hostage," the magician protested.

"C'mon, Quigley," I argued. "We aren't taking her anyplace. She'll be right here on the field in full sight of you and everybody else."

"And you can all skip off to another dimension any time you want," Quigley pointed out. "No deal."

That was uncomfortably close to the truth, but if there's one thing I've learned from Aahz, it's how to bluff with a straight face.

"Now, look, Quigley," I snarled. "I'm trying to be fair about this, but it occurs to me you're taking advantage of my promise."

"Of course," the magician nodded. "But tell you what. Just to show you I'm a sport, I'll let you have Tanda."

"Swell." I grinned.

"If . . . and I repeat, *if* you let me keep Aahz in exchange."

"What?" I exclaimed. "I mean, sure. Go ahead. He's already out cold."

"Very well." He nodded. "This will just take a few seconds."

"What does this do to our plans?" Gus asked, drawing me aside.

"Nothing," I informed him through gritted teeth. "We go as soon as it's clear."

"What?" The gargoyle gaped. "What about Aahz?"

"It's his orders," I snarled. "Before the game started he made me promise that if he got in trouble I wouldn't endanger myself or the team trying to save him."

"And you're going to skip out on him?" Gus sneered. "After all he's done for you?"

"Now don't you start on me, Gus!" I grimaced. "I don't want to . . ."

"Hi, handsome," Tananda chirped, joining our discussion. "If it isn't too much trouble, could someone fill me in as to why this august assemblage has assembled, why we're standing in the middle of a pasture, and what all these people are doing staring at us? And where's Quigley going with Aahz?"

"There's no time," I declared. "We've got to get going."

"Get going where?" She frowned.

"Back to Klah," Gus grumbled. "Skeeve here is in the middle of abandoning Aahz."

"He's what?" Tananda gasped.

"Gus . . ." I warned.

"Save it, handsome. I'm not budging until someone tells me what's going on, so you might as well start now."

It took surprisingly little time to bring her up to date once I got started. I deliberately omitted as many details as possible to keep from getting Tananda riled. I had enough problems on my hands without fighting her, too! It seemed to work, as she listened patiently without comment or frown.

". . . and so that's why we've got to get out of here before play resumes," I finished.

"Bull feathers," she said firmly.

"I'm glad you . . . how's that again?" I sputtered.

"I said 'Bull feathers,' " she repeated. "You guys have been knocked around, trampled, and otherwise beaten on for my sake and now we're going to run? Not me! I say we stay right here and teach these bozos a lesson."

"But . . ."

"I don't know if your D-Hopper can move the whole team," she continued, "but I'll bet it can't do the job if we aren't cooperating."

"That's telling him," Gus chortled.

". . . so retreat is out. Now, if you're afraid of getting hurt, just stay out of our way. We aren't leaving until we finish what you and Aahz started."

"Well said." Badaxe nodded.

"Count me in," the gargoyle supplied.

"You'll be the death of me yet, little sister," Chumly sighed.

I managed to get a grip on Gleep's nose before he could add his vote to the proceedings.

"Actually," I said slowly, "Aahz had always warned me about how dangerous it is to travel dimensions alone. And if I'm going to stay here, it occurs to me the safest place would be surrounded by my teammates."

"All right, Skeeve!" Gus grinned, clapping me on the back.

"Then it's decided." Tananda nodded. "Now then, handsome, what's the plan?"

Somehow, I had known she was going to say that.

"Give me a minute," I pleaded. "A second ago the plan was to just split, remember? These plans don't just grow on trees, you know."

I plunged into thought, considering and discarding ideas as they came to me. That didn't take long. Not that many ideas were occurring to me.

I found myself staring at Chumly. He was craning his neck to look at the stands.

"What are *you* doing?" I asked, irritated by his apparent lack of concern with our situation.

"Hmmm? Oh. Sorry, old boy," the troll apologized. "I

was just curious as to how many Deveels were in the crowd. There's a lot of them."

"There are?" I blinked, scanning the crowd. "I don't see any."

"Oh, they're disguised, of course." Chumly shrugged. "But you can see their auras if you check. With the odds that were being given on this bloody game, it was a sure thing they'd be here."

He was right. I'd been so preoccupied with the game I had never bothered to check the stands. Now that I looked, I could see the auras of other demons scattered throughout the crowd.

"It's too bad we can't cancel their disguises," I muttered to myself.

"Oh, we could do that easy enough," the troll answered.

"We could?"

"Certainly. Deveels always use the cheapest, easiest disguises available. I know a spell that would restore their normal appearance quick enough."

"You do?" I pressed. "Could it cover the whole stadium?"

"Well, not for a terribly long time," Chumly said, "but it would hold for a minute or two. Why do you ask?"

"I think I've got an idea," I explained. "Be back in a minute."

"Where are you going?" the troll called after me as I started for the sidelines.

"To talk to Griffin," I retorted, not caring that the explanation didn't really explain anything.

XXVII:

"Ask not for whom the bell tolls—"

—M. ALI

The ball carrier was somewhere under Gleep when the whistle blew. That wouldn't have been too bad, if it weren't for the fact that Chumly had already thrown the ball carrier to the ground and jumped on him prior to my pet joining in the fracas. As I said before, Gleep had *really* gotten into the spirit of things.

"I say," came an agonized call from the troll, "do you mind?"

"Sorry!" I apologized, backing the dragon onto more solid footing.

"Say, Skeeve," Gus murmured, sliding up beside me, "how much longer until we're set for the big play?"

"Should be any minute now," I confided. "Why do you ask?"

"He's afraid of additional casualties you and that dragon will inflict on the team while we're stalling for time," Badaxe chimed in sarcastically.

"Gleep," my pet commented, licking the general's face.

"You might as well forget the hard guy act, Hugh,"

the gargoyle observed. "The dragon's got you pegged as a softie."

"Is that so?" Badaxe argued, gasping a bit on Gleep's breath. "Well, allow me to point out that with the master plan about to go into effect, we don't have the ball!"

"Skeeve'll get it for us when we need it," Tananda protested, rising to my defense. "He always comes through when we need him. You've just never followed him into battle before."

"I believe I can testify," Chumly growled, limping back to join us, "that it's safer to be following him than in front of him."

"Sorry about that, Chumly," I winced. "It's just that Gleep . . ."

"I know, I know," the troll interrupted. " 'Spooked under fire' . . . remember, *I* gave you that excuse originally. He seems to have recovered admirably."

"I hate to interrupt," Gus interrupted, "but isn't that our signal?"

I followed his gaze to the sidelines. Griffin was there waving his arms wildly. When he saw he had my attention, he crossed the fingers on both hands, then crossed his forearms over his head. That was the signal.

"All right," I announced. "Fun time is over. The messages have been delivered. Does everyone remember what they're supposed to do?"

As one, the team nodded, eager grins plastered on their faces. I don't know what they were so cheerful about. If any phase of this plan didn't work, some or all of us would be goners.

"Tanda and Chumly make one team. Badaxe, you stick with Gus. He's your ticket home," I repeated needlessly.

"We know what to do." The general nodded.

"Then let's do it!" I shouted, and wheeled Gleep into position.

This time, as the ball came into play, we did not swarm toward the ball carrier. Instead, our entire team backpedaled to cluster in the mouth of our goal.

Our opponents hesitated, looking at each other. We had emptied over three quarters of their reserve teaching them

to respect our strength, and now that lesson was bearing
fruit. No one seemed to want to be the one to carry the
ball into our formation. They weren't sure what we were
up to but they didn't want any part of it.

Finally, the ball carrier, a Ta-hoe player, turned and
threw the ball to his Rider, apparently figuring the bug
had the best chance of breaking through to the goal.
That's what I had been waiting for.

Reaching out with my mind, I brought the ball winging, not to me, but to Hugh Badaxe. In a smooth, fluid
motion, the axe came off the general's belt and struck at
the missile. I had never seen Hugh use his axe before, and
I'll admit I was impressed. Weapon and ball met, and the
weapon won. The ball fell to the ground in two halves as
the axe returned to its resting place on the general's belt.

The crowd was on its feet, screaming incoherently. If
they didn't like that, they didn't really get upset over our
next move.

"Everybody, mount up!" I shouted.

On cue, Tananda jumped on Chumly's back and Badaxe did the same with Gus. I levitated half the ball to each
twosome, then did a fast disguise spell.

What our opponents saw now was three images of me
astride three images of Gleep. Each image of me had half
a ball proudly in its possession.

The more mathematically oriented of you might realize
that that adds up to three halves. Very good. Fortunately
for us, Jahks aren't big on math. The question remains,
however, where did the third half come from?

You don't think I was standing by idly while all this
was going on, do you? While my teammates were mount-
ing up, I took advantage of the confusion to do one more
levitation/disguise job. As a result, the Trophy was now
resting in front of me on Gleep's back disguised as half
a ball. It was the same stunt I had pulled in Veygus, but
this time I draped my shirt over it.

"Chumly!" I called. "Start your spell!"

"Done!" He waved back.

"We meet back in Klah!" I shouted.

"Now go for it!"

My teammates started up opposite sidelines, heading for both our opponents' goals simultaneously. I waited a few beats for them to draw off the tacklers, then started for my objective. Gleep and I were going for Aahz.

With all due modesty, my plan worked brilliantly. The appearance of Deveels throughout the crowd sent the Jahks into a state of panic. The crossbowmen were too busy trying to get a shot of these new invaders to pay any attention to me, but they were poorly aimed. For some reason the beings shooting at me seemed a bit rattled.

I caught sight of Quigley, standing on his seat and waving his arms. Catchy phrases like "Begone foul spirits!" and "I vanquish thee!" were issuing from his lips as he did his routine.

This didn't surprise me. Not that I felt Quigley was particularly quick thinking in a crisis. It had to do with the messages I had sent to both him and Massha before the play started.

The messages were simple:

STAND BY TO REPEL AN INVASION OF DEMONS!
P.S. GO THROUGH THE MOTIONS. I'LL TAKE CARE OF
THE DEMONS.

SKEEVE

I caught his eye and winked at him. In return, one of his "demon dispelling" waves got a little limp-wristed as he nodded slightly, bidding me adieu. In the middle of saving his employers from an invasion of demons, who could blame him if a few departed who were supposed to stay put.

Aahz's unconscious body came wafting toward us in response to my mental summons. Gleep stretched out his long neck and caught my mentor's tunic in his mouth as he floated by.

It wasn't quite the way I planned it but I was in no position to be choosy. Tightening my legs around Gleep's middle, I hit the button on the D-Hopper, and . . .

The walls of my room were a welcome change from the hostile stadium.

"We did it!" I exclaimed, then was startled by the volume of my voice. After the din of the stadium, my room seemed incredibly quiet.

"Kid," came a familiar voice, "would you tell your stupid dragon to put me down before I die from his breath?"

"Gleep?" my pet asked, dropping my mentor in an undignified heap.

"Aahz?" I blinked. "I thought you were . . ."

"Out cold? Not hardly. Can you think of a better way to get Tanda out on the field? For a while there I was afraid you wouldn't figure it out and call for a replacement."

"You mean you were faking all along?" I demanded. "I was scared to death! You could have warned me, you know."

"Like you warned me about your vanishing act?" he shot back. "And what happened to my orders to head for home once Tanda was in the clear?"

"Your orders?" I stammered. "Well . . ."

There was a soft *BAMF* and Gus and Badaxe were in the room. Gus was holding the general cradled in his arms like a babe, but they both seemed in good spirits.

"Beautiful!!" Hugh chortled, hugging the gargoyle around the neck. "If you ever need a back-up man . . .".

"If you ever need a partner," Gus corrected, hugging him back. "You and I could . . ."

BAMF!

Chumly and Tananda appeared sprawling on the bed. Both her nostrils were bleeding, but she was laughing uproariously. Chumly was panting for breath and wiping tears of hilarity from his big moon eyes.

"I say," he gasped. "That was a spot of fun. We haven't double-teamed anyone like that since the last family reunion, when Auntie Tizzie got Tiddley and . . ."

"What happened?" I bellowed.

"We won!" Gus cheered. "One and a half to one and a half to one! They never knew what hit 'em."

"It's one for the record book," Tananda agreed, dabbing at her nose.

"For the record book?" Gus challenged. "This game'll fill a book by itself."

"Aahz, old bean," Chumly called. "Do you have any wine about? The assemblage seems up for a celebration."

"I know where it is." Badaxe waved, starting for the barrels we had secreted under the work table.

"Hold it!" Aahz roared. "Halt, stop, desist, and TIME OUT!!"

"I think he wants our attention," Tananda told the group.

"If you're all *quite* through," my mentor continued, shooting her a black look, "I have one question."

"What's that?" Tananda asked in her little girl voice.

"Quit bleeding on the bed." Aahz scowled. "It lacks class. What I want to know is, did any of you superstars think to pick up the Trophy? That was the objective of this whole fiasco, you know."

The team gestured grandly at me. With a grin, I let the disguise drop away from the Trophy.

"Ta-da!" I warbled. "Happy birthday, Aahz."

"Happy birthday!!" the team echoed.

Aahz looked at their grins, then at the Trophy, then at their grins again.

"All right," he sighed. "Break out the wine."

The roar of approval for this speech rivaled anything that had come from the stands that afternoon as the team descended on the wine barrels like a swarm of hungry humming mice.

"Well, Aahz." I grinned, levitating the Trophy to the floor and sliding from Gleep's back. "I guess that just about winds it up."

I was starting for the wine barrels when a heavy hand fell on my shoulder.

"There are a *few* loose ends to be tied up," my mentor drawled.

"Like what?" I asked fearfully.

"Like the invitation you gave Massha to drop by for a visit."

"Invitation?" I echoed in a small voice.

"Badaxe told me about it." Aahz grimaced. "Then

there's a little matter of a quick trip to Deva."

"To Deva?" I blinked. "What for? I mean, swell, but . . ."

"I've got to pick up our winnings," my mentor informed me. "I took the time to place a few small bets on the game while we were there. Profits don't just happen, you know."

"When do we start?" I asked eagerly.

"We don't," Aahz said firmly. "This time I'm going alone. There's something about you and the Bazaar that just don't mix well."

"But Aahz . . ."

"And besides," he continued, grinning broadly, "there's one more loose end from this venture that will be occupying your time. One which only you can handle."

"Really?" I said proudly. "What's that?"

"Well," my mentor said, heading for the wine, "you can start thinking about how we're going to get that stupid dragon out of our room. He's too big to fit through the door or window."

"Gleep!" said my pet, licking my face.

HIT OR MYTH

I:

"There's something to be said for relatives . . . it has to be said because it's unprintable!"

— A. EINSTEIN

Perhaps if I hadn't been so preoccupied with my own thoughts when I walked into my quarters that day, I wouldn't have been caught unawares. Still, who expects to get caught in a magikal attack just walking into their own room?

Okay, okay! So I *am* the Court Magician of Possiltum, and maybe I *have* been getting a bit of a reputation lately. I still should be able to walk into my own room without getting jumped! I mean, if a magician isn't safe in his own quarters, can he be safe anywhere?

Scratch that question!

It's the kind of thing my teacher says to convince me that choosing magic for a career path is not the best way to insure living out one's normal life span. Of course, it doesn't take much convincing. Actions speak louder than words, and the action since I signed on as his apprentice has been loud enough to convince me that a magician's life is not particularly quiet. I mean, when you realize that within days of meeting him, we both got lynched by an angry mob . . . as in hung by the neck . . .

But I digress.

We started out with me simply walking into my room. Yeah, simple! There was a demon waiting for me, a Pervect to be exact. This in itself wasn't unusual. Aahz, the teacher I mentioned earlier, is a Pervect. In fact, he shares my quarters with me. What *was* unusual was that the demon waiting for me wasn't Aahz!

Now I haven't met many Pervects ... heck, the only one I know is Aahz ... but I know Aahz very well, and this Pervect wasn't him!

This demon was shorter than my mentor, his scales were a lighter shade of green, and his gold eyes were set closer together. What's more, he wasn't smiling ... and Aahz always smiles, even when he's mad ... *especially* when he's mad. To the average eye Aahz and this stranger might look alike, but to me they were as different as a Deveel and an Imp. Of course, there was a time when I couldn't tell the difference between a Deveel and an Imp. It says something about the company I've been keeping lately.

"Who are you?" I demanded.

"You Skeeve?"

"Yeah. Me Skeeve. Who you?"

For an answer, I suddenly felt myself snatched into the air by an invisible hand and spun end over end until I finally stopped, dangling head down four feet off the floor.

"Don't get smart with me, punk. I understand you're holding a relative of mine in some kind of bondage. I want him back. Understand?"

He emphasized his point by lowering me to within a few inches of the floor, then using that surface to rap my head sharply.

I may not be the greatest magician ever, but I knew what he was doing. He was using his mind to levitate me about the room. I've done it myself to small objects from time to time. Of course, it occurred to me that I wasn't a small object and that I was dealing with someone a bit better versed in the magikal arts than myself. As such, I deemed it wiser to keep my temper and my manners.

"You know Aahz?"

"Sure do. And I want him back."

The latter was accompanied by another head rap. So much for holding my temper.

"Then you should know him well enough to know that nobody holds him against his will!"

My head started for the floor again, but stopped short of its target. From my inverted position I could get a partial view of the demon tapping himself thoughtfully on the chin.

"That's true," he murmured. "All right . . ."

I was turned into an upright position once more.

". . . Let's take it from the top. Where's Aahz, and what's keeping him in this backwater dimension?"

"I think *and* talk better with my feet on the ground."

"Hmm? Oh! Sorry."

I was lowered into a normal standing position. Now that I was self-supporting again, I realized the interrogation had left me with a splitting headache.

"He's back in General Badaxe's quarters arguing military tactics," I managed. "It was so boring I came back here. He should be along soon. They were almost out of wine when I left."

"Tactics and wine, eh?" My visitor grimaced. "That sounds like Aahz. What's the rest of it? Why is he staying around a nowhere dimension like Klah and how did he get mixed up with the Great Skeeve?"

"You've heard of me?"

"Here and there around the dimensions," the demon acknowledged. "In some circles they think you're pretty hot stuff. That's why I started wondering if you'd managed to cage Aahz somehow. I was braced for a real battle royale when you walked in."

"Well, actually I'm not all that good," I admitted. "I've only really started making headway in the last couple years since I started studying under Aahz. I'd still be a total nothing if he hadn't lost his powers and taken me on as an apprentice."

"Bingo!" my visitor declared, holding up his hand. "I think you just explained everything. Aahz lost his powers and took on a new apprentice! No wonder he hasn't been home in a while. And all this talk about the Great Skeeve is just a standard Aahz-managed hype job for a new talent. Right?"

"We *have* taken on a few rough assignments," I said defensively.

"In which Aahz choreographed, then set you up to take the credit. Right?"

"What's 'choreographed'?" I asked. Obviously the family similarity was more than scale deep.

"Well, I hope you're up to operating on your own, Skeeve, 'cause I'm taking your mentor back to Perv with me."

"But you don't have to rescue him from me!" I protested. "He's free to come and go as he wants."

"I'm not saving him from you, I'm saving him from Aahz. Our colleague has an overblown sense of responsibility that isn't always in his own best interest. Do you know how lucrative a practice he's letting fall apart on Perv while he clowns around with you?"

"No," I admitted.

"Well, he's losing money every day he's gone . . . and that means the family is losing money."

Right there I gave up the argument. Early on in my association with Aahz I learned the futility of trying to talk a Pervect out of money. The fact that Aahz was willing to sacrifice a steady income to work with me was an incredible tribute to our friendship . . . or his sense of duty. Of course, there's more than one way to win an argument.

"Well, as I said before, I can't keep him here," I said innocently. "If you can convince him he's not needed anymore . . ."

"No way, punk," the demon sneered. "We both know that won't get him to desert an apprentice. I'm going to lure him back to Perv with a blatant lie. And *you're* going to keep your mouth shut."

"But . . ."

". . . Because if you don't, I'll make sure there's nothing left to keep him in Klah . . . meaning you! Now before you even think about trying to match magik with me,

remember something. *You've* been studying under Aahz
for a couple years now. *I* graduated after over three hundred years of apprenticeship. So far, I'm willing to live
and let live. You should be able to earn a living on what
you've learned so far, maybe even pick up a few new
tricks as you go along. *However*, if you cross me now,
there won't be enough of you to pick up with a sponge.
Do we understand each other?"

I was suddenly aware why nobody we met in our
dimension-crawling ever wanted to tangle with a Pervect.
I was also aware that someone had just walked into the
room behind me.

"Rupert!"

"Uncle Aahz!"

The two pounded each other on the back. I gave them
lots of room.

"Hey, kid, this is my nephew Rupert . . . but I see
you've already met."

"Unfortunately," I grumbled.

That earned me a black look from Rupert, but Aahz
missed it completely.

"So what brings you to Klah, nephew? A bit off your
normal prowl pattern, isn't it?"

"It's Dad. He wants you."

"Sorry." Aahz was suddenly his normal self again.
"I've got too many irons in the fire here to get drawn into
some family squabble."

"But he's dying."

That stopped Aahz for a moment.

"My brother? Nonsense. He's too tough to kill. He
could even beat me in an unfair fight."

"He got into a fight with Mom."

A look of concern crossed Aahz's face. I could see he
was wavering.

"That serious, huh? I don't know, though. If he's really
dying, I don't see what I can do to help."

"It shouldn't take long," Rupert urged. "He said something about his will."

I groaned inwardly. Trust a Pervect to know a Pervect's weaknesses.

"Well, I guess my business here can keep for a few days," Aahz declared with false reluctance. "Stay out of trouble, kid. I'll be back as soon as I can."

"Let's get going," Rupert suggested, hiding his triumphant grin. "The sooner we get to Perv, the sooner you can be back."

"But Aahz . . ."

"Yeah, kid?"

I saw Rupert's brow darken.

"I . . . I just wanted to say 'goodbye.' "

"Hey, don't make a big thing of this, kid. It's not like I was going forever."

Before I could respond, Rupert clapped an arm around Aahz's shoulder and they both faded from view.

Gone.

Somehow I couldn't make myself believe it had happened. My mentor had been spirited away . . . permanently. Whatever I had learned from Aahz would have to do, because now I was totally on my own.

Then I heard a knock at my door.

II:

"When things are blackest, I just tell myself 'cheer up, things could be worse!' And sure enough, they get worse!"

—SKEEVE

I decided that as Court Magician of Possiltum, my response should be gracious.

"Go away!"

That *was* gracious. If you knew what my actual thoughts were, you'd realize that. Very few people ever visited me in my chambers, and I didn't want to see any of them just then.

"Do you know who you're talking to?" came a muffled voice from the other side of the door.

"No! And I don't care! Go away!"

"This is Rodrick the Fifth. Your King!"

That stopped me. Upset or not, that title belonged to the man who set and paid my wages. As I said earlier, I *have* learned a few things from Aahz.

"Do you know who *you're* talking to?" I called back, and hoped.

There was a moment's pause.

"I assume I'm talking to Skeeve the Magnificent, Court Magician of Possiltum. At best, he'll be the one to bear the brunt of my wrath if I'm kept waiting outside his chambers much longer."

So much for hoping. These things never work in real life the way they do in jokes.

Moving with undignified haste, I pounced on the door handle and wrenched it open.

"Good afternoon, Lord Magician. May I come in?"

"Certainly, Your Majesty," I said, standing aside. "I never refuse a fifth."

The King frowned.

"Is that a joke? If so, I don't get the point."

"Neither do I," I admitted calmly. "It's something Aahz my apprentice says."

"Ah, yes. Your apprentice. Is he about?"

Rodrick swept majestically into the room, peering curiously into the corners as if he expected Aahz to spring forth from the walls.

"No. He's . . . out."

"Good. I had hoped to speak with you alone. Hmmm . . . these are really quite spacious quarters. I don't recall having been here before."

That was an understatement. Not only had the King never visited my room in his palace, I couldn't recall having seen him when he wasn't either on the throne or in its near vicinity.

"Your Majesty has never graced me with his presence since I accepted position in his court," I said.

"Oh. Then, that's probably why I don't recall being here," Rodrick responded lamely.

That in itself was strange. Usually the King was quite glib and never at a loss for words. In fact, the more I thought about it, the stranger this royal visit to my private chambers became. Despite my distress at Aahz's unplanned and apparently permanent departure, I felt my curiosity beginning to grow.

"May I ask the reason for this pleasant, though unexpected audience?"

"Well . . ." the King began, then shot one more look about the room. "Are you sure your apprentice isn't about?"

"Positive. He's . . . I sent him on a vacation."

"A vacation?"

"Yes. He's been studying awfully hard lately."

The King frowned slightly.

"I don't remember approving a vacation."

For a moment, I thought I was going to get caught in my own deception. Then I remembered that in addition to the various interdimensional languages, Aahz had also been teaching me to speak "bureaucrat."

"I didn't really feel your authorization was necessary," I said loftily. "Technically, my apprentice is not on your Majesty's payroll. I am paying him out of *my* wages, which makes him my employee, subject to my rules including vacations . . . or dismissal. While he is subject to your laws, as is any subject of Possiltum, I don't feel he actually is governed by Subparagraph G concerning palace staff!"

My brief oration had the desired effect: It both confused and bored my audience. Aahz would have been proud of me. I was particularly pleased that I had managed to sneak in that part about dismissals. It meant that when Aahz didn't return, I could claim that I had dismissed him without changing the wage paid me by the crown.

Of course, this got me brooding again about Aahz not coming back.

"Well, whatever. I'm glad to see your philosophy regarding vacations mirrors my own, Lord Magician. Everyone should have a vacation. In fact, that's why I came to see you this afternoon."

That threw me.

"A vacation? But your Majesty, I don't need a vacation."

That threw the King.

"You? Of course not. You and that apprentice of yours spend most of your time gallivanting around other worlds. You've got a lot of nerve asking for a vacation."

That did it. All the anger I had been storing up since Rupert's arrival exploded.

"I didn't *ask* for a vacation!"

"Oh! Yes. Of course."

"And furthermore, that 'gallivanting around other worlds' you mentioned is stock in trade for magicians, court or otherwise. It enables us to work our wonders . . . like saving your kingdom from Big Julie's army. Remember?"

"How could I forget. I . . ."

"If, however, your Majesty feels I have been lax in fulfilling my duties as his court magician, he need only ask for my resignation and it's his. If he recalls, *he* approached *me* for this position. I didn't ask for *that* either!"

"Please, Lord Magician," Rodrick interrupted desperately, "I meant no offense. Your services have been more than satisfactory. In fact, any reluctance I expressed regarding your vacation was based on a fear of having to run the kingdom for a period without your powers available. If you really feel you want a vacation, I'm sure we could work out something to . . ."

"I don't *want* a vacation. All right? Let's drop the subject."

"Certainly. I just thought . . . very well."

Shaking his head slightly, he headed for the door.

Winning the argument put me in a much better mood. After the beating my ego had taken from Rupert, it was nice to hear *someone* say they thought my powers were worth something.

It occurred to me, however, that winning the argument with the man who paid my wages might not have been the wisest way to bounce back.

"Your Majesty?"

The King stopped.

"Aren't you forgetting something?"

He frowned.

". . . Like the original reason for your visit? Since I wasn't asking for a vacation, and you weren't offering one, I assume you had something else on your mind?"

"Oh, yes. Quite right. But all things considered, this might not be the time to discuss it."

"What? Because of our misunderstanding? Think nothing of it, your Majesty. These things happen. Rest assured

I am still your loyal retainer, ready to do anything in my power to assist you in the management of your kingdom."

As I said before, I was getting pretty good at shoveling when the situation called for it.

Rodrick beamed.

"I'm glad to hear that, Master Skeeve. That is precisely why I came to you today."

"And how may I be of service?"

"It's about a vacation."

I closed my eyes.

For a brief moment, I knew . . . *knew*, mind you . . . how Aahz felt. I knew what it felt to be sincerely trying to help someone, only to find that that someone seems bound and determined to drive you out of your mind.

The King saw my expression and continued hastily, "Not a vacation for you. A vacation for me!"

That opened my eyes. Figuratively and literally.

"You, your Majesty? But Kings don't take vacations."

"That's the whole point."

Rodrick began pacing the floor nervously as he spoke.

"The pressures of being a King mount up like they do on any other job. The difference is that as a King you never get a break. No time to rest and collect your thoughts, or even just sleep late. From the coronation when the crown hits your head until it's removed by voluntary or forcible retirement, you are the King."

"Gee, that's tough, your Majesty. I wish there was something I could do to help."

The King stopped pacing and beamed at me again.

"But you can! That's why I'm here!"

"Me? I can't approve a vacation for you! Even if it were in my power, and it isn't, the kingdom needs a king on the throne all the time. It can't spare you, even for one day!"

"Exactly! That's why I can't leave the throne unattended. If I wanted a vacation, I'd need a stand-in."

An alarm bell went off in my mind.

Now, however much Aahz may have nagged me about being a slow student, I'm not stupid. Even before I met Aahz . . . heck, before I learned my letters . . . I knew how to add two and two to get four. In this case, one two was the king's need for a stand-in; the second two was his presence in my quarters, and the four was . . .

"Surely your Majesty can't mean me!"

"Of course I mean you," Rodrick confirmed. "The fact is, Lord Magician, I had this in mind when I hired you to your current position."

"You did?"

I could feel the jaws of the trap closing. If this was indeed why the King had hired me, I would be ill-advised to refuse the assignment. Rodrick might decide my services were no longer needed, and the last thing I needed with Aahz gone was to get cut off from my source of income. I wasn't sure what the job market was like for ex-court magicians, but I was sure I didn't want to find out first hand.

"As you said earlier, the powers of the Court Magician are at my disposal, and one of the powers you demonstrated when we first met was the ability to change your own shape, or the shape of others, at will."

The disguise spell! It was one of the first spells Aahz had taught me and one of the ones most frequently used over our last several adventures. After all the times it's bailed me out of tight spots, who would have guessed it would be the spell to get me into trouble? Well, there was the time it had gotten me hung. . . .

"But, your Majesty, I couldn't possibly substitute for you. I don't know how to be a King!"

"Nothing to it." Rodrick smiled. "The nice thing about being a King is that even when you're wrong, no one dares to point it out."

"But. . . ."

"And besides, it will only be for one day. What could possibly go wrong in one day?"

III:

*"Once a knight, always a knight,
But once a King is once too often!"*

— SIR BELLA OF EASTMARCH

Now, I don't want you to think I'm a pushover. I
drove a hard bargain with the King before giving in.
I not only managed to get him to agree to a bonus, but
to cough up a hefty percentage in advance before accepting the assignment. Not bad for a fledgling magician who
was over a barrel.

Of course, once I accepted, I was no longer over a
barrel, I was in over my head!

The more I thought about it, the worse the idea of
standing in for the King seemed. The trouble was, I didn't
have a choice . . . or did I? I thought about it some more
and a glimmer of hope appeared.

There was a way out! The only question was, how far
could I run in a day? While not particularly worldly (or
off-worldly for that matter) I was pretty sure that double-
crossing kings wasn't the healthiest of pastimes.

It was going to be a big decision, definitely the biggest
I ever had to make on my own. The King (or to be exact,
his stand-in) wasn't due to make an appearance until noon
tomorrow, so I had a little time to mull things over. With

that in mind, I decided to talk it out with my last friend left in the palace.

"What do you think, Gleep? Should I take it on the lam, or stick around and try to bluff it out for one day as king?"

The response was brief and to the point.

"Gleep!"

For those of you who've tuned in to this series late, Gleep is my pet. He lives in the Royal Stables. He's also a twenty-foot long blue dragon . . . half grown. (I shudder to think what he'll be like when he's fully grown! Groan!) As to his witty conversation, you'll have to forgive him. He only has a one-word vocabulary, but he makes up for it by using that word a lot. Wordy or not, I turned to him in this moment of crisis because with Aahz gone, he was the only one in this dimension who would be even vaguely sympathetic to my problem. That in itself says a lot about the social life of a magician.

"Come on, Gleep, get serious. I'm in real trouble. If I try to stand in for the King, I might make a terrible mistake . . . like starting a war or hanging an innocent man. On the other hand, if I double-cross the King and disappear, you and I would spend the rest of our lives as hunted fugitives."

The unicorn in the next stall snorted and stamped a foot angrily.

"Sorry, Buttercup. The *three* of us would be hunted fugitives."

War unicorns aren't all that common, even in Royal Stables. That particular war unicorn was mine. I acquired him as a gift shortly after I acquired Gleep. As I said before, this life-style is more than a little zooish.

"In a kingdom with a bad king, a lot of people would get hurt," I reasoned, "and I'd be a terrible king. Heck, I'm not all that good a magician."

"Gleep," my pet argued sternly.

"Thanks for the vote of confidence, but it's true. I don't want to hurt anybody, but I'm not wild about being a hunted fugitive, either."

Tired of verbalizing his affection, Gleep decided to

demonstrate his feelings by licking my face. Now, aside from leaving a slimy residue, my dragon's kisses have one other side effect. His breath is a blast of stench exceeded only by the smell of Pervish cooking.

"G . . . Gleep, old boy," I managed at last, "I love you dearly, but if you do that twice a week, we may part company . . . permanently!"

"Gleep?"

That earned me a hurt expression, which I erased simply enough by scratching his head. It occurred to me that dragons had survived because each of them only became emotionally attached to one being in its lifetime. If their breath reached the entire population instead of a single individual, they would have been hunted into extinction long ago. No, it was better that only one person should suffer than . . .

Another part of my mind grabbed that thought and started turning it over.

"If I run, then I'll be the only one in trouble, but if I try to be king, the whole kingdom suffers! That's it! I have to leave. It's the only decent thing to do. Thanks, Gleep!"

"Gleep?"

My pet cocked his head in puzzlement.

"I'll explain later. All right. It's decided. You two stock up on food while I duck back to my room to get a few things. Then it's 'Goodbye, Possiltum!' "

I've had pause to wonder what would have happened if I'd followed my original plan: just headed for my room, gathered up my belongings, and left. The timing for the rest of the evening would have changed, and the rest of this story would have been totally different. As it was, I made a slight detour. Halfway to my room, Aahz's training cut in. That is, I started thinking about money.

Even as a hunted fugitive, money would come in handy . . . and the King's advance would only last so long. With a little extra cash, I could run a lot farther, hide a lot longer . . . or at the very least live a lot better. . . .

Buoyed by these thoughts, I went looking for J. R. Grimble.

The Chancellor of the Exchequer and I had never been what you would call close friends. Blood enemies would be a better description. Aahz always maintained that this was because of my growing influence in court. Not so. The truth was that my mentor's greed for additional funding was surpassed only by Grimble's reluctance to part with the same. Literally the same, since my wages came out of those coffers so closely guarded by the Chancellor.

I found him, as expected, in the tiny cubicle he used for an office. Scuttlebutt has it he repeatedly refused larger rooms, trying desperately to impress the rest of the staff by setting an example of frugality. It didn't work, but he kept trying and hoping.

His desk was elbow deep in paper covered by tiny little numbers which he alternately peered at and changed while moving various sheets from stack to stack. There were similar stacks on the floor and on the only other available chair, leading me to believe he had been at his current task for some time. Seeing no available space for sitting or standing, I elected to lean against the door frame.

"Working late, Lord Chancellor?"

That earned me a brief, dark glare before he returned to his work.

"If I were a magician, I'd be working late. As Chancellor of the Exchequer, these *are* my normal hours. For your information, things are going rather smoothly. So smoothly, in fact, I may be able to wrap up early tonight, say in another three or four hours."

"What are you working on?"

"Next year's Budget and Operating Plan, and it's almost done. That is, providing someone doesn't want to risk incurring my permanent disfavor by trying to change a number on me at the last minute."

The last was accompanied by what can only be described as a meaningful stare.

I ignored it.

I mean, what the heck! I was already on his bad side, so his threats didn't scare me at all.

"Then it's a good thing I caught you before you finished your task," I said nonchalantly. "I want to discuss something with you that will undoubtedly have an impact on your figures. Specifically, a change in my pay scale."

"Out of the question!" Grimble exploded. "You're already the highest paid employee on the staff, including myself. It's outrageous that you would even think of asking for a pay increase."

"Not a pay *increase*, Lord Chancellor, a pay cut."

That stopped him.

"A pay cut?"

"Say, down to nothing."

He leaned back in his chair and regarded me suspiciously.

"I find it hard to believe that you and your apprentice are willing to work for nothing. Forgive me, but I always distrust noble sacrifice as a motive. Though I dislike greed, at least it's a drive I can understand."

"Perhaps that's why we've always gotten along so well," I purred. "However, you're quite right. I have no intention of working for free. I was thinking of leaving the court of Possiltum to seek employment elsewhere."

The chancellor's eyebrows shot up.

"While I won't argue your plan, I must admit it surprises me. I was under the impression you were quite enamored of your position here in 'a soft job,' I believe is how your scaly apprentice describes it. What could possibly entice you to trade the comforts of court life for an uncertain future on the open road?"

"Why, a bribe, of course," I smiled. "A lump sum of a thousand gold pieces."

"I see," Grimble murmured softly. "And who's offering this bribe, if I might ask?"

I stared at the ceiling.

"Actually, I was rather hoping that *you* would."

There was a bit of haggling after that, but mostly on the terms of our agreement. Grimble *really* wanted Aahz and me out of his accounts, though I suspect he

would have been less malleable if he had realized he was
only dealing with me. There was a bit of name calling
and breast beating, but the end result is what counts, and
that end result was my heading for my quarters, a thousand gold pieces richer in exchange for a promise that it
was the last money I would ever receive from Grimble.
It was one more reason for my being on my way as soon
as possible.

With light heart and heavy purse, I entered my quarters.

Remember the last time I entered my quarters? How
there was a demon waiting for me? Well, it happened
again.

Now don't get me wrong. This *isn't* a regular occur-
rence in my day-to-day existence. One demon showing up
unannounced is a rarity. Two demons . . . well, no matter
how you looked at it, this was going to be a red-letter day
in my diary.

Does it seem to you I'm stalling? I am. You see, this
demon I knew, and her name was Massha!

"Well hel-lo, high roller! I was just in the neighborhood and thought I'd stop by and say 'Hi!' "

She started forward to give me a hug, and I hastily
moved to put something immobile between us. A 'hi!'
and a hug might not sound like a threat to you. If not,
you don't know Massha!

I have nothing against hello hugs. I have another demon friend named Tananda (yes, I have a *lot* of demon
friends these days) whose hello hugs are high points in
my existence. Tananda is cute, curvaceous, and cuddly.
Okay, so she's also an assassin, but hello hugs can
get a rise out of a statue.

Massha, on the other hand, is *not* cute and cuddly.
Massha is immense . . . and then some. I didn't doubt the
sincere goodwill behind her greeting. I was just afraid that
if she hugged me, it would take days to find my way out
again . . . and I had a getaway to plan.

"Um . . . Hi, Massha. Good to see you . . . all of you."

The last time I had seen Massha, she was disguised as
a gaudy circus tent, except it wasn't a disguise. It was

actually the way she dressed. This time, though, she had apparently kicked out the jams . . . along with her entire wardrobe and any modicum of good taste. Okay, she wasn't completely naked. She was wearing a leopard-skin bikini, but she was showing enough flesh for four *normal* naked people. A bikini, her usual wheelbarrow full of jewelry, light green lipstick that clashed with her orange hair, and a tattoo on her bicep. That was Massha. Class all the way.

"What brings you to Klah? Aren't you still working Jahk?" I asked, mentioning the dimension where we met.

"The boys will just have to work things out without me for a while. I'm on a little . . . vacation."

There was a lot of that going around.

"But what are you doing here?"

"Not much for small talk, are you? I like that in a man."

My skin started to crawl a little on that last bit, but she continued.

"Well . . . while I'm here, I thought I'd take another little peek at your General Badaxe, but that's not the real reason for my visit. I was hoping you and me could talk a little . . . business."

My life flashed before my eyes. For a moment, neither Aahz's departure nor the King's assignment was my biggest problem . . . pun intended.

"Me?" I managed at last.

"That's right, hot stuff. I've been giving it a lot of thought since you and your scaly green sidekick rolled through my territory, and yesterday I made up my mind. I've decided to sign on as your apprentice."

IV:

"Duty: A fee paid for transacting in good(s)."

—U.S. DEPT. OF COMMERCE

"**B**ut your Majesty, he promised me he'd pay the other half before spring, and . . ."

"I did not."

"Did too."

"Liar!"

"Thief!"

"Citizens," I said, "I can only listen to one side at a time. Now then, you! Tell me what you remember being said."

That's right. *I* said. There I was, sitting on the very throne I had decided to avoid at all cost.

Actually, this king business wasn't all that rough. Rodrick had briefed me on basic procedure and provided me with a wardrobe, and from there it was fairly simple. The problems paraded before me weren't all that hard to solve, but there were lots of them.

At first I was scared, then for a while it was fun. Now it was just boring. I had lost count of how many cases I had listened to, but I had developed a new sympathy for Rodrick's desire to get away for a while. I was ready for a vacation before lunch rolled around. It was beyond my comprehension how he had lasted for years of this nonsense.

You may wonder how I went from talking with Massha to sitting on the throne. Well, I wonder myself from time to time, but here's what happened as near as I can reconstruct it.

Needless to say, her request to work as my apprentice caught me unprepared.

"M . . . my . . . but Massha. You already *have* a job as a court magician. Why would you want to apprentice yourself to me?"

In response, Massha heaved a great sigh. It was a startling phenomenon to watch. Not just because there was so much of Massha moving in so many different directions, but because when she was done, she seemed to have deflated to nearly half her original size. She was no longer an imposing figure, just a rather tired looking fat woman.

"Look, Skeeve," she said in a low voice that bore no resemblance to her normal vampish tones. "If we're going to work together, we've got to be honest with each other. Court magician or not, we both know that I don't know any magik. I'm a mechanic . . . a gimmick freak. I've got enough magik baubles to hold down a job, but any bozo with a big enough bankroll could buy the same stuff at the Bazaar at Deva.

"Now, mind you, I'm not complaining. Old Massha's been kicked around by some of the best and nobody's ever heard her complain. I've been happy with what I have up to now. It's just when I saw you and your rat pack put one over on *both* city-states at the Big Game with some *real* magik, I knew there was something to learn besides how to operate gimmicks. So whattaya say? Will you help me learn a little of the stuff I really got into the magik biz for?"

Her honesty was making me more than a little uncomfortable. I wanted to help her, but I sure didn't want an apprentice right now. I decided to stall.

"Why did you choose magik for a profession, anyway?"

That got me a sad smile.

"You're sweet, Skeeve, but we were going to be honest with each other, remember? I mean, look at me. What am I supposed to do for a living? Get married and be a housewife? Who would have me? Even a blind man could figure out in no time flat that I was more than he had bargained for . . . a lot more. I resigned myself to the way I look a long time ago. I accepted it and covered up any embarrassment I felt with loud talk and flamboyant airs. It was only natural that a profession like magik that thrives on loud talk and flamboyant airs would attract me."

"We aren't *all* loud talk," I said cautiously.

"I know." She smiled. "You don't have to act big because you've got the clout to deliver what you promise. It impressed me on Jahk, and everyone I talked to at the Bazaar on Deva said the same thing. 'Skeeve doesn't strut much, but don't start a fight with him.' That's why I want you for my teacher. I already know how to talk loud."

Honesty and flattery are a devastating one-two punch. Whatever I thought about her before, right now Massha had me eating out of the palm of her hand. Before I committed myself to anything I might regret later, I decided to try fighting her with her own weapons.

"Massha . . . we're going to be honest with each other, right? Well, I can't accept you as an apprentice right now for two reasons. The first is simple. I don't know that much magik myself. No matter what kind of scam we pull on the paying customers, including the ones on Deva, the truth is that I'm just a student. I'm still learning the business myself."

"That's no problem, big bwana." Maasha laughed, regaining some of her customary composure. "Magik is like that: the more you learn, the more you find there is to know. That's why the really big guns in our business spend all their time closeted away studying and practicing. You know *some* magik, and that's more than I know. I'll be grateful for anything you're willing to teach me."

"Oh," I said, a bit surprised that my big confession

hadn't fazed her at all. "Well, there's still the second reason."

"And that is?"

". . . That I'm in a bit of trouble myself. In fact, I was just getting ready to sneak out of the kingdom when you showed up."

A small frown wrinkled Massha's forehead.

"Hmm . . ." she said, thoughtfully. "Maybe you'd better give me some of the details of this trouble you're in. Sometimes talking it out helps, and that's what apprentices are for."

"They are?" I countered skeptically. "I've been apprenticed twice, and I don't remember either of the magicians I studied under confiding in me with their problems."

"Well, that's what *Massha's* for. Listening happens to be one of the few things I'm *really* good at. Now give. What's happened to put a high-stepper like you on the run?"

Seeing no easy alternative, I told her about the King's assignment and my subsequent deal with Grimble. She was right. She was an excellent listener, making just enough sympathetic noise to keep me talking without actually interrupting my train of thought.

When I finally wound down, she sighed and shook her head.

"You're right. You've got a real problem there. But I think there are a few things you've overlooked in reaching your final decision."

"Such as . . . ?"

"Well, first, you're right. A bad king is worse than a good king. The problem is that a bad king is better than no king at all. Roddie Five is counting on you to fill his chair tomorrow, and if you don't show up, the whole kingdom goes into a panic because the king has disappeared."

"I hadn't thought about it that way," I admitted.

"Then there's the thing with Grimble. We all pick up a little extra cash when we can, but in this case if it comes out that Grimble paid you to skip out when the King was counting on you, *his* head goes on the chopping block for treason."

I closed my eyes.

That did it. It was bad enough to hurt the faceless masses, but when the mass had a face, even if it was Grimble's, I couldn't let him face a treason charge because of my cowardice.

"You're right." I sighed. "I'm going to have to sit in for the King tomorrow."

"With me as your apprentice?"

"Ask me after tomorrow . . . if I'm still alive. In the meantime, scurry off and say 'Hello' to Badaxe. I know he'll be glad to see you."

"**Y**our Majesty?"

I snapped back to the present, and realized the two arguers were now looking at me, presumably to render a decision.

"If I understand this case correctly," I stalled, "both of you are claiming ownership of the same cat. Correct?"

Two heads bobbed in quick agreement.

"Well, if the two of you can't decide the problem between you, it seems to me there's only one solution. Cut the cat in two and each of you keep half."

This was supposed to inspire them to settle their difference with a quick compromise. Instead they thanked me for my wisdom, shook hands, and left smiling, presumably to carve up their cat.

It occurred to me, not for the first time today, that many of the citizens of Possiltum don't have both oars in the water. What anyone could do with half a dead cat, or a whole dead cat for that matter, was beyond me.

Suddenly I was very tired. With an offhanded wave I beckoned the herald forward.

"How many more are waiting out there?" I asked.

"That was the last. We deliberately kept the case load light today so your Majesty could prepare for tomorrow."

"Tomorrow?"

The question slipped out reflexively. Actually, I didn't

really care what happened tomorrow. My assignment was done. I had survived the day, and tomorrow was Rodrick's problem.

"Yes, tomorrow . . . when your bride arrives."

Suddenly I was no longer tired. Not a bit. I was wide awake and listening with every pore.

"My bride?" I asked cautiously.

"Surely your Majesty hasn't forgotten. She specifically scheduled her arrival so that she would have a week to prepare for your wedding."

Case load be hanged. Now I knew why dear Rodrick wanted a vacation. I also knew, with cold certainty, that he wouldn't be back tonight to relieve me of my duties. Not tonight, and maybe not ever.

V:

"The only thing worse than a sorcerer is a sorcerer's apprentice."

—M. MOUSE

For once, I successfully suppressed the urge to panic. I had to! Without Aahz around to hold things together until I calmed down, I couldn't afford hysterics.

Instead, I thought . . . and thought.

I was in a jam, and no matter how I turned it over in my mind, it was going to take more than just me to get out of it.

I thought of Massha.

Then I thought about suicide.

Then I thought about Massha again.

With firm resolve and weak knees, I made my decision. The question was, how to locate Massha? The answer came on the heels of the question. Standing in for the King had been nothing but a pain so far. It was about time I started making it work *for* me for a change.

"Guard!"

A uniformed soldier materialized by the throne with impressive speed.

"Yes, your Majesty?"

"Pass the word for General Badaxe. I'd like to see him."

"Umm . . . begging your Majesty's pardon. He's with a lady just now."

"Good. I mean, bring them both."

"But . . ."

"Now."

"Yes, your Majesty!"

The guard was gone with the same speed with which he had appeared.

I tried not to grin. I had never gotten along particularly well with the military of Possiltum. Of course, the fact that my first exposure to them was when Aahz and I were hired to fight their war for them might have something to do with it. Anyway, the thought of some poor honor guard having to interrupt his general's tête-a-tetê was enough to make me smile, the first in several days.

Still, sending a guard to fetch the person I wanted to see was certainly better than chasing them down myself. Perhaps being a king *did* have its advantages.

Two hours later, I was still waiting. In that time, I had more than ample opportunity to reconsider the benefit of issuing a kingly summons. Having sent for Badaxe, I was obligated to wait for him in the throne room until he appeared.

At one point I considered the horrible possibility that he had taken Massha riding and that it might be *days* before they were located. After a little additional thought, I discarded the idea. There wasn't a steed in the Kingdom, including Gleep, who could carry Massha more than a few steps before collapsing.

I was still contemplating the image of Massha, sitting indignant on the ground with horse's legs protruding grotesquely from beneath her rump, when the herald sprang into action.

"Now comes General Badaxe . . . and a friend."

With that, the man stood aside. Actually, he took several sideways steps to stand aside.

I've already described Massha's bulk. Well, Hugh Badaxe wasn't far behind her. What he lacked in girth, he made up for in muscle. My initial impression of the General remained unchanged; that he had won his rank by taking on the rest of the army . . . and winning. Of course, he was wearing his formal bearskin, the clean one, which made him appear all the larger. While I had been there when they met, I had never actually seen Badaxe and Massha standing side by side before. The overall effect was awe-inspiring. Together, they might have been a pageant of a barbarian invasion gone decadent . . . if it weren't for the General's axe. His namesake, a huge, double-bitted hand axe, rode comfortably in its customary place on the General's right hip, and the glitter from it wasn't all decorative. Here, at least, was one barbarian who hadn't let decadence go to his sword arm.

"Your Majesty."

Badaxe rumbled his salutation as he dropped to one knee with an ease that denied his size. One could almost imagine the skull of a fallen enemy crackling sharply beneath that descending knee. I forced the thought from my mind.

"Greetings, General. Won't you introduce me to your . . . companion?"

"I . . . certainly, your Majesty. May I present Massha, Court Magician of Ta-hoe, and friend of both myself and Lord Skeeve, Magician to your own court here at Possiltum."

"Charmed, your Majesty."

I realized with a start that Massha was about to attempt to imitate Badaxe by dropping to one knee. Even if she were able to execute such a maneuver, it would require sufficient effort as to invite ridicule from the other court retainers present . . . and somehow I didn't want that.

"Ah . . . there is no need for that," I asserted hastily. "It was not our intention to hold formal court here, but rather an informal social occasion."

That caused a minor stir with the court, including the general who frowned in slight puzzlement. Still, I was already committed to a line of conversation, so I blundered on.

"In fact, that was the only reason for the summons. I

wished to meet the lady dazzling enough to lure our general from his usual position by my side."

"Your Majesty gave his permission for my absence today," the general protested.

"Quite right. As I said, this is a social gathering only. In fact, there are too many people here for casual conversation. It is our wish that the court be adjourned for the day and the room cleared that I might speak freely with this visiting dignitary."

Again there was a general ripple of surprise, but a royal order was a royal order, and the various retainers bowed or curtsied to the throne and began making their way out.

"You too, general. I would speak with Massha alone."

Badaxe began to object, but Massha nudged him in the ribs with an elbow, a blow which would have been sufficient to flatten most men, but was barely enough to gain the general's attention. He frowned darkly, then gave a short bow and left with the others.

"So, you're a friend of our lord Magician," I asked after we were finally alone.

"I have that . . . honor, your Majesty," Massha replied cautiously. "I hope he's . . . well?"

"As a matter of fact, he's in considerable trouble right now."

Massha heaved a great sigh.

"I was afraid of that. Something to do with his last assignment?"

I ignored the question.

"General Badaxe seems quite taken with you. Are you sure you want to stay in the magik biz? Or are you going to try your hand at a new lifestyle?"

Massha scowled at me.

"Now how did you hear that? You haven't been torturing your own magician, have you?"

I caught the small motion of her adjusting her rings, and decided the time for games was over.

"Hold it, Massha! Before you do anything, there's something I have to show you."

"What's that?"

I had already closed my eyes to remove my disguise spell . . . faster than I ever had before.

"Me," I said, opening my eyes again.

"Well, I'll be . . . you really had me going there, hot stuff."

"It was just a disguise spell," I waved off-handedly.

"Nice. Of course, it almost got you fried. Why didn't you let me know it was you?"

"First of all, I wanted to see if my disguise spell was good enough to fool someone who was watching for it. This is my first time to try to disguise my voice as well as my appearance. Secondly . . . well, I was curious if you had changed your mind about being my apprentice."

"But why couldn't you have just asked me . . . I see. You're really in trouble, aren't you? Bad enough that you didn't want to drag me into an old promise. That's nice of you, Skeeve. Like I said before, you run a class act."

"Anybody would have done the same thing," I argued, trying to hide my embarrassment at her praise.

She snorted loudly.

"If you believed that, you wouldn't have survived as long as you have. Anyway, apprentice or not, a friend is a friend. Now out with it. What's happened?"

Sitting on the steps to the throne, I filled her in about the forthcoming wedding and my suspicions about the King's conveniently scheduled vacation. I tried to sound casual and matter-of-fact about it, but towards the end my tone got rather flat.

When I was done, Massha gave a low whistle of sympathy.

"When you big leaguers get in trouble, you don't kid around, do you? Now that you've filled me in, I'll admit I'm a little surprised you're still here."

I grimaced.

"I'm a little slow from time to time, but you only have to lecture me once. If one day without a king is bad for a kingdom, a permanent disappearance could be disastrous. Anyway, what I need right now is someone to track down the real King and get him back here, while I keep bluffing from the throne."

Massha scowled.

"Well, I've got a little trinket that could track him, if you've got something around that he's worn, that is . . ."

"Are you kidding? You think court magicians dress this way in Possiltum? Everything I'm wearing and two more closetsful in his quarters belong to the King."

". . . But what I can't figure out is why you need me? Where's your usual partner . . . whatsisname . . . Aahz? It seems to me he'd be your first choice for a job like this. Wherever he is, can't you just pop over to that dimension and pull him back for a while?"

Lacking any other option, I decided to resort to the truth, both about Aahz's permanent departure and my own lack of ability to travel the dimensions without a D-Hopper. When I was done, Massha was shaking her head.

"So you're all alone and stranded here and you were *still* going to give me an out instead of pressuring me into helping? Well, you got my help, mister, and you don't have to bribe me with an apprenticeship, either. I'll get your king back for you . . . before that wedding. *Then* we'll talk about apprentices."

I shook my head.

"Right idea, but wrong order. I wasn't going to bribe you with an apprenticeship, Massha. I told you before I don't know much magik, but what I know I'll be glad to teach you . . . whether you find the King or not. I'm not sure that's an apprenticeship, but it's yours if you want it."

She smiled, a smile quite different from her usual vamp act.

"We'll argue about it later. Right now, I've got a king to find."

"Wait a minute! Before you go, you're pretty good with gadgets, right? Well, I've got a D-Hopper in my quarters. I want you to show me two settings: the one for Deva, and the one for Klah. You see, I'm not all *that* noble. If things get too rough or it takes you longer than a week to find the King, I want a little running room. If I'm not here when you get back, you can look for your 'noble' Skeeve at the Yellow Crescent Inn at the Bazaar at Deva."

Massha snorted.

"You're putting yourself down again, Hot Stuff. You're going to try before you run, which is more than I can say for most in our profession. Besides, whatever you think your motives are, they're deeper than you think. You just asked me to show you two settings. You only need one to run."

VI:

"Good information is hard to get. Doing anything with it is even harder!"

—L. SKYWALKER

I had long since decided that the main requirement for Royalty or its impersonators was an immunity to boredom. Having already chronicled the true tedious nature of performing so-called "duties of state," I can only add that *waiting* to perform them is even worse.

There was certainly no rush on my part to meet the King's bride-to-be, much less marry her. After word had come that her arrival would be delayed by a full day, however, *and* as the day waxed into late afternoon waiting for her "early morning" reception, I found myself wishing that she would get here so we could meet and get it over with already.

All other royal activity had ground to a halt in an effort to emphasize the importance of Possiltum's greeting their queen-to-be. I hardly thought it was necessary, though, as the citizens decked the street with flowers and lined up three deep in hopes of catching a glimpse of this new celebrity. The wait didn't seem to dampen their spirits, though the flowers wilted only to be periodically replaced by eager hands. If nothing else, this reception was going to put a serious dent in Possiltum's flower crop for a while. Of course, it might also put a dent in *all* our crops, for the streets remained packed with festive people who showed not the slightest inclination to return to their fields or guild shops when word was passed of each new delay.

"Haven't the citizens anything better to do with their time than stand around the streets throwing flowers at each other?" I snarled, turning from the window. "*Somebody* should be keeping the kingdom during all this foolishness."

As usual, J. R. Grimble took it on himself to soothe me.

"Your Majesty is simply nervous about the pending reception. I trust his wisdom will not allow his edginess to spill over onto his loyal subjects?"

"I was assured when she crossed the border that she would be here this morning. Morning! Ever see the sun set in the morning before?"

"Undoubtedly she was delayed by the condition of the roads," General Badaxe offered. "I have told your Majesty before that our roads are long overdue for repair. In their current state, they hinder the passage of travelers . . . *and* troops should our fair land come under attack."

Grimble bared his teeth.

"And his Majesty has always agreed with *me* that repairing the roads at this time would be far too costly . . . unless the general would be willing to significantly reduce the size of his army that we might use the savings from wages to pay for the road work?"

The general purpled.

"Reduce the size of the army and you'll soon lose that treasury that you guard so closely, Grimble."

"Enough, gentlemen," I said, waving them both to silence. "As you've both said, we've discussed this subject many times before."

It had been decided that rather than having the King of Possiltum sit and fidget in front of the entire populace, that he should sweat it out in private with his advisors until his bride actually arrived. Royal image and all that. Unfortunately this meant that since morning I had been confined in a small room with J. R. Grimble and Hugh Badaxe for company. Their constant bickering and sniping was sufficient to turn my already dubious mood into something of record foulness.

"Well, while we're waiting, perhaps you can each brief me on your opinions of my future bride and her kingdom."

"But your Majesty, we've done that before. Many times."

"Well, we'll do it again. You're supposed to be my advisors, aren't you? So advise me. General Badaxe, why don't you start?"

Badaxe shrugged.

"The situation is essentially unchanged from our last briefing. Impasse is a small kingdom; tiny really—less than a thousand citizens altogether. They claim the entire Impasse mountain range, from which the kingdom gets its name, and which is the bulk of their military defense. Their claim stands mostly because the mountains are treacherous and there is little or no reason to venture there. At least ninety-five percent of their population is concentrated along the one valley through the mountains. They have no formal military, but rather a militia, which suffices as there are no less than five passes in the main valley where a child with a pile of rocks could hold off an army . . . and they have plenty of rocks. Their main vulnerability is food. The terrain is such that they are unable to support even their small population, and as they are still at odds with the kingdom at the other end of the valley who originally owned it, they are forced to buy all their food from us . . . at prices even a generous man would call exorbitant."

"Supply and demand," Grimble said with a toothy smile.

"Wait a minute, general," I interrupted. "If I understand this right, Impasse is not a threat to us militarily because of its size. If anything, it guards our flank against attack from the pass. Right?"

"Correct."

"Which it is already doing."

"Also correct."

Seeing an opening, I hurried on.

"We can't attack them, but from what you say they don't have anything we want. So why are we bothering with this marriage/alliance?"

The general looked pointedly at Grimble.

"Because even though Impasse is people-few and crop-light, they are sitting on the largest deposit of precious metal on the continent," the Chancellor of the Exchequer supplied.

"Precious met . . . oh! You mean gold."

"Precisely. With the alliance, Possiltum will become the richest kingdom ever."

"That hardly seems like sufficient reason to get married," I mumbled.

"Your Majesty's opinions on the subject are well known to us," Grimble nodded. "You have expressed them often and long every time the possibility of this marriage was broached. I am only glad that you finally gave your consent when the citizens of Possiltum threatened to revolt if you didn't accept the betrothal offer."

"That was only after you spread the word that such an alliance would significantly lower taxes, Grimble," Bad-axe scowled.

"I said it *might* lower taxes," the Chancellor corrected innocently. "Can I help it if the common folk jumped to conclusions?"

Now that I had a clearer picture of the situation, I might have mustered a bit of sympathy for the King's predicament, if he hadn't stuck me in it in his stead.

"Enough about Impasse. Now give me your opinions of my bride-to-be."

There was a brief moment of uncomfortable silence.

"Impasse doesn't have a monarchy," Grimble said carefully. "That is, until recently. It was more a tribal state, where the strongest ruled. When the last king died, however, his daughter Hemlock somehow managed to take over and maintain the throne, thereby establishing a royal line of sorts. Exactly how she did it is unclear."

"Some say that prior to the king's death she managed

to gain the . . . loyalty of all the able-bodied fighters in the kingdom, thereby securing her claim from challenge," Badaxe supplied.

I held up a restraining hand.

"Gentlemen, what you're telling me are facts. I asked for your *opinions*."

This time, there was a long uncomfortable silence.

"That good, eh?" I grimaced.

"Your Majesty must remember," Grimble protested, "we are being asked to express our hidden feelings about a woman who will soon be our Queen."

"Not until the marriage," I growled. "Right now, I am your King. Get my drift?"

They got it, and swallowed hard.

"The words 'cold-blooded' and 'ruthless' come to mind," the general said, "and that's the impression of a man who's made a career of the carnage of war."

"I'm sure the rumors that she murdered her father to gain control of the kingdom are exaggerated," Grimble argued weakly.

". . . But your Majesty would be well advised to insist on separate sleeping quarters, and even then sleep lightly . . . and armed," the general concluded firmly.

"No difficulty should be encountered with separate quarters." Grimble leered. "It's said Queen Hemlock has the morals of an alley cat."

"Terrific," I sighed.

The Chancellor favored me with a paternal smile.

"Oh, there's no doubt that the entire kingdom, myself included, admires your Majesty for the sacrifices he is willing to make for his people."

The trouble was, only *I* knew who the King was willing to sacrifice!

I studied Grimble's smile through hooded eyes, seeking desperately through my mind for something to disrupt his smug enjoyment of the situation. Suddenly, I found it.

"I've been meaning to ask, does anyone know the current whereabouts of our Court Magician?"

Grimble's smile disappeared like water on a hot skillet.

"He's . . . gone, your Majesty."

"What? Out on another of his madcap adventures?"

The Chancellor averted his eyes.

"No, I mean, he's . . . gone. Tendered his resignation and left."

"Tendered his resignation to whom?" I pressed. "On whose authority has he quit his post during this, my darkest hour?"

"Ahh . . . mine, your Majesty."

"What was that, Grimble? I couldn't quite hear you."

"Mine. I told him he could go."

Grimble was sweating visibly now, which was fine by me. In fact, an idea was beginning to form in my mind.

"Hmm . . . knowing you, Lord Chancellor, I would suspect money is behind the Great Skeeve's sudden departure."

"In a way," Grimble evaded, "you might say that."

"Well, it won't do," I said firmly. "I want him back . . . and before this accursed marriage. What's more, since you approved his departure, I'm holding you personally responsible for his return."

"B-ut, your Majesty! I wouldn't know where to start looking. He could be anywhere by now."

"He can't have gone far," Badaxe volunteered casually. "His dragon and unicorn are still in the Royal Stables."

"They are?" The Chancellor blinked.

"Yes," the general smiled, "as you might know if you ever set foot outside your counting house."

"See, Grimble," I said. "The task I set before you should be easy for a man of your resources. Now off with you. The longer you tarry here, the longer it will be before you find our wayward magician."

The Chancellor started to say something, then shrugged and started for the door.

"Oh, Grimble," I called. "Something you might keep in mind. I heard a rumor that the Great Skeeve has recently been disguising himself as me for an occasional prank. Like as not the scamp is parading around somewhere with the royal features on his face. That tidbit alone should help you locate him."

"Thank you, your Majesty," the Chancellor responded

glumly, reminded now of the shape-changing abilities of his supposed quarry.

I wasn't sure, but I thought General Badaxe was stifling a laugh somewhere in the depths of his beard as his rival trudged out.

"How about you, general? Do you think your men could assist in passing word of my royal summons to the Great Skeeve?"

"That won't be necessary, your Majesty."

With sudden seriousness he approached me, laid a hand on my shoulder, and stared into my eyes.

"Lord Magician," he said, "the King would like to see you."

VII:

"There is no counter for a spirited woman except spirited drink."

—R. BUTLER

"**Y**ou've known for some time that I'm a fighting man. What you *don't* seem to realize is what that implies."

We were sitting over wine now, in a much more relaxed conversation than when I had been pretending to be King Rodrick.

"Fighting men recognize people as much by movement and mannerism as they do by facial feature. It's a professional habit. Now, you had the appearance and voice of the King, but your carriage and gestures were that of the Great Skeeve, not Rodrick the Fifth."

"But if you knew I was an imposter, why didn't you say something?"

The general drew himself up stiffly.

"The King had not taken me into his confidence in this matter, nor had you. I felt it would have been rude to intrude on your affairs uninvited."

"Weren't you afraid that I might be a part of some plot to murder the King and take his place?"

"Lord Magician, though we met as rivals, prolonged exposure to you has caused my respect for you to grow to no small matter. Both in your convincing Big Julie and his army to defect from the Mob and join Possiltum as honest citizens, and in fighting at your side in the Big Game when you risked life and limb to rescue a comrade in peril, you have shown ingenuity, courage, and honor. While I may still speak of you from time to time in less than glowing terms, my lowest opinion of you does not include the possibility of your having a hand in murdering your employer."

"Thank you, general."

". . . And besides, only a total idiot would want to assume Rodrick's place so soon before his marriage to Queen Hemlock."

I winced.

"So much for your growing respect."

"I said 'ingenuity, courage, and honor.' I made no mention of intelligence. Very well, then, a total idiot or someone under orders from his king."

"How about a bit of both?" I sighed.

"I suspected as much." Badaxe nodded. "Now that we're speaking candidly, may I ask as to the whereabouts of the King?"

"Good question."

In a few depressing sentences, I brought him up to date on my assignment and Rodrick's disappearance.

"I was afraid something like this would happen," the general said when I concluded. "The King has been looking desperately for some way out of this marriage, and it looks like he's found it. Well, needless to say, if there's anything I can do to help, just ask."

"Thanks, general. As a matter of fact, I . . ."

". . . As long as it doesn't go against the good of the kingdom," Badaxe amended. "Like helping you to escape. Possiltum needs a king, and for the time being, you're it!"

"Oh. Well . . . how about using your men to help find the king?"

Badaxe shook his head.

"Can't do it. Massha has that assignment. If I sent my men to back her up, she'd think I didn't have any faith in her."

Terrific! I had an ally, if I could get around his loyalties and amorous entanglements.

The General must have noticed my expression.

"Anything else I'll be willing to do."

"Like what?"

"Well . . . like teaching you to defend yourself against your bride-to-be."

That actually sounded promising.

"Do you think we'll have enough time?"

With that, there was a heavy knocking at the door.

"Your Majesty! The carriage of Queen Hemlock is approaching the palace!"

"No," said the General with disheartening honesty.

We barely made it to our appointed places ahead of the Queen's procession. The throne of Possiltum had been temporarily moved to a position just inside the doors to the palace, and only by sprinting through the corridors with undignified abandon were Badaxe and I able to reach our respective positions before the portals were thrown open.

"Remind me to have a word with you about the efficiency of your army's early warning system," I said to the general as I sank into my seat.

"I believe it was the Court Magician who complained about the excessive range of the military spy system," Badaxe retorted. "Perhaps your Majesty will see fit now to convince him of the necessity of timely information."

Before I could think of a sufficiently polite response, the Queen's party drew to a halt at the foot of the stairs.

The kingdom of Impasse had apparently spared no expense on the Queen's carriage. If it was not actually fashioned of solid gold, there were sufficient quantities of the metal in the trim and decorations as to make the difference academic. I took secret pleasure that Grimble was not present to gloat at the scene. The curtains were drawn, allowing us to see the rich embroidery upon them, but not who or what was within. A team of eight matched horses completed the rig, though their shaggy coats and short stature suggested that normally the mountainfolk put them to far more practical use than dragging royalty around the countryside.

With the carriage, however, any semblance of decorum about the Queen's procession vanished.

Her escort consisted of at least twenty retainers, all mounted and leading extra horses, though whether these were relief mounts or the bride's dowry I couldn't tell. The escort was also all male, and of a uniform appearance; broad-shouldered, narrow-waisted, and musclebound. They reminded me of miniature versions of the opposing teams Aahz and I had faced during the Big Game, but unlike those players, these men were armed to the teeth. They fairly bristled with swords and knives, glittering from boot-tops, arm sheaths, and shoulder scabbards, such that I was sure the combined weight of their weapons offset that of the golden coach they were guarding. These weren't pretty court decorations, but well handled field weapons worn with the ease fighting men accord the tools of their trade.

The men themselves were dressed in drab tunics suited more for crawling through thickets with knives clenched in their teeth than serving as a royal escort. Still, they wrinkled their broad, flat features into wide smiles as they alternately gawked at the building and waved at the crowd which seemed determined to unload the earlier noted surplus of flowers by burying the coach with them. The escort may have seemed sloppy and undisciplined in the eyes of Badaxe or Big Julie, but I wouldn't want to be the one to try to take anything away from them; Queen, coach, kingdom, or even a flower they had taken a fancy to.

Two men in the procession were notable exceptions to the rule. Even on horseback they looked to be a head and shoulder taller than the others and half again as broad. They had crammed their massive frames into tunics which were clean and formal, and appeared to be unarmed. I noted, however, that instead of laughing or waving, they sat ramrod stiff in their saddles and surveyed their surroundings with the bored, detached attention to detail I normally associated with predators . . . big predators.

I was about to call Badaxe's attention to the pair when the carriage door opened. The woman who appeared was obviously akin to most of the men in the escort. She had the same broad, solid build and facial features, only more so. My first impression was that she looked like the bottom two-thirds of an oak door, if the door were made of granite. Unsmiling, she swept the area with a withering stare, then nodded to herself and stepped down.

"Lady in waiting," Badaxe murmured.

I'm not sure if his comment was meant to reassure me, but it did. Only after did it occur to me that the general had volunteered the information to keep me from running, which I had been seriously considering.

The next figure in view was a radical departure from the other Impassers in the party. She was arrow thin and pale with black stringy hair that hung straight past her shoulders. Instead of the now expected round, flat face, her features looked like she had been hung up by her nose to dry. She wasn't unpleasant to look at; in fact, I guessed that she was younger than I was, but the pointed nose combined with a pair of dark, shiny-alert eyes gave her a vaguely rodent-like appearance. Her dress was a long-sleeved white thing that would have probably looked more fetching on a clothes-hanger. Without more than a glance at the assembled citizens she gathered up what slack there was in the skirt, hopped down from the carriage, and started up the stairs toward me with the athletic, leggy grace of a confirmed tomboy.

"*That* is Queen Hemlock," the general supplied.

I had somehow suspected as much, but having received confirmation, I sprang into action. *This* part, at least, I knew how to handle, having had it drilled into me over and over again by my advisors.

I rose to my feet and stood regally until she reached the throne, then timed my bow to coincide with her curtsey . . . monarch greeting monarch and all that.

Next, I was supposed to welcome her to Possiltum, but before I could get my mouth open, she came up with her own greeting.

"Sorry I didn't curtsey any lower, but I'm not wearing a thing under this dress. Rod, it's beastly hot here in the lowlands," she said, giving me a wide but thin-lipped smile.

"Aahh . . ." I said carefully.

Ignoring my response, or lack thereof, she smiled and waved at the throng, which responded with a roar of approval.

"What idiot invited the rabble?" she asked, the smile never leaving her face.

"Aahh . . ." I repeated.

General Badaxe came to my rescue.

"No formal announcement was made, your Majesty, but word of your arrival seems to have leaked out to the general populace. As might be expected, they are very eager to see their new Queen."

"Looking like this?" she said, baring her teeth and waving to those on the rooftops. "Six days on the road in this heat without a bath or a change of clothes and instead of a discreet welcome, half the kingdom gets to see me looking like I was dragged along behind the coach instead of riding in it. Well, it's done and we can't change it. But mind you, if it happens again . . . General Badaxe, is it? I thought so. Anyway, as I was saying, if it happens again, heads will roll . . . and I'm not speaking figuratively."

"Welcome to Possiltum," I managed at last.

It was a considerably abbreviated version of the speech I had planned to give, but it was as much as I could remember under the circumstances.

"Hello, Roddie," she said without looking at me, still waving at the crowd. "I'm going to scamper off for my quarters in a second. Be a love and try not to get underfoot during the next week . . . there's so much to do. Besides, it looks like you're going to have your hands full with other business."

"How's that?"

"You've got a wee bit of trouble coming your way, at least according to the gentleman I met on the road. Here he comes now. Bye."

"But . . ."

Queen Hemlock had already disappeared, vanishing
into the depths of the palace like a puff of smoke. Instead,
I found myself focusing on the man who had stepped from
the carriage and was currently trudging up the stairs toward my throne. I observed that he had the same weasel
features and manners of J. R. Grimble. Mostly, though, I
noticed that the two broadshouldered predators previously
assumed to be part of the Queen's escort, had suddenly
materialized at his side, towering over him like a pair of
bookends . . . mean looking bookends.

I sat down, in part because the approaching figure did
not seem to be royalty, but mostly because I had a feeling
I wanted to be sitting down for this next interview.

The man reached my throne at last, drew himself up,
and gave a curt nod rather than a bow. This, at least,
looked polite, since his flankers didn't acknowledge my
presence at all.

"Forgive me for intruding on such a festive occasion,
your Majesty," the man said, "but there are certain matters
we need to discuss."

"Such as . . . ?"

"My name is Shai-ster, and I represent a . . . consor-
tium of businessmen. I wish to confer with one of your
retainers concerning certain employees of ours who failed
to report in after pursuing our interests in this region."

As I mentioned earlier, I was getting pretty good at
speaking "bureaucrat." This man's oration, however, lost
me completely.

"You want to what about who?"

The man sighed and hung his head for a moment.

"Let me put it to you this way," he said at last. "I'm
with the Mob, and I want to see your Magician, Skeeve.
It's about our army, Big Julie's boys, that sort of disappeared after tangling with him. Now do you understand
me?"

VIII:

"Choose your friends carefully. Your enemies will choose you!"

— Y. ARAFAT

Within a few days of Queen Hemlock's arrival, the palace of Possiltum had the happy, relaxed air of a battlefield the night before the battle. The Queen's party and the mob representatives were housed in the palace as "royal guests," giving me a two-front war whether I wanted it or not.

Queen Hemlock was not an immediate problem; she was more like a time bomb. With specific orders to "stay out of her way," I didn't have to deal with her much, and even General Badaxe admitted that if she were going to try to kill me, it wouldn't be until after the wedding when she was officially Queen of Possiltum. Still, as the wedding day loomed closer, I was increasingly aware that she would have to be dealt with.

The Mob representatives, however, were an immediate problem. I had stalled them temporarily by telling them that the Court Magician was not currently in the palace, but had been sent for, and as a token of good faith had given them the hospitality of the palace. They didn't drink much, and never pestered me with questions about

"Skeeve's" return. There was no doubt in my mind, however, that at some time their patience would be exhausted and they would start looking for the Court Magician themselves. I also had a felling that "some time" would be real soon.

Needing all the help I could get, I had Badaxe send one of his men for Big Julie. With minimal difficulty we smuggled him into the palace, and the three of us held a war council. On Badaxe's advice, I immediately dropped my disguise and brought our guest up to date on the situation.

"Ah'm sorry," Julie said to open the meeting, "but I don't see where I can help you, know what I mean?"

Terrific. So much for Big Julie's expert military advice.

"I'd *like* to help," he clarified. "You've done pretty good by me and the boys. But I used to work for the Mob, you know? I know what they're like. Once they get on your trail, they never quit. I tried to tell you that before."

"I don't see what the problem is," General Badaxe rumbled. "There are only three of them, and their main spokesman's a non-combatant to boot. It wouldn't take much to make sure they didn't report anything to anybody . . . ever again."

Big Julie shook his head.

"You're a good man, Hugh, but you don't know what you're dealing with here. If the Mob's scouting party disappears, the Big Boys will know they've hit paydirt and set things in motion. Taking out their reps won't stop the Mob . . . it won't even delay them. If anything, it will speed the process up!"

Before Badaxe had a chance to reply, I interrupted with a few questions of my own.

"Wait a minute, Big Julie. When we first met, you were commanding the biggest army this world had ever seen. Right?"

"That's right." He nodded. "We was rolling along pretty good until we met you."

". . . And we didn't stop you militarily. We just gave you a chance to disappear as soldiers and retire as citizens of Possiltum. You and your boys were never beaten in a fight."

"We were the best," Big Julie confirmed proudly. "Anybody messed with us, they pulled back a bloody stump with no body attached, know what I mean?"

"Then why are you all so afraid of the Mob? If they try anything, why don't you and your boys just hook up with General Badaxe's army and teach 'em a lesson in maneuvers?"

The ex-commander heaved a deep sigh.

"It don't work that way," he said. "If they was to march in here like an army, sure, we could send 'em packing. But they won't. They move in a few musclemen at a time, all acting just as polite as you please so there's nothing you can arrest 'em for. When enough of 'em get here, though, they start leaning on your citizens. Little stuff, but nasty. If somebody complains to you, that somebody turns up dead along with most of their family. Pretty soon, all your citizens are more afraid of the Mob than they are of you. Nobody complains, nobody testifies in court. When that happens, you got no more kingdom. The Mob runs everything while you starve. You can't fight an invasion like that with an army. You can't fight it at all!"

We all sat in uncomfortable silence for a while, each avoiding the other's gaze while we racked our brains for a solution.

"What I don't understand," Badaxe said at last, "is if the system you describe is so effective and so unstoppable, why did they bother having an army at all?"

"I really hate to admit this," Big Julie grimaced, "but we was an experiment. Some of the Mob's bean-counters got it into their heads that even though an army was more expensive, the time savings of a fast takeover would offset the additional cost. To tell you the truth, I think their experiment was a washout."

That one threw me.

"You mean to say your army wasn't effective?"

"Up to a point we were. After that, we were too big. It costs a lot to keep an army in the field, and toward the end there, it was costing more to support my boys for a week than we were getting out of the kingdoms we were conquering. I think they were getting ready to phase us out . . . and that's why it's taken so long for them to come looking for their army."

I shook my head quickly.

"You lost me on that last loop, Big Julie. *Why* did they delay their search?"

"Money," he said firmly. "I'll tell you, nothing makes the Big Boys sit up and take notice like hard cash. I mean, they wrote the book when it came to money motivation."

"Sounds like Grimble," Badaxe muttered. "Doesn't anybody do anything for plain old revenge anymore?"

"Stow it, General," I ordered, leaning forward. "Keep going, Big Julie. What part does money have in this?"

"Well, the way I see it, the Mob was already losing money on my army, you know? To me, that means they weren't about to throw good gold after bad. I mean, why spend more money looking for an army that, when you find it, is only going to cost you more money?"

"But they're here now."

"Right. At the same time Possiltum's about to become suddenly rich. It looks to me like the Big Boys have found a way to settle a few old scores and turn a profit at the same time."

"The wedding!" I said. "I should have known. That means that by calling off the wedding, I can eliminate two problems at once: Queen Hemlock *and* the Mob!"

Badaxe scowled at me.

"I thought we had already discarded that option. Remember Grimble and the citizenry of Possiltum?"

Without thinking, I slammed the flat of my hand down on the table with a loud slap.

"Will you forget about Grimble and the citizenry of Possiltum? I'm tired of being in a box, general, and one way or another I'm going to blast a way out!"

From the expressions of my advisors, I realized I might have spoken louder than I had intended. With a conscious effort, I modulated my tone and my mood.

"Look, general . . . Hugh," I said carefully. "You may be used to the pressures of command, but this is new to me. I'm a magician, remember? Forgive me if I get a little razzled trying to find a solution to the problem that your . . . I mean, *our* King has dropped in my lap. Okay?"

He nodded curtly, but still didn't relax.

"Now, your point has merit," I continued, "but it overlooks a few things. First, Grimble isn't here. When and *if* he does get back, he'll have the King in tow, and friend Rodrick can solve the problem for us . . . at least the problem with the Queen. As for the citizenry of Possiltum . . . between you and me I'm almost ready to face their protests rather than have to deal with Queen Hemlock. Now if you weigh the disappointment of our people over having to continue the status quo against having both the Queen *and* the Mob move in on a permanent basis, what result do you get? Thinking of the welfare of the kingdom, of course!"

The general thought it over, then heaved a great sigh.

"I was never that much in favor of the wedding, anyway," he admitted.

"Just a minute, boys," Big Julie said, holding up a weary hand. "It's not quite that easy. The money thing may have slowed up their search a bit, but now that the Mob is here, there are a couple other matters they're gonna want to settle."

"Such as?" I asked, dreading the answer.

"Well, first off, there's me and my boys. Nobody just walks away from the Mob, you know. Their pay scale is great, but their retirement plan stinks."

"I thought you said they didn't want their army anymore," Badaxe grumbled.

"Maybe not as an army, but they can always use manpower. They'll probably break us up and absorb us into various positions in the organization."

"Would you be willing to go back to work for them?"

Big Julie rubbed his chin with one hand as he considered the general's question.

"I'd have to talk to the boys," he said. "Like I said, this kingdom's been pretty good to us. I'd hate to see anything happen to it because we were here . . . especially if we'd end up working for them again anyway."

"No," I said flatly.

"But . . ."

"I said 'No!' You've got a deal with Possiltum, Big Julie. More important, you've got a deal with me. We don't turn you over to the Mob until we've tried everything we can do to defend you."

"And how do you propose to defend them from the Mob?" Badaxe asked, sarcastically.

"I don't know. I'm working on it. Maybe we can buy them off. Offer them Queen Hemlock to hold for ransom or something."

"Lord Magician!"

"Okay, okay. I said I was still working on it, didn't I? What's next, Big Julie? You said there were a couple things they wanted besides money."

"You," he said bluntly. "The Mob isn't going to be happy until they get the Great Skeeve, Court Magician of Possiltum."

"Me?" I said in a small voice.

"The Mob didn't get to the top by ignoring the competition. You've made some pretty big ripples with your work, and the biggest as far as they're concerned is making their army disappear. They know you're big. Big enough to be a threat. They're gonna want you neutralized. My guess is that they'll try to hire you, and failing that, try for some sort of non-aggression deal."

"And failing that . . . ?" Badaxe asked, echoing my thoughts.

Big Julie shrugged.

"Failing that, they're gonna do their best to kill you."

IX:

"I don't know why anyone would be nervous about going to see royalty."

—P. IN BOOTS

"**B**ut why do *I* have to come along?" Badaxe protested, pacing along at my side as we strode towards the Queen's chambers.

"Call it moral support," I growled. "Besides, I want a witness that I went into the Queen's chambers . . . and came out again, if you get my drift."

"But if this will only solve one of our problems . . ."

". . . Then it will be one less problem for us to deal with. Shh! Here we are."

I had switched back to my Rodrick disguise. That combined with the general's presence was enough to have the Honor Guards at the Queen's chambers snap to rigid attention at our approach. I ignored them and hammered on the door, though I did have a moment to reflect that not long ago, I thought the biggest problem facing a king was boredom!

"For cryin' out loud!" came a shrill voice from within. "Can't you guards get *anything* right? I told you I didn't want to be disturbed!"

One of the guards rolled his eyes in exasperation. I

favored him with a sympathetic smile, then raised an eyebrow at Badaxe.

"King Rodrick the Fifth of Possiltum seeks an audience with Queen Hemlock!" he bellowed.

"I suppose it's all right," came the reply. "How about first thing in the morning?"

"Now," I said.

I didn't say it very loud, but it must have carried. Within a few heartbeats the door flew open, exposing Queen Hemlock . . . literally. I can't describe her clothing because she wasn't wearing any. Not a stitch!

"Roddie!" she chirped, oblivious to the guards and Badaxe, all of whom gaped at her nakedness. "Come on in. What in the world are you doing here?"

"Wait for me," I instructed Badaxe in my most commanding tone.

"C-certainly, your Majesty!" he responded, tearing his eyes away from the Queen long enough to snap to attention.

With that, I stepped into the Queen's lair.

"So, what have you got for me?" She shut the door and leaned back against it. The action made her point at me, even though her hands were behind her back.

"I beg your pardon?"

"The audience," she clarified. "You wanted it, you got it. What's up?"

Somehow under the circumstances, I found that to be another embarrassing question.

"I . . . um . . . that is . . . could you please put something on? I'm finding your attire, or lack thereof, to be quite distracting."

"Oh, very well. It *is* beastly hot in here, though."

She flounced across the room and came up with a flimsy something which she shrugged into, but didn't close completely.

"Right after the wedding," she declared, "I want that window enlarged, or better yet, the whole wall torn out. Anything to get a little ventilation in this place."

She plopped down in a chair and curled her legs up

under her. It eased my discomfort somewhat, but not much.

"Ahh . . . actually, that's what I'm here to talk to you about."

"The window?" She frowned.

"No. The wedding."

That made her frown even more.

"I thought it was agreed that I would handle all the wedding arrangements. Oh, well, if you've got any specific changes, it isn't too late to . . ."

"It isn't that," I interrupted hastily. "It's . . . well, it's come to my attention that the high prices Possiltum is charging your kingdom for food is forcing you into this marriage. Not wishing to have you enter into such a bond under duress, I've decided to cut our prices in half, thereby negating the need for our wedding."

"Oh, Roddie, don't be silly. That's not the reason I'm marrying you!"

Rather than being upset, the Queen seemed quite amused at my suggestion.

"It isn't?"

"Of course not. Impasse is so rich that we could buy your yearly crop at double the prices if we wanted to and still not put a dent in our treasury."

My stomach began to sink.

"Then you *really* want this marriage? You aren't being forced into it for political reasons?"

The Queen flashed all her teeth at me in a quick smile.

"Of course there are political reasons. I mean, we are royalty, aren't we? I'm sure you're a pleasant enough fellow, but I can get all the pleasant fellows I want without *marrying* them. Royalty marries power blocks, not people."

There was a glimmer of hope in what she was saying, and I pounced on it with all fours.

". . . Which brings us to the other reason we should call off the wedding," I said grandly.

The Queen's smile disappeared.

"What's that?" she said sharply.

For my reply, I let drop my disguise spell.

"Because I'm not Royalty. I'm people."

"Oh, that." The Queen shrugged. "No problem. I knew that all along."

"You did?" I gulped.

"Sure. You were embarrassed . . . twice. Once when I arrived at the palace, and again just now when I opened the door in my all-together. Royalty doesn't embarrass. It's in the blood. I knew all long you weren't Rodrick. It's my guess you're the Great Skeeve, Court Magician. Right? The one who can shape change?"

"Well, it's a disguise spell, not shape changing, but except for that, you're right."

Between Badaxe and Queen Hemlock, I was starting to wonder if anyone was really fooled by my disguise spells.

The Queen uncoiled from her seat and began pacing back and forth as she spoke, oblivious to her nakedness which peeked out of her wrap at each turn.

"The fact that you aren't the King doesn't change my situation, if anything it improves it. As long as you can keep your disguise up enough to fool the rabble, I'll be marrying two power blocks instead of one."

"Two power blocks," I echoed hollowly.

"Yes. As the 'King' of Possiltum, you control the first block I was after: land and people. Impasse by itself isn't large enough to wage an aggressive war, but uniting the respective powers of the two kingdoms, we're unstoppable. With your armies backed by my capital, I can sweep as far as I want, which is pretty far, let me tell you. There's nothing like growing up in a valley where the only view is the other side of the valley to whet one's appetite for new and unusual places."

"Most people content themselves with touring," I suggested. "You don't have to conquer a country to see it."

"Cute," Queen Hemlock sneered. "Naive, but cute. Let's just say I'm not most people and let it ride, okay? Now then, for the second power base, there's you and your magic. That's a bonus I hadn't expected, but I'm sure that, given a day or two, I can expand my plans to take advantage of it."

At one time, I thought I had been scared by Massha. In hindsight, Massha caused me only faint discomfort. Talking with Queen Hemlock, I learned what fear was all about! She wasn't just a murderess, as Badaxe suspected. She was utter mayhem waiting to be loosed on the world. The only thing between her and the resources necessary to act out her dreams was me. Me, and maybe . . .

"What about King Rodrick?" I blurted out. "If he shows up, the original wedding plans go into effect."

"You mean he's still alive?" she exclaimed, arching a thin eyebrow at me. "I've overestimated you, Skeeve. Alive he could be a problem. No matter. I'll alert my escort to kill him on sight if he appears before the wedding. After we're married, it would be a simple matter to declare him an imposter and have him officially executed."

Terrific. Thanks to my big mouth, Massha would be walking into a trap if she tried to return the King to the castle. If Queen Hemlock's men saw him, then . . .

"Wait a minute!" I exclaimed. "If I'm walking around disguised as the King, what's to keep your men from offing me by mistake?"

"Hmm. Good thing you thought about that. Okay! Here's what we'll do."

She dove into her wardrobe and emerged with a length of purple ribbon.

"Wear this in full view whenever you're outside your chambers," she instructed, thrusting it into my hands. "It'll let my men know that you're the man I want to marry instead of their target."

I stood with the ribbon in my hand.

"Aren't you making a rather large assumption, your Majesty?"

"What's that?" She frowned.

"That I may not want to marry you?"

"Of course you do." She smiled. "You've already got the throne of Possiltum. If you marry me, you not only have access to my treasury, it also rids you of your other problem."

"My other problem?"

"The Mob, silly. Remember? I rode in with their representative. With my money, you can buy them off. They'll forget anything if the price is high enough. Now, isn't being my husband better than running from their vengeance *and* mine for the rest of your life?'

I had my answer to that, but in a flash of wisdom kept it to myself. Instead, I said my goodbyes and left."

"From your expression, I take it that your interview with the Queen was less than a roaring success," Badaxe said dryly.

"Spare me the 'I told you so's,' general," I snarled. "We've got work to do."

Shooting a quick glance up and down the corridor, I cut my purple ribbon in half on the edge of his axe.

"Keep a lookout for Massha and the King," I instructed. "If you see them, be sure Rodrick wears this. It'll make his trip through the palace a lot easier."

"But where are you going?"

I gave him a tight smile.

"To see the Mob representatives. Queen Hemlock has graciously told me how to deal with them!"

X:

"Superior firepower is an invaluable tool when entering into negotiations."

—G. PATTON

The Mob representatives had been housed in one of the less frequented corners of the palace. In theory, this kept them far from the hub of activity while Badaxe and I figured out what to do with them. In fact, it meant that now that I was ready to face them, I had an awfully long walk to reach my destination.

By the time I reached the proper door, I was so winded I wasn't sure I'd have enough breath to announce my presence. Still, on my walk I had worked up a bit of a mad against the Mob. I mean, who did they think they were, popping up and disrupting my life this way? Besides, I was too unnerved by Queen Hemlock to try anything against her, which left the Mob as the only target for my frustration.

With that in mind, I drew a deep breath and knocked on the door.

I needn't have worried about announcing myself. Between the second and third knocks, the door opened a crack. My third knock hit the door before I could stop it, but the door remained unmoved by the impact.

"Hey, Shai-ster! It's the King!"

"Well, let him in, you idiot!"

The door opened wide, revealing one of Shai-ster's massive bodyguards, then a little wider to allow me entry space past him.

"Come in, come in, your Majesty," the Mob's spokesman said, hurrying forward to greet me. "Have a drink . . . Dummy! Get the King something to drink!"

This last was addressed to the second hulking muscleman who heaved himself off the bed he had been sprawled upon. With self-conscious dignity he picked up the end of the bed one-handed, set it down again, then picked up the mattress and extracted a small, flat bottle from under it.

I wondered briefly if this was what Big Julie meant when he referred to the Mob tradition of "going to the mattresses." Somehow the phrase had always brought another image to mind . . . something involving women.

Accepting the flask from his bodyguard, Shai-ster opened the top and offered it to me, smiling all the while.

"Am I correct in assuming that your Majesty's visit indicates news of the whereabouts of his court magician? Perhaps even an estimated time as to when he is expected back?"

I accepted the flask, covertly checking the locations of the bodyguards before I answered. One was leaning against the door, while the other stood by the bed.

"Actually, I can do better than that. The Great Skeeve . . ."

I closed my eyes and dropped my disguise spell.

". . . is here."

The bodyguards started visibly at my transformation, but Shai-ster remained unmoved except for a narrowing of the eyes and a tightening of his smile.

"I see. That simplifies things a bit. Boys, give the Great Skeeve here a chair. We have some business to discuss."

His tone was not pleasant, nor were the bodyguards smiling as they started for me.

Remember how Rupert jumped me so easily? Well, he took me by surprise, and had three hundred years plus of magical practice to boot. Somehow, I was not particularly surprised by the bodyguards' action . . . in fact, I had been expecting it and had been gathering my powers for just this moment.

With a theatric wave of my hand and a much more important focusing of my mental energies, I picked the two men up and spun them in midair. Heck, I wasn't adverse to stealing a new idea for how to use levitation . . . even from Rupert. I did like a little originality in my work, though, so instead of bouncing them on their heads, I slammed them against the ceiling and held them pinned there.

"No, thanks," I said as casually as I could, "I'd rather stand."

Shai-ster looked at his helpless protectors, then shot a hard stare at me.

"Perhaps this won't be as simple as I thought," he admitted. "Say, you've got a unicorn, don't you?"

"That's right," I confirmed, surprised by the sudden change in topic.

"I don't suppose you'd be particularly scared if you woke up in the morning and found him in your bed . . . not all of him, just his head?"

"Scared? No, not particularly. In fact, I'm pretty sure I'd be mad enough to quit playing games and get down to serious revenge."

The Mob spokesman sighed heavily.

"Well, that's that. If we can't make a deal, we'll just have to do this the hard way. You can let the boys down now. We'll be heading back in the morning."

This time, it was my turn to smile.

"Not so fast. Who said I didn't want to make a deal?"

For the first time since I met him, Shai-ster's poise was shaken.

"But . . . I thought . . . if you can . . ."

"Don't assume, Shai-ster. It's a bad habit for businessmen to get into. I just don't like to get pushed around, that's all. Now then, as you said earlier, I believe we have some business to discuss."

The spokesman shot a nervous glance at the ceiling.

"Um . . . could you let the boys down first? It's a bit distracting."

"Sure."

I closed my eyes and released the spell. Mind you, unlike the disguise spell, I don't have to close my eyes to remove a levitation spell. I just didn't want to see the results.

The room shook as two loud crashes echoed each other. I distinctly heard the bed assume a foolproof disguise as kindling.

I carefully opened an eye.

One bodyguard was unconscious. The other rolled about, groaning weakly.

"They're down," I said, needlessly.

Shai-ster ignored me.

"Big bad bodyguards! Wait'll the Big Boys hear how good dumb muscle is against magik!"

He paused to kick the groaner in the side.

"Groan quieter! *Mister* Skeeve and I have some talking to do."

Having already completed one adventure after antagonizing the military arm of a large organization, I was not overly eager to add another entire group of plug-uglies to my growing list of enemies.

"Nothing personal," I called to the bodyguard who was still conscious. "Here! Have a drink."

I levitated the flask over to him, and he caught it with a weak moan I chose to interpret as "thanks."

"You said something about a deal?" Shai-ster said, turning to me again.

"Right. Now, if my appraisal of the situation is correct, the Mob wants three things: Big Julie's army back, me dead or working for them, and a crack at the new money coming into Possiltum after the wedding."

The Mob spokesman cocked his head to one side.

"That's a bit more blunt than I would have put it, but you appear to have captured the essential spirit of my clients' wishes. My compliments on your concise summation."

"Here's another concise summation to go with it.

Hands off Big Julie and his crew; he's under my protection. By the same token, Possiltum is my territory. Stay away from it or it will cost you more than you'll get. As to my services, I have no wish to become a Mob employee. I would consider an occasional assignment as an outside contractor for a specific fee, but full-time employment is out."

The Mob spokesman was back in his element, face stony and impassive.

"That doesn't sound like much of a deal."

"It doesn't?"

I reviewed the terms quickly in my mind.

"Oh! Excuse me. There is one other important part of my offer I neglected to mention. I don't expect your employers to give up their objectives without any return at all. What I have in mind is a swap: an army and maybe a kingdom for an opportunity to exploit an entire world."

Shai-ster raised his eyebrows.

"You're going to give us the world? Just like that? Lord Magician, I suspect you're not bargaining with a full deck."

"I didn't say I would give you the world, I said I would give you *access* to a world. Brand new territory full of businesses and people to exploit; one of the richest in the universe."

The spokesman frowned.

"Another world? And I'm supposed to take your word as to how rich it is and that you can give us access?"

"It would be nice, but even in my most naive moments I wouldn't expect you to accept a blind bid like that. No, I'm ready to give you a brief tour of the proposed world so that you can judge for yourself."

"Wait a minute," Shai-ster said, holding up his hands. "This is so far beyond my negotiating parameters that even if I liked what I saw, I couldn't approve the deal. I need to bring one of the Big Boys in on this decision."

This was better than I had hoped. By the time he could bring one of the Mob's hierarchy to Possiltum, I could deal with some of my other problems.

"Fine. Go and fetch him. I'll hold the deal until your return."

The spokesman gave one of his tight-lipped smiles.

"No need to wait," he said. "My immediate superior is on call specifically for emergencies such as this."

Before I could frame a reply, he opened the front of his belt-buckle and began rubbing it, all the while mumbling under his breath.

There was a quick flash of light, and an old, hairy-jowled man appeared in the room. Looking round, he spied the two bodyguards sprawled on the floor and gripped the sides of his face with his open hands in an exaggerated expression of horror.

"Mercy!" he wheezed in a voice so hoarse I could barely understand him. "Shai-ster, you bad boy. If there was trouble, you should have called me sooner. Oh, those poor, poor boys."

The Mob spokesman's face was once again blank and impassive as he addressed me.

"Skeeve, Lord Magician of Possiltum, let me introduce Don Bruce, the Mob's fairy godfather."

XI:

*"Tell you what. Let me sweeten the deal
a bit for you. . . ."*

—BEELZEBUB

"**O**h! This is simply *mar*-velous! Who would have ever
thought . . . another dimension, you say?"

"That's right," I said off-handedly. "It's called Deva."

Of course, I was quite in agreement with Don Bruce.
The Bazaar on Deva was really something, and every time
I visited it, I was impressed anew. It was an incredible
tangle of tents and displays stretching as far as the eye
could see in every direction, crammed full of enough magikal devices and beings to defy anyone's imagination and
sanity. It was the main crossroads of trade for the dimensions. Anything worth trading money or credits for was
here.

This time, however, I was the senior member of the
expedition. As much as I wanted to rubberneck and ex-
plore, it was more important to pretend to be bored and
worldly . . . or other-worldly as the case might be.

Don Bruce led the parade, as wide-eyed as a farm-kid
in his first big city, with Shai-ster, myself, and the two
bodyguards trailing along behind. The bodyguards seemed
more interested in crowding close to me than in protecting

their superiors, but then again, they had just had some bad experiences with magik.

"The people here all look kinda strange," one of them muttered to me. "You know, like foreigners."

"They are foreigners ... or rather *you* are," I said. "You're on their turf, and a long way from home. These are Deveels."

"Devils?" the man responded, looking a little wild-eyed. "You're tellin' me we're surrounded by devils?"

While it was reassuring to me to see the Mob's bully-boys terrified by something I had grown used to, it also occurred to me that if they were *too* scared, it might ruin the deal I was trying to set up.

"Look ... say, what is your name, anyway?"

"Guido," the man confided, "and this here's my cousin Nunzio."

"Well look, Guido. Don't be thrown by these jokers. Look at them. They're storekeepers like storekeepers anywhere. Just because they look funny doesn't mean they don't scare like anybody else."

"I suppose you're right. Say, I meant to thank you for the drink back there at the castle."

"Don't mention it." I waved. "It was the least I could do after bouncing you off the ceiling. Incidentally, there was nothing personal in that. I wasn't trying to make you two look bad, I was trying to make myself look good ... if you see the difference."

Guido's brow furrowed slightly.

"I ... think so. Yeah! I get it. Well, it worked. You looked real good. I wouldn't want to cross you, and neither would Nunzio. In fact, if we can ever do you a favor ... you know, bend someone a little for you ... well, just let us know."

"Hey, what's that?"

I looked in the direction Don Bruce was pointing. A booth was filled with short painted sticks, all floating in midair.

"I think he's selling magic wands," I guessed.

"Oh! I want one. Now, don't go anywhere without me."

The bodyguards hesitated for a moment, then followed as Don Bruce plunged into negotiations with the booth's proprietor, who gaped a bit at his new customer.

"Does he always dress like that?" I asked Shai-ster. "You know, all in light purple?"

The Mob spokesman raised an eyebrow at me.

"Do you always dress in green when you travel to other dimensions?"

Just to be on the safe side, I had donned another disguise before accompanying this crew to Deva. It occurred to me that if I were successful in my negotiations, it wouldn't be wise to be known at the Bazaar as the one who introduced organized crime to the dimension.

Unfortunately, this had dawned on me just as we were preparing to make our departure, so I hadn't had much time to choose someone to disguise myself as. Any of my friends were out, as were Massha, Quigley, Garkin . . . in desperation I settled on Rupert . . . I mean, there was one being I owed a bad turn or two. Consequently, I was currently parading around the Bazaar as a scaly green Pervert . . . excuse me, Pervect.

"I have my reasons," I dodged loftily.

"Well, so has Don Bruce." Shai-ster scowled. "Now if you don't mind, I've got a few questions about this place. If we try to move in here, won't language be a problem? I can't understand anything these freaks are saying."

"Take a look," I instructed, pointing.

Don Bruce and the Deveel proprietor were haggling earnestly, obviously having no difficulty understanding each other, however much they disagreed.

"No Deveel worth his salt is going to let a little thing like language stand in the way of a sale."

"Hey, everybody! Look what I got!"

We turned to find Don Bruce bearing down on us, proudly waving a small rod the same color as his clothes.

"It's a magic wand!" he exclaimed. "I got it for a song."

"A song plus some gold, I'd wager," Shai-ster observed dryly. "What does it do?"

"What does it do?" Don Bruce grinned. "Watch this."

He swept the wand across the air with a grand gesture, and a cloud of shiny dust sparkled to the ground.

"That's it?" Shai-ster grimaced.

Don Bruce frowned at the wand.

"That's funny. When the guy back there did it, he got a rainbow."

He pointed the wand at the ground and shook it . . . and three blades materialized out of thin air, lancing into the dust at our feet.

"Careful!" Shai-ster warned, hopping back out of range. "You'd better read the instructions on that thing."

"I don't need instructions," Don Bruce insisted. "I'm a fairy godfather. I know what I'm doing."

As he spoke, he gestured emphatically with the wand, and a jet of flame narrowly missed one of the bodyguards.

". . . But this can wait," Don Bruce concluded, tucking the wand into his waistband. "We've got business to discuss."

"Yes. We were just . . ." Shai-ster began.

"Shuddup! I'm talking to Skeeve here."

The force behind Don Bruce's sudden admonishment, combined with the Shai-ster's quick obedience, made me hastily revise my opinion of the Mob leader. Strange or not, he was a force to be recognized.

"Now then, Mister Skeeve, what's the police situation around here?"

"There aren't any."

Shai-ster's eyebrows shot up.

"Then how do they enforce the laws?" he asked, forgetting himself.

"As far as I can tell, there are no laws either."

"How 'bout that, Shai-ster?" Don Bruce laughed. "No police, no laws, no lawyers. You'd be in trouble if you were born here."

I started to ask what a lawyer was, but the godfather saved me from my own ignorance by plunging into the next question.

"How about politicians?"

"None."

"Unions?"

"None."

"Bookies?"

"Lots," I admitted. "This is the gambling capital of the dimensions. As near as I can tell, though, they all operate independently. There's no central organization."

Don Bruce rubbed his hands together gleefully.

"You listening to this, Shai-ster? This is some world Mister Skeeve is givin' us here."

"He's not giving it to us," Shai-ster corrected. "He's offering *access* to it."

"That's right," I said quickly. "Exploiting it is up to your organization. Now, if you don't think your boys can handle it . . ."

"We can handle it. A layout like this? It's a piece of cake."

Guido and Nunzio exchanged nervous glances, but held their silence as Don Bruce continued.

"Now if I understand this right, what you want in return for letting us into this territory is that we lay off Big Julie and Possiltum. Right?"

I count real good up to three.

"And me," I added. "No 'getting even with the guy who thrashed our army plans,' no 'join the Mob or die' pressure. I'm an independent operator and happy to stay that way."

"Sure, sure," Don Bruce waved. "Now that we've seen how you operate, no reason we can't eat out of the same bowl. If anything, we owe you a favor for opening up a new area to our organization."

Somehow, that worried me.

"Um . . . tell you what. I don't want any credit for this . . . inside the Mob or outside. Right now, nobody but us knows I had a hand in this. Let's keep it that way, okay?"

"If that's what you want." Don Bruce shrugged. "I'll just tell the Big Boys you're too rough for us to tangle with, and that's why we're going to leave you alone. Anytime our paths cross, we go ahead with your approval or we back off. Okay?"

"That's what I want."

"Deal?"

"Deal."

We shook hands ceremoniously.

"Very well," I said. "Here's what you need to travel between here and home."

I fished the D-Hopper out of my sleeve.

"This setting is for home. This one is for here. Push this button to travel."

"What about the other settings?" Shai-ster asked.

"Remember the magic wand?" I countered. "Without instructions, you could get lost with this thing. I mean, *really* lost."

"Come on, boys," Don Bruce said, setting the D-Hopper. "We gotta hurry home. There's a world here to conquer, so we gotta get started before somebody else beats us to it. Mister Skeeve, a pleasure doin' business with you."

A second later, they were gone.

I should have been elated, having finally eliminated one set of problems from my horizon. I wasn't.

Don Bruce's last comment about world conquering reminded me of Queen Hemlock's plans. Now that the Mob was neutralized, I had other problems to solve. As soon as I got back to the palace, I would have to . . .

Then it hit me.

The Mob representatives had taken the D-Hopper with them when they left. That thing was my only route back to Klah! I was stranded at the Bazaar with no way back to my own dimension!

XII:

"I'm making this up as I go along!"

—I. JONES

But I didn't panic. Why should I?

Sure, I was in a bit of a mess, but if there was one place in all the dimensions I could be confident of finding help, it was here at the Bazaar. Anything could be had here for a price, and thanks to Aahz's training, I had made a point of stocking my pouch with money prior to our departure from Klah.

Aahz!

It suddenly occurred to me that I hadn't thought about my old mentor for days. The crises that had erupted shortly after his departure had occupied my mind to an extent where there was no time or energy left for brooding. Except for the occasional explanation of his absence, Aahz was playing no part in my life currently. I was successfully handling things without him.

Well . . .

Okay. I had successfully handled *some* things without him . . . the Mob, for example. Of course, the training he had gotten me into earlier in our relationship had also provided me with confidence under fire . . . another much-needed commodity these days.

"Face it, kid," I said to myself in my best imitation of Aahz. "You owe a lot to your old mentor."

Right. A lot. Like not making him ashamed of his prize pupil . . . say by leaving a job half done.

With new resolve, I addressed my situation. First, I had to get back to Klah . . . or should I look for a solution right here?

Rather than lose time to indecision, I compromised. With a few specific questions to the nearest vendor, I set a course for my eventual destination, keeping an eye out as I went for something that would help me solve the Queen Hemlock problem.

This trip through the Bazaar was different from my earlier visits. Before, my experience had been of wishing for more time to study the displays at leisure while hurrying to keep up with Aahz. This time, it was me that was pushing the pace, dismissing display after display with a casual "interesting, but no help with today's problem." Things seemed to have a different priority when responsibility for the crisis was riding on *my* shoulders.

Of course, I didn't know what I was looking for. I just knew that trick wands and instant thunderstorms weren't it. Out of desperation, I resorted to logic.

To recognize the solution, I needed to know the problem. The problem was that Queen Hemlock was about to marry me instead of Rodrick. Scratch that. Massha was bringing Rodrick back, and I couldn't help her. I just had to believe she could do it. The problem was Queen Hemlock.

Whether she married me or Rodrick, she was determined to use Possiltum's military strength to wage a war of expansion. If her husband, whoever it was, tried to oppose her, he would find himself conveniently dead.

Killing the Queen would be one solution, but somehow I shrank from cold-blooded murder . . . or hot-blooded murder for that matter. No. What was needed was something to throw a scare into her. A big scare.

The answer walked past me before I recognized it. Fortunately, it was moving slowly, so I turned and caught up with it in just a few steps.

Answers come in many shapes and sizes. This one was in the form of a Deveel with a small tray display hung by a strap around his neck.

"What you just said, was it true?"

The Deveel studied me.

"I said, 'Rings. One size fits all. Once on, never off.' "

"That's right. Is it true?"

"Of course. Each of my rings are pre-spelled. Once you put it on, it self-adjusts so that it won't come off, even if you want it to."

"Great. I'll take two."

". . . Because to lose a ring of such value would be tragedy indeed. Each one worth a king's ransom . . ."

I rolled my eyes.

"Look," I interrupted. "I know it's a tradition of the Bazaar to bargain, but I'm in a hurry. How much for two? Bottom price."

He thought for a moment and named a figure. My training came to the fore and I made a counteroffer one-tenth of his.

"Hey! You said 'no haggling,' " he protested. "Who do you think you are?"

Well, it was worth a try. According to Massha, I was getting a bit of a reputation at the Bazaar.

"I think I'm the Great Skeeve, since you asked."

". . . And the camel you rode in on," the vendor sneered. "Everyone knows the Great Skeeve isn't a Pervert."

The disguise! I had forgotten about it completely. With a mental wave, I restored my normal appearance.

"No, I'm a Klahd," I smiled. "And for your information, that's Pervect!"

"You mean you're really . . . no, you must be. No one else would voluntarily look like a Klahd . . . or defend Perverts . . . excuse me, Pervects."

"Now that that's established," I yawned, "how much for two of your rings?"

"Here," he said, thrusting the tray forward. "Take your

pick, with my compliments. I won a bundle betting on your team at the Great Game. All I ask is permission to say that you use my wares."

It was with a great deal of satisfaction that I made my selection and continued on my way. It was nice to have a reputation, but nicer to earn it. Those two little baubles now riding in my pouch were going to get me out of the Possiltum dilemma . . . if I got back in time . . . and if Massha had found the King.

Those sobering thoughts brought my hat size back to normal in a hurry. The time to gloat was after the battle, not before. Plans aren't victories, as I should be the first to know.

With panic once again nipping at my heels, I quickened my pace until I was nearly running by the time I reached my final destination: the Yellow Crescent Inn.

Bursting through the door of the Bazaar's leading fast food establishment, I saw that it was empty of customers except for a troll munching on a table in the corner.

Terrific.

I was expecting to deal with Gus, the gargoyle proprietor, but I'd settle for the troll.

"Skeeve!" the troll exclaimed. "I say, this is a surprise. What brings you to the Bazaar?"

"Later, Chumly. Right now I need a lift back to Klah. Are you busy with anything?"

The troll set his half-eaten table to one side and raised the eyebrow over one mismatched moon eye.

"Not to be picky about formality," he said, "but what happened to 'Hello, Chumly. How are you?' "

"I'm sorry. I'm in a bit of a hurry. Can we just . . ."

"Skeeve! How's it going, handsome?"

A particularly curvaceous bundle of green-haired loveliness had just emerged from the ladies' room.

"Oh. Hi, Tananda. How 'bout it, Chumly?"

Tananda's smile of welcome disappeared, to be replaced by a puzzled frown.

" 'Oh. Hi, Tananda?' " she repeated, shooting a look at the troll. "Does anything strike you as strange about that rather low-key greeting, big brother?"

"No stranger than the greeting I just got," Chumly confided. "Just off-hand, I'd say that either our young friend here has forgotten his manners completely, or he's gotten himself into a spot of trouble."

Their eyes locked and they nodded.

"Trouble," they said together.

"Cute." I grimaced. "Okay, so I'm in a mess. I'm not asking you to get involved. In fact, I think I've got it worked out myself. All I want is for you to pop me back to Klah."

Brother and sister stepped to my side.

"Certainly." Chumly smiled. "You don't mind if we tag along, though, do you?"

"But I didn't ask you to . . ."

"When have you had to ask for our help before, handsome?" Tananda scolded, slipping an arm around my waist. "We're your friends, remember?"

"But I think I've got it handled . . ."

". . . In which case, having us along won't hurt," the troll insisted.

"Unless, of course, something goes wrong," Tananda supplied. "In which case, we might be able to lend a hand."

". . . And if the three of us can't handle it, we'll be there to pull you out again," Chumly finished.

I should have known better than to try to argue with the two of them when they were united.

"But . . . if . . . well, thanks," I managed. "I didn't really expect this. I mean, you don't even know what the trouble is."

"You can tell us later," Tananda said firmly, starting her conjuring to move us through the dimensions. "Incidentally, where's Aahz?"

"That's part of the problem," I sighed.

And we were back!

Not just back on Klah, back in my own quarters in the palace. As luck would have it, we weren't alone. Someday I'll have time to figure out if it was good luck or bad.

The King was trussed up hand and foot on my bed, while Massha and J. R. Grimble were each enjoying a goblet of wine, and apparently each other's company. At least, that was the scene when we arrived. Once Massha and Tananda set eyes on each other, the mood changed dramatically.

"Slut," my new apprentice hissed.

"No-talent mechanic," Tananda shot back.

"Is that freak on our payroll?" Grimble interrupted, staring at Chumly.

"Spoken like a true bean-counter," the troll sneered.

I tried to break it up.

"If we can just . . ."

That brought Grimble's attention to me.

"You!" he gasped. "But if you're Skeeve, then who's . . ."

"King Rodrick of Possiltum," I supplied, nodding to the bound figure on the bed. "And now that everybody knows each other, can you all shut up while I tell you what our next move is?"

XIII:

"Marriage, being a lifelong venture, must be approached with care and caution."

—BLUEBEARD

The wedding went off without a hitch.

I don't known why I had been worried. There were no interruptions, no missed lines, nobody protested or even coughed at the wrong time. As was previously noted, Queen Hemlock had handled the planning to the last minute detail . . . except for a few surprises we were holding back.

That's why I was worried! My cronies and I knew that as gaudy and overdone as the Royal Wedding was, it was only the warm-up act for the main event. There was also the extra heat on me of knowing that I hadn't shared *all* of my plans with my co-conspirators. It seemed that was another bad habit I had picked up from Aahz.

Grimble and Badaxe were at their usual places as mismatched bookends to the throne, while Chumly, Tananda, Massha, and I, courtesy of my disguise spells and Badaxe's pull as general, were lined up along the foot of the throne as bodyguards. Everything was set to go . . . if we ever got the time!

As dignitary after dignitary stepped forward to offer

his or her congratulations and gifts, I found little to oc-
cupy my thoughts except how many things could go
wrong with my little scheme. I had stuck my neck out a
long way with my plan, and if it didn't work, a lot of
people would be affected, starting with the King and subjects of Possiltum.

The more I thought, the more I worried until, instead
of wishing the dignitaries would hurry, I actually found
myself hoping they would take forever and preserve this
brief moment of peace.

Of course, no sooner did I start hoping things would
last than they were over. The last well-wisher was filing
out and the Queen herself rising to leave when Grimble
and Badaxe left their customary positions and stepped before the throne.

"Before you go, my dear," Rodrick said, "our retainers
wish to extend their compliments."

Queen Hemlock frowned slightly, but resumed her
seat.

"The Chancellor of the Exchequer stands ready to support their Majesties in any way," Grimble began. "Of
course, even with the new influx of wealth into the treasury, we must watch needless expenses. As always, I
stand ready to set the example in cost savings, and so
have decided that to purchase a present for you equal to
my esteem would be a flagrant and unnecessary expense,
and therefore . . ."

"Yes, yes, Grimble," the King interrupted. "We understand and appreciate your self-sacrifice. General Badaxe?"

Grimble hesitated, then yielded the floor to his rival.

"I am a fighting man, not a speechmaker," the general
said abruptly. "The army stands ready to support the kingdom and the throne of Possiltum. As for myself . . . here
is my present."

He removed the axe from his belt and laid it on the
stairs before the throne.

Whether he was offering his pet weapon or his personal
allegiance, I found the gesture eloquent beyond words.

"Thank you, General Badaxe, Grimble," Queen Hemlock said loftily. "I'm sure I can . . ."

"My dear," the King interrupted softly. "There *is* another retainer."

And I was on.

Screwing up my courage, I dropped my disguise and stepped before the throne.

"Your Majesties, the Great Skeeve gives you his congratulations on this happy event."

The Queen was no fool. For one beat her eyes popped open and on the next she was staring at the King. You could almost hear her thoughts: "If the Magician is there, then the man I just married is . . ."

"That's right, your Majesty. As you yourself said in our earlier conversations, 'Royalty has married royalty.' "

While it might have been nice dramatically to savor that moment, I noticed the Queen's eyes were narrowing thoughtfully, so I hurried on.

"Before you decide how to express your joy," I warned, "perhaps I should explain *my* gift to the throne."

Now the thoughtful gaze was on me. I expressed my own joy by sweating profusely.

"My gift is the wedding rings now worn by both King and Queen. I hope you like them, because they won't come off."

Queen Hemlock made one brief attempt to remove her ring, then her eyes were on me again. This time, the gaze wasn't thoughtful.

"Just as the fate of the kingdom of Possiltum is linked to the throne, as of the moment you donned those rings, your fates are linked to each other. By the power of a spell so simple it cannot be broken or countered, when one of you dies, so does the other."

The Queen didn't like that at all, and even the King showed a small frown wrinkle on his forehead, as if contemplating something he had not previously considered. That was my signal to clarify things for him . . . that there *was* an implication to the rings that I hadn't mentioned to him.

"This is not intended as a 'one-sided' gift, for just as Queen Hemlock must now protect the health and well-being of her king, so must King Rodrick defend his queen against all dangers . . . *all* dangers."

The King was on his feet now, eyes flashing.

"What is that supposed to mean, Lord Magician?"

As adept as I was becoming at courtly speech, there were things which I felt were best said in the vernacular.

"It means if you or anybody else kills her, say, on your orders, then, *you're* dead. Now *SIT DOWN AND LISTEN!!*"

All the anger and frustration I had felt since figuring out the King was trying to double-cross me, but had been too busy to express, found its vent in that outburst. It worked. The King sank back into his chair, pale and slightly shaken.

I wasn't done, though. I had been through a lot, and a few words weren't enough to settle my mind.

"Since I accepted this assignment, I've heard nothing but how ruthless and ambitious Queen Hemlock is. Well, that may be true, *BUT SHE ISN'T GETTING ANY PRIZE EITHER!* Right now, *King* Rodrick, I have more respect for her than I have for you. *She* didn't abandon her kingdom in the middle of a crisis."

I began to pace back and forth before the thrones as I warmed to my topic.

"Everybody talks about 'our duty to the throne.' It's the guiding directive in the walk-a-day life of commoners. What never gets mentioned is 'the throne's duty to the people.' "

I paused and pointed directly at the King.

"I sat in that chair for a while. It's a lot of fun, deciding people's lives for them. Power is heady, and the fringe benefits are great! All that bowing and scraping, not to mention one heck of a wardrobe. Still, it's a job like any other, and with any job you sometimes have to do things you don't like. Badaxe doesn't just parade and review his troops, he has to train them and lead them into battle . . . you know, as in 'I could get killed out here' battle. Grimble spends ungodly hours poring over those numbers of his for the privilege of standing at your side.

"Any job has its pluses and minuses, and if the minuses

outweigh the pluses, you screw up your courage and quit . . . unless, of course, you're King Rodrick. Then, instead of abdicating and turning the pluses and minuses over to someone else, you stick someone else with doing the job in your name and sneak out a back door. Maybe that's how people do their jobs where you were raised, but I think it's conduct a peasant would be ashamed of."

I faced them, hands defiantly on my hips.

"Well, I've done *my* job. The kingdom has been protected from the immediate threat. With any luck, you two will learn to work together. I trust King Rodrick can dilute the Queen's ambition. I only hope that Queen Hemlock's fiery spirit can put a little more spine and courage into the King."

This time it was Queen Hemlock who was on her feet.

"Are you going to let him talk to you like that, Roddie? You're the King. Nobody pushes a king around."

"Guards!" Rodrick said tightly. "Seize that man."

It had worked! King and Queen were united against a common foe . . . me! Now all I had to do was survive it.

One more mind pass, and my comrades stood exposed as the outworlders they were.

Queen Hemlock, unaccustomed to my dealings with demons, dropped into her seat with a small gasp. The King simply scowled as he realized the real reason for the presence of my friends.

"Your Majesties," Badaxe said, stepping forward. "I am sworn to protect the throne and would willingly lay down my life in your defense. I do not see a physical threat here, however. If anything, it occurs to me both throne and kingdom would be strengthened if the Great Skeeve's words were heard and heeded."

"I am not a fighting man," Grimble said, joining Badaxe, "so my duty here is passive. I must add, though, that I also feel the Lord Magician's words have merit and should be said to every ruler."

His eyes narrowed and he turned to face me.

"I challenge, though, whether they should be said by a retainer to the court. One of our first duties is to show respect to the throne, in word *and* manner."

"That much we agree on, Grimble," Badaxe nodded, adding his glare to the many focused on me.

"Strange as it may sound," I said, "I agree, too. For that reason, I am hereby tendering my resignation as Court Magician of Possiltum. The kingdom is now secure militarily and financially, and in my opinion there is no point in it bearing the expense of a full-time magician . . . especially one who has been insolent to the throne. There is no need to discuss severance pay. The King's reward for my last assignment, coupled with the monies I have already received from the Exchequer, will serve my needs adequately. I will simply gather my things and depart."

I saw Grimble blanch slightly when he realized that I would not be returning his bribe. I had faith in his ability to hide anything in his stacks of numbered sheets, though.

With only the slightest of nods to the throne, I gathered my entourage with my eyes and left.

Everything had gone perfectly. I couldn't have asked for the proceedings to have turned out better. As such, I was puzzled as to why I was sweat-drenched and shaking like a leaf by the time I reached my own quarters.

XIV:

"Some farewells are easier than others."

—P. Marlowe

"So, where do you go from here?" Tananda asked.

She and Chumly were helping me pack. We had all agreed that having incurred the combined wrath of the King and Queen, it would be wisest to delay my departure as little as possible. Massha was off seeing to Gleep and Buttercup as well as saying her goodbyes to Badaxe.

"I don't really know," I admitted. "I was serious when I said I had accumulated enough wealth for a while. I'll probably hole up someplace and practice my magic for a while . . . maybe at that inn Aahz and I used to use as a home base."

"I say, why don't you tag along with little sister and me?" Chumly suggested. "We usually operate out of the Bazaar at Deva. It wouldn't be a bad place for you to keep your hand in, magik-wise."

It flashed through my mind that the Mob must have started its infiltration of the Bazaar by now. It also occurred to me that, in the pre-wedding rush, I hadn't told Tananda or Chumly about that particular portion of the caper. Having remembered, I found myself reluctant to admit my responsibility for what they'd find on their return.

"I dunno, Chumly," I hedged. "You two travel pretty light. I've got so much stuff, I'd probably be better off settling down somewhere permanent."

It was a pretty weak argument, but the troll seemed to accept it . . . maybe because he could see that mountain of gear we were accumulating, trying to clear my quarters.

"Well, think it over. We'd be glad to have you. You're not a bad sort to have around in a tight spot."

"I'll say," Tananda agreed with a laugh. "Where did you find those rings, anyway?"

"Bought them from a street vendor at the Bazaar."

"On Deva?" Chumly said with a frown. "Two spelled rings like that must have set you back a pretty penny. Are you *sure* you have enough money left?"

Now it was my turn to laugh.

"First of all, they aren't spelled. That was just a bluff I was running on their royal Majesties. The rings are plain junk jewelry . . . and I got them for free."

"Free?"

Now Tananda was frowning.

"Nobody gets anything for free at the Bazaar."

"No, really. They were free . . . well, the vendor did get my permission to say that I use his wares, but that's the same as free, isn't it? I mean, I didn't pay him any money."

As I spoke, I found myself suddenly uncertain of my "good deal." One of my earliest lessons about dealing with Deveels was "If you think you've made a good deal with a Deveel, first count your fingers, then your limbs, then your relatives. . . ."

"Permission to use your name?" Tananda echoed. "For two lousy rings? No percentage or anything? Didn't Aahz ever teach you about endorsements?"

There was a soft *BAMPH* in the air.

"Is someone taking my name in vain?"

And Aahz was there, every green scaly inch of him, making his entrance as casually as if he had just stepped out.

Of the three of us, I was the first to recover from my surprise. Well, at least I found my voice.

"Aahz!"

"Hi, kid. Miss me?"

"But, Aahz!"

I didn't know if I should laugh or cry. What I really wanted to do was embrace him and never let go. Of course, now that he was back, I would do no such thing. I mean, our relationship had never been big in the emotional displays department.

"What's the matter with everybody?" my mentor demanded. "You all act like you never expected to see me again."

"We ... Aahz! I ..."

"We didn't," Tananda said flatly, saving me from making an even bigger fool of myself.

"What little sister means," Chumly put in, "is that it was our belief that your nephew, Rupert, had no intention of letting you return from Perv."

Aahz gave a derisive snort.

"Rupert? That upstart? Don't tell me anybody takes him seriously."

"Well, maybe not if your powers were in full force," Tananda said, "but as things are ..."

"Rupert?" Aahz repeated. "You two have known me a long time, right? Then you should get it through your heads that nobody holds me against my will."

Somehow that quote sounded familiar. Still, I was so glad to have Aahz back, I would have agreed to anything just then.

"Yeah!" I chimed in eagerly. "This is Aahz! *Nobody* pushes him around."

"There!" My mentor grinned. "As much as I hate to agree with a mere apprentice, the kid knows what he's talking about ... this time."

Chumly and Tananda looked at each other with that special gaze that brother and sister use to communicate non-verbally.

"You know, big brother," Tananda said, "this mutual

admiration society is getting a bit much for my stomach. How about you?"

"Ectually," the troll responded. "I wasn't hearing all that much *mutual* admiration. Somehow the phrase 'mere apprentice' sticks in my mind."

"Oh, come on, you two," Aahz waved. "Get real, huh? I mean, we all like the kid, but we also know he's a trouble magnet. I've never met anyone who needs looking after as badly as he does. Speaking of which . . ."

He turned his yellow eyes on me with that speculative look of his.

". . . I notice you're both here . . . *and* I definitely heard my name as I phased in. What I need more than fond 'hellos' is a quick update as to exactly what kind of a mess we have to bail the Great Skeeve out of this time."

I braced myself for a quick but loud lesson about "endorsements," whatever that was, but the troll surprised me.

"No mess," he said, leaning back casually. "Little sister and I just dropped by for a visit. In fact, we were just getting ready to leave."

"Really?" My mentor sounded both surprised and suspicious. "Just a visit? No trouble?"

"Well, there was a *little* trouble," Tananda admitted. "Something to do with the King. . . "

"I knew it!" Aahz chortled, rubbing his hands together.

". . . But Skeeve here handled it himself," she finished pointedly. "Currently, there are no problems at all."

"Oh."

Strangely, Aahz seemed a bit disappointed.

"Well, I guess I owe you two some thanks, then. I really appreciate your watching over Skeeve here while I was gone. He can . . ."

"I don't think you're listening, Aahz," Chumly said, looking at the ceiling. "Skeeve handled the trouble. We just watched."

"Oh, we would have pitched in if things got tight," Tananda supplied. "You know, the way we do for *you*, Aahz. As it turned out, we weren't needed. Your 'mere apprentice' was more than equal to the task."

"Finished the job rather neatly, you know?" the troll added. "In fact, I'm hard pressed to recall when I've seen a nasty situation dealt with as smoothly or with as little fuss."

"All right, all right." Aahz grimaced. "I get the message. You can fill me in on the details later. Right now, the kid and I have some big things to discuss . . . and I mean *big*."

"Like what?" I frowned.

"Well, I've been giving it a lot of thought, and I figure it's about time we left Possiltum and moved on."

"Um, Aahz?" I said.

"I know, I know," he waved. "You think you need practice. You do, but you've come a long way. This whole thing with the trouble you handled only proves my point. You're ready to . . ."

"Aahz?"

"All right. I know you've got friends and duties here, but eventually you have to leave the nest. You'll just have to trust my judgment and experience to know when the time is right to . . ."

"I've already quit!"

Aahz stopped in midsentence and stared at me.

"You have?" He blinked.

I nodded and pointed at the pile of gear we had been packing. He studied it for a moment as if he didn't believe what he was seeing.

"Oh," he said at last. "Oh well, in that case, I'll just duck over to talk to Grimble and discuss your severance pay. He's a tight-fisted bird, but if I can't shake five hundred out of him, I'll know the reason why."

"I know the reason why," I said carefully.

Aahz rolled his eyes.

"Look, kid. This is *my* field of expertise, remember? If you go into a bargaining session aiming low, they'll walk all over you. You've got to . . ."

"I've already negotiated for a thousand!"

This time Aahz's "freeze" was longer . . . and he didn't look at me.

"A thousand?" he said finally. "In gold?"

"Plus a hefty bonus from the King himself," Tananda supplied helpfully.

"We've been trying to tell you, Aahz old boy," Chumly smiled. "Skeeve here has been doing just fine without you."

"I see."

Aahz turned away and stared silently out the window.

I'll admit to being a bit disappointed. I mean, maybe I hadn't done a first-rate job, but a *little* bit of congratulations would have been nice. The way my mentor was acting, you'd think he . . .

Then it hit me. Like a runaway war-chariot it hit me. Aahz was jealous! More than that, he was hurt!

I could see it now with crystal clarity. Up until now I had been blinded by Aahz's arrogant self-confidence, but suddenly the veil was parted.

Aahz's escape from Perv wasn't nearly as easy as he was letting on. There had been a brawl—physical, verbal, or magikal—some hard feelings, and some heavy promises made or broken. He had forced his way back to Klah with one thing on his mind: his apprentice . . . his *favorite* apprentice, was in trouble. Upon returning, what was his reception? Not only was I not in trouble, for all appearances, I was doing better without him!

Tananda and Chumly were still at it, merrily chattering back and forth about how great I was. While I appreciated their support, I wished desperately I could think of a way of getting it through to them that what they were really doing was twisting a knife in Aahz.

"Umm . . . Aahz?" I interrupted. "When you've got a minute, there *are* a few things I need your advice on."

"Like what?" came the muffled response. "From the sound of things, you don't need anybody, much less a teacher with no powers of his own."

Tananda caught it immediately. Her gadfly manner dropped away like a mask and she signaled desperately to Chumly. The troll was not insensitive, though. His re-action was to catch my eye with a pleading gaze.

It was up to me. Terrific.

"Well, like . . . um."

And Massha exploded into the room.

"Everything's ready downstairs, hot stuff, and . . . oh! Hi there, green and scaly. Thought you were gone for good."

Aahz spun around, his eyes wide.

"Massha?" he stammered. "What are you doing here?"

"Didn't the man of the hour here tell you?" She smiled, batting her expansive eyelashes. "I'm his new apprentice."

"Apprentice?" Aahz echoed, his old fire creeping into his voice.

"Um . . . that's one of the things I wanted to talk to you about, Aahz." I smiled meekly.

"Apprentice?" he repeated, as if he hadn't heard. "Kid, you and I have got to talk . . . NOW!"

"Okay, Aahz. As soon as I . . ."

"Now!"

Yep. Aahz was back.

"Um, if you'll excuse us, folks, Aahz and I have to . . ."

For the second time, there was a *BAMPH* in the room.

This one was louder, which was understandable, as there were more beings involved. Specifically, there were now four Deveels standing in the room . . . and they didn't look happy.

"We seek the Great Skeeve," one of them boomed.

My heart sank. Could my involvement with the Mob have been discovered so fast?

"Who's asking?"

Aahz casually placed his bulk between me and the intruders. Tananda and Chumly were also on their feet, and Massha was edging sideways to get a clear field of fire. Terrific. All I needed to complete my day was to have my friends soap up the trouble I had started.

"We are here representing the merchants of the Bazaar on Deva, seeking an audience with the Great Skeeve."

"About what?" my mentor challenged.

The Deveel fixed him with an icy glare.

"We seek the Great Skeeve, not idle chit-chat with a Pervert."

"Well, this particular Per-*vect* happens to be the Great

Skeeve's business manager, and he doesn't waste his time with Deveels unless *I* clear them."

I almost said something, but changed my mind. Concerned or not, this was not the time to take a conversation away from Aahz.

The Deveel hesitated, then shrugged.

"There is a new difficulty at the Bazaar," he said. "A group of organized criminals has gained access to our dimension threatening to disrupt the normal flow of business unless they are paid a percentage of our profits."

Tananda and Chumly exchanged glances, while Massha raised an eyebrow at me. I studied the ceiling with extreme care. Aahz alone was unruffled.

"Tough. So what does that have to do with the Great Skeeve?" he demanded.

Anticipating the answer, I tried to decide whether I should fight or run.

"Isn't it obvious?" The Deveel frowned. "We wish to retain his services to combat this threat. From what we can tell, he's the only magician around up to the job."

That one stopped me. Of all the strange turns events could have taken, this had to be the most unanticipated and . . . well, bizarre!

"I see," Aahz murmured, a nasty gleam in his eye. "You realize, of course, that the Great Skeeve's time is valuable and that such a massive undertaking would require equally massive remuneration?"

Every alarm in my system went off.

"Um . . . Aahz?"

"Shut up, k . . . I mean, be patient, Master Skeeve. This matter should be settled in a moment."

I couldn't watch.

Instead, *I* went to the window and stared out. Listening over my shoulder, I heard Aahz name an astronomical figure, and realized there might be a way out of this yet. If Aahz was greedy enough, and the Deveels stingy enough . . .

"Done!" said the spokesman.

". . . Of course, that's only an advance," Aahz pressed.

"A full rendering will have to wait until the job is completed."

"Done," came the reply.

". . . And that is the fee only. Expenses will be reimbursed separately."

"Done! The advance will be awaiting your arrival. Anything else?"

In tribute to the Deveel's generosity, Aahz was unable to think of any other considerations to gouge out of them.

There was another *BAMPH*, and the delegation was gone.

"How about that!" Aahz crowed. "I finally put one over on the Deveels!"

"What's that thing you always say about anyone who thinks they've gotten a good deal from a Deveel, Aahz?" Tananda asked sweetly.

"Later," my mentor ordered. "Right now we've got to get our things together and pop over to the Bazaar to scout the opposition."

"We already know what the opposition is."

"How's that, kid?"

I turned to face him.

"The opposition is the Mob. You remember, the organized crime group that was sponsoring Big Julie's army?"

A frown crossed Aahz's face as he regarded me closely.

"And how did you come by that little tidbit of information, if I may ask?"

I regarded him right back.

"That's the other little thing I wanted your advice on."

XV:

"In a war against organized crime, survival is a hit or myth proposition."

—M. BOLAN

"**N**ow let me see if I've got this right." Aahz scowled, pacing back and forth in front of our worried gazes. "What we've got to do is keep the Mob from taking over the Bazaar, without letting them know we're opposing them or the Deveels know we were the ones who loosed the Mob on the Bazaar in the first place. Right?"

"You can do it, Aahz," I urged eagerly.

This time it required no false enthusiasm on my part. While I had done an adequate job operating on my own, when it came to premeditated deviousness, I was quick to acknowledge my master. There might be someone out there in the multitude of dimensions better than Aahz at finding under-handed ways out of dilemmas, but I haven't met them yet.

"Of course I can do it," my mentor responded with a confident wink. "I just want everyone to admit it isn't going to be easy. All this talk about the Great Skeeve has made me a little insecure."

"A little?" Tananda smirked.

"I think it's a bit of all right," Chumly said, nudging

his sister with an elbow. "I've always heard how formi-
dable Aahz is when he swings into action. I, for one, am
dying to see him handle this rather sticky situation all by
himself."

Aahz's shoulders sagged slightly as he heaved a small
sigh.

"Whoa! Stop! Perhaps in my enthusiasm I overspoke.
What I *meant* to say is that my slimy but agile mind can
provide a *plan* to pull off this assignment. Of course, the
execution of said plan will rely upon abilities and goodwill of my worthy colleagues. Is that better, Chumly?"

"Quite," the troll nodded.

"Now that that's settled," Gus interrupted impatiently,
"can we get on with it? This *is* my place of business, you
know, and the longer I keep the place closed, the more
money I lose."

For those of you who missed the earlier references,
Gus is a gargoyle. He is also the owner/proprietor of the
Yellow Crescent Inn, the Bazaar's leading fast-food establishment and our current field headquarters. Like
Chumly and Tananda, he's helped me out of a couple
scrapes in the past and, as soon as he heard about our
current crisis, volunteered again. Like anyone who earns
their living at the Bazaar, however, he habitually keeps
one eye on the cash register. Even though he had closed
his doors to give us a base of operations for the upcoming
campaign, there was still a reflexive bristling over missed
profits.

An idea struck me.

"Relax, Gus," I ordered. "Come up with a daily figure
for your normal trade, bump it for a decent profit, and
we'll reimburse you when this thing's over."

"What!" my mentor screeched, losing momentary control. "Are you out of your mind, kid? Who do you think
is paying for this, anyway?"

"The merchants of Deva," I answered calmly. "We're
on an expense account, remember? I think renting a place
while we're on assignment isn't an unreasonable expense,
do you?"

"Oh. Right. Sorry, Gus. Old reflexes."

Aahz's confusion was momentary. Then his eyes narrowed thoughtfully.

"In fact, if we put all of you on retainer, your help will fall under the heading of 'consultant fees' and never come near our own profits. I like it."

"Before you get too carried away," Tananda put in quickly, "I think big brother and I would rather work for a piece of the action than on a flat fee."

"But, honey," Massha blinked, "you haven't even heard his plan yet. What makes you think a percentage will net you more than a fee? . . . just between us girls?"

"Just between us girls," Tananda winked, "you've never worked with Aahz before. I have, and while he may not be the pleasantest being to team with, I have unshakeable faith in his profit margins."

"Now that we're on the subject," Aahz said, staring hard at Massha, "we never *have* worked together before, so let's get the rules straight early on. I've got my own style, see, and it usually doe'sn't allow much time for 'please' and 'thank you' and explanations. As long as you do what you're told, when you're told, we'll get along fine. Right?"

"Wrong!"

My reply popped out before Massha could form her own response. I was vaguely aware that the room had gotten very quiet, but most of my attention was on Aahz as he slowly cranked his head around to lock gazes with me.

"Now look, kid. . . ." he began dangerously.

"No, *you* look, Aahz," I exploded. "I may be your apprentice, but Massha is *mine*. Now if she wants to dump that agreement and sign on with you, fine and dandy. But until she does, she's *my* student and *my* responsibility. If you think she can help, then you suggest it to me and *I* decide whether she's up to it. There's one lesson you've drummed into my head over and over, mentor mine, whether you meant to or not. Nobody leans on your apprentice but you . . . nobody! If you didn't want to teach that lesson, then maybe you'd better be more careful with the example you set the next time you take on an apprentice."

"I see," Aahz murmured softly. "Getting pretty big for your britches, aren't you, kid?"

"Not really. I'm very much aware of how little I know, thank you. But this is my assignment, or at least it was accepted in my name, and I mean to give it my best shot . . . however inadequate that might be. Now for that assignment, I need your help, Aahz . . . heck, I'll always probably need your help. You're my teacher and I've got a lot to learn. But, I'm not going to roll over and die without it. If getting your help means turning my assignment and my apprentice over to you, then forget it. I'll just have to try to handle things without you."

"You'll get your brains beat out."

"Maybe. I didn't say I'd win, just that I'd try my best. *You* bring out my best, Aahz. You push me into things that scare me, but so far I've muddled through somehow. I *need* your help, but I don't *have* to have it. Even if you don't want to admit it to me, I think you should admit it to yourself."

With that, we both lapsed into silence.

Me, I couldn't think of anything else to say. Up until now, I had been carried along by my anger and Aahz's responses. All of a sudden, my mentor wasn't responding. Instead, he stared at me with expressionless yellow eyes, not saying a thing.

It was more than a little unnerving. If there is one characteristic of Aahz's I could always count on, it was that he was expressive. Whether with facial expression, gestures, grunts, or verbal explosions, my mentor usually let everyone in the near vicinity know what he felt or thought about any event or opinion expressed. Right now, though, I didn't know if he was about to explode or just walk away.

I began having regrets over instigating this confrontation. Then I toughened up. What I had said was right and needed to be said. It flashed across my mind that I could lose Aahz over this argument. My resolve wavered. Right or not, I could have said it better . . . gentler. At least I

could have picked a time when all our friends weren't
watching and listening. Maybe . . .

Aahz turned away abruptly, shifting his stance to face
Tananda and Chumly.

"*Now* I'm ready to believe you two," he announced.
"The kid here really *did* handle that mess on Klah all by
himself, didn't he?"

"That's what we've been trying to tell you, old boy."
The troll winked. "Your apprentice is growing up, and
seems to us more than capable of standing on his own
two feet lately."

"Yeah, I noticed."

He looked at me again, and this time his eyes were
expressive. I didn't recognize the expression, but at least
there was one.

"Kid . . . Skeeve," he said. "If I've ever wondered why
I bothered taking you under my wing, you just gave me
the answer. Thanks."

"Um . . . Thanks. I mean, you're welcome. No. I
mean . . ."

As always, I was very glib in the face of the unexpected. I had gotten used to weathering Aahz's tirades,
but *this* I didn't know how to handle. Fortunately my pet
came to my rescue.

"Gleep?" he queried, shaking his head in through the
door.

". . . But if you take anything I've showed you, I mean
spell one, and teach it to that dragon," my mentor roared,
"you and I are going to go a couple rounds. Do we understand each other, apprentice?"

"Yes, Aahz."

Actually, I didn't. Still, this didn't seem like the time
to call for a clarification.

"Butt out, Gleep," I ordered. "Go play with Buttercup
or something."

"Gleep!" and my dragon's head was gone as fast as it
had appeared.

"Say, hot stuff," Massha drawled. "As much as I appreciate your standing up for me, I'm kinda curious to
hear what Big Green has for a plan."

"Right!" I nodded, glad to be off the hot seat. "Sorry, Aahz, I didn't mean to interrupt. What's the plan?"

"Well, first," Aahz said, taking his accustomed place as center of attention once more, "I've got a question for Gus. What's the Mob been doing so far to move in?"

"Judging from what I heard," the gargoyle responded, "a bunch of them move in on a merchant and offer to sell him some 'insurance.' You know, 'pay us so much of your revenue and nothing happens to your business.' If anyone's slow to sign up, they arrange a small demonstration of what could go wrong: some 'accidental' breaking of stock or a couple plug-uglies standing outside hassling customers. So far it's been effective. Deveels don't like to lose business."

"Good." My mentor grinned, showing every last one of his numerous pointed teeth. "Then we can beat them."

"How?"

If nothing else, I've gotten quite good at feeding Aahz straight lines.

"Easy. Just ask yourselves this: If you were a Deveel and paid the Mob to protect your business, and things started going wrong anyway, what would you do?"

"I can answer that one," Massha said. "I'd either demand better protection, scream for my money back, or both."

"I don't get it." I frowned. "What's going to happen to a Mob-protected business?"

"We are." Aahz grinned.

"What our strategist is trying to say," Chumly supplied, "is that the best defense is a good offense. Not terribly original, but effective nonetheless."

"You're darn right it's effective," my mentor exclaimed. "Instead of us defending against the Mob, we're going to start a crime wave right here at the Bazaar. Then let's see how good the Mob is at defending against us!"

XVI:

"It's always easier to destroy than to create."

— ANY GENERAL, ANY ARMY, ANY
AGE

"Hey, Guido! How's it going?"

The big bodyguard spun around, scanning the crowd to see who had hailed him by name. When he saw me, his face brightened.

"Mister Skeeve!"

"Never expected to run into you here!" I lied.

From Gus's description, I had known that both Guido and his cousin Nunzio were part of the Mob's contingent at the Bazaar. This "chance meeting" was the result of nearly half a day's worth of searching and following rumors.

"What are you doing here?" he asked confidentially. "Shopping for a few little items to wow 'em with back at Possiltum?"

"Just taking a bit of a vacation. That new Queen and I don't get along so well. I thought things might ease up if I disappeared for a while."

"Too bad. If you was shoppin', I could line you up with some 'special deals,' if you know what I mean."

"You guys are really moving in, then?" I marveled. "How is it going? Any problems?"

"Naw," the bodyguard bragged, puffing out his chest. "You was right. These Deveels are like shopkeepers anywhere. Lean on 'em a little and they fall in line."

"Don't tell me you're handling this all by yourself! I mean I know you're good, but . . ."

"Are you kiddin'? I'm an executive now . . . well, at least a team leader. Both Nunzio and me have a dozen men to order around, courtesy of our 'extensive knowledge of the Bazaar.' Pretty good, huh?"

"You mean you're running the whole operation?"

"That's Shai-ster's job. Me and Nunzio report to him, but it's us gives the orders to the boys."

I looked around expectantly.

"Is your team around? I'd like to meet them."

"Naw. We worked this area a couple days ago. I'm on my way to meet 'em and give out today's assignments. We're going after the area by the livestock pens today."

"How about Nunzio's team?"

"They're about three hours west of here. You know, this is a really big place!"

I put on my most disappointed face.

"Too bad, I would have liked to have met some of the ones who do the *real* work."

"Tell ya' what," Guido exclaimed, "why don't you drop by Fat's Spaghetti Parlor sometime? That's where we're all hanging out. If we're not there, they can tell you where we are."

"I'll do that. Well, don't work too hard . . . and be careful. These guys can be meaner than they look."

"Piece of cake." He laughed as he headed off.

I was still waving merrily at his retreating figure as the rest of my "gang" faded out of the crowd around me.

"Did you get all that?" I asked out of the corner of my mouth.

"Two teams, neither one in this area. Shai-ster's running the show and therefore holding the bag," Tananda recited. "This area is both clear and under protection."

"Fat's Spaghetti Parlor is their headquarters, which is

where we can find Shai-ster," Chumly completed. "Anything else?"

"Yeah." Aahz grinned. "Skeeve has a standing invite to drop by, and when he does, they're ready to tell him which team is working what area that day. Nice work."

"Lucky," I admitted with no embarrassment. "Well, shall we start?"

"Right." Aahz nodded. "Just like we planned, Tananda and Chumly are a team. Gus, you're with me. Skeeve and Massha, you start here. We all move out in different directions and space our hits so there's no pattern. Okay?"

"One more thing," I added. "Keep an eye on your disguises. I'm not sure of the exact range I can hold that spell at. If your disguise starts to fade, change direction to parallel mine."

"We meet back at the Yellow Crescent Inn," Gus finished. "And all of you watch your backs. I don't stock that much first aid gear."

"Good thought," I said. "Okay. Enough talk. Let's scatter and start giving the Mob a headache."

The other two teams had melted into the crowd of shoppers before I had even turned to Massha.

"Well, anything catch your eye for us to have a go at?"

"You know, you're starting to sound a bit like that troll."

That sounded a bit more abrupt than was Massha's normal style. I studied her curiously.

"Something bothering you?"

"Just a little nervous, I guess," she admitted. "Has it occurred to you all this plan has a major flaw? That to implement it potentially means getting the entire Bazaar after us, as well as the Mob?"

"Yes, it has."

"Doesn't it scare you?"

"Yes, it does."

"Well, how do you handle it?"

"By thinking about it as little as possible," I said flatly. "Look, apprentice, aside from doing shtick in court for the amusement of the masses, this profession of ours is pretty dangerous. If we start dwelling on everything that can go wrong in the future, we'll either never move or blunder headlong into the present because our minds aren't on what we're doing right *now*. I try to be aware of the potential danger of a situation, but I don't worry about trouble until it happens. It's a little shaky, but it's worked so far."

"If you say so," she sighed. "Oh, well, gear me up and let's get started."

With a pass of my mind, I altered her features. Instead of being a massive woman, she was now a massive man . . . sort of. I had been experimenting with color lately, so I made her purple with reddish sideburns that ran all the way down her arms to her knuckles. Add some claw-like horns at the points of the ears and rough-textured, leathery skin on the face and hands, and you had a being *I* wouldn't want to mess with.

"Interesting." Massha grimaced, surveying what she could see of herself. "Did you make this up yourself, or is there a nasty dimension I haven't visited yet?"

"My own creation," I admitted. "The reputation you're going to build I wouldn't wish on any dimension I know of. Call it a Hoozit from the dimension Hoo."

"Who?"

"You've got it."

She rolled her eyes in exasperation.

"Hot stuff, do me a favor and only teach me magik, okay? Keep your sense of humor for yourself. I've already got enough enemies."

"We still need a target," I said, slightly hurt.

"How about that one? It looks breakable."

I looked where she was pointing and nodded.

"Good enough. Give me a twenty count head start. If they're not protected, I'll be back out. If you don't see me in twenty, they're fair game. Do your worst."

"You know," she smiled rubbing her hands together, "this could be fun."

"Just remember that *I'm* in there before you decide exactly what today's 'worst' is."

The display she had chosen was a small, three-sided tent with a striped top. It was lined with shelves that were crowded with an array of stoppered bottles of all sizes and colors. As I entered, I noticed there was something in each of the bottles—smoky things that shifted as if they were alive.

"May I help you, sahr?" the Deveel proprietor asked, baring what he doubtless thought was a winning smile.

"Just browsing." I yawned. "Actually, I'm seeking refuge from gossip. All anyone can talk about is this pack of ruffians that's selling insurance."

The Deveel's face darkened and he spat out the door.

"Insurance! Extortion I call it. They ruined two of my treasures before I could stop them long enough to subscribe to their services. It was a dark day when they first appeared at the Bazaar."

"Yes, yes. Believe me, I've heard it before."

Having established that this shop was indeed under the protection of the Mob, I turned my attention to the displays.

With studied nonchalance, I plucked up a small bottle, no more than a hand's-width high, and peered at the contents. Murky movement and a vague sparkle met my gaze.

"Be careful," the proprietor cautioned. "Once a Djin is released, it can only be controlled if you address it by name."

"A Djin?"

The Deveel swept me with a speculative gaze. Since I wasn't doing the heavy work, I wasn't in disguise and looked like . . . well, me.

"I believe in Klah, they're referred to as Genies."

"Oh. You have quite a collection here."

The Deveel preened at the praise.

"Do not be fooled by the extent of my poor shop's selection, young sahr. They are extremely rare. I personally combed the far reaches of every dimension . . . at great personal expense, I might add . . . to find these few specimens worthy of . . ."

I had been wondering when Massha was going to make her entrance. Well, she made it. Hoo-boy, did she make it. Right through the side of the tent.

With an almost musical chorus, the stand along the

wall went over, dumping the bottles onto the floor. The released Djin rose in a cloud and poured out the open tent side, shrieking with inhuman joy as they went.

The Deveel was understandably upset.

"You idiot!" he shrieked. "What are you doing?"

"Pretty weak shelves," Massha muttered in a gravelly bass voice.

"Weak shelves?"

"Sure. I mean, all I did was this . . ."

She shoved one of the remaining two shelves, which toppled obligingly into the last display.

This time the Djin didn't even bother using the door. They streaked skyward, taking the top of the tent with them as they screamed their way to freedom.

"My stock! My tent! Who's going to pay for this?"

"That's Hoozit," Massha retorted, "and I'm certainly not going to pay. I don't have any money."

"No money?" The proprietor gasped.

"No. I just came in here to get out of the rain."

"Rain? Rain? But it isn't raining!"

"It isn't?" My apprentice blinked. "Then, goodbye."

With that she ambled off, making a hole in yet another tent side as she went.

The Deveel sank down in the shattered remains of his display and cradled his face in his hands.

"I'm ruined!" he moaned. "Ruined!"

"Excuse me for asking," I said. "But why didn't you call out their names and get them under control?"

"Call out their names? I can't remember the name of every Djin I collect. I have to look them up each time I sell one."

"Well, at least that problem's behind you."

That started him off again.

"Ruined!" he repeated needlessly. "What am I going to do?"

"I really don't know why you're so upset," I observed. "Weren't you just saying that you were insured?"

"Insured?"

The Deveel's head came up slowly.

"Certainly. You're paying to be sure things like this

don't happen, aren't you? Well, it happened. It seems to me whoever's protecting your shop owes you an explanation, not to mention quite a bit of money."

"That's right!" The proprietor was smiling now. "More the latter than the former, but you're right!"

I had him going on now. All that was left to be done was the *coup de grace*.

"Tell you what. Just so your day won't be a total washout, I'll take this one. Now you won't have to stay open with just one Djin in stock."

I flipped him the smallest coin in my pouch. True to his heritage, he was sneering even as he plucked it out of the air.

"You can't be serious," he said. "This? For a Djin? That doesn't even cover the cost of the bottle!"

"Oh come, come, my good man," I argued. "We're both men of the world . . . or dimensions. We both know that's clear profit."

"It is?" he frowned.

"Of course," I said, gesturing at the broken glass on the floor. "No one can tell how many bottles were just broken. I know you'll just include this one on the list of lost stock and collect in full from your insurance in *addition* to what I just gave you. In fact, you could probably add five or six to the total if you were really feeling greedy."

"That's true," the Deveel murmured thoughtfully. "Hey, thanks! This might not turn out so bad after all."

"Don't mention it." I shrugged, studying the small bottle in my hand. "Now that we're in agreement on the price, though, could you look up the name of my Djin?"

"I don't have to. That one's new enough that I can remember. It's name is Kalvin."

"Kalvin?"

"Hey, don't laugh. It's the latest thing in Djins."

XVII:

"The best laid plans often go fowl."

— WILE E. COYOTE

"**W**ell, except for that, how are things going?"

"Except for that?" Shai-ster echoed incredulously. "Except for that? Except for that things are going rotten. This whole project is a disaster."

"Gee, that's tough," I said, with studied tones of sympathy.

I had gotten to be almost a permanent fixture here at Fat's Spaghetti Palace. Every night I dropped by to check the troops' progress . . . theirs and mine.

It was nice to be able to track the effectiveness of your activities by listening to the enemy gripe about them. It was even nicer to be able to plan your next move by listening to counter-attacks in the discussion stage.

"I still don't get it," Guido protested, gulping down another enormous forkful of spaghetti. "Everything was goin' terrific at first. No trouble at all. Then BOOM, it hits the fan, know what I mean?"

"Yeah! It was like someone was deliberately workin' to put us out of business."

That last was from cousin Nunzio. For the longest time

I thought he was physically unable to talk. Once he got used to having me around, though, he opened up a little. In actuality, Nunzio was shy, a fact which was magnified by his squeaky little voice which seemed out of place coming from a muscleman.

"I warned you that Deveels can be a nasty lot," I said, eager to get the subject away from the possibility of organized resistance. "And if the shopkeepers are sneaky, it only stands to reason that the local criminal element would have to have a lot on the ball. Right, Guido?"

"That's right." The goon nodded vigorously, strands of spaghetti dangling from his mouth. "We criminal types can beat any honest citizen at anything. Say, did I ever tell you about the time Nunzio and me were . . ."

"Shut up, dummy!" Shai-ster snapped. "In case you haven't noticed, *we're* footing the bill for these local amateurs. We're getting our brains beat out financially, and it's up to you boys to catch up with the opposition and return the favor . . . physically."

"They're scared of us," Guido insisted. "Wherever we are, they aren't. If we can't find 'em, they can't be doin' *that* much damage."

"You know, brains never were your long suit, Guido," Shai-ster snarled. "Let me run this past you once real slow. So far, we've paid out six times as much as we've taken in. Add all our paychecks and expenses to that, and you might have a glimmer as to why the Big Boys are unhappy."

"But we haven't been collecting very long. After we've expanded our clientele . . ."

"We'll be paying claims on that many more businesses," Shai-ster finished grimly. "Don't give me that 'we'll make it up on volume' guff. Either an operation is self-supporting *and* turning a profit from the beginning, or it's in trouble. And we're in trouble so deep, even if we could breathe through the tops of our heads we'd *still* be in trouble."

"Maybe if we got some more boys from back home. . . ." Nunzio began.

Shai-ster slapped his hand down on the table, stopping his lieutenant short.

"No more overhead!" he shouted. "I'm having enough trouble explaining our profit/loss statement to the Big Boys without the bottom line getting any worse. Not only are we not going to get any more help, we're going to start trimming our expenses, and I mean *right* now. Tell the boys to . . . what are *you* grinning at?"

This last was directed at me.

"Oh, nothing," I said innocently. "It's just that for a minute there you sounded just like someone I know back on Klah . . . name of Grimble."

"J. R. Grimble?" Shai-ster blinked.

Now it was my turn to be surprised.

"Why, yes. He's the Chancellor of the Exchequer back at Possiltum. Why, do you know him?"

"Sure. We went to school together. Chancellor of the Exchequer, huh? Not bad. If I had known he was working the court of Possiltum, I would have stuck around and said 'hi' when I was there."

Somehow, the thought of Shai-ster and Grimble knowing each other made me uneasy. There wasn't much chance of the two of them getting together and comparing notes, and even if they did, Grimble didn't know all that much about my *modus operandi*. Still, it served as a grim reminder that this was a very risky game I was playing, with some very dangerous people.

"I still think there's another gang out there somewhere," Nunzio growled. "There's too much going down for it to be independent operators."

"You're half right," Shai-ster corrected. "There's too much going down for it to be a gang. Nobody's into that many things . . . not even us!"

"You lost me there, Shai-ster," I said, genuinely curious.

The mobster favored me with a patronizing smile.

"That's right. As a magician, you don't know that much about how organized crime works. Let me try to explain. When the Mob decides to move in, we hit one specialty field at a time . . . you know, like protection or the numbers. Like that. Focusing our efforts yields a better saturation as well as market penetration."

"That makes sense," I nodded, not wanting to admit he had lost me again.

"Now you take a look at what's happening here. We're getting all sorts of claims: vandalism, shoplifting, armed robbery, even a couple cases of arson. It's too much of a mix to be the work of one group. We're dealing with a lot of small-time independents, and if we can make an example of a few of them, the others will decide there are easier pickings elsewhere."

In a way, I was glad to hear this. I owed Aahz one more back-pat. He was the one who had decided that the efforts of our team were too limited. To accelerate our "crime wave," he had introduced the dubious practice of "insurance fraud" to Deva . . . and the Deveels were fast learners.

Is your stock moving too slow? Break it yourself and turn in a claim for vandalism. Trying to sell your shop, but nobody wants to buy, even at a discount? Torch the place and collect in full. Better still, want to fatten up your profit margin a little? Dummy up a few invoices and file a claim for "stolen goods." All profit, no cost.

The Deveels loved it. It let them make money and harass the Mob at the same time. No wonder Shai-ster's table was fast disappearing under a mountain of claims and protests.

It was terrific . . . except for the part about making an example out of everyone they caught. I made a mental note to warn the team about being extra careful.

"If it's not a gang, and they aren't working against us," Nunzio scowled, "why is everything happening in *our* areas? My dad taught me to be suspicious of coincidences. He got killed by one."

"How do you know it's just happening in our area?" Shai-ster countered. "Maybe we picked a bad area of the Bazaar to start our operation. Maybe the whole Bazaar is a bad area. Maybe we should have been suspicious when Skeeve here told us there were no police. You get this much money floating around with no police, of course there'll be crooks around."

"So what are we supposed to do?" Guido snarled, plucking his napkin from under his chin and throwing it on the table. "My boys can't be two places at once. We can't watch over our current clients and sign on new accounts, too."

"That's right," Shai-ster agreed, "so here's what we're going to do. First, we split up the teams. Two-thirds of the boys patrol the areas we've got under protection. The others go after new clients . . . *but* we don't just take anybody. We investigate and ask questions. We find out how much trouble a new area or a new shop has had *before* we take them as a client. Then we know who the bad risks are, and if we protect them at all, they pay double. *Capish?*"

Both Guido and Nunzio were thinking, and it was obvious the process hurt.

"I dunno," Nunzio squeaked at last. "Sumpin' sounds kinda funny about that plan."

"Crime wouldn't pay if the government ran it," I murmured helpfully.

"What's that?" Shai-ster snapped.

"Oh, just something my teacher told me once." I shrugged.

"Hey! Skeeve's right," Guido exclaimed.

"What you're sayin' is that we're going to be policemen and insurance investigators."

"Well, I wouldn't use those words. . . ."

" 'Well' nothin'. We ain't gonna do it!"

"Why not?"

"C'mon, Shai-ster. We're the bad guys. You know, crooks. What's it going to do to our reputation if it gets back to the Mob that we've turned into policemen?"

"They'll think we're valuable employees who are working hard to protect their investment."

"Yeah?" Guido frowned, unconvinced.

"Besides, it's only temporary," Shai-ster soothed. "Not only that, it's a smoke screen for what we'll *really* be doing."

"What's that?" I asked blandly.

Shai-ster shot a quick look around the restaurant, then leaned forward, lowering his voice.

"Well, I wasn't going to say anything, but remember that I was telling you about how the Mob focuses on one field at a time? The way I see it, maybe we picked the wrong field here at Deva. Maybe we shouldn't have tried the protection racket."

"So you're going to change fields?" I urged.

"Right." Shai-ster smiled. "We'll put the protection racket on slow-down mode for a while, and in the meantime start leaning on the bookies."

"Now you're talking," Guido crowed. "There's always good money to be made at gambling."

"Keep your voice down, you idiot. It's supposed to be a secret."

"So who's to hear?" Guido protested.

"How about them?"

Shai-ster jerked his thumb toward a table of four enormous beings, alternately stuffing their faces and laughing uproariously.

"Them? That's the Hutt brothers. They're in here about once a week. They're too busy with their own games to bother us."

"Games? Are they gamblers?"

"Naw ... well, except maybe Darwin. He's the leader of the pack. But he only gambles on businesses."

"Which one is he?"

"The thinnest one. I hear his fiancée has him on a diet. It's making him mean, but not dangerous to us."

Shai-ster turned back to our table.

"Well, keep your voice down anyway. How about it, Skeeve? The gambling, I mean. You've been here at the Bazaar before. Do you know any bookies we can get hold of?"

"Gee, the only one I know of for sure is the Geek," I said. "He's a pretty high-roller. If you boys are going to try to pull a fast one on him, though, don't tell him I was the one who singled him out."

Shai-ster gave me a broad wink.

"Gotcha. But anything we get from him, you're in for a percentage. You know, a finder's fee. We don't forget our friends."

"Gee, thanks," I managed, feeling more than a little guilty. "Well, I'd better be going. C'mon, Gleep."

"Gleep!" echoed my dragon, pulling his head up out of a tub of spaghetti at the sound of his name.

Fats had taken an instant liking to my pet, founded I suspect on Gleep's newfound capacity for the maggot-like stuff barely hidden by blood-red sauce that was the parlor's mainstay.

I had never been able to screw up my courage enough to try spaghetti, but my dragon loved it. Knowing some of the dubious things, edible and in, living and non, that also met with Gleep's culinary approval, this did little toward encouraging me to expand my dietary horizons to include this particular dish. Still, as long as I had Gleep along, we were welcome at Fats, even though my pet was starting to develop a waddle reminiscent of the parlor's proprietor.

"Say, Skeeve. Where do you keep your dragon during the day?"

I glanced over to find Shai-ster studying my pet through narrowed, thoughtful eyes.

"Usually he's with me, but sometimes I leave him with a dragon-sitter. Why?"

"I just remembered an 'interruption of business' claim we had to pay the other day . . . had to pay! Heck, we're still paying it. Anyway, this guy sells dragons, see, except for over a week now he hasn't sold a one. Usually sells about three a day and says since he paid us to be sure nothing happens to his business, we should make up the difference in his sales drop . . . and, you know, those things are *expensive!*"

"I know," I agreed, "but what does that have to do with Gleep?"

"Probably nothing. It's just that this guy swears that just before everything went to pot, some little dragon came by and talked to his dragons. Now they won't roar or blow fire or nothing. All they do is sleep and frolic . . .

and who wants to buy a dragon that frolics, you know?"

"Talked to his dragons?" I asked uneasily.

For some reason, I had a sudden mental image of Gleep confronting Big Julie's dragon, a beast that dwarfed him in size, and winning.

"Well . . . they didn't exactly talk, but they did huddle up and put their heads together and made mumbly puffy noises at each other. Wouldn't let this guy near 'em until it was over. The only thing he's sure of is the little one, the one he says messed up his business, said something like 'Peep!' Said it a couple of times."

"Peep?" I said.

"Gleep!" answered my dragon.

Shai-ster stared at him again.

"C'mon, Shai-ster," Guido said, giving his superior a hearty shove. "Talking dragons? Somebody's pullin' your leg. Sounds to me like he got a bad shipment of dragons and is trying to get us to pay for them. Tell him to take a hike."

"It's not that easy," Shai-ster grumbled, "but I suppose you're right. I mean, all dragons look pretty much alike."

"True enough," I called, heading hastily for the nearest exit. "C'mon, Peep . . . I mean, Gleep!"

Maybe Shai-ster's suspicions had been lulled, but I still had a few of my own as we made our way back to the Yellow Crescent Inn.

"Level with me, Gleep. Did you do anything to louse up somebody's dragon business?"

"Gleep?" answered my pet in a tone exactly like my own when I'm trying too hard to sound innocent.

"Uh-huh. Well, stay out of this one. I think we've got it in hand without you getting in the line of fire."

"Gleep."

The answer was much more subdued this time, and I realized he was drooping noticeably.

"Now don't sulk. I just don't want anything to happen to you. That's all."

I was suddenly aware that passers-by were staring at

us. As strange as the Bazaar was, I guess they weren't used to seeing someone walking down the street arguing with a dragon.

"Let's hurry," I urged, breaking into a trot. "I don't know what we can do about the Mob moving in on the bookies, but I'm sure Aahz will think of something."

XVIII:

"Life can be profitable, if you know the odds."

—RIPLEY

The sports arena we were in was noticeably smaller than the stadium on Jahk where we had played in the Big Game, but no less noisy. Perhaps the fact that it was indoors instead of being open-air did something to the acoustics, but even at half-full the crowd in the arena made such a din I could barely hear myself think.

Then again, there was the smell. The same walls and ceiling that botched up the acoustics did nothing at all for ventilation. Even a few thousand beings from assorted dimensions in these close quarters produced a blend of body odors that had my stomach doing slow rolls . . . or maybe it was just my nerves.

"Could you explain to me again about odds?"

"Not now," the Geek snarled, nervously playing with his program. "I'm too busy worrying."

"I'll give it a try, hot stuff," Massha volunteered from my other side. "Maybe I can say it in less technical jargon than our friend here."

"I'd appreciate it," I admitted.

That got me a black look from the Geek, but Massha was already into it.

"First, you've got to understand that for the most part, bookies aren't betting their own money. They're acting as agents or go-betweens for people who are betting different sides of the same contest. Ideally, the money bet on each side evens out, so the bookie himself doesn't have any of his own money riding on the contest."

"Then how do they make their money?"

"Sometimes off a percentage, sometimes . . . but that's another story. What we're talking about is odds. Okay?"

"I guess so." I shrugged.

"Now, the situation I described is the ideal. It assumes the teams or fighters or whatever are evenly matched. That way, some people bet one side, some the other, but overall it evens out. That's even odds or 1-1."

She shifted her weight a bit, ignoring the glares from our fellow patrons when the entire row of seats wobbled in response.

"But suppose things were different. What if, instead of an even match, one side had an advantage . . . like say if Badaxe were going to fight King Rodrick?"

"That's easy." I smiled. "Nobody would bet on the King."

"Precisely." Massha nodded. "Then everybody would bet one side, and the bookies would have to cover all the bets with their own money . . . bets they stood a good chance of losing."

"So they don't take any bets."

"No. They rig things so that people will bet on the King."

I cocked an eyebrow at her.

"They could try, but I sure wouldn't throw my gold away like that. I'd back Badaxe."

"Really?" Massha smiled. "What if, instead of betting one gold piece to win one gold piece, you had to bet ten gold pieces on Badaxe to win one back?"

"Well . . ."

"Let me make it a little harder. How about if you bet one gold piece on the King, and he won, that instead of getting one gold piece back, you got a hundred?"

"I . . . um . . . might take a long shot on the King," I said, hesitantly. "There's always a chance he could get lucky. Besides, if I lose, I'm only out one gold piece."

". . . And *that's* how bookies use odds to cover themselves. Now, how they figure out how many bets they need on the King at 'x' odds to cover the bets they have on Badaxe at 'y' odds is beyond me."

I looked at the Deveel next to me with new respect.

"Gee, Geek. I never really realized how complicated your work is."

The Deveel softened a bit. They're as susceptible to flattery as anyone else.

"Actually, it's even more complicated than that," he admitted modestly. "You've got to keep track of several contests at once, sometimes even use the long bets from one to cover the short bets on another. Then there are side bets, like who will score how often in which period in the Big Game. It isn't easy, but a sharp being can make a living at it."

"So what are the odds tonight?"

The Deveel grimaced.

"Lousy. It's one of those Badaxe and the King matchups, if I was following your example right. In this case, the team you'll see in red trunks are Badaxe. They're hotter than a ten dollar laser and have won their last fifteen bouts. The weak sisters . . . the King to you . . . will be in white trunks and haven't won a bout in two years. When the Mob put their bet down, the odds were running about two hundred to one against the whites."

I whistled softly.

"Wow. Two hundred in gold return on a one-gold-piece bet. Did you remember to act surprised when they put their money down?"

"I didn't have to act," the Geek said through tight lips. "Not with the size bet they came up with. Being forewarned, I had expected they wouldn't be going small, but still . . ."

He shook his head and lapsed into silence.

I hadn't really paused to consider the implication of

the odds, but I did now. If betting one piece could get you two hundred back, then a bet of a thousand would have a potential payback of two hundred thousand! And a ten thousand bet . . .

"How big was their bet?" I asked fearfully.

"Big enough that if I lose, I'll be working for the Mob for the rest of my life to pay it off . . . and Deveels don't have short life-spans."

"Wait a minute. Didn't Aahz tell you that if you lost, we'd cover it out of our expense money?"

"He did," the Deveel said. "And he also pointed out that if you were covering my losses, you'd also take all winnings if things went as planned. I opted to take the risk, and the winnings, myself."

Massha leaned forward to stare.

"Are you that confident, or that greedy?"

"More the latter," the Geek admitted. "Then again, I got burnt rather badly betting against Skeeve here in the Big Game. I figure it's worth at least one pass backing the shooter who's working a streak."

I shook my head in puzzlement.

"Aren't you afraid of losing?"

"Well, it did occur to me that it might be me and not the Mob who's being set up here. That's why I'm sitting next to you. If this turns out to be a double cross . . ."

"You're pretty small to be making threats, Geek," Massha warned.

". . . And you're too big to dodge fast if I decide I'm being had," the Deveel shot back.

"Knock it off, both of you," I ordered. "It's academic anyway. There won't be any problems . . . or if there are, I'll be as surprised as you are, Geek."

"More surprised, I hope," the Deveel sneered. "I'm half expecting this to blow up, remember?"

"But Aahz has assured me that the fix is in."

"Obviously. Otherwise, the Mob wouldn't be betting so heavily. The question is, which fix is going to work, theirs or yours?"

Just then a flurry of activity across the arena caught my eye. The Mob had just arrived . . . in force. Shai-ster

was there, flanked by Guido and Nunzio and backed by
the remaining members of the two teams currently as-
signed to the Bazaar. Seen together and moving, as op-
posed to individually feeding their faces at Fats', they
made an impressive group. Apparently others shared my
opinion. Even though they were late, no one contested
their right to prime seats as they filed into the front row.
In fact, there was a noticeable bailing out from the desired
seats as they approached.

It was still a new enough experience for me to see other
beings I knew in a crowd at the Bazaar that I stood up
and waved at them before I realized what I was doing.
Then it dawned on me! If they saw me sitting with the
Geek and then lost a big bet, they might put two and two
together and get five!

I stopped waving and tried to ease back into my seat,
but it was too late. Guido had spotted my gyrations and
nudged Shai-ster to point me out. Our eyes met and he
nodded acknowledgment before returning to scanning the
crowd.

Crestfallen, I turned to apologize to the Geek, only to
find myself addressing a character with a pasty complexion and hairy ears who bore no resemblance at all to the
Deveel who had been sitting beside me.

I almost . . . almost! . . . looked around to see where the
Geek had gone. Then I did a little mental arithmetic and
figured it out.

A disguise spell!

I'd gotten so used to fooling people myself with that
spell that when someone did the same to me, I was completely taken in.

"Still kinda new at this intrigue stuff, aren't you?" he
observed dryly from his new face.

Fortunately I was saved the problem of thinking up a
suitable response by the entrance of the contestants. With
the scramble of planning and launching our counter-
offensive, I hadn't really been briefed on what the Mob
was betting on except that it would be a tagteam wrestling
match. No one said what the contestants would be like,

and I had assumed it would be like the matches I had seen back on Klah. I should have known better.

The two teams were made up of beings who barely stood high enough to reach my waist! I mean they were *small!* They looked like kids . . . if you're used to having kids around with four arms each.

"What are those?" I demanded.

"Those are the teams," the Geek said helpfully.

"I mean, *what* are they? Where are they from?"

"Oh. Those are Tues."

"And you bet on them? I mean, I've heard of midget wrestling, but this is ridiculous!"

"Don't knock it." The Deveel shrugged. "They're big on the wrestling circuit. In fact, teams like this are their dimension's most popular export. Everyone knows them as the Terrible Tues. They're a lot more destructive than you'd guess from their size."

"This is a put-on, right?"

"If you really want to see something, you should catch their other export. It's a traveling dance troupe called the Tue Tours."

Massha dropped a heavy hand on my shoulder.

"Hot stuff, remember our deal about my lessons?"

"Later, Massha. The match is about to start."

Actually, it was about to finish. It was that short, if you'll pardon the expression.

The first member of the favored red trunk team simply strolled out and pinned his white-trunked rival. Though the pin looked a bit like someone trying to wrap a package with tangled string, the red-trunker made it seem awfully easy. All efforts of his opponent's partner to dislodge the victor were in vain, and the bout was over.

"Well, that's that," the Geek said, standing up. "A pleasure doing business with you, Skeeve. Look me up again if you tie on to a live one."

"Aren't you going to collect your bet?"

The Deveel shrugged.

"No rush. Besides, I think your playmates are a little preoccupied just now."

I looked where he was pointing and saw Shai-ster

storming toward the dressing rooms with Guido and Nunzio close behind. None of them looked particularly happy, which was understandable, given the circumstances.

"Whoops. That's my cue. See you back at the Yellow Crescent, Massha."

And with that, I launched myself in an interceptor course with the angry mobsters.

XIX:

*"These blokes need to be taught to re-
spect their superiors."*

—GEN. CORNWALLIS

I almost missed them. Not that I was moving slow, mind
you. It's just that they had a real head of steam on.

"Hi guys!" I called, just as Shai-ster was raising a fist
to hammer on the dressing room door. "Are you going to
congratulate the winners, too?"

Three sets of eyes bored into me as my "friends" spun
around.

"Congratulate!" Guido snarled. "I'll give 'em congratulate."

"Wait a minute," Shai-ster interrupted. "What did you.
mean, 'too'?"

"Well, that's why *I'm* here. I just won a sizable bet on
the last match."

"How sizable?"

"Well, sizable for me," I qualified. "I stand to collect
fifty gold pieces."

"Fifty." Guido snorted. "You know how much we *lost*
on that fiasco?"

"Lost?" I frowned. "Didn't you know the Reds were
favored?"

"Of course we knew," Shai-ster snarled. "That's why we were set to make a killing when they lost."

"But what made you think they were going to . . . Oh! Was that what you were talking about when you said you were going into gambling?"

"That's right. The red team was supposed to take a graceful dive in the third round. We paid them enough . . . more than enough, actually."

He sounded so much like Grimble I couldn't resist taking a cheap shot.

"Judging from the outcome, it sounds to me that you paid them a little less than enough."

"It's not funny. Now, instead of recouping our losses, we've got *another* big loss to explain to the Big Boys."

"Oh come on, Shai-ster." I smiled. "How much can it cost to fix a fight?"

"Not much," he admitted. "But when you figure in the investment money we just lost, it comes to . . ."

"Investment money?"

"He means the bet," Guido supplied.

"Oh. Well, I suppose that's the risk you take when you try to make a killing."

An evil smile flitted across Shai-ster's face.

"Oh, we're going to make a killing, all right," he said. "It's time the locals at this Bazaar learned what it means to cross the Mob."

With that, he nodded at Guido who opened the dressing room door.

All four wrestlers were sharing the same room, and they looked up expectantly as we filed in. That's right. I said we. I kind of tagged along at the end of the procession and no one seemed to object.

"Didn't you clowns forget something out there?" Shai-ster said for his greeting. "Like who was supposed to win?"

The various team members exchanged glances. Then the smallest of the red team shrugged.

"Big deal. So we changed our minds."

"Yeah," his teammate chimed in. "We decided it would

be bad for our image to lose . . . especially to these stumblebums."

That brought the white team to its feet.

"Stumblebums?" one of them bellowed. "You caught us by surprise, that's all. We was told to take it easy until the third round."

"If you took it any easier, you'd be asleep. We were supposed to be wrestling, not dancing."

Shai-ster stepped between them.

"So you all admit you understood your original instructions?"

"Hey, get off our backs, okay? You'll get your stinking money back, so what's your beef, anyway?"

"Even if you gave us a full refund," Shai-ster said softly, "there's still a matter of the money we lost betting on you. I don't suppose any of you are independently wealthy?"

"Oh, sure," one of the reds laughed. "We're just doin' this for kicks."

"I thought not. Guido. Nunzio. See what you can do about squaring accounts with these gentlemen. And take your time. I want them to feel it, you know?"

"I dunno, Shai-ster." Guido scowled. "They're awfully small. I don't think we can make it last too long."

"Well, do your best. Skeeve? Would you join me outside? I don't think you're going to want to see this."

He was closer to being right than he knew. Even though I had been through some rough and tumble times during recent years, that didn't mean I enjoyed it—even to watch.

The door was barely shut behind us when a series of thuds and crashes erupted inside. It was painful just to listen to, but it didn't last long.

"I told them to take their time," Shai-ster said, scowling at the silence. "Oh well, I guess . . ."

The door opened, revealing one of the white team.

"If you've got any more lessons out there, I suggest you send them in. These two didn't teach us much at all."

He shut the door again, but not before we caught a glimpse of the two bodyguards unconscious on the floor.

Well, Guido was on the floor. Nunzio was kind of standing on his head in the corner.

"Tough little guys," I remarked casually. "It must be
the four arms. Think you could find work for them in the
Mob?"

Shai-ster was visibly shaken, but he recovered quickly.

"So they want to play rough. Well, that's fine by me."

"You aren't going in there alone, are you?" I asked,
genuinely concerned.

He favored me with a withering glance.

"Not a chance."

With that, he put his fingers in his mouth and blew a
loud blast. At least, that's what it looked like. I didn't
hear a thing.

Before I could ask what he was doing, though, a thun-
der of footsteps announced the arrival of two dozen Mob
reinforcements.

Neat trick. I guess the whistle had been too high for
me to hear . . . or too low.

"They got Guido and Nunzio," Shai-ster shouted before the heavies had come to a complete halt. "Let's show
'em who's running things around here. Follow me!"

Jerking the door open, he plunged into the dressing
room with the pack at his heels.

I'm not sure if Shai-ster had ever actually been in a
fight before, much less led a team into a fight. I *am*, however, sure he never tried it again.

The screams of pain and anguish that poured out of
that room moved me to take action. I walked a little further down the hall and did my waiting there. It turned out
my caution was needless. The wall didn't collapse, nor
did the ceiling or the building itself. Several hunks of
plaster did come loose, however, and at one point someone poked a hole in the wall . . . with his head.

It occurred to me that if the fight fans in the arena
really wanted to get their money's worth, they should be
down here. Additional thought made me decide it was just
as well they didn't. There were already more than enough
beings crowded into that dressing room . . . which was as
good a reason as any for my staying in the hall.

Eventually the sounds of battle died away, leaving only ominous silence. I reminded myself that I had every confidence in the outcome. As the length of silence grew, I found it necessary to remind myself several times.

Finally the door opened, and the four Tues filed out laughing and chatting together.

"Cute," I called. "Don't hurry or anything. I can worry out here all day."

One of the white team ran up and gave me a hug and a kiss.

"Sorry, handsome. We were having so much fun we forgot about you."

"Um . . . could you do something about the disguises before you kiss me again?"

"Whoops. Sorry about that!"

The taller red team member closed his eyes, and the Tues were gone. In their places stood Aahz, Gus, Tananda, and Chumly. That's why I hadn't been worried . . . much.

"Nice work, Gus," I said, nodding my approval. "But I still think I could have handled the disguises myself."

"Have you ever seen a Tue before?" Aahz challenged.

"Well . . . no."

"Gus has. That's why he handled the disguises. End of discussion."

"Used to have a secretary named Etheyl," the gargoyle explained, ignoring Aahz's order. "She was a big fan of the wrestling circuit."

"A secretary?" I blinked.

"Sure, haven't you ever heard of a Tue Fingered Typist?"

"Enough!" Aahz insisted, holding up his hand. "I vote we head back to the Yellow Crescent Inn for a little celebration. I think we've thwarted the Mob enough for one night."

"Yeah." Tananda grinned. "That'll teach 'em to pick on someone their own size."

"But you are their size." I frowned.

"I know." She winked. "That's the point."

"I say, are you sure, Aahz?" Chumly interjected. "I

mean, we gave them a sound thrashing, but will it hold them until morning?"

"If they're lucky." My mentor grinned. "Remember, once they wake up, they're going to have to report in to their superiors."

"Do you think they'll try to recoup their losses with another stab at gambling?" I asked.

"I hope so," Aahz said, his grin getting broader. "The next big betting event on the docket is the unicorn races, and we've got that covered easily."

"You mean Buttercup? You can't enter him in a race. He's a war-unicorn."

"I know. Think about it."

XX:

*"Figure the last thing you would expect
the enemy to do, then count on him doing precisely that!"*

— RICHELIEU

The Mob did not try another gambit right after their
disastrous attempt to move in on Deva's bookies. In
fact, for some time afterward, things were quiet . . . too
quiet, as Aahz put it.

"I don't like it," he declared, staring out the front window of the Yellow Crescent Inn. "They're up to something. I can feel it."

"Fats says they haven't been around for nearly a
week," I supplied. "Maybe they've given up."

"Not a chance. There's got to be at least one more try,
if for nothing else than to save face. And instead of getting
ready, we're sitting around on our butts."

He was right. For days now, the team's main activity
had been hanging around Gus's place waiting for some
bit of information to turn up. Our scouting missions had
yielded nothing, so we were pretty much reduced to relying on the normal Bazaar gossip network to alert us to
any new Mob activity.

"Be reasonable, Aahz," Chumly protested. "We can't
plan or prepare without any data to work with. You've

said yourself that action in an absence of information is wasted effort, eh what? Makes the troops edgy."

Aahz stalked over to where the troll was sprawled.

"Don't start quoting me at me! You're the one who usually argues with everything I say. If everybody starts agreeing with me, we aren't using all the mental resources we can."

"But you're the one saying that we should be planning," I pointed out.

"Right." My mentor smiled. "So we might as well get started. In absence of hard facts, we'll have to try to second-guess them. Now, where is the Bazaar most vulnerable to Mob takeover? Tananda, have you seen . . . Tananda?"

She abandoned her window-gazing to focus on the discussion.

"What was that, Aahz? Sorry. I was watching that Klahd coming down the street dressed in bright purple."

"Purple?"

Massha and I said it together.

I started to race her for the window, then changed my mind. What if I won? I didn't want to be between the window and her mass when she finally got there. Instead, I waited until she settled into position, then eased in beside her.

"That's him all right," I said out loud, confirming my unvoiced thoughts. "That's Don Bruce. Well, now we know what the Mob's been doing. They've been whistling up the heavy artillery. The question is, what is he doing here at the Bazaar? When we get the answer to that, we'll be able to plan our next move."

"Actually, the question should be what is he doing here at the Yellow Crescent Inn," Gus commented dryly from my elbow. "And I think we're about to get the answer."

Sure enough, Don Bruce was making a beeline for the very building we were watching him from. With his walk, it had taken me a minute to zero in on his direction.

"All right. We know who he is and that he's coming here. Now, let's quit gawking like a bunch of tourists."

Aahz was back in his familiar commander role again.

Still, I noticed he was no quicker to leave the window than any of the rest of us.

"Everybody sit down and act natural. Skeeve, when he gets here, let me do the talking, okay?"

"Not a chance, Aahz," I said, sinking into a chair. "He's used to dealing with me direct. If we try to run in a middleman he'll know something's up. Sit at this table with me, though. I'm going to need your advice on this one."

By the time Don Bruce opened the door, we were all sitting. Aahz and I at one table, and two others accommodating Massha and Gus, and the Chumly-Tananda team respectively. I noticed that we had left two-thirds of the place empty to sit at adjoining tables, which might have looked a little suspicious. I also noticed we had reflexively split up into two-person teams again, but it was too late to correct either situation.

"Hi there," Don Bruce called, spotting me at once. "Thank goodness I found you here. This Bazaar is great fun to wander, but simply *beastly* at finding what or who you're looking for."

"You were looking for me?"

This was not the best news I had heard all day. Despite his affected style of speech, I had a healthy respect for Don Bruce. From what I had seen of the Mob, it was a rough group, and I figured no one could hold down as high a position as Don Bruce did, unless there was some real hard rock under that soft exterior. Friendly greeting or not, I began to feel the fingers of cold fear gripping my stomach.

"That's right. I've *got* to have a meet with you, you know? I *was* hoping I could speak with you in private."

The last thing in the world I wanted right now was to be alone with Don Bruce.

"It's all right," I said expansively. "These are my friends. Any business I have with your . . . organization we're in on together . . . I mean, can be discussed in front of them."

"Oh, very well."

The Mob chieftain flounced onto a chair at my table.

"I didn't mean to be rude, and I *do* want to meet you all. It's just that, first thing, there are some pressing matters to deal with."

"Shoot," I said, then immediately wished I had chosen another word.

"Well, you know we're trying to move in on this place, and you know it hasn't been going well . . . no, don't deny it. It's true. Shai-ster has mentioned you often in his reports, so I know how well informed you are."

"I haven't seen Shai-ster lately, but I do know he's been working hard at the project."

"That's right," Aahz chimed in. "From what Skeeve's been telling us, Shai-ster is a good man. If he can't pull it off, you might as well pack up and go home."

"He's an idiot!" Don Bruce roared, and for a moment we could see the steel inside the velvet glove. "The reason you haven't seen him is that I've pulled him from the project completely. He thought we should give up, too."

"You aren't giving up?" I said, fearfully.

"I can't. Oh, if you only knew what I go through on the Council. I made such a thing out of this Deva project and how much it could do for the Mob. If we pulled out now, it would be the same as saying I don't know a good thing when I see it. No sir. Call it family politics or stubborn pride, we're going to stay right here."

My heart sank.

"But if the operation is losing money—" I began, but he cut me off with a gesture.

"So far . . . but not for long. You see, I've figured out for myself what's going wrong here."

"You have? How? I mean, this is your first visit here since the project started."

I was starting to sweat a bit. Don Bruce was regarding me with an oily reptilian smile I didn't like at all.

"I saw it in the reports," he declared. "Clear as the nose on your face. That's why I know Shai-ster's an idiot. The problem was right here in front of him and he couldn't see it. That problem is you."

My sweat turned cold. At the edge of my vision I saw Tananda run her fingers through her hair, palming one of her poison darts in the process, and Massha was starting to play with her rings. Chumly and Gus exchanged glances, then shifted in their chairs slightly. Of our entire team, only Aahz seemed unconcerned.

"You'll have to be a little clearer for the benefit of us slow folks," he drawled. "Just how do you figure that Skeeve here is a problem?"

"Look at the facts," Don Bruce said, holding up his fingers to tick off the count.

"He's been here the whole time my boys were having trouble; he knows the Bazaar better than my boys; he knows magik enough to do things my boys can't handle; and now I find out he's got a bunch of friends and contacts here."

"So?" my mentor said softly.

"So? Isn't it obvious? The problem with the operation is that he should have been working for us all along."

By now I had recovered enough to have my defense ready.

"But just because I . . . what?"

"Sure. That's why I'm here. Now I know you said before you didn't want to work for the Mob full time. That's why I'm ready to talk a new deal with you. I want you to run the Mob's operation here at the Bazaar . . . and I'm willing to pay top dollar."

"How much is that in gold?"

Aahz was leaning forward now.

"Wait a minute! Whoa! Stop!" I interrupted. "You can't be serious. I don't have the time or the know-how to make this a profitable project."

"It doesn't have to be profitable," Don argued. "Break even would be nice, or even just lose money slower. Anything to get the Council to look elsewhere for things to gripe about at our monthly Meetings. You could do it in your extra time."

I started to say something, but Aahz put a casual hand on my shoulder. I knew that warning. If I tried to interrupt or correct him, that grip would tighten until my bones creaked.

"Now let me see if I've got this right," he said, showing *all* his teeth. "You want my man here to run your operation, but you don't care if it doesn't show a profit?"

"That's right."

"Of course, with things as shaky as they are now, you'd have to guarantee his salary."

Don Bruce pursed his lips and looked at me.

"How much does he cost?"

"Lots," Aahz confided. "But less than the total salary of the force you've got here now."

"Okay. He's worth it."

"Aahz . . ." I began, but the grip on my shoulder tightened.

". . . *And* you aren't so much concerned with the Mob's reputation here on Deva as you are with how the Council treats you, right?"

"Well . . . yeah. I guess so."

". . . So he'd have free rein to run the operation the way he saw fit. No staff forced on him or policies to follow?"

"No. I'd have to at least assign him a couple bodyguards. Anybody running a Mob operation has got to have a couple of the Family's boys to be sure nothing happens to him."

Aahz scowled.

"But he's already got . . ."

"How about Guido and Nunzio?" I managed, through gritted teeth.

Abruptly the grip on my shoulder vanished.

"Those losers?" Don Bruce frowned. "I was going to have a severe talk with them after this disaster, but if you want 'em, they're yours."

". . . But since *you're* the one insisting on them, they don't show up on *our* overhead. Right?" Aahz said firmly.

I leaned back, working my shoulder covertly, and tried to ignore the horrified stares my friends were exchanging. I didn't know for sure what Aahz was up to, but knew better than to get in his way when he smelled money.

I could only cross my fingers and hope that he knew what he was doing . . . for a change.

XXI:

"Stayin' alive! Stayin' alive!"

— V. DRACULA

The representatives of the Bazaar Merchants didn't look happy, but then Deveels never do when they're parting with money.

"Thank you, gentlemen." Aahz beamed, rubbing his hands together gleefully over the substantial pile of gold on the table.

"You're sure the Mob is gone?" the head spokesman asked, looking plaintively at the gold.

"Positive. We've broken their reign of terror and sent them packing."

The Deveel nodded.

"Good. Now that that's settled, we'll be going."

". . . Of course," Aahz yawned, "there's no guarantee they won't be back tomorrow."

That stopped the delegation in their tracks.

"What? But you said . . ."

"Face it, gentlemen. Right now, the only thing between the Mob and the Bazaar is the Great Skeeve here, and once he leaves . . ."

The Deveels exchanged glances.

"I don't suppose you'd consider staying," one said hopefully.

I favored him with a patronizing smile.

"I'd love to, but you know how it is. Expenses are high, and I've got to keep moving to eke out a living."

"But with your reputation, clients will be looking for you. What you really need is a permanent location so you can be found."

"True enough." Aahz smiled. "But to be blunt, why should we give you for free what other dimensions are willing to pay for? I should think that if anybody could understand that, you Deveels would."

"Now we're getting to the heart of the matter." The lead spokesman sighed, pulling up a chair. "Okay. How much?"

"How much?" Aahz echoed.

"Don't give me that," the Deveel snapped. "Innocence looks ridiculous on a Pervert. Just tell us what kind of retainer would be necessary to keep the Great Skeeve around as the Bazaar's magician in residence."

Aahz winked at me.

"I'm sure you'll find his fee reasonable," he said. "Well, reasonable when you stop to think what you're getting for your money. Of course, the figure I'm thinking of is just for making the Bazaar his base of operations. If any specific trouble arises, we'll have to negotiate that separately."

"Of course." The Deveel winced.

I settled back to wait patiently. This was going to take a while, but I was confident of the eventual outcome. I also knew that whatever fee Aahz was thinking of originally just got doubled when the Deveel made that 'Pervert' crack. As a Pervect, Aahz is very sensitive about how he's addressed . . . and this time I wasn't about to argue with him.

"I love it!" Aahz crowed, modestly. "Not only are we getting a steady income from both the Mob and the Deveels, we don't have to do a thing to earn it! This is even better than the setup we had at Possiltum."

"It's a sweet deal, Aahz."

"And how about this layout? It's a far cry from that shack you and Garkin were calling home when we first met."

Aahz and I were examining our new home, provided as an extra clause in our deal with the Bazaar merchants. It was huge, rivaling the size of the Royal Palace at Possiltum. The interesting thing was that from the outside it looked no bigger than an average Bazaar stall.

"Of course, holding out for a lifetime discount on anything at the Bazaar was a stroke of genius, if I do say so myself."

"Yeah, Aahz. Genius."

My mentor broke off his chortling and self-congratulations to regard me quizzically.

"Is something bothering you, Skeeve? You seem a little subdued."

"It's nothing, really."

"Come on. Out with it," he insisted. "You should be on top of the world right now, not moping around like you just heard that your dragon has a terminal illness or something."

"Well, it's a couple of things," I admitted grudgingly. "First, I've got a bad feeling about those deals you just put together."

"Now wait a minute." My mentor scowled. "We talked all this out before we went after the merchants and you said that double-dealing wouldn't bother you."

"It doesn't. If anything, I'm glad to see both the Mob and the Deveels getting a little of their own back for a change."

"Then what's wrong? I got you everything I could think of!"

"That's what's wrong."

My mentor shook his head sharply as if to clear his vision.

"I've got to admit, this time *you* lost *me*. Could you run that one past again, slow?"

"Come on, Aahz. You know what I'm talking about.

You've gotten me more money than I could spend in a lifetime, a beautiful house ... not just anywhere, mind you, but at the Bazaar itself ... steady work anytime I want it ... in short, everything I need to not only survive, but prosper. Everything."

"So?"

"So are you setting me up so you can leave? Is that what this is all about?"

I had secretly hoped that Aahz would laugh in my face and tell me I was being silly. Instead, he averted his eyes and lapsed into silence.

"I've been thinking about it," he said finally. "You're doing pretty well lately and, like you say, this latest deal will insure you won't starve. The truth of the matter is that you really don't need me anymore."

"But, Aahz!"

"Don't 'But, Aahz' me! All I'm doing is repeating what you shoved down my throat at the beginning of this caper. You don't need me. I've been giving it a lot of thought, and you're right. I thought you always wanted to hear me say that."

"Maybe I don't like being right," I said plaintively. "Maybe I wish I *did* need you more and things could go on forever like they have in the past."

"That's most of growing up, kid." Aahz sighed. "Facing up to reality whether we like it or not. You've been doing it, and I figure it's about time I did the same. That's why I'm going to stick around."

"But you don't have to ... what?"

My mentor's face split in one of his expansive grins.

"In this case, the reality that I'm facing is that whether you need me or not, I've had more fun since I took you on as an apprentice than I've had in centuries. I'm not sure exactly what's going to happen to you next, but I wouldn't miss it for all the gold on Deva."

"That's great!"

"... Of course, there's still a lot I can teach you, just like there's a lot I have to learn from you."

"From me?" I blinked.

"Uh huh. I've been learning from you for some time

now, kid. I was just never up to admitting it before. You've got a way of dealing with people that gets you respect, even from the ones who don't like you. I haven't always been able to get that. Lots of folks are afraid of me, but not that many respect me. That's why I've been studying your methods, and have every intention of continuing."

"That's . . . umm . . . interesting, Aahz. But how come you're telling me this now?"

"Because if I stay around, it'll be on one condition: that you wake up and accept the fact that you're a full partner in our relationship. No more of this 'apprentice' crud. It's getting too rough on my nerves."

"Gee, Aahz . . . I . . ."

"Deal?"

"Deal."

We shook hands solemnly, and I remembered he had refused this simple act when he first accepted me as an apprentice. A full partner. Wow!

"Now what's the other thing?"

"Hmm, excuse me?"

"If I recall correctly, you said there were a couple of things bothering you. What's the other?"

"Well . . . it's this house."

"What about the house?" Aahz exploded, slipping easily back into his old patterns. "It's got enough room for us *and* our friends *and* your bodyguards when they show up *and* Buttercup and Gleep and anyone else who wanders by."

"That's true."

"What's more, we got it for free. It's a good deal."

"Say that again, Aahz."

"I said, 'It's a good . . .'Oh."

"From the Deveels, right?"

"Oh come on, Skeeve. It's just a house. What could be wrong?"

"To use your phrase, 'The mind boggles.' I've been trying to spot the catch, and I want you to check me to see if my facts and logic are correct."

"Okay."

"Now. Deveels are experts at dimension travel. If I understand it right, they manage these 'bigger inside than outside' houses by offsetting the dimensions just a bit. That is, if we numbered the dimensions, and Deva was one, then our door is in dimension one and the rest of our house is in dimension one point four or something."

"Now *that's* one I hadn't thought about before," Aahz admitted. "The Deveels have been pretty tight-lipped about it. Makes sense, though. It would be rough to play the poverty-stricken shopowner with a place like this just over your shoulder. If I had thought about it I would have realized a Deveel needs someplace secret to keep his wealth."

"So we've effectively been given our own dimension," I continued, "an unlisted dimension that's all ours. For free, no less."

"That's right." Aahz nodded, but there was a note of doubt in his voice now.

"What I wonder about is how many of these offset dimensions do the Deveels have access to, and why is this particular one standing vacant? What's in this dimension?"

"Our house?" my mentor suggested tentatively.

"And what else?" I urged. "I've noticed there are no windows. What's outside our back door that the Deveels were so eager to give away?"

"Back door?"

I pulled away the tapestry to reveal the door I had spotted during our first tour. It was heavy wood with strange symbols painted on it. It also had a massive beam guarding it, and several smaller but no less effective-looking locks around the edge.

"I tried to say something at the time, but you kept telling me to shut up."

"I did, didn't I."

We both stared at the door in silence for several minutes.

"Tell you what," Aahz said softly. "Let's save investigating this for another day."

"Right," I agreed, without hesitation.

"... And until we do, let's not mention this to the others."

"My thoughts precisely."

"... And, partner?"

"Yes, Aahz?"

"If anyone knocks at this door, don't answer unless I'm with you."

Our eyes met, and I let the tapestry fall back into place.

About the Author

Robert (Lynn) Asprin was born in 1946. While he has written some stand-alone novels such as *Cold Cash War*, *Tambu*, *The Bug Wars*, and also the *Duncan and Mallory* illustrated stories, Bob is best known for his series: *The Myth Adventures of Aahz and Skeeve*; the *Phule* novels; and, more recently, the *Time Scout* novels written with Linda Evans. He also edited the groundbreaking *Thieves World* anthologies with Lynn Abbey. His most recent collaboration is *License Invoked*, written with Jody Lynn Nye. It is set in the French Quarter, New Orleans, where he currently lives.